DAWN OF THE SORCERER

SORCEROUS PURSUITS
BOOK ONE

ROBERT M. KERNS

KFP

Published by Knightsfall Press
PO Box 280
Mineral Wells, WV 26150

ABOUT THIS BOOK

Gianna is a young novice in one of Earth's oldest secret societies. She faces a nigh-impossible task: search the Archives for references to the recent Blood Moon.

Jake craves challenge. He stagnates in his hometown, but feels it hides his greatest challenge yet.

What Gianna and Jake each find will change the world.

If you love stories where Earth is a high-magic world...

If you love stories with intelligent animal companions...

If you love Contemporary / Urban Fantasy...

Make *Dawn of the Sorcerer* your next read.

CHAPTER

ONE

THE SMELL OF OLD PAPER, books, and scrolls pervaded the underground level given over to the Archives, and Gianna trapped her foot on a dense mass in her futile search for the light switch. Her right arm windmilled as she caught her glasses with her other hand. Fall averted, she stopped and took a deep, calming breath. She closed her eyes and pictured herself communing with the structure. Oneness with the brick-and-mortar edifice achieved—or so she thought—she slapped her hand to the wall where she *knew* the light switch to be. It wasn't there. Frustration charged the gates of her serenity, but the defenses held, valiant and steadfast.

"Three paces into the room along the right wall," Gianna muttered the memorized location of the switch. "I'll just back up to the door and re-orient myself."

A half-step back. A second. Her confidence swelled. She took a full step, and... she backed into something at knee height, then sat heavily on a crate. Had the room been lit, Gianna would have seen an epic mushroom cloud of dust rising into the air from her nuclear-grade failure.

Not for the first time, Gianna cursed her supposed mentor's oddball criteria for advancing her novitiate. *Find the Archives light switch without a light... while on an assigned search.*

"I'd like to see **him** find this never-sufficiently-damned light switch," Gianna growled as she fished a tiny flashlight out of her pocket. A quick click of a button, and the palm-sized modern torch illuminated a circle in front of her. She swung the light around and gaped at the distance to the entrance. She sat on a crate over twice as far into the Archives as she thought she was.

For just a moment—no longer than two heartbeats—she gave into frustration and allowed her shoulders to slump. But after that moment... she stood, tromped to the switch, and flicked on the lights.

The Archives of the New York City Field Office didn't quite rival the warehouse at the end of *Raiders of the Lost Ark*, but it was a near thing. She had yet to pace out the basement level, but just looking down the rows and aisles of shelves filled to bursting with crates, tomes, grimoires, scrolls, and countless other items, the space appeared to be **at least** twice the size of the building's exterior footprint.

She turned off her flashlight and returned it to her pocket as she examined the note that Master Gregory gave her. "Benedictine collection, Box 57."

She went to the index that was slightly more accurate than a card catalog assembled and curated by a blind drunk and sought the entry for the Benedictine collection.

"Ah, ha. Aisles 76 through 99, part of the Italian Relocation during World War II." Gianna closed the index with care—lest another explosion of dust assault her senses—and marched off in search of her quarry.

A SHORT TIME LATER, Gianna lugged the wooden file box into her mentor's office and tried not to drop it on his desk. She failed. It must've weighed close to thirty pounds.

Master Gregory looked up from his newspaper and smiled. "Excellent work, Apprentice. Your next task is to comb through that box for any reference to a blood-red moon. I remember something about a blood moon being important, but I can't recall why. I do know I read it somewhere in the Benedictine collection."

"It's amazing you remembered which box it was in. The collection looked like it had hundreds of these things," Gianna remarked, her tone betraying how impressed she was with her mentor.

Master Gregory blew a raspberry and shook his head. "Perish the thought. There are one-thousand-seventy-three boxes in the Benedictine collection, and I have no idea where I read it. I just like to start my searches with box numbers that match my age. Proceed as you like if your search takes you past that one."

Gianna clenched her fists around the box's carry handles and lugged it across the room to her meager desk. She contemplated whether she had sufficient provocation for justifiable homicide. Surely, no one in the Society would miss him... right?

THREE DAYS, several paper cuts, and the occasional splinter later, Gianna sat cross-legged on the floor of the Archives, working her way through Box 94 of the Benedictine collection. Box 94 seemed to contain half the collected writings of Silas, a monk of the Carthusian order of Benedictines in the 1300s. What his surname was—if he had one at all—appeared lost to time. What's more, he must've been some kind of vintner for the Carthusians, because every document seen thus far held at least one wine spot. At least, she **hoped** they were wine spots.

The sheaf of writings that held her current interest chronicled Silas's work to translate a writing brought to him by a monk from Rome. The writing defied every attempt at translation up till then, and Silas was renowned for his translations... in his own mind, anyway.

Gianna couldn't make heads nor tails of Silas's narrative, as she hadn't learned Latin yet, but it seemed someone had. A crumpled note occupied a corner of the box, and upon inspection, it revealed someone had enjoyed him- or herself translating Silas's Latin.

Hark, ye hapless souls, as I forewarn.
One day, another Titan shall be born.
Know ye the time of birth is nigh
When shade devours the sun on high.
Yet eclipse alone doth not the birth foretell.
The child comes within a fortnight; mark ye well
The night when hangs a blood moon o'er the dell.

GIANNA STARED at the wrinkled paper. It looked old, maybe late 1800s or early 1900s, and the verse was an assault upon the senses. Still, she dare not discount it. It was the first mention of a blood moon she'd found thus far.

Hope swelled within her soul, and she collected both Silas's Latin narrative and the crumpled paper before returning Box 94 to its place on the shelf. Now, to see if she was finished with her despised search.

. . .

4

"Master Gregory?" Gianna asked as she approached her mentor's desk. "Sir?"

He snorted himself awake and dropped his feet to the floor, angling his chair upright. "Yes, Apprentice? Have you found something?"

"Yes, sir." She presented the documents for evaluation.

Master Gregory looked at the rag paper first. "Ah, good old Silas. Some of his documents are so wine-soaked we have no idea what he wrote." Then he eyed the crumpled note and snorted. "Yes... yes. This abysmal verse. This was what I remembered. Apprentice, do you know why I sent you to find this?"

"Because of the blood moon the night of the twenty-first?"

"Very good, child. And why might that blood moon be important?"

Gianna wracked her brain for something besides the moon shining red as blood for a whole night. Her eyes shot wide when she connected the dots. "The total eclipse at noon a week ago!"

"Excellent. I have high hopes for you. Take these with my compliments to Headmistress Selene, if you please."

Gianna collected the rag paper and crumpled note from her mentor and turned. Before she counted her tenth step, she heard snoring behind her.

The Office of the Headmistress looked as though someone decided to cram a library and tea parlor into the same physical space. Every flat surface groaned under the weight of many tomes, papers, and scrolls. Deep pile carpet stretched from wall to wall, and the smell of a citrus tea struck Gianna when she crossed the threshold.

Headmistress Selene sat behind a massive handmade oaken desk that bore the crushing weight of its uncounted years in subtle dignity. Wavy hair the color of driven snow cascaded past the woman's shoulders, though her unwrinkled skin belied her age. When the leader of the field office betrayed no awareness of Gianna's presence after several minutes, the young apprentice rapped her knuckles on the doorframe.

Selene's head shot up, and she peered at her visitor over pince-nez glasses. "Yes, child? How can I help you?"

Gianna approached the desk and held out her delivery. "Master Gregory asked me to bring these to you. He seemed to think them important."

The older woman erupted out of her seat and charged around the desk. She snatched Gianna's cargo and perused it at speed. When she read the crumpled paper, her shoulders slumped.

"Damn and blast." Selene stalked back to her seat. "Our order's greatest labor has begun."

Gianna frowned, then spoke. "I'm sorry, ma'am? I don't understand."

"Did you read what you carried, child?"

A rueful chuckle escaped Gianna's self-control. "Carried, ma'am? I scoured the Benedictine collection for three days at Master Gregory's behest. I did more than **read** them, though I haven't learned Latin yet."

The headmistress leaned back in her seat and plucked the pince-nez off her nose. She held one end between her finger and thumb while she bit the opposite corner of the frame. After several moments of evaluation, she broke into a smile.

"By all that's holy, child, you have a fire about you. I like that. You're wasted on that lazy git Gregory. The Harpocratic Society does not just catalog and preserve documents too valuable to be lost to time. Our order evolved into that mission when our primary task showed no signs of beginning after several centuries. A task made all the more difficult by the modern age. Do you know how many children are born—on average—every day? Three-hundred eighty-five thousand, and that is doubled, because the blood moon shone on both the twenty-first and the twenty-second. That's seven-hundred seventy thousand babies we must watch and evaluate, because **one** of them is the first Titan to be born since ancient times."

"Please, forgive me, ma'am. I still don't see how Greek Mythology connects with all this."

Selene tossed the pince-nez to the top of her desk and gave Gianna a patient, understanding smile. "Because the Titans and Olympians of Greek Mythology were not gods, though they seemed as such to the common people. Tell me what you know of the classes of crafters as delineated in Rasputin's *Ruminations on Crafting*."

Gianna fought to keep her surprise from showing. "Uhm... the weakest crafters are warlocks and witches. They possess no affinities to any of the Arcane Spheres and can only work rituals and use imbued items triggered by command word. Next are the Divine crafters. Through True Faith and Belief, they can channel their chosen deity's power on Earth; they are **very** rare, but their power is limited only by how well their deity favors them. The third group are Druids. These crafters possess a hyper-affinity to Nature, which is a subset of the Life Sphere. Inside their chosen groves, they are like gods, but beyond those spaces, it's rare for them to be more powerful than any other single-affinity crafter. The fourth and final are the Mages. These crafters possess affinities to one or more of the Arcane Spheres, with more affinities meaning a more powerful mage. Mages with one to two affinities are common. Powerful mages have three to four and are rare. Legendary mages have five, and multiple sources claim Merlin had **six**."

"Very good," Selene complimented, "but you're missing one group: the sorcerers."

"Nothing I've read thus far mentioned such a group, ma'am."

Selene threw back her head and laughed. "I'm not surprised. The Parthians killed the last **known** sorcerer somewhere around 36 BC. Every group of supernaturals feared the sorcerers. Every. Single. One. Thankfully, they were always rather rare, for they possess affinity with all twelve Spheres."

The room spun around her as Gianna contemplated the headmistress's words. Affinities for all the Spheres? How was that possible? Merlin—the most powerful mage ever known and founder of the Magocracy—possessed five affinities that were well-documented, though many scholars argued he possessed a sixth. What could a crafter do with *twelve*?

"And that, dear child, is why the ancient Greeks called them *Titans*."

CHAPTER
TWO

Hornbeam, Illinois
14 May 2025, 08:35am

THORNTON ADAMS DESPISED his given name. The sole other instance of it he'd ever encountered was John Wayne's character in *The Quiet Man*, and he had yet to work up the courage to ask his parents if that's where it came from. He went by Jake instead and managed to win his parents over to the idea after a valiant and relentless effort spanning years.

Jake stood six feet and two inches tall, before hair or shoes, and sported broad shoulders and toned muscles that he developed after surviving puberty and maintained across uncounted hours of extreme physical labor. There was just something about the kind of physical work anyone else would call back-breaking torture that left Jake feeling satisfied and complete.

The best part was how his body never complained and demonstrated uncanny resilience. No matter how extreme a day's work, the soreness never endured beyond the next evening. Cuts, tears, bruises, or pulled muscles never lasted past the second day, and tiny injuries like paper cuts often disappeared within hours, if not minutes.

JAKE SWALLOWED his emotions as he trudged across the parking lot that led to Percy's Grocery. It was his least favorite job: bag boy and stocker. Oh, sure... it was nice helping the town's older citizens to their vehicles, but no part of his work at Percy's **challenged** him. He craved challenge. He hungered to test himself and win like a starving man craved food. It had been a long time since any work around his hometown delivered that satisfaction.

Feminine laughter reached his ears, and he gave no outward sign that he knew Jolene Chesterfield held court in one corner of the parking lot. Jolene had been the captain of the varsity cheerleading team **and** Prom Queen their senior year, and she ruled her crowd of vapid sycophants like the small-town royalty she knew she was. Every guy Jake's age and three years above or below wanted to date her, and she played them all against each other in a virtuoso performance of well-choreographed social symphony.

The laughter faded as he reached the closest point of approach to Her Majesty, and Jake knew the ladies watched him as he passed. More than one of his fellow guys bemoaned Jake's toned physique and begged him to teach them how he kept his body so perfect. Which might lead one to think Jake could have Jolene—or really, any lady—whenever he chose.

But such was not the case.

Jake carried an unsettling aura about him. A subtle **something** that set most people's nerves on edge. It tripped a survival sense buried deep in the human psyche, honed across many thousands of years to know when dangerous predators stalked unseen through the shadows just beyond the campfire's light.

The bullies and other n'er-do-wells around town felt it, too. They stayed well away from Jake, lest he take offense and choose to act...

not that he ever did. Still, at the mere sight of Jake across the street, more than one petty thief graciously returned purloined items with anxious, rapid apologies before fleeing in a full sprint.

This was the true tragedy of Jake's young adulthood, for he was a kind and gentle soul, who greeted everyone with a welcoming smile. Regardless of how much he hungered to find greater personal challenges, Jake enjoyed helping people when he could and possessed not the slightest idea **why** most people shied away from him or tensed at his approach.

That would've probably driven most people to seek answers... some form of explanation for how everyone reacted to him. But as far back as he could remember, he'd carried a sense of... *difference*. He knew beyond any doubt that he was fundamentally different in some way from those around him and especially his peer group. Not better. Not worse. Not greater. Not less. Just... *different*. So, he held that feeling around him like a blanket and went from day to day as best he could.

"Good day, ladies," Jake said, nodding his greetings and paying Her Majesty all due respect.

As Jake increased his distance from them, the ladies of Her Majesty's court exploded into urgent whispers. His hearing wasn't acute enough to pick up what they hissed, but in the long run, it was probably just as well. He had no desire to pursue any of them; he saw how they treated people. He continued walking across the parking lot to the store.

"Good day to you, young Jake," Percy Senior intoned as Jake approached the pavilion where the older man perched most pleasant days. Percy Senior took over the store from his father and re-named it at his father's posthumous request in the will, then rebuilt it in the wake of the Independence Day attacks. Now, he was retired and had entrusted the store to Percy Junior.

"Hello, Mister Hendricks. How are you today?"

"Oh, I'm fine, young man, just fine. It'll be a busy day in the back. Today's a truck day."

Jake nodded and smiled indulgently at the information he already knew. Today's truck was the sole reason Percy Junior called him to work. "Thanks for the warning, sir."

"Well, you better go on in. I'd hate to make you late just because you're too polite to tell an old man to shut up so you can get to work." Percy Senior chuckled.

"All right, sir. Have a great day." Jake gave him a nod of respect, taking the place of tipping his non-existent hat to the man.

Percy Senior was what his parents called 'good people;' more than once, Jake had seen him send people home with armloads of groceries, regardless of their ability to pay. He oftentimes allowed an exchange of work for groceries if a family simply did not have the money. Recessions tended to hit Hornbeam harder than most places, but Percy Senior—and his son after him—never let anyone go hungry.

Entering the store felt like stepping into a cooler to Jake, but he didn't mind. The store's loading docks were not air-conditioned, so he'd be able to work up a good, honest sweat. He wasn't sure why Percy Junior kept the store just a little on the cool side; he would've thought people lingering would be better, maybe buying more as they remembered items they forgot to put on the list. But either way, it was none of Jake's business; he was only here to help unload the delivery.

～

Hornbeam, Illinois
    14 May 2025, 02:47pm

Emilia Harcourt fought the urge to look for banjo players as her mom drove into the sleepy little town of Hornbeam, Illinois. A city girl born and raised, Emilia already missed *everything* about her home. Where were the streetlights? Taxis? Did the place even have traffic lights? What about nail spas? Or clothing boutiques? Okay, so she didn't expect one of the continent's premiere Druids to settle in Central Park, but damn... her time here would be nothing short of roughing it.

Emilia was a Tri-Sphere mage—possessing a full affinity with Life and strong affinities with Mind and Spirit—and when she graduated from NYU with a Bachelor's in Biology, her mother suggested she might find value in training up her magic a little before pursuing advanced degrees. After all, many universities tended to give preference to applicants with some experience—especially mages—over those fresh out of school.

But she never thought she'd have to leave civilization to get said experience.

"I know, I know... it's not New York City," her mom said, unconsciously echoing her thoughts. "But give it a chance. Gerald and Bianca are two of my oldest friends, and no one else in North America knows Nature magic like Bianca. On top of that, Gerald just earned his Grandmaster certification in the Life Sphere a couple of months ago, and he's still in his forties. There is *a lot* you can learn from them, and it will better position you to become a doctor or work in any other field of medicine you choose."

"Mom... seriously... Harvard or Johns Hopkins are the *only* paths for me. How can you think I'd choose some lesser school?"

Her mom gave one of those parent chuckles that implied more experience and greater understanding of life's mysteries, and Emilia just rolled her eyes and turned to look out the passenger window. What did her mom know about any of this anyway? She was a freaking *librarian* of all things. It wasn't like she knew anything about major life goals or the calling to advance the frontiers of medicine.

Her mom braked for a 4-way stop sign before turning right, and Emilia blinked her surprise. A guy about her age trudged along the sidewalk. He kept his head down and his hands stuffed in his pockets, but she didn't care. He was *dreamy*. The sleeves of his t-shirt strained to surround his biceps at rest, and his hair was the perfect shade of milk-chocolate brown. The car rolled past him as her mom drove, and she turned to check the caboose. Oh, yeah... the complete package right there.

"See anything you like?" her mom asked, jerking Emilia out of her laser-focused examination so hard she flinched.

"What? Huh?"

Another mom-chuckle, only this one edged toward a full-on mom-laugh. "That's what I thought."

Emilia looked in the side mirror, but it was the 'objects are closer than they appear' one... which meant a horrid view. It totally did zero justice to whoever that hottie was. Then, she sighed her frustration, contemplating ways to meet him. Gerald and Bianca would give her time off from studies, right? Let her explore the town?

"So, where is this grove exactly?" Emilia asked, aiming for total innocence in her voice.

Another mom-laugh. "Only a few miles outside of town, but don't worry. I'll leave you the car."

Emilia frowned her confusion. "But if you leave me the car, how will you get home?"

"There's an Amtrak line that runs through here; I'll just hop a train to Chicago and fly home out of O'Hare. I'd prefer a portal, honestly, but I don't think there are any Spatial Mages close who could gate me all the way back to New York."

The Spatial Sphere was one of the three rarest Spheres in terms of affinities. It was second in rarity only to the Time Sphere.

"What are Gerald's affinities?" Emilia asked, her mind shifting to how she could make the most of this educational exile.

The corner of her mom's mouth curled into a half-smile, but she didn't comment on Emilia's change of heart. "He has full affinity with Life and strong affinity with Shadow, and Bianca of course only has her hyper-affinity to Nature magic with the rest of the Life Sphere being a strong affinity at best."

Well, that seemed a little anti-climactic. These people could only help her with one of her Spheres. But then, understanding clicked. Druids were the best alchemists bar none. Bianca could teach her things about the discipline Harvard or Johns Hopkins didn't even know existed, because no Druid ever considered teaching at such an institution, regardless of the prestige. They avoided cities like the plague.

Maybe this wouldn't be such a hardship assignment after all...

JAKE PAID no attention to the cars passing him as he walked home, thinking about his time at the grocery. The burn in his muscles was not quite satisfying. He experienced **exactly** what he expected at the grocery store, so there was that. On the other hand, though, he felt an underlying disappointment.

But was it disappointment? Was that the most accurate description for what he felt? Yes, kind of. Disappointment was a part of the complicated furball that was his emotional state, especially when he considered his physical exertion at the grocery store. He knew it wouldn't challenge him today, and it didn't. So, aside from helping Percy Junior and getting paid for his time, the effort was of no practical value to him.

On the other hand, if he included all of his values as part of his consideration, the day was not a total loss. He **helped** Percy Junior. He **made a difference** today for the better. That much was beyond apparent when he walked in on Percy Junior learning his other stocker called off sick. So, Jake was all the man had... for the whole day. On the 'other people' side, the day was a huge success.

He needed to find **something** to keep challenging his body. He couldn't explain it, but he knew—knew beyond any doubt—that he had not even scratched the surface of his potential. There was **more** just waiting for him to reach it, and it felt oh so tantalizingly close. Almost close enough to grasp. And yet far beyond his reach, all at the same time. Because in all of his exercise and challenging his body,

Jake never felt that he tapped into whatever it was that seemed to hover so close. It was a hummingbird dancing around him, taunting him to catch it, all the while ensuring that he didn't.

Another facet of the problem was how he felt drawn to Hornbeam. He'd gone on class trips and such throughout his school years, but he always felt... **something**... pulling him back to Hornbeam. Somehow, the little town was where he needed to be, and he didn't understand that.

His parents had told him during his middle school years that he was adopted. They didn't go into a lot of detail about it, but from what they said, he knew he was a foundling. Left at a church near where they had lived at the time. As far as anyone had ever told him, no one knew anything about his birth parents or where he was from or if he even had a name before Thornton Adams.

It was frustrating.

JAKE'S THOUGHTS swirled around the topic the rest of his walk home. Jake's adoptive parents owned a large piece of land on the northern edge of town. It was kind of a long walk to and from anything in Hornbeam, but Jake appreciated his home and felt no need for a car. In fact, Jake persuaded his parents to put the money that would've gone to his first car into a care package for his best friends. They were—admittedly—very recent friends to be considered his best friends, but Jake didn't doubt their loyalty to—or regard for—him in the slightest.

He walked through the gate separating the sidewalk and street from the large front yard and remained so focused on his thoughts that he almost missed the surprise attack from one of his friends. A sixth—or maybe **seventh**?—sense penetrated his focus in time for him to drop flat on the ground so his friend sailed over him in what would've been a chest-high flying tackle.

The melanistic jaguar's front paws touched grass first, and the rest of him returned to ground in a graceful landing. Jake pushed himself back to his feet as the big cat spun and trotted back to him, then brushed against Jake's left leg in a silence that somehow managed to communicate images of welcome and love in Jake's mind. Not to be undone, the black cat's white—and only—littermate trotted up to Jake's right side and brushed that leg, adding her own welcome and love.

Jake reached down—but not **that** far—and scratched each jaguar behind his and her ears, then proceeded to rub his way along their spines as they pushed against his hand to communicate their appreciation and interest in more rubs.

* *We missed you today. Welcome home.* * The white jaguar—Smokey—didn't speak; after all, jaguars did not possess the necessary equipment for human speech. But Jake **heard** them both in his mind as if they did.

He 'heard' them for the first time shortly after rescuing them, and it had freaked him out to no end. However, after a few experiments, he had decided that he was indeed 'hearing' them and that his mind wasn't making it all up.

* *Yeah! You missed all the fun.* * The melanistic jaguar—Bandit—said as Jake stopped the 'welcome home' rub and started walking with them to the house. * *There was a new mail carrier.* *

Jake froze and scanned the yard for any discarded pieces of mail. The kids—as he liked to think of his jaguars—enjoyed playing with Vern, the regular mail carrier, and they—well, Bandit at least—didn't always make allowances for substitutes when Vern had to take a day off. And no matter how many times Vern warned the subs, they **always** flipped out when Bandit came charging toward them at a full sprint, mere seconds after they passed through the gate. More than one hardy soul—supremely confident that he or she could handle **anything** the postal service threw at them—resigned in a screaming fit after meeting Bandit.

He didn't see any envelopes or other out-of-place items on the lawn, so the carrier must've held the presence of mind to stuff the mail back into the shoulder bag. If that was indeed the case, maybe this sub would stand the test of time.

Returning his focus to the house, Jake saw that the kids were a cat-length or two ahead of him, from where he stopped to look for tossed mail. They both paused to wait for him to catch up, and Bandit asked, * *Hey... when are you going to claim a female and bring her home to the den?* *

Smokey immediately expressed her displeasure with her brother through a half-strength and no-claws slap across his jaw. * *Shut up, fur-butt. That's not how humans handle mating.* * Then, she looked back to Jake. * *Don't listen to him. He doesn't hang around for the afternoon shows your mom and I watch. But the point is a little bit valid; you need a female in your life.* *

Jake fought the urge to sigh. This wasn't the first time the kids had brought up that topic, and his position on it hadn't changed, either. He wasn't asexual or interested in guys, but he hadn't met anyone who held his interest or—heaven forbid—impressed him. Besides, he was only twenty-five; he had plenty of time to find someone who wouldn't object to sharing him with a couple of (mostly) friendly jaguars.

"We've been over this before," he replied, "and nothing has changed. I don't feel... I don't know... there's just no one around here who holds my interest."

* *That just means you need to explore a different batch of females.* * Bandit immediately shot back. Feelings of faint sorrow tinged Bandit's 'voice.' * *I miss Momma.* *

Smokey moved closer and brushed against her brother, expressing her care and support. * *I miss her, too, fur-butt.* *

Jake marveled at how their mental development had grown over time. When he first brought them home, their thoughts were not complex. In fact, their communication with him amounted to little more than raw emotion. But... as he interacted with them, caring for them and raising them, their mental acuity had improved by leaps and bounds to the point that he now felt they were on par with an average adolescent human, depending on one's definition of 'average.'

He wasn't sure if he should be concerned about that or not. It wasn't like he could go to anyone with more experience and show them what was happening, then ask for advice. It was almost like they were increasing not just their knowledge around him but also their base intelligence. And he had no idea how that could happen.

Regardless, they were as much a part of his life as his parents were, and he worried that someone would one day come to take them. After all, he was pretty sure having them outside an accredited zoo was probably illegal.

But that was a problem for another time. Now, it was time to shower, then have dinner with his parents.

CHAPTER

THREE

The Wainwright Grove
  Five miles north of Hornbeam, Illinois
  14 May 2025, 3:17pm

EMILIA WATCHED her surroundings shift from a small town to the small town's attempt at suburbs... and then all at once, most signs of modern civilization stopped. The pavement ended in a roundabout that had a gravel road leave it, heading a few points west of north, and no other turn-offs. She wanted to be concerned, but her mother drove on without missing a beat.

"Uhm, Mom?"

"Yes, Sweetheart?"

Emilia wrestled with how to express her concerns. The terrain was so unlike everything she was used to, everything she wanted or loved.

"I don't know how to ask what I want to know. Will my cell phone work there?"

Emilia saw a smile curl one side of her mom's mouth as she

replied, "No, I'm afraid not. Gerald and Bianca have a land-line phone, and the telephone company does a good job of keeping the local infrastructure working... unlike some places I've seen. They don't have internet access or television. They get their news from various newspaper and magazine subscriptions. Yes, they may be a day or so late in getting the news, but they consider that a small price to pay to live how they prefer."

The crushing weight of her sentence hit Emilia full force. No internet? No cell phone service? How was she supposed to live? How was she supposed to keep in touch with her friends?

"That's the main reason I'm leaving you the car, dear," her mom continued. "That way, you can drive into town and visit a local coffee shop or cafe and keep in touch with everyone. But don't think you'll be running into town willy nilly. If they conduct their training even slightly like how we were trained, don't expect to have more than two days for your own time each week, usually just one. And those days probably won't always line up with the weekend."

There was no doubt about it now. As much as this experience might benefit her in the long run, it was most definitely a sentence, definitely worse than a hardship post. She stared out the window and tried to keep from scowling at the countryside as it rolled past. Not even Central Park was this green and undeveloped.

Emilia fought back a snort at her own thought; there wasn't *anything* undeveloped about Central Park. It was all carefully land-scaped and maintained, every square inch of it. This... this was raw, untapped Nature. She would never admit it to her mom, but it scared her a little. She *knew* the city. Knew the mores. Knew where to go, where not to go, and when she could get away with going where she wasn't supposed to go. She knew how to be *safe*, no matter where she was in the city. But here? Where were the sirens? The subway? The police? It was so *peaceful* here, and that was a subtle itch she couldn't reach.

"I know what you're thinking," her mom said as she slowed for a farmer to herd sheep across the road, "but it's not so bad. You'll adapt quickly. You always have. Gerald and Bianca are good people, and don't be surprised if they already know a few things about you. I'm a very proud mom, you know."

Emilia tore her gaze away from unending green to regard her mom. "How did you meet them?"

"We all had the same arcane internship during high school. All three of us manifested before we graduated, so they adjusted our schedules to permit the necessary basic training all mages must complete."

"Is it common to manifest so early?" Emilia asked. Her affinities had not manifested until her sophomore year of NYU. Until then, she had no idea that she was a mage like her mom; most of the instructors said it could—and often did—skip generations.

Her mom snorted and managed a shrug as she drove. "Who knows? The Magocracy would have you believe they're all-knowing and have everything well in hand, but I can tell you such is not the case. Nowhere close to it, in fact. It would terrify you to know just how much we **don't know** about magic. Why we're mages when others are witches or warlocks. Why some people are Druids. What determines the strength of our affinities. What determines how many affinities we have. And these are just the first things the Magocracy can't explain that popped into my mind. You could probably fill a decent-sized book with the list of everything we know for certain our supposed 'greatest minds' simply do not understand. Oh, here's a good one. Why do people with a weak affinity to Life sometimes live far longer than those with strong or full affinities? No idea. Magic is like magnetism to a great extent. We can work with it—make it do what we want **most of the time**—but we cannot explain **why** it works the way it does. Just like we can't explain why magnetism works. Or what causes it. Or what it is. We define both magic and magnetism based on what we perceive them doing."

Okay... Mom was right. That **was** kinda scary. For someone who liked being in control of herself and her immediate surroundings, the idea that such a fundamental part of her life was unknown to such a degree was more than a little unnerving.

They approached what looked like a fence or wall made of hedge, rising some ten to fifteen feet into the air. The hedge ran perpendicular to the road as far as she could see in either direction, leaving a space large enough for delivery trucks to pass through. A span that was at most a foot thick curved over the road, joining the two sections, and a mixture of red, yellow, and orange flowers spelled 'Wainwright Grove' in living letters that followed the curve of the hedge arch.

"Oh, wow," Emilia said, her voice somewhere between normal volume and a whisper, saturated with awe.

Her mom chuckled. "Bianca was doing this kind of stuff in school within a month of her manifestation. The Magocracy never devised gradients for the different levels of affinity, so there's no way to know, but I suspect Bianca is easily among the top three most powerful Druids in North America... if not the Western Hemisphere. Nature just **responds** to her, like it's part of her or she's part of it. I've never seen anything else like it."

They drove through the opening in the hedge, and Emilia felt **something** during their passing. Something brushed her mind; that much she knew. But she either wasn't strong enough in Mind or wasn't trained enough to recognize whatever it was. After a few brief moments, the sensation passed, and a feeling of a deep, unwavering, warm welcome suffused her entire being.

"Mom..."

"It's okay, dear; I felt it, too. There's no reason to be concerned. It was only Beauregard."

Emilia sent both a confused frown and a mild hairy eyeball toward her mom. "Huh? You wanna try again? Maybe in English this time?"

Her mom chuckled. "Bianca has tended and evolved this grove for so long that it has developed an... awareness, for lack of a better term. And when it comes to Bianca and Gerald, 'protective' does not even *begin* to describe it... well... him. The awareness identifies as 'he' and 'him.' Bianca spent the better part of a year going through names, until he finally settled on Beauregard."

"Protective? Really? What can a hedge and some trees do against mage-haters with Molotov cocktails and firearms?"

Emilia frowned when she saw a shudder escape her mother's control. "I was here during the last upswell of anti-mage sentiment in the country, when a group of 'good ole boys' came to 'save Hornbeam from the influence of these devil-worshippers.' For one thing, the hedge doesn't burn. Trust me; I know it *should*, but it doesn't. They finally tried spraying it with gasoline and only succeeded in lighting themselves on fire. But that was nothing next to the earth constructs."

Her mom's voice trailed off to the point that Emilia turned to look at her, concerned. After several moments of silence, her mom spoke again.

"I don't think I'll ever forget it. Some idiot climbed the sole tree outside the grove and managed to shoot Bianca with his deer rifle. Beauregard went *nuts*. Five massive constructs—made completely of rock—rose out of the ground and stomped through the hedge. They were human-shaped to a degree; their heads were just rounded protrusions on top of the bodies, no faces or anything like that. The arms ended in stone spheres covered in spikes, like the medieval spiked maces. And they *destroyed* the mob. Ruined over ten vehicles, some of them brand new electric models. Out of something like thirty people, I think maybe five escaped unharmed, and no more than fifteen lived. The constructs were halfway to town before Gerald healed Bianca enough that she could talk Beauregard down."

"But the authorities cleared Bianca and Gerald, right?" Emilia asked. "I mean, they're still here and doing their thing."

Her mom eased the car to a stop beside a sedan and truck. The sedan was a newer, top-of-the-line electric model, but the truck was not.

"The Arcane Division of the US Marshals and the US Attorney's office for the state ruled the incident as justified self-defense, but honestly, I think they were too afraid of having to do something about it if they ruled otherwise. The Magocracy sent in a team when the Feds chose not to touch it with a ten-foot pole and spent about an hour trying to get through the hedge before they dismissed the case," her mom answered as she unbuckled her seat belt.

Emilia gaped. "What? I've **never** heard of the Magocracy dismissing a case."

"Beauregard met them at the hedge with two constructs. And no matter how hard Bianca talked, he would not stand down. One of the mages—a Tri-Sphere with full affinity to Death and strong affinities to Earth and Fire—decided he was going to put Beauregard in his place. Well... Beauregard's still here, and the Magocracy acts as though the Wainwright Grove doesn't exist. I've had nightmares about what happens if Bianca dies from something that isn't natural causes."

"So, how did he get to be so strong?" Emilia asked as she helped her mother unload the luggage.

"Again, it comes back to how little we truly understand magic. The Druid recognized as the preeminent Grandmaster in the world visited to research or investigate Beauregard and the grove in general after the Magocracy dropped their case. She left without developing any meaningful conclusions. She did certify to the Magocracy that Bianca didn't set out to create Beauregard, so Bianca's off the hook for that if anything ever happens. But as for how he came to be so strong or why he is? No one really knows."

Emilia collected her luggage and followed her mom out from behind the car and promptly fought the urge to freeze in surprise at the sight of the two people approaching. To many, the term 'Druid' or 'Druids' conjured images of an unwashed soul in primitive clothing with twigs and flowers and who knew what else in his or her hair. To a certain generation and in certain places, it was almost synonymous with 'hippie.' The two people walking down the path from the house shattered those preconceptions.

The gentleman looked like he was around the age of Emilia's mother. Strands of gray dominated his temples and haphazardly streaked through the rest of his dark hair. He wore a polo shirt, khaki cargo shorts, and what looked like deck shoes without socks. He looked exactly like Emilia pictured her dad looking, if he had lived to reach a similar age.

When she directed her attention to the woman, Emilia's breath caught in her throat. Yes, she did have a flower woven into her wavy strawberry blond hair, but that was the only similarity to the stereotypes. She wore a floral print t-shirt and cut-off denim shorts that were a few inches too long to be called Daisy Dukes, and strappy sandals clung to her feet. The woman's light blue eyes shone with a vibrancy Emilia would not have expected to see even in someone her own age.

Before Emilia and her mother could reach their hosts, though, a swarm of animals converged on them. Squirrels, chipmunks, birds, two deer, and a small family of rabbits ringed the parking area. The birds flitted around Emilia like fighter pilots dodging flak cannons during World War II.

* Hello. *

* You're tall. *

* Do you want to see my nest? I have a very nice nest. Where's your nest? *

All these voices and more invaded in Emilia's mind, threatening to overwhelm her.

"Here, now," the woman said, "ease off. They're our guests, not interrogation subjects. You'll have more than enough time to meet them and visit with them, once they've settled from their trip."

The birds pulled back to the fringe of the parking area with the rest of the non-human welcoming committee. As Emilia rejoiced in the sudden silence within her mind, the woman who spoke swarmed her mom, enfolding her in a tight hug.

"Gia, it has been **too** long," she said, her voice betraying the fierceness of the hug. "How was the drive?"

Emilia's mom—Gianna, or Gia for short—smiled and returned the hug. "It was okay. Long but okay."

The gentleman stepped in and hugged Gianna then, offering his greetings. And all three turned to her.

"This is my daughter, Emilia," Gianna said. "Emi, this is Gerald and Bianca Wainwright, two of my oldest friends."

"It's nice to meet you both," Emilia responded, shaking their hands in turn, "and thank you for agreeing to teach me."

Bianca beamed. "Think nothing of it. You and your mother will always have a place here. Beauregard already likes you. He's of the opinion you've come home at last."

Emilia blinked her surprise. "Uhm... I don't want to offend him, but..."

Bianca chuckled and dismissed the concern with a wave. "Pay it no mind at all, dear. I gave up trying to understand even half of what Beauregard tells me a long time ago. Would you believe he's been nattering on about a Titan being in the area for twenty-some years now?" If Bianca was aware of how Emilia's mother froze at the mention of 'Titan,' she gave no indication. "I don't even know how he learned Greek mythology; it's not like I have any of it in the library. The only thing I can think of is that it's just Beauregard being Beauregard. But! You two must be wrung out after two days of driving. Come on. Both of you have your own room, each with its own ensuite. Ger and I will get dinner ready while you freshen up."

CHAPTER

FOUR

The Wainwright Grove
   15 May 2025, 8:15am

EMILIA ENTERED THE WAINWRIGHTS' kitchen and found her mom and the Wainwrights already gathered in the breakfast nook. She ambled over to them, accepting a cup of coffee as she slid in next to her mom.

"Time zones..." her eyes flitted to her audience as she allowed her voice to trail off, unsure of the language customs.

"...suck?" Gerald Wainwright offered.

She nodded her agreement. "Yes. They thoroughly suck. I wish they would do away with Daylight Savings Time altogether and put us all on Standard Time. I know the time change was in March, but it is ridiculous to do this to ourselves twice a year."

"Preaching to the choir, dear," Bianca remarked. "So, your mother told us you just graduated NYU with a course load for Pre-Med?"

Emilia nodded. "Either Harvard or Johns Hopkins are my first choices. I watched one of my closest friends die in the hallway when we were in the tenth grade, and there was no reason for it. She had a rare blood disorder that has not enjoyed a lot of research because there aren't enough cases to draw the big money. Well, I have decided that I will find a way to stop it... either through medicine or magic. I will not settle for anything less than complete eradication in my lifetime."

Gerald and Bianca shared a look before Gerald replied, "That is a very tall order. Are you prepared for the possibility that you might not succeed?"

"There is always the chance that I won't succeed," Emilia agreed, "but I refuse to allow that to happen."

"Dear," Bianca began, "it's not always within your control."

Gianna nodded, interjecting, "I've been trying to tell her that for over five years now."

Emilia felt a little swell of anger. Weren't these people supposed to teach her? What business was it of theirs anyway?

*They desire to spare you heartache, Young Mistress. *

Emilia froze, coffee cup halfway to her waiting lips, and her eyes shot wide.

"What is it, Sweetheart?" Gianna asked.

Emilia's eyes flitted between the three of them as her mind scrambled for what to say so she wouldn't sound crazy. Nothing immediately came to mind.

Amusement danced in Bianca's eyes. "Just say it, dear. I promise you that we've heard crazier, probably this week even."

"I... I just heard another voice in my head, but it didn't sound like the birds. It didn't sound like anything I've ever heard."

The amusement fled from Bianca's demeanor. "Kinda deep, undertones of relentless patience?"

Emilia nodded.

"Why would Beauregard speak to her?" Gerald asked. "He hasn't had time to get to know her yet."

*I have known her since I accepted my purpose, Father. *

The expressions staring back at Emilia told her **all four** of them heard the voice that time.

"And just what is your purpose, Beauregard?" Bianca asked.

I await the coming of the Titan. Forgive me, Mother; the rest is not for you to know.

Before she fully considered it, Gianna blurted, "And why do you await the Titan?"

That is even beyond thy ken, Disciple of Harpocrates. I shall not speak of it.

At mention of 'Harpocrates,' a strangled "eep!" escaped Gianna's lips, and the color drained from her face.

"Harpocrates..." Emilia repeated. "That sounds Greek. Any relation to Hippocrates?"

To some extent, Young Mistress. Harpocrates was their appropriated god of secrets and confidentiality. Thy mother is not a mere librarian as you believe.

"Beauregard!" Bianca's voice cracked like a whip. "That secret is not yours to share."

I make my own choices, Mother, and there are truths Young Mistress must know if she is to achieve her brightest destiny. Excuse me. Poachers approach the northern hedge.

The silence that settled over the breakfast nook was deafening. Moreover, the subtle presence Emilia had sensed all around her after passing through the hedge the evening before seemed... elsewhere... now. Her brightest destiny? What did **that** mean? And what was that business about a Titan? Weren't the Titans just part of the ancient Greeks' origin myth?

A quick glance at her mom showed Emilia she still wore something of a haunted, unsettled look. It was like her entire demeanor radiated uncertainty and a figurative lack of footing now. Like she didn't know what to do or how to proceed.

"Well, there are some errands to run in town," Bianca abruptly said, shattering the awkward silence. "Who wants to go with me?"

At first, Emilia thought her hosts going shopping would give her an excellent opportunity to get her mother alone and find out what was going on, but Gerald demurred any interest in the trip. Damn... she might as well go into town then. Maybe she'd get to meet that fine example of masculinity she saw last evening.

"I'll go." Emilia tried not to notice how relaxed—perhaps even *relieved?*—her mother seemed in the wake of her statement.

THE TOWN of Hornbeam was not the first town or settlement to exist on the site it occupied. On July 4th, 2001, a terrorist group used mages to bring the horror of overseas terrorism to the United States through a series of crippling attacks across the country and sparked a decades-long War on Terror in the process. They spared no American holding; Hawaii, Alaska, Puerto Rico, Guam, American Samoa, the US Virgin Islands... all territories endured at least one attack timed to coincide with those on the mainland.

One of those attacks on the mainland was a cross-planar rift to a dimension of pure water; before the Magocracy could respond with an emergency team comprised of *all* the grandmasters of the Spatial Sphere in the world, the rift dumped over five hundred trillion gallons into the upper Mississippi River just north of the Minnesota state line... in the span of an hour, two at the most. The sheer volume of water created a torrent of raging destruction reminiscent in size to an Ice-Age glacier that swept clear a swath of land almost ten miles across.

St. Louis—like several small towns and hamlets up-river—ceased to exist; even its famous arch did not survive. The small town of Cairo, Illinois, which had stood at the confluence of the Ohio and Mississippi Rivers since shortly after the Civil War and survived countless economic crises, simply vanished... along with every other town, city, or settlement in the water's path.

The river delta where New Orleans once thrived became the site of a monument to all those lost in the Independence Day attacks. Over a million souls across all the devastation.

EMILIA STARED out the window as Bianca drove down the gravel road. They weren't back to pavement yet. She still couldn't believe how verdant it was, how unlike New York City.

"It's so green and peaceful here," she said, giving voice to her thoughts. "It's... I think I might learn to call it beautiful."

Bianca sighed. "It is now. It wasn't when Gerald and I first came out here."

"Really?"

Bianca nodded as she drove. "The mass of water from the Independence Day attack here stripped away everything—houses, pavement, topsoil, trees... *everything*—from the Minnesota state line to the Gulf of Mexico. It was like a liquid glacier that stretched five miles to either side of the Mississippi River. Where our house stands now was bare bedrock. Given my status as a Druid and Gerald's full affinity to Life, the government offered us an obscene amount of money to join the resettlement effort and oversee part of the restoration, but the money wouldn't have mattered."

Emilia frowned, expressing her confusion. "Why not?

"Shortly after the water receded, revealing the true extent of the devastation, I felt... a call for lack of a better term... toward the west. Even today, I can't really explain it. I just **knew** my future was out here somewhere. That I belonged out here. It wasn't until we stood on the site of the former national forest several miles north of here, that whatever it was drew me south. When I felt it change to something like 'right here,' we stopped and set our campsite. It took hundreds of thousands of people putting in countless man-hours just to restore the topsoil. Gerald and I founded our core grove once the topsoil was restored, but we still spent the better part of fifteen years on the road traveling as far north as the Minnesota-Iowa border and as far south as Tennessee, encouraging growth to return.

It was *brutal*. But we did it. If it weren't for the pictures at the Mississippi Monument down at the delta or old maps in libraries, you'd never know the river country wasn't always like this. We still make four to six trips a year, just making sure all the ecosystems are thriving as they should."

Emilia couldn't help but marvel at the sheer scope of the effort Bianca described. The Independence Day attacks happened before she was born, so she only knew of them from classes in school. Talking to someone who experienced them was different... powerful.

She shook her head. "I can't imagine. I simply cannot imagine what that was like. Do the history classes do it justice?"

"I doubt it," Bianca answered. "My soul wept."

The conversation faded into a companionable silence at that point. There wasn't really any way to segue off from such a topic. At least Emilia finally understood why the town's suburbs seemed so fresh and made her think they were trying too hard, especially compared to the 'big city' suburbs she knew.

The fields soon gave way to the outskirts of Hornbeam, and before long, Bianca turned into the parking lot of one of the town's banks. She put the car in Park and tapped the button to turn off the engine.

Emilia unlatched her seatbelt and was out of the car before Bianca, falling into step with the Druid once she emerged.

"Okay, so we have a little account business to handle here, and then, I'd like to visit the library. They called yesterday to tell me that one of my inter-library loans arrived," Bianca remarked as they approached the lobby's doors and entered the bank.

Passing through the second set of double doors, Emilia scanned the lobby. Its architecture was modern in style with lots of glass and angles and shiny metal surfaces. The maintenance staff had waxed the tiled floor to the point it was almost a mirror, and she couldn't help but smile in return when several of the personnel waved and greeted Bianca.

Then, Emilia scanned the people waiting in line and felt the icy claws of shock reach for her heart. There he was! The gorgeous hunk from the sidewalk last evening! He stood in the line they approached, only three people ahead of where they would be. She would not stare. She would not! She was made of sterner stuff than that.

They stopped at the end of the line for the teller windows, and Emilia forced herself to pay closer attention to the paintings along one wall. They resembled pieces she remembered from her Art Appreciation class in college, but she couldn't *quite* place them. But then again, she wasn't devoting her full faculties to art identification.

Emilia heard the inner doors move over her right shoulder, and she turned to look in time to see four people in masks and trench coats reveal shotguns.

One of them shouted, "Everyone on the floor! This is a robbery!"

CHAPTER
FIVE

Hornbeam, Illinois
15 May 2025, 8:45am

JAKE SIGHED as he trudged along the sidewalk. He journeyed to the bank that morning. The Adams's elderly neighbor, Mrs. Feldman, asked Jake if he would take a check to the bank and bring her the money from cashing it. The sweet old dear had to be one of the few people in the town—maybe the state—who didn't use a debit card. Checks and cash all the way, with her. Still, though... it wasn't the worst thing to do after breakfast, and he did enjoy the leisurely walk. It was a beautiful day.

He turned the corner and laid eyes on his destination. He passed a white panel van with an Oklahoma license plate, and the oddest feeling overtook him. There was something *wrong* about that van. Or there would be something wrong with it... *soon*. The feeling was little more than a fleeting impression, not lasting in his mind long enough to examine and try to understand, but there was no denying the strength of it for all its brevity. His first reflex was to turn and take a closer look, but the part of his brain that had never evolved past thinking fire was the bleeding edge of technology implied **very firmly** that he should keep right on walking.

Never one to ignore his hunches, Jake did exactly that; he kept right on walking. He did, however, slip his phone out of his pocket in what he hoped was a nonchalant manner and texted his friend Mike, who just happened to be one of the town's police officers. Hornbeam tended to be a rather quiet place, so it wasn't unusual for there to be only one or two officers on any given shift.

His phone buzzed in his hand, and he checked it, discovering a reply from Mike.

> A white panel van with Oklahoma plates?
> You SURE?

> Very sure. It gave me an odd feeling. Want me to turn and grab a pic?

> NO!!!! Keep doing what you're doing. Where are you?

> Walking along Fourth Street to the bank on Main. Why?

> You say you're going to the bank?

> Yeah, Mrs. Feldman asked me to cash a check for her.

> Sure you're not hungry or something?
> Maybe want to grab a bite at Marci's diner before heading over there?

Jake growled. **Something** had Mike spooked, but what?

> Mike... seriously, bud, what's going on?

No response came, and Jake already stood at the bank's entrance. He shook his head and returned the phone to his hip pocket as he opened the first set of doors and walked inside, only to see long lines at every teller window. Several tellers smiled and waved as he entered the lobby, and Jake returned their smiles and waves as he ambled to the end of the closest line.

Over the next ten minutes or so, the line creeped forward, and a couple other people moved to stand behind him. He was lost in the world of =his thoughts—not focusing on much of anything—when the door opening again caught his attention. He turned to look and felt all moisture vanish from his mouth.

Bianca Wainwright entered the bank with a young woman Jake didn't know, and the young woman was stunning. Wavy blond hair over the classic Mediterranean olive complexion. More of an athletic build than Jake usually favored, but she carried herself very well.

Her head started to turn toward him, and panic swelled in his chest. He jerked his head back and focused on his toes, praying she hadn't caught him staring. He glanced the opposite way, toward the manager's 'office' with its glass walls and the security desk outside the offices. Ned Packingham sat at the desk, the phone's handset held to his head, and his expression looked grim. Jake watched him nod several times in quick succession as his lips moved, then hang up the phone and scurry over to the manager. He entered the office without knocking and walked straight to the manager. He gestured for her to swivel away from the lobby and leaned close to speak near her ear.

Seriously... what was going on around here? First, Mike. Now, Ned.

He heard the lobby doors move and turned to look that way. Four people in black ski masks and black trench coats entered the lobby. They opened their coats long enough to pull shotguns as the one in front shouted, "Everyone on the floor! This is a robbery!"

"Don't move!" Ned Packingham shouted from behind Jake. "Hornbeam PD is already on the way, and they've notified Illinois State Police. Don't make this any worse; just lay down the shotguns and surrender."

The leader swung his firearm around to point it at Ned. As the barrel flashed across several people in line—including the gorgeous stunner with Bianca—they all dropped to the floor, crossing their arms over their heads.

"Why don't *you* surrender, Mister Security Man? You have a lobby full of people. Care to find out how many I can kill before you take me down? Clickety-BOOM, baby!"

Jake knew he should be terrified. *Knew it*. But he wasn't. His lizard brain didn't broadcast any fear signals. No... instead, he felt *something* gradually saturating his very being. Whatever it was defied his efforts to describe or name it. The only thing he could think of was potential energy from physics class in high school. Yes... *that* made sense. His body readied energy stores in preparation for something, but what? And what kind of preparation didn't trigger his fight-or-flight response?

"Hey, kid! I've about had it with you. Get on the floor or get in a grave. Move it!"

Jake blinked, refocusing his attention to the situation at hand, and realized the muzzle of a pump shotgun pointed right at him from a distance of about ten feet. He turned his head, looking side to side, and saw he was the only person still standing aside from the robbers and Ned.

"Huh... I guess you were talking to me," Jake remarked, his voice not carrying even a scrap of fear or terror.

Jake saw the pair of eyes behind the mask narrow, just as the robber said, "Ah... hell with it. It's been a while since we delivered a lesson anyway."

The robber's finger squeezed the shotgun's trigger, and Jake's awareness exploded. For less than a tenth of the time it takes to snap one's fingers, he *felt time itself*. From its beginning all the way through to its end. In the wake of that overwhelming sensation, his awareness shifted, and he sensed the vibration of every atom and molecule around him... except everything barely moved. The world around him—down to the atomic scale, maybe even the quantum—seemed to move exponentially slower than even the slowest slow-motion replay he'd ever seen. He felt like he could reach out and *touch* the molecules in the air.

It was then that he first felt a little fear. He didn't hear his heartbeat or feel his body breathing. Oh, shit... was he dead? But how could he be dead? He still moved his head and arms.

DUB

Understanding flared in his mind as he felt the first half of his heartbeat, except it was drawn out and *beyond* slow. It was like he existed *between* the seconds. Or maybe each second filled the span of a minute? He wasn't sure.

But the one thing he was sure of was that this weird time effect was fading. He didn't know *how* he knew; he just knew. It wouldn't be long before he answered to time once more, instead of time answering to him.

Jake shot a glance behind him and saw Ned was out of the direct line behind him in case his idea didn't work; the manager wasn't in sight. Then, he jumped forward, ripped the shotgun out of the robber's hands, reversed it, and placed it back *into* the robber's hands, being sure to squeeze the guy's fingers as tight against the firearm as he could. Then, he returned to a spot as close to his starting point as he could manage, hoping no one would notice the difference.

DUB

As Jake felt the second half of his heartbeat, time reasserted itself with the ***BANG!*** of the robber's own shotgun appearing to obliterate his chest. Several pellets ripped through his back and peppered two of his associates, with at least one even shattering the window beyond them.

The robber collapsed to the floor like a puppet with cut strings, and after a split-second's hesitation, Ned charged into the confusion with his sidearm drawn, yelling for the remaining robbers to get down on the floor. The town's police force erupted through the doors behind the robbers, adding their shouts to Ned's, and those robbers still standing under their own power quickly complied.

EMILIA WAS ashamed that she'd cowered on the floor with her arms over her head, afraid of watching Death come to claim her.

Then... she wasn't sure what happened. She'd never felt anything like it before in her life. An explosion of power erupted that reduced every mage she'd ever met to a tiny candle before a raging bonfire. It settled on and around the bank's lobby, enshrouding everyone— even her—like the favorite, heavy quilt that's always so snuggly warm on the coldest days of winter.

She should feel fear. That much power should terrify her right down to her bones. But... it didn't. Somehow, it felt protective. No. Not protective. Defensive. It was a wall thirty feet thick standing between her and anyone who might even consider harming her. In that instant, she knew beyond any doubt that she and every other customer in the bank was safer than if they were babes wrapped in their mothers' arms.

It made no sense. How could such raw power make her feel so protected? So defended? She didn't understand it, but at the same time, there was no question in her mind. No harm would come to the innocents in the bank. No harm at all.

The **BOOM** of a shotgun made her flinch across her entire body, and for the first few moments, she hunched her head even closer to her torso before she processed that she was still alive. She risked a glance upward just in time to see the loudmouth with the shotgun hit the floor, the center of his torso a bloody mess. After that, every-thing seemed to happen all at once and too fast for her to follow, but the remaining robbers soon lay on the floor with their hands cuffed behind their backs.

But what struck her as the oddest part of all was the expression Bianca directed toward the hunk. It was almost an appraising frown, like she wasn't sure if the hunk was a good guy or not and leaned in favor of the thought that he wasn't.

"Miss, are you hurt?" a young man in a police uniform asked, crouching at her side.

"Hmmm? Oh... no, I'm fine. No harm."

The officer nodded and moved on, but Emilia's eyes never left the Druid and how she stared at the hunk, the only customer in the bank who never dropped to the floor.

CHAPTER
SIX

The Wainwright Grove
15 May 2025, 9:00am

GIANNA LOOKED up as Gerald arrived at her side. She sat on a decorative retaining wall in what Bianca and Gerald called their backyard. For the first several minutes after Emilia and Bianca left, she simply wandered the property, hoping Beauregard would speak to her again. He didn't.

When she gave up on trying to coax the awareness to converse with her, Gianna returned to the house and settled on the retaining wall that didn't retain much of anything; it merely separated the patio from the yard that surrounded the house.

Gerald walked over to sit beside her. "Feel better after your walk?"

"I guess I do… maybe. Did you or Bianca ever tell Beauregard about the Society?"

Gerald snorted and shook his head. "You should know better

than that. Just because Bianca was called here to establish the grove —and I followed her—doesn't mean we ignored our oaths."

"Sorry... sorry. I should have known better."

Gerald laid his hand on her shoulder. "No, it's okay. You've had the rug jerked out from under you in a big way. If you weren't unsettled a little bit, I'd be worried."

"It hasn't been easy letting Emilia think I'm just a librarian. I'm sure there have been times she was ashamed of me and what she thought I did."

Gerald nodded his understanding. "That's the one thing Bianca and I are still discussing. The decision to have children. We're both undecided on the matter, but it's not like we're running out of time. With our affinities being as strong as they are, I imagine we'll live at least a few hundred years, and that's plenty of time."

Before Gianna could respond, reality itself seemed to blink.

"Did you feel that?" Gianna asked.

"What was it?" Gerald replied.

Gianna threw up her hands and shrugged. "How am I supposed—"

The subtle presence of Beauregard dominated the area.

*At last—at long last—the Titan has manifested. *

CORNER OF SEVENTH & Main Streets

15 May 2025, 11:53am

JAKE WAS HALFWAY home when it hit him. He killed that guy. He didn't quite understand **how** he managed it, but that robber would still be alive if Jake hadn't reversed the guy's shotgun. Why had he done that? Why hadn't he simply stepped far enough to one side that the buckshot sailed right on by him?

Bile swelled, surging up from the pit of his stomach like the reliable eruption of Old Faithful in Yosemite. He knew he couldn't hold it and cast around for some solution. There! He was just a short distance from an alley, and he sprinted to it. He dashed to the dumpster about halfway down the alley and grabbed the edge of the bar the truck used to hoist it for emptying. He made sure to keep his clothes tight against his torso as he leaned forward and stopped fighting. All at once, his stomach heaved, and he sprayed the ground and base of the dumpster with the remains of his breakfast.

It was the most violent and forceful vomiting he could ever remember experiencing, and it left him staggered at the end, even as his stomach went through convulsions as it fought to eject what it no longer possessed.

It took a moment for the dry heaves to subside, and he staggered back out of the alley, desperately wishing he had a cloth or napkin or something to wipe his face. He made it as far as a nearby bench, where he unceremoniously collapsed.

His perch was one of the benches that dotted the sidewalks all over town. Local fifth graders—well, local fifth graders of about two years ago now—had decorated this one before someone sealed it in polyurethane. He rested his elbows on his knees and laid his forehead against his interlaced fingers. Why had he reversed the shotgun? What motivated him—drove him—in that instant?

The robber was a threat... a threat that Ned or the police might not have subdued without harm to or the death of someone in the bank. But Jake had the initiative to resolve the threat. So, he did.

Shouldn't he feel guilty about killing the robber, though? Killing someone was a bad thing, right? The more Jake considered it, the more he felt like he *thought* he should feel guilty. But the simple fact was that the robber could have killed anyone in the bank with that shotgun, and had Jake acted in any other way, there's no telling what might have happened.

Jake heard a car roll to a stop in front of him, moments before his buddy Mike said, "You okay, Jake?"

He looked up and saw Mike sitting in one of the town's police cruisers, the passenger window down. He nodded, saying, "I think so, Mike. Thanks."

Mike shifted the car into Park. He tapped the button to turn off the car and grabbed his radio as he exited the vehicle. He stopped at the trunk, unlocking it with his key fob and opening it to reach inside. Jake didn't see what Mike retrieved, but whatever it was must've been small enough to fit in his palm.

"Dispatch, Two-Oh-Four... over," Mike spoke into the mic of his belt radio as he walked toward Jake's bench.

"Go ahead, Two-Oh-Four."

"I'm going on lunch. Can still respond to emergencies. Over."

The radio crackled as the dispatcher replied, "Copy that, Two-Oh-Four."

Mike sat on the open half of the bench and let the silence extend for a moment. He wordlessly handed Jake two wet wipes in tiny packages little bigger than alcohol swabs.

Jake nodded his thanks as he tore open the first one and swabbed down his face from cheeks to jawline, focusing on the area around his mouth. Even though that first wipe didn't seem to find anything, Jake still tore open the second and gave the area around his mouth a more thorough scrubbing.

"Thanks, Mike."

His long-time friend waved it away. "Sorry I couldn't tell you, buddy, but thank you for the text messages; we didn't have a clue they were in town. Those guys have been going state-to-state for the last couple months, and they always leave people in the hospital, if not the morgue. The guy that shot himself—man... how am I going to write up *that* report? Anyway, that guy killed a woman at their last robbery; three kids now have to grow up without their mom because of him. There's a guy in Kansas who might never walk again because of him, too."

Jake nodded his understanding. After a couple heartbeats, he asked, "So... what you're saying is that he wasn't exactly the best guy?"

"Yes, but not just that," Mike countered. "Jake, that guy would've harmed **someone** before they skipped town, and the way everyone told it, that someone had an excellent chance of being you. Until his shotgun somehow reversed in the blink of an eye, and he turned his own chest into Swiss cheese. You know anything about that?"

"Should I?"

Mike shrugged. "Dunno. Just asking. I'm on lunch, remember? Say... you ever watch any film student projects, like first-time film student projects?"

Jake blinked at the non-sequitur. "Uhm, no... I don't think so. Why?"

"Well, back in the day, they didn't have video editing software or digital cameras, so making cuts for a movie was literally unrolling the film and making actual cuts with a razor blade. And sometimes... every once in a while... they wouldn't get the cut right. And the actors on the screen would suddenly be in different places than they had been just the second before. It looked weird, right? Like they just blinked to the new spot." Mike fell silent for a few moments. He rubbed his hands together like he was nervous about something and didn't know what to do with them. "Sarge had me go over the bank's security cameras and make copies of the feeds from this morning's incident, and I saw the damnedest thing, you know? So, the whole thing—from the time they walked in the door to the time we charged in as Ned shouted for them to surrender—was not even ten minutes. And that's probably overestimating it. Two things stood out to me while I watched the feeds, Jake. Can you guess what they were?"

Jake had a pretty good idea what Mike was going to say, but he decided to play stupid at the last second. "Uhm, the guy shot himself with his own shotgun?"

"You might think that, but no. See... I don't think he shot himself. I think he fully intended to blast **your** chest to ribbons. No. The funny things were, one, you never acted or looked afraid during the entire event and, two, there was a blip in the feeds across the span of less than half a second where you jumped between two spots... just like one of those old-school film student projects. It looked like you moved close to a full inch to the side from one frame to the next. I would've thought it was a recording glitch, except **no one else** in any of the frames moved."

Jake felt his heartbeat go from a walk to a sprint in the blink of an eye. Mike **knew**. He knew that Jake was involved in the robber dying.

"Jakey," Mike said, almost sighing it out, "we've been friends since grade school. Hell, you saved my ass from the bullies when my family first moved to town. There is nothing that will change our friendship, buddy... nothing. So, in all seriousness, is there something you maybe ought to tell me?"

And there it was.

Jake didn't want to tell anyone anything. Not until he knew what it meant, at least. But Mike was his friend. He tried to go through life without lying to anyone... well, except when Bandit ate half a box of treats and still wanted more. He one-hundred-percent straight up lied about the treat box being empty, then. But with people in his day-to-day interactions, he did his best not to lie, and he absolutely did not lie to his friends. There were so few of them that he didn't want to risk losing any.

"Mike, Mrs. Feldman asked me to cash a check for her. That was the only reason I was in the bank. Is there any way you maybe could ask me that question tomorrow morning over a bagel at Marci's diner?"

Mike smiled and nodded. "Sure, buddy. I can do that. You already call the fam?"

"I think Mom tried to crawl through the phone to make sure I was all right, but yeah, I called home."

"So, when are we meeting tomorrow?"

Jake sighed and scratched his jaw. "It takes me about twenty minutes to walk to the diner, and I always feed the kids at seven-thirty, so eight-thirty?"

"That's fine, but I'll pick you up. Tomorrow's my day off, so we can linger while we catch up."

"All right, Mike. Thanks."

Mike pushed his fist into Jake's shoulder. "Forget about it. It's what friends do. See you at your gate in the morning!"

Jake stood as his friend did and watched Mike amble back to the police cruiser. As he walked, Mike pulled his cell phone from one of the pouches on his duty belt and tapped at the screen. Just as Jake resumed walking home, he heard Mike say, "Marci, hi... this is Mike. I was hoping to place an order to go."

THE WAINWRIGHT GROVE
15 May 2025, 6:35pm

EMILIA BIT down on the urge to feel embarrassed. She worked at unpacking her luggage as she listened to a rather heated conversation through a window that was open just far enough to allow the voices through. Her mom, Bianca, and Gerald sat down in the patio below her window, and they seemed too worked up to realize her window was open above them.

"Oh, come on, Bianca," Gianna protested. "You can't believe he's really the Titan of prophecy. You remember how we searched, right? It was one of the last things we did together before you two left the Society. I don't see how anyone—let alone a helpless infant—could have escaped the Society's notice."

"Okay, sure," Bianca shot back, "he may just be a Time mage. But stop to think about *that*. When was the last time you heard of a mage with a full affinity to Time?"

"Stop, Bianca. Just stop," Gianna said. "Of course, he's more powerful than a single-Sphere mage. We won't *know* all his affinities until the Magocracy evaluates him. Even if he is special, I doubt he's more than a Tri-Sphere. The Society only pays lip service to that old prophecy anymore, anyway. I don't think we've tried to identify the supposed Titan since the Independence Day attacks."

Gerald—having been silent throughout the entire exchange thus far—asked, "When did the robber shoot himself with his own shotgun?"

"Around nine o'clock, maybe nine-oh-five, hon," Bianca answered. "Why?"

"That was the same time Beauregard told us the Titan had manifested."

"Oh, not you, too," Gianna groaned. "You yourselves told me you quit listening to half of what Beauregard says. Why should this be any different?"

Bianca and Gerald remained silent for several moments until Bianca spoke in an almost-fearful tone. "Gerald, honey... what if Beauregard has been right all these years? What if the Titan has grown up under our very noses? If he's right, do we dare let the Magocracy evaluate him?"

"I cannot believe what I'm hearing," Gianna interjected. "Are the two of you honestly proposing to hide a newly manifested mage from the Magocracy? Seriously? Do you realize what will happen when they catch you? Druid or not, Life Grandmaster or not, no matter if you saved half the Mississippi River basin... the two of you will spend the rest of your lives in the Triangle. You two need to step the hell back and get your minds right."

Emilia bit her lip to prevent a gasp. The Triangle—despite its almost prosaic name—was the Magocracy's prison that floated somewhere in the Atlantic. No one outside the Magocracy knew precisely where, and a geas constructed by two Grandmaster-certified Mind mages prevented anyone who had the dubious privilege of enjoying its hospitality from discussing the place, its location, or the experience.

"You weren't there, Gia," Bianca shot back. "I don't care what some evaluation crystal says. There was more raw power in that manifestation than I've ever felt."

Gianna's expression betrayed her disbelief, but Bianca was not deterred.

"I'm serious. It... I don't know how to describe it. Power flooded that bank lobby. Saturated it like too much incense in a pothead's room. It was like one of the gods of old descended from Olympus to stand between us and danger. I've never felt anything like that before. The thought of facing a mage of that power—even within the safety of the Grove—outright *terrifies* me, Gia."

Gianna sat almost motionless as she regarded one of her oldest friends. It was clear that she considered Bianca's words. After several moments, she took a deep breath and slowly exhaled it.

"You're right. I wasn't there. I have no idea what you felt or experienced. But even if you're right, does it really change anything?"

"No... I guess not," Bianca remarked after several moments of silence. "It's never wise to buck the system, is it, Ger?"

"Hrmmm?" Gerald sounded distracted. "Oh... no, it's not."

Silence ensued for several moments, interrupted only by the stride of her mother's heels on the wooden deck. As soon as the door opened and closed, Bianca said, "We can't let her report this to the Magocracy, Ger. We just *can't*. If we're right and that boy is the Titan, I give it even money that they just kill him before he leaves the testing center. Seriously, do you expect them to react rationally to this?"

"No, I really don't, especially since I doubt the Magocracy even knows of the prophecy. The Society has never been all that talkative about its archives. And it's been long enough that it's not more than a footnote or maybe a one-line record in one of their old, moth-eaten tomes. Silas translated it in... what... the early 1300s?"

Bianca shrugged. "About that."

"So, if we're going to do this, what about Emilia?" Gerald asked. "Gia will know something's up if we send her daughter back with her."

Bianca let out an exasperated huff. "I don't like involving Emilia. Yes, she's old enough to make her own decisions, but I don't see how she could make a truly informed one without implicating herself if we're ever discovered. Wait... here comes Gia."

The door to the back deck opened again, and Emilia heard her mother say, "I was thinking of raiding your fridge for a sandwich. One, do you mind? And two, do either of you want one?"

"That sounds like an excellent idea," Gerald said. "I'll come help."

Gerald's heavy footsteps overshadowed any movement Emilia might have heard her mother make, and she hustled to head downstairs, so she could 'happen to run into' her mom... in case her mom came up to mention the sandwiches and discovered her eavesdropping.

Bianca leaned back in her seat as Gerald went inside to help Gia make sandwiches, and her eyes went to the open window above. One of the windows in Emilia's room. She had said she was going to go unpack and get settled, but was she also listening in? And what would it matter if she was?

The world was a complex place, even more complex than the supposedly transparent Magocracy would have you believe. On the whole, the Magocracy filled a necessary role. Yes, there needed to be an established curriculum for training crafters. Yes, there needed to be an authority to police said crafters, because they were just as human as everyone else. And for the most part, the Magocracy stayed in their lane. Most governments in the world had their own laws regarding the arcane, along with crafters employed in every level of law enforcement. The Founding Fathers even created a Department of Magic as a Cabinet-level position in the Constitution of the United States, right up there with the Departments of State and War and all the rest, and the last Bianca checked, about ten percent of Congress possessed at least a weak affinity with one Sphere. Magic and crafters were accepted... had been for ages.

So, why did she feel like the supposed Titan was in danger if he went to an Arcane Evaluation Center? Was it because Beauregard was acting weird? Was it because he somehow managed to avoid discovery by the Harpocratic Society for twenty-five years? Was it something else she couldn't *quite* label? Some kind of sixth sense maybe?

No answers seemed readily forthcoming, but the fact remained that she could not allow her dear friend, Gianna, to report the manifestation. Which meant the first thing she needed to do was arrange some clean-up.

She retrieved her phone from the small side table to her right and thumbed through the contacts until she found whom she sought. She quickly tapped out a message that she needed to talk, preferably in their usual place. Then, she accessed the local discussion boards to see if there was any chatter about the Time manifestation. Nothing yet. The bright spot to all this was that the town's newspaper was weekly, and the new issue published the day before. That gave her plenty of time to handle everything.

It still left the thorny problem of what to do about Emilia, but Bianca believed she could sort that out once Gia was on her way back to the Big Apple. Gerald called out that they had sandwiches, and she pushed herself to her feet and entered the house with a happy smile.

CHAPTER
SEVEN

Marci's Diner
16 May 2025, 8:35am

LESS THAN HALF THE tables were full as Jake led Mike into the diner. He saw Marci through the window between the counter and the kitchen, and she smiled and waved, which he returned. He had a favorite booth that he always tried to use every time he came to the diner, and seeing it open made him happy. He needed as many little things to help him keep up his courage as possible.

He let Mike slide into the side of the booth with his back to the wall and eased in across from him, and it wasn't long until Marci offered them menus and laid two sets of napkin-wrapped silverware on the table.

"So, you boys know what you're drinking?"

"Tea for me, thanks," Jake answered.

Mike chimed in with, "Coffee, please."

Marci wrote both on her order pad. "Alrighty, gents... back in a bit."

Mike opened the menu and looked it over, but Jake didn't bother. He always ordered the same thing at the diner... well, depending on the time of day.

Mike laid his menu aside before Marci returned with their drinks, and Jake gestured for him to order first. Mike did so, and then, Marci turned to him. She quirked an eyebrow and said, "Two asiago cheese bagels, toasted and sliced, with chive and onion cream cheese?"

Jake grinned. "Thank you, Marci."

She laughed and shook her head. "It's easy when you always order the same thing. Okay, boys... I'll be back when it's ready."

Mike busied himself with doctoring his coffee to preference while Jake took a swallow of his tea. After a few moments, Mike said, "So, wanna tell me what *really* happened?"

"I don't *know*, Mike, not for certain. But yes, I switched the shotgun around to point at his chest."

Jake watched his long-time friend lean back against the booth, as all trace of tension faded from him. He punched the air with his fist. "Ha! I knew it! What else can you do?"

Jake blinked. "Uhh... what? I don't even know how I did *that*, Mike, and you're asking what else I can do?"

"Hey, you know I'm a fanboy when it comes to mages, Jakey. And you, my friend, are a Time mage at the very least."

Whoa... a Time mage? Seriously? Jake wasn't sure how to handle that. Affinity to the Time Sphere was so rare that the high school classes that were basically Magic 101 never discussed it in detail. They admitted it existed. They covered how it was the rarest of the twelve affinities. And... that was pretty much it. It should've occurred to him that he might be... okay, probably was... a Time mage, and he felt a little bit like an idiot for not connecting the dots.

"What do you mean by 'at the very least?'"

Mike shrugged as he leaned forward again to rest his arms on the booth's table, wrapping his hands around his coffee. "The Magocracy has released statistics on mages going back as far as the 1500s. How they managed to *record* those statistics when it all had to be done by hand is another animal, but if their records are accurate, there has never been a single-Sphere mage with an affinity to Time. And... there has never been a mage with an affinity to Time that was less than strong. So, yeah... you being a Time mage is the very least you can be." Mike erupted in ecstatic giggles. "Oh, man... wouldn't it be awesome if you have the power pair? Time *and* Spatial affinities? You could really do some mind-bending stuff, then. Have you thought about visiting an AEC yet?"

Jake blinked. AEC? What... oh... an Arcane Evaluation Center. Yeah. That *was* supposed to be the next step. It was like the Selective Service registration when he turned eighteen, except there was no age deadline. It was a law that everyone who manifested go for evaluation at an official AEC within two weeks.

"I honestly hadn't even thought that far, Mike. But doesn't that kind of depend on our *other* conversation?"

Now, Mike blinked. "Our 'other' conversation? What 'other' conversation?"

"The one where we go to the station to discuss how I killed that robber?"

Mike blew a raspberry and waved that away. "That's a non-issue, buddy. I already told Sarge what I thought happened, and we ran it by Penelope at the State's Attorney's office. Even if we wrote everything up and brought it to her, she wouldn't file charges, Jake. First, it was a clear-cut case of self-defense. Everyone who was involved in the discussion agreed on that. Second, it happened as part of your manifestation, and the law is *very* clear about those. Unless there is overwhelming evidence of intent to harm without justification, the State's Attorney rules any injuries or deaths caused by a mage manifesting as accidental. Always."

"But Mike... I chose to flip that shotgun. I could've just stepped out of the way."

"Yeah, but the bank manager was still in her office. Did you think to look at her while you were doing your thing?"

"Yeah," Jake answered, "but I didn't see her. Wasn't she on the floor like everyone else?"

Mike chuckled. "You know, I could see how you might think that, but the fact is... she was in the process of standing. If you had simply stepped aside without reversing that shotgun, I think the bank manager would be in the hospital today, if not the morgue. She would've stood up, right into the path of the buckshot. So, yeah... you kinda saved her. Too bad she's like your mom's age, or I would totally tell you to ask her out. Oh, and there's the small matter of the reward. Well, **rewards**, with an 's.'"

"Rewards? What rewards?"

"These guys made a lot of folks unhappy, Jake. Lessee... there's a fund in Kansas that has a reward offering a hundred thousand for any information leading to their arrest with an extra fifty thousand if it leads to a conviction. Oklahoma has the same. Texas, though... Texas really wants them. The crew killed two officers down there. People in Texas raised two-hundred and fifty thousand for any information leading to their arrest and/or conviction. Heh... even Uncle Sam got in on the action; the Feds posted a hundred-thousand-dollar reward for them last week. So, all told, you're looking at... somewhere around seven-hundred thousand dollars before taxes."

Jake frowned. "Wait... you said 'convictions.' Wouldn't that mean the states that offer the extra for convictions would require the convictions be in their states?"

"Not the way they're worded," Mike replied. "And besides, more often than not, bank robbery gets kicked up the chain to federal jurisdiction anyhow, especially if the banks are FDIC insured."

Whoa. Jake had never been the kind of person to chase money. He worked his jobs to offset what the kids ate and help his parents with expenses around the house, plus clothes and stuff like that. But by and large, Jake never thought about having a lot of money. He just didn't need it.

"So, you doing anything today?" Mike asked, pulling Jake out of his spiraling thoughts.

"Uhm, no?"

Mike beamed. "Well, then... why don't we run up to Springfield and put you through the AEC there? I think it's the closest one."

"What are we going to tell my parents, Mike? I didn't tell them what really happened."

"Ehh..." Mike shrugged. "Don't tell them anything right now. Let's just tell them we're going for a drive since it's been an age since we hung out." Mike's eyes lit up, and he barked a laugh. "We'll even fold the back two rows flat in the Explorer and take the kids. I'll bet they'd love it."

Jake just shook his head. "I'm not sure if we ought to do that, Mike. I mean, I'm pretty sure it isn't legal for me to have them."

"Actually, I'm pretty sure you're covered."

"Oh? Why do you say that?"

"Well, there's an exception in the federal and state laws that covers exotic pets," Mike explained, "and that exception is why I expected you to manifest eventually. But I expected Life or Nature, to tell you the truth. I never thought for the world you'd be a Time mage."

Understanding dawned. Oh. Yeah. The Familiar Exception. Not familiar as in 'well known' but as in the bonded animal companions of crafters. But it wasn't common for crafters outside of Druids or Life mages to attract animal companions. And since Druids never had any affinity beyond the hyper-affinity to the Nature subset of Life, with the rest of Life being merely a strong affinity at best, he was probably a Life mage, too, in addition to Time.

"Come to think of it," Mike said, his voice sounding absent as if speech wasn't his main focus, "we probably don't have a choice about taking the kids. I'd have to check, but I think prospective mages are supposed to bring any possible animal companions for evaluation as well."

Jake took a deep breath and forced himself to exhale in a calm and controlled manner. "So, no one will take them from me?"

Mike snorted. "Hell, no. Not if I'm right, and I'm pretty sure I am.

It's a crime at the same level as kidnapping to take a mage's familiar without a court order countersigned by the local Magocracy council."

"So, we need to get them evaluated *soon*."

"Yup... and registered."

Jake nodded just as Marci returned with their food, saying, "Okay. Let's do that as soon as we're finished here."

∼

THE WAINWRIGHT GROVE
16 May 2025, 8:43am

BIANCA SAT at the base of her favorite oak tree, a little over a hundred yards into the forest that surrounded her home. A blanket protected her from the morning's dew while she waited for a friend just as dear to her as Gia. It was a pleasant morning, the sky overhead a cloudless perfection, and more than ten varieties of birds serenaded her.

At eight-forty-five on the dot, a man looking a few years older than Gerald appeared at the edge of the blanket. Bianca smiled her welcome and gestured for him to sit, which he did.

"Bianca, it has been too long," he said as he folded into a half lotus. "How is Gerald?"

"He's doing well, Brian," Bianca answered. "You'll have to visit sometime. It would make for an excellent cover to my favor, actually."

Brian nodded. "Possibly, but I haven't agreed to the favor yet. What would you like me to clean up?"

"A mage manifested during a bank robbery yesterday, here in Hornbeam. Beauregard says he's the Titan the Harpocratic Society was so frantic about back at the turn of the millennium. I want your help in removing memories or adjusting them so we can hide the boy —well, young man—from the Magocracy."

He let out an incredulous whistle. "That... that is not a small favor, Bianca. And you're basically setting me at odds with the Magocracy. Are you sure that's the path you want to take?"

"But what if Beauregard's right, Brian? The Magocracy will **kill** him when they have proof of his affinities."

"You don't know that, Bianca. You've talked yourself into believing that, and sure, he'll cause some waves in the community when it gets out that he has all twelve affinities. But I can't see how that would be cause to kill him."

Bianca gaped at Brian. How could he not *see* it? The Magocracy relied on being the most powerful mages 'in the room.' A mage didn't even bother hoping to apply for a job with them unless he or she was a dual Sphere with two full affinities. They usually preferred Tri-Spheres or better. She closed her eyes and took a deep breath, exhaled it very slowly, then decided to approach it as if she addressed a child.

"Brian, what's to stop them from whisking him off somewhere to be a professional lab rat the rest of his life?

He replied with a skeptical expression, saying, "Oh, I don't know. His civil rights? The only place the Magocracy could discover him is at one of the AECs, and every one of those—at least in the United States—has government oversight. They couldn't just whisk him off —as you put it—without a ton of paperwork and due process. Besides, unless he shows himself to be a serial killer, he's fundamentally entitled to his freedom, just like everyone else in the country."

Bianca fought the urge to growl. "So, are you denying me the favor?"

"I don't want to do it, but no, I'm not denying you the favor. But I want you to take a moment and listen to me. If you insist on making this the favor, we're through, Bianca. Once I'm finished, you should lose my number, because I will damn-sure block yours. So, take a second and make certain that's the path you really want."

Bianca floundered. She never expected Brian to throw down such a gauntlet. The sad thing was, she didn't **want** to lose his friendship... but she didn't see any other choice. She knew—beyond any doubt—that the young man could not come to the attention of the Magocracy. Every fiber of her being almost **shouted** that such would be a disaster. But Brian was one of her oldest friends, the same as Gia.

"Gia says it's folly to think about hiding him," Bianca admitted.

Brian chuckled, nodding. "Yeah... Gianna has always had a good head on her shoulders. Why aren't you listening to her?"

"Because... I don't know, really. I feel like we're at a tipping point, and I'm terrified of choosing the wrong path."

"Okay. Let's unpack that. Who is 'we?'"

"Society, maybe. It's not personal. I don't feel that I'm at the tipping point, and the same for Gerald. Maybe I just let ancient anxiety from my short time with the Society infect me again. I don't know. I'm starting to feel a little silly for freaking out, now."

Brian offered her a tolerant smile. "Well, I'm not saying a little freaking out is unjustified. If there really is a sorcerer walking around for the first time in over two thousand years, that's kind of a big deal. But maybe we should wait and be **sure** he's a sorcerer before we possibly throw our lives away?"

Bianca sighed, then nodded her acceptance. "Fine. Okay. You win."

Brian beamed like a child presented with a giant birthday cake. "Excellent. I love winning."

"Sorry I freaked out and called you here for nothing."

"Oh, no. It wasn't 'nothing,'" Brian remarked as he stood. "After all, I seem to have helped my friend step back from a path of no return. We good? You're not going to call up some other Mind mage in your contact list and twist their arm to erase or modify a bunch of memories?"

Bianca shook her head. "No. I'm going to let it ride and see how everything turns out. Who knows, he may even avoid being evalu-ated somehow. It's not like Hornbeam is the center of American civilization. Besides, you're the only Mind mage I know who also has a full affinity to Spatial. Thank you, Brian."

"You're welcome, Bianca." Then, he vanished with a small whoosh of air rushing in to fill the sudden void.

Bianca stood and proceeded to collect and fold the blanket. She **really** hoped he and Gia were right.

❧

SPRINGFIELD, Illinois
16 May 2025, 1:45pm

BANDIT PUSHED his head between the two front seats of Mike's Explorer to look out the windshield. *Are we there yet?*

Jake took a deep breath and sighed it back out in a slow exhalation. This was only the eighth or ninth time Bandit had asked, and Mike had **no** idea, because he couldn't hear the jaguar... either of them. The bright side was that, yes, they were almost there. The buildings of downtown Springfield surrounded them, and the AEC occupied a section of the basement in the federal building that was less than two blocks away.

"Not quite, buddy," Jake replied, "but almost."

How does the nice lady in the box know where we're going?

A white paw struck Bandit on his shoulder loud enough that Mike heard it. *Quit being stupid, fur-butt. That's a mobile phone. Jake already explained them to us. It's like a baby computer.*

Oh. How long until it grows up then? And what do you feed it?

Smokey replied with a chuff laced with exasperation. *I don't know why I try. I really don't.* Another chuff. *It's not a baby like we were. It's not alive. It doesn't grow or change.*

Oh. Okay. Bandit remarked as Mike turned the Explorer into the federal building's parking lot and then chose one of the vacant spots. * *Ooooh... does this mean we're there? The car stopping means we're there, right?* *

* *Yes, fur-butt. It means we're here.* * When Smokey continued, the 'flavor' of her mind-voice changed, and somehow, Jake knew she 'spoke' only to him. * *Did he hit his head a lot when we were cubs?* *

Jake grinned and shook his head, thinking his reply. * *Not that I noticed, but it's always possible, I suppose. No... I think he's just excited to be on his first trip since I brought you two home, so he ends up sounding more stupid than he really is.* *

* *He needs to work on that. I'm not sure I like having a littermate who sounds so mentally challenged.* *

And with those words, Smokey blew Jake's mind yet again. As far as he knew, he had never discussed the phrase 'mentally challenged' with either of them, so she must've learned it somewhere else. Where? No idea. Probably from watching TV with his mom, but there was no guarantee. Smokey easily sounded like she was on par with a junior or maybe a senior in high school. He suspected Bandit mirrored her development, but his excitable nature overshadowed it.

Jake unbuckled his seatbelt and turned in his seat as best he could to face the kids. "Okay. So, we've talked about this. Stay at my side at all times. If anyone acts like they're afraid of you, either lean into me like you're afraid of them or lay flat on the floor. Don't approach any children, and if any children approach you—especially if they escape their parents to do so—freeze and don't move. We good?"

Both jaguars bobbed their heads in obvious nods, and Jake turned to Mike. "Well, I think we're good. Let's do this."

EIGHT

Jake let Mike lead the way into the federal building. If there was a security desk, he suspected Mike's credentials as a police officer would keep the kids from getting shot or tased long enough to explain. After all, Jake hadn't heard of too many jaguars as familiars; he thought they were usually dogs or cats or birds... smaller animals like that. Upon passing through the doors and entering the main vestibule or foyer, Jake felt a twinge of disappointment. It didn't look any different than any other office building he'd visited. Tile floors waxed until they shined. Fluorescent lights in the drop ceilings. Signs everywhere. And yes... the security desk he feared.

A lady with dark curly hair sat at the security desk, wearing the uniform of the Federal Protective Service, and she watched them enter. She especially paid attention to how the jaguars stopped and waited for Jake to hold each set of double doors for them.

Mike approached the desk and offered the lady his best Cary Grant smile as he began, "Hi, I—"

"Mage and familiar evaluation?" She interrupted Mike to ask, not taking her admiring eyes off the big cats.

"Uhm, yes... that's right," Jake answered.

"Take the second elevator down to B1. The signs will direct you." The lady paused for a moment, then glanced down the hall both ways. "So, I *know* it's almost rude to ask, but I would love to feel their fur."

Jake grinned. Yeah... he knew that feeling. He loved spending an evening sitting with them on the floor, just rubbing their backs or sides. He looked down to find them looking up at him, almost hopeful, if he interpreted their expressions correctly.

"Up to you two... it's your fur."

At which point, they both went behind the security desk, each choosing the opposite side so that the lady ended up sandwiched between jaguars. She held her hands out for them to sniff, and they promptly dropped their heads and pushed them up against her hands. Taking that as a sign, she stroked their fur from their heads to their shoulder blades.

"They are so beautiful. How old are they?"

"About four years, I think," Jake replied. "Give or take a few months. I found them when they were little, barely old enough to chew solid food."

After a couple more strokes along their spines, she pulled her hands away, but it was obvious the decision was reluctant. "You two should probably get back on the other side of the desk now. My partner for this shift should be back any minute, and he's a real stickler for the rules."

The jaguars bobbed their heads in a nod, then backed out for more room before they turned to walk back to Jake's side.

"Oh, wow... they understand English?" she asked.

Jake chuckled as several memories came to the surface of his thoughts. "When they want to, but Bandit is worse about it than Smokey."

She snorted a laugh before she could stop herself. "You named them Smokey and Bandit?"

"Seemed appropriate."

The squeaky hinge of a door off to Jake's right prompted the lady to bring her face back to a neutral non-expression. "Well, best of luck in your evaluation today, sir. You want the second elevator down this side of the hall."

Jake noticed a guy about his dad's age—also in the uniform of the Federal Protective Service—enter the hall from the Men's room and approach the security desk. He frowned at the sight of the jaguars but didn't otherwise react when they stayed glued to Jake's side. Jake fought to keep a straight face as he thought that the guy's visit to the restroom must've been unsuccessful, given his constipated expression.

They entered the elevator, and as soon as the doors closed, Mike turned to Jake and gave him a bewildered look. "It's like I was invisible. I've never had that happen."

Jake almost made a *very* crude joke, but he kept his peace and simply shrugged.

THE RECEPTION AREA of the Springfield AEC was a well-lit and tastefully appointed room just off the elevator. Two half-windows lined with security wire allowed natural light into the room, and a woman sat at the reception desk. Chairs lined the walls, and people with the occasional animal occupied about half of them.

It was clear from her expression that she fought the urge to gush over the jaguars like the lady at the security desk, and Jake held back his own smile at her reaction.

"Good day, and welcome to the Springfield AEC. I'm Melanie. How can I help you today?"

Jake stepped forward, saying, "Hi. I think I might have manifested yesterday, and my friend drove me up here for evaluation."

"And we're evaluating which one of these lovely jaguars as a potential familiar?"

"Uhm, can we do both?"

Melanie replied with a tolerant smile. "Of course. It never hurts to be sure."

She swiveled her chair and grabbed a clipboard off the credenza behind her. She secured three forms in its clip before swiveling back to them. "Please fill out these forms to the best of your knowledge. There are pens right there in the cup if you need one."

Jake pulled his pen from where he had it clipped to the outside of his thigh pocket and accepted the clipboard. Then, he led Mike and the kids to an unoccupied section and picked a seat. Mike sat beside him, and Smokey and Bandit curled up at Jake's feet... as much as adult jaguars curl up at all.

The forms went into almost excruciating detail about family history of affinities. It wasn't the first time that he had encountered forms asking about his family history. But his records from DCFS didn't give even a hint about who his biological parents were. So, he wrote 'Adopted—Presumed Orphaned' in every section asking about family history and paid it no further thought.

By the time he finished the forms, even taking as little time as he did, he stood and looked down on two sleeping jaguars and fought the urge to chuckle. Maybe they'd been so excited about going for a ride that they were already drained from just the trip to Springfield... or maybe—and more probably—they were faking it. Either way, it wasn't the first time he had to step over them, and neither one even twitched as he did so. Jake returned the forms to Melanie before resuming his seat to await his turn.

"So, you're the resident expert on mages between the two of us," Jake said, his voice low. "How does this evaluation work?"

Mike frowned, then leaned back and tapped his chin as he adopted a thoughtful expression. "You know, I'm not sure. I don't think I've ever read anything about it, beyond everyone saying it's quick and painless."

"Huh. Do you think they tell people not to talk about it?"

Mike shrugged. "Maybe? I dunno. I guess we'll find out."

Over the next hour or so, officials called everyone who was ahead of Jake. They went through the single door out of the reception area that wasn't the entrance, and they returned within minutes... often looking either relaxed or bewildered. Jake and Mike chatted back and forth as the minutes passed until the door opened once more, and the lady who had called about half the people stepped out, saying, "Thornton Adams?"

At first, Jake didn't react, but Mike jabbed him in the ribs with his elbow.

"What?" Jake asked.

Mike rolled his eyes. "Dude, she just called your name."

"She did?"

"Thornton Adams?" she helpfully repeated, amusement dancing in her eyes.

"Oh, yeah... that's me," Jake said as he stood, then looked down at the napping jaguars at his feet. "Okay, you two. You can quit faking. Let's go."

Both jaguars languidly stretched as they stood, and when Jake walked toward the lady, they fell in beside him. She stepped back through the door first, and Jake held it for the jaguars then followed himself. As soon as the door closed, the woman turned to him as she led them down the short hallway and smiled, saying, "Hi, I'm Abby, and I'll be your evaluation specialist today. I'm what's known as a Tri-Sphere among mages; I have full affinity with the Air Sphere, strong affinity with Spirit, and a weak affinity with Death. Do you have any suspicions what your affinity might be?"

"Mike, my friend outside, seems rather convinced one of them is Time."

"Oh? Why is that?" Abby asked, her expression patient... maybe even patronizingly indulgent.

"Well, he's a self-confessed fanboy when it comes to anything mage-related. He reads everything he can about all this." Jake felt his cheeks flush with embarrassment. "And when I manifested yesterday, I think I kinda froze time."

Abby froze mid-step for just a heartbeat before she resumed her easy gait. "Are you *certain* you froze time?"

"Oh, yeah... pretty certain."

"And may I ask *why* you are so certain?"

Jake took a breath, then a second. "Because everything seemed to stop when a bank robber pulled the trigger of a shotgun he pointed at me, and I was able to move to him and reverse the shotgun in his grip before it fired."

Abby froze again and slowly turned her head to stare at Jake. Her jaw trembled like it wanted to drop but she fought it. "You... you mean that not only did time freeze around you but you were also able to walk around and manipulate objects inside the frozen moment?"

"Yeah... there's something else really weird, too. It felt like I could feel the cyclic vibrations of all the atoms and molecules around me. I think I could've touched the different molecules that make up the air if I had tried really hard and put my full focus to it."

Abby paled in the blink of an eye, faster than a finger-snap. Her jaw worked as if to speak, but no sound escaped. Jake didn't know how long they stood in the middle of the hallway like that, but Abby seemed beyond unsettled by what he said.

After several moments, she blinked and shook her head, then pivoted and opened a door. She stepped through the doorway that led to what seemed to be a normal office, except there was only a small waist-high table in the center of the room. A large smokey-white crystal laid atop it.

Abby waited for Jake and the jaguars to enter the room, then closed the door.

"O-okay... the evaluation procedure is fairly straightforward. Just approach the table when you're ready and pick up the crystal. It will turn one or more colors that match those on a twelve-point color wheel. Each color represents a specific Sphere, and the relative brightness—if there's more than one color—indicates the strength of each affinity. Go ahead when you're ready."

"That's it? Just pick up the crystal, and it will do the rest?"

Abby nodded. "That's it."

"How do we evaluate them to see if they're familiars?"

"Pretty much the same thing," Abby answered, though she still seemed rattled. "After the initial evaluation, you'll put the crystal back on the table, then call one of them to you. Pick up the crystal again while you're touching each of them. If you're bonded, the color or colors will be brighter than they were when it was just you."

"Huh... there's so little information out there about this that I kinda had myself psyched up for an ordeal."

Without waiting for Abby to respond, Jake stepped forward. The crystal itself was about eight to ten inches long and maybe three inches in diameter at its widest point. The moment Jake lifted it off the table, the off-white cloud in the crystal vanished for several heartbeats before it came back a pure white that glowed bright enough to hurt his eyes.

"What the hell..." Abby's professional demeanor slipped even further that time. She strode toward the table and stopped maybe six feet away, her eyes locked on the crystal. "That's not right. Something's wrong. Put it back on the table."

Jake complied, and as soon as he no longer touched the crystal, the white radiance faded, returning to the off-white smoke. Abby leaned over and grabbed the crystal. The off-white cloud separated into three distinct colors.

"Okay," Abby said, her tone uncertain.

She returned the crystal to the table. "Pick it up again."

Jake shrugged and picked it up with his right hand that time. The off-white cloud inside the crystal almost instantly shifted to a brilliant white radiance.

"What the ever-loving f—" Abby's eyes shot wide, and her hand flew up to cover her mouth. "Sorry. Sorry." Then, she closed her eyes and slowly shook her head side to side as if exaggerating a 'no' answer. "Get your head right, Abby girl. You're a professional; act like it."

She took a deep breath. Then, a second. And a third before she opened her eyes once more. "Okay... well, something is obviously wrong. But let's try testing your friends before we move on."

69

"Smokey, over here, please," Jake said as he laid the crystal back on the table.

The white jaguar dutifully padded to Jake's side, and he crouched to place his hand right between her shoulders. When he picked up the crystal this time, it flared so bright—and still pure white—that he saw spots when he put it back on the table.

"Thank you, Smokey," Jake said as he blinked his eyes. "Bandit, buddy, you're up."

The jaguars switched, and Jake almost feared to pick up the crystal. He still saw so many spots that a second round might blind him. With his hand touching Bandit between his shoulders, he lifted the crystal once more and winced at the brightness as he hurried to return it to the tabletop.

"Well, it seems you have *two* familiars... on top of everything else that's odd about all this."

"Familiars aren't common?"

Abby shook her head. "Heavens, no. Just because little Johnny really likes his ferret and his ferret really likes him does not mean the ferret is a familiar. I've never seen a mage below a Tri-Sphere with a familiar, either. Wait here, please. I'll be right back."

Abby pivoted on her heel and strode from the room. A few minutes passed before she returned, her arms laden with black velvet bags with draw-string closures. As she placed them on the table, Jake heard a glass-like tinkling.

"These are all the evaluation crystals we have. We're going to try them all until we find one that works for you. Go."

Jake went through the whole stack. Every single one displayed the same pure-white radiance when he touched it.

By the time he returned the final crystal to its bag and placed it back on the table, Abby's expression had shifted from disbelief mixed with astonishment to suspicious anger.

"Seriously, dude... what the shit? Is this some kind of joke? Did someone put you up to this to haze the new girl? If that's what's going on, it's really not nice, you know."

Jake backed up and lifted his hands in the classic 'surrender' gesture. "I'm sorry, Abby. I don't know what you mean. Mike drove me here from Hornbeam, because I don't own a car and know nothing about mages beyond the basics they teach in high school."

She glared at him as she clenched her jaw. After several heart-beats of silence, she pivoted toward the door and stomped out, almost slamming the door behind her. It seemed like she was gone a minute—at most—before she returned... almost dragging an African American woman who appeared middle-aged with her.

"Do it again," Abby ordered. "Use the very first one."

Jake picked up the crystal that didn't have a velvet bag and held it out to the ladies, glowing a bright white light.

"See? See!" Abby demanded, waving one arm in Jake's general direction. "What the *hell* is up with that?"

The older lady clicked her tongue. "Language, Abigail. We must comport ourselves at all times like the honored professionals of the Magocracy that we are."

"The hell with comportment!" Abby shot back, and Jake winced. "That shit ain't right!"

"Abigail, calm yourself," the older lady said before she turned to Jake. "Young man, you may return the crystal to the tabletop. I'm Martha Culpepper, by the way, senior evaluator here at the Spring-field AEC."

"Jake Adams."

"It's a pleasure to make your acquaintance," Martha replied before turning back to Abby. "Now... Abigail, recite how the crystals work, if you please."

Abby seemed like she wanted to glare at her elder, but she huffed a breath, then said, "The crystals are spelled to respond to a mage's affinities. They will show each Sphere as a color on the common twelve-point color wheel. The brightness of the color shows the strength of the affinity."

"And if the crystal glows white?"

"How the f—" Abby stopped, closed her eyes for a moment. She then opened her eyes and continued. "That never came up in training for this job, ma'am."

"That's very true. It didn't come up in mine, either. But do you remember your high school physics? Specifically, the sections on visible light?"

Abby frowned. "Sure. Each color is a different wavelength of light."

Martha nodded like a parent pleased that a child saw the obvious answer. "And if there are all the different wavelengths of visible light present?"

"You have white light, of course," Abby replied. It took a few seconds, but then, her eyes shot wide, and her jaw dropped as she stared at the naked crystal laying on the table. Her eyes snapped back to Jake, and she edged back a step.

Martha turned to Jake, adopting a patient smile. "We find ourselves in some uncharted waters, Mister Adams. I'm not quite sure *how* to record this, because our system only allows us to enter up to five affinities. If the crystal is accurate—and it *always* is—you appear to have all twelve affinities. Off the top of my head, I can't remember ever reading or hearing about this happening before."

"And there's no chance he's faking it somehow?" Abby asked.

"I don't see how," Martha replied. "Grandmasters of each Sphere collaborated to design and create the evaluation crystals. I have never heard of a case where faking an evaluation was even suspected."

"Then, what do we do?" Abby's voice edged perilously close to the wail of a frightened child.

Martha sighed. "That does bear some thought. It's already been a long day, dear. Why don't you go ahead and clock out? I'll handle this."

Abby's expression and shoulders relaxed, betraying her utter relief. "Thank you."

Without even saying goodbye to Jake, she fled the room.

As soon as the door latched, Martha worked the fingers of her left hand through a complex gesture, and two wooden chairs suddenly appeared, one by her and the other by Jake. Jake gaped at them, especially when he saw they bore no tool marks.

"Have a seat, lad," Martha said, as she eased herself into taking her own advice.

Jake sat with extreme caution, half expecting the chair to vanish out from under him. "How...?"

"Full affinity with the Earth Sphere," Martha replied. "Abigail is an excellent worker when it comes to the rote, everyday tasks... but she is not suited for totally new and unfamiliar situations, no pun intended. I fully expect her to drown today's stress and wake up tomorrow with a vicious hangover. I'll be amazed if she remembers *any* of this when she comes to work Monday morning. But that doesn't help us decide what to do with you. Tell me... how would *you* handle this?"

Jake shrugged. "I don't really know. I... never wanted to be a mage. I hadn't figured out what my ambitions were, beyond not wanting anyone to take them," nodding to the jaguars, "away from me. As far as I know, they're the only survivors of that big train wreck just north of Hornbeam, back in 2021."

"Well, we can certainly register them both as your familiars. That won't be a problem." Martha leaned back against her seat and tapped her lips in a thoughtful pose. After several moments, she sighed. "I remember when the Civil Rights movement and the riots really kicked off in the sixties. My parents lived through slavery and the Civil War. They weren't slaves, of course; no one in their right mind tries to enslave a mage, even a single Sphere, but they *saw* it. History overflows with evidence that humans—regardless of type—do not like anyone or anything they perceive as 'different.' No matter if 'different' is only skin deep, and your 'different' is way more than that. Even if I could record that you have all twelve affinities, I don't think I would. I'd like to think our fellow mages would be good and upstanding people, but we both know that's a load of bull. Gimme a second."

Martha heaved herself to her feet and left the room. She returned not even a minute later with a chart that delineated every Sphere and what color represented them in the crystal. She held it out to him and said, "Pick three. I'll record that you're an exceptional Tri-Sphere with full affinities across the board. Just make damn sure you never publicly display any affinities beyond the three you pick. Savvy?"

"Well, my friend says I manifested as a Time mage, and I have two familiars, so there's Life. I hate having to hunt for a flashlight, so let's go with Light for the third."

Martha eyed him, lifting one eyebrow. "You sure? Once we do this, we can't change it."

Jake looked over the list again and nodded. "Yeah... I'm sure."

"Very well. Hang out here for a little bit, and I'll come back when I have your record and registration certificates. Oh... and do they have names?"

Jake pointed to the white jaguar. "Smokey." Then, pointed to the melanistic one. "Bandit."

Martha barked a laugh, then turned and crossed the room. As she walked through the door, Jake heard her mutter, "Kids, these days."

CHAPTER
NINE

A few minutes later, Martha returned. She held a manila envelope under her arm, while her hands overflowed with what looked like harnesses in more colors than a rainbow. When she laid them out on the table, Jake saw that they were indeed animal harnesses with the words 'REGISTERED FAMILIAR' on each of the top bands that ran along their spine. Each harness further had what looked like MOLLE straps and hook-and-loop attachment points just about everywhere.

"Okay, my dears," Martha said, "I tried to guess the sizes, and these all allow for a certain amount of adjustment. Since you're already adults for your species, I skipped the harnesses we provide for pups or cubs. Let's pick color first, and then, we'll see about sizing."

Jake approached the table and picked up one of the harnesses, giving it a closer look. "So, what's with all the MOLLE straps and industrial velcro?"

Martha smiled. "Well, some crafters take their familiars into a service, like police or fire department or even the military, and these attachment points provide the opportunity for the familiars to carry their own food and snacks or spell components, if the crafter needs such. Spell components aren't really a thing for us as mages, unless we allow ourselves to develop bad habits, but the witches and warlocks—poor souls—can only do ritual magic or use imbued items that trigger with a command word."

I like that one. Bandit said, lifting his nose to point at the black harness in Jake's hands. The 'REGISTERED FAMILIAR' was bold white lettering, and the harness had large, reflective white strips to increase visibility.

Jake smiled. "Bandit picks this one."

"Excellent," Martha replied, then turned to Smokey. "And what about you, dear? See anything you like?"

Martha held several harnesses at a level where Smokey could see them, and she went through several groups before Smokey responded.

There! I like the pink one.

"She likes the pink one with the text in black," Jake said.

"Excellent choice, dear," Martha remarked. "I think it will look quite fetching on you. Now... shall we see about fit?"

Over the next few minutes, Martha taught Jake how to put the harnesses on the jaguars, making sure they were not too tight while still being snug enough not to foul their legs or catch on anything.

Martha smiled, "And I was right. Very pretty, my dear."

Smokey leaned in and brushed her head against Martha's leg to express her gratitude. *Please tell the nice lady 'thank you' for me, Jake.*

"She asked me to tell you 'thank you,'" Jake dutifully conveyed.

"And you're very welcome, Smokey."

Please thank her for me, too. Bandit said, as he settled down from moving and shifting his body to get a feel for the harness, then brushed his head along Martha's other leg.

Jake did so.

"You're welcome, too, Bandit. Familiars are so rare that it's a very special treat to meet just one, let alone two."

"So, what do I owe you for the harnesses?" Jake asked, reaching for his wallet.

Martha waved that question away. "The Magocracy provides the first harness for all new registered familiars. Just like there's no charge for the mage evaluation." She turned and retrieved the manila envelope. "This envelope contains your official certification as an exceptional Tri-Sphere and the registration certificates for Bandit and Smokey. In a few days, you'll receive cards for your wallet you can laminate. Please, have those cards with you any time you're out in public with either or both of them. For now, I printed temporary ones that you can cut out until the permanent cards arrive; they're in the envelope, too. Any questions?"

Jake accepted the envelope and pursed his lips, unsure how to ask. "So, what should I do about training? I mean, if I have all the affinities, shouldn't I learn to control that at a minimum?"

Martha reached into her pocket and withdrew an index card. She turned it so Jake could see and revealed his name, address, cell number, and email address written on it. "I thought you might ask about something like that, so I took the liberty of violating your personal privacy by copying your contact information. When you've been around as long as I have, you tend to develop social networks, and I'll see what I can do about arranging for some off-the-books training. When it comes to Nature and Life, you're very close to the two I'd recommend anyway. Gerald and Bianca Wainwright live at the Wainwright Grove right outside of Hornbeam; if the Magocracy certified Druids, she would easily be Grandmaster by now, and her husband Gerald just passed the exam for Grandmaster of the Life Sphere. It's been an age since I said hello, so I'll give them a call after work to catch up with them."

A weight he hadn't fully realized he carried evaporated off Jake's shoulders. "Thank you... for everything."

"Think nothing of it, lad. I don't see how the so-called 'right thing' in this case would do anything other than ruin your life. If I shared the fact that every evaluation crystal here says you have all twelve affinities, the Magocracy would hound you for the rest of your life; you'd never have a moment's peace... and that's assuming the Magocracy were the only ones hounding you. Besides, if the Magocracy believed possessing all twelve affinities was possible, their registration system would allow that. As long as you don't do anything that attracts attention and forces another evaluation, no one will give you a second look... unless they're head-hunting for a job or something. Everyone loves to hire Tri-Spheres and will pay top-dollar for them. Now then, is there anything else you'd like to ask?"

Jake wracked his mind and came up empty. He slowly shook his head. "I'm sure there are all kinds of things I should ask, but my mind's blank at the moment."

"That's often how these things happen. You'll wake up in the middle of the night—or be walking down the street next week—and have all manner of questions invade your mind. Well, let's get you back to your friend, so you can go home."

MARTHA OPENED THE DOOR, and Jake watched his friend jerk his head up, then erupt in a huge grin when he saw both Bandit and Smokey wore a familiar harness. Mike surged to his feet and crossed the room, kneeling to look them over and compliment their new accessory. After giving the kids their due, he stood and directed an expectant expression toward Jake.

"Well?"

Jake took a breath, not liking what he was about to do. "Exceptional Tri-Sphere. Full affinities to Time, Life, and Light."

Mike flexed his arm and clenched his fist in a silent cheer. "I *knew* it! Well, not that you'd be a Tri-Sphere, but I knew you weren't just a Time mage. That's awesome, dude! Come on; we need to go celebrate."

"Slow down," Jake replied, then turned to Martha. "Thank you much for all your help, Martha. I really appreciate it."

Martha beamed. "Think nothing of it, young man. I'm glad I could help you. Have a good afternoon and evening."

She retreated through the door to the back offices as Jake turned back to Mike. "So, what does 'celebrate' look like in *your* mind?"

"Well, we *are* starting the weekend," Mike remarked as he led Jake and the kids to the exit, then shot Jake a mischievous look, "but you've never really been the type for strippers and beer. Tell you what... how about I take you home so you can talk to your folks about all this, and I'll call you tomorrow? It's my other day off in this schedule rotation, so we can do something fun... like take Bandit and Smokey to the park or something."

Both jaguars perked up at the mention of exploring the town, and Jake feared Mike just created a couple monsters. But he had always felt kinda bad about having to hide them all the time. So, he might as well embrace the new reality.

"That sounds like fun, actually," Jake replied, and both jaguars rubbed against him.

∾

MARTHA CULPEPPER'S Residence
 Springfield, Illinois
 16 May 2025, 6:45pm

MARTHA OPENED the drawer of the bureau at one end of her dining room and retrieved a cell phone inside an antistatic bag with a built-in Faraday mesh and an old, hardcopy address book. She collected a battery from a different drawer. The antistatic bag with a built-in Faraday mesh wasn't perfect, but overall, it performed acceptably to block signals to or from the device. She withdrew the phone and fitted its battery back into its slot, then replaced the battery cover and held the power button to start the boot-up sequence. It was one of the original mobile phones with no camera or GPS, and she only used it in very specific circumstances. On her way home from work, she bought a pre-paid block of minutes and resigned herself to going through the torturous process of picking a new number.

Once the phone was fully active, Martha opened the address book and thumbed through it until she arrived at the entry she desired. She tapped the numbers into the ancient flip phone and pressed the button to initiate the call.

She heard three rings before a voice she recognized said, "Draco Investigations."

Martha first met the woman she knew as Isabel Taylor in her young adulthood. Isabel was investigating a string of murders at the time, and Martha's parents were the two latest victims.

"Isabel, hi... it's Martha Culpepper. Thank you for taking my call."

There was a slight pause before warmth suffused Isabel's voice, "Martha, it has been quite some time. How have you been?"

"Oh, I'm fine. I'm the senior evaluator at the AEC in Springfield, Illinois, and I had an odd case come into the center today. A **very** odd case."

"Is that so?" Isabel replied.

"Oh, yes. A young man—twenty-five, or there about—came in for evaluation. He brought two jaguars with him for familiar evaluation—one melanistic and the other white—and when he touched the crystal, it glowed white."

Silence extended for long enough that Martha feared the call dropped. Just as she was about to ask if Isabel was still on the line, Isabel said, "It glowed **white**. You're sure?"

"My newest evaluator went through every crystal we have, with the same results. It unsettled her quite a bit, let me tell you. Have you ever heard of something like that?"

"Oh, yes, Martha; I have indeed. Even though they are technically still mages, arcane scholars in ancient times grouped them separately. The common name for them was 'sorcerer,' but the ancient

Greeks called them Titans. The Olympians in Greek mythology were based on the children of sorcerers and humans with no affinities."

"I... I see. Why doesn't the Magocracy teach about them?"

"Because I'd be amazed if the Magocracy **knows** about them... in the institutional sense. The Magocracy didn't really get established until the Byzantine Empire under Justinian, and by that point, it had been something like six-hundred years since the Parthians killed the last known sorcerer. They were never **common**, you understand, but they were plentiful enough that knowledge of them passed as whispers from parent to child. 'Be good, or a sorcerer will come for you' kind of thing."

Martha frowned. "But why? I know that crafters haven't always enjoyed wide acceptance, but they've never been ostracized or been any kind of bogeyman."

"No, they haven't, and you're right," Isabel answered. "The reason why is the sorcerers. Everyone feared them, Martha. **Everyone**. Even my people. Compared to sorcerers, even a Quad-Sphere mage is little more than a child. I still remember seeing a sorcerer in action; I was a young hatchling at the time, and I think it was during Caesar's conquest of Gaul. I never did know **why** Caesar had a sorcerer with him, but regardless, I watched that sorcerer fend off the concerted attacks of over twelve mages... and a handful of them displayed affinities with **five** Spheres. Think about that for a second, Martha. Merlin—the founder of the Magocracy, for all intents and purposes, who is verified as having five Spheres—would not have been even worrisome to a sorcerer."

More than anything else, Martha felt overwhelmed from the conversation. "Are... will you try to kill him? I mean, if he's as dangerous as you say?"

Isabel snorted. "He hasn't done anything heinous, has he?"

"Well, no... but what if—"

"I do not deal in 'what ifs,' Martha, and neither should you. Unless or until he presents himself as a threat to humanity, he has as much right to live as anyone else. But if he chooses evil... well... I will try."

Martha's blood went cold. Isabel would *try* to kill him if he turned evil? And she heard the uncertainty in Isabel's voice at the thought of facing this sorcerer in combat. Who the hell were these people that Isabel doubted her ability to win a fight?

"Isabel, I—"

"No, Martha. You were right to call me. I presume you wanted to ask me to teach him the Fire Sphere?"

"Yes. I will owe—"

Again, Isabel interrupted her. "No, Martha. The debt will be the sorcerer's, and I will negotiate with him directly. Who and where is he?"

Martha read off the information she wrote on the blank index card. Jake's name, address, mobile number, and email address.

Once Martha finished, Isabel snorted. "Damn. If my parents hung a shingle on me like 'Thornton,' I'd go by 'Jake,' too. I almost feel sorry for him. Very well. I don't have any open cases right now, and the supernatural world has been fairly quiet. Kai can keep an eye on things here for a while and contact me if there are any flare-ups. I'll be in Hornbeam no later than Monday, and I'll oversee his training from there."

Martha didn't know what to say. She hadn't expected Isabel to move on it quite like that. "Uhm, I don't know what to say, Isabel. Thank you."

"No thanks necessary. It behooves us all for me to meet him and get a sense of his character before he learns the full extent of his power. As long as I'm in the area, I may nip up to Springfield and invite you to lunch."

"I'd like that," Martha replied. "Well, I won't keep you. Safe travels, Isabel."

"Safe travels to you, too."

The call ended, and Martha went through the steps to return the phone to its inactive and protected state before turning her attention to dinner.

~

THE ADAMS RESIDENCE
Hornbeam, Illinois
16 May 2025, 6:35pm

JAKE HELD the door for the jaguars and asked them to wait until he called them before coming into the living room. They promptly sat and settled into wait for his call.

He wasn't really looking forward to this. Never in his life had he doubted his parents' love, but he was still adopted. He wasn't truly **theirs**. How would that affect things? His mind was unshakable in his certainty that his parents would love him regardless, but fear was hardly ever rational.

Jake entered the living room that shared space with the dining 'room.' That part of the house was more of an open concept design than strict divisions between rooms, so his parents noticed him almost immediately as they set the table for dinner.

"There he is," his dad—Frank—said. "Did you enjoy the day with Mike?"

His mom—Sarah—swarmed around the table and pulled him into a tight hug. "I've been so worried about you ever since that nastiness at the bank. I'm glad you're home."

Jake returned his mother's hug, savoring the unconditional love that poured into him. "Mom, Dad... there's something we should probably discuss."

"What is it, son?" his dad asked.

"Well," Jake began, then sighed. "It's about yesterday... at the bank. I switched the shotgun around in the robber's grip. He had already pulled the trigger, so it was going to fire regardless. I... well... I killed that man."

His mother released him from the hug and stepped back to her arms' length. "That doesn't make any sense, honey. How could you have switched it? You wouldn't have had time."

"Yeah, Mom... I kinda did." Jake turned his head toward the house's foyer. "Okay, you two... come on in."

Soon enough, the jaguars trotted into view, and it was a heart-beat or three before his parents processed what was different. Smokey helped by turning sideways, so they could read the text embroidered into her harness.

His mom understood first, and her eyes shot wide as her hand flew to her mouth. "Oh my goodness! My baby is a *mage*?"

Jake simply nodded as his dad almost charged around the table and pulled him into a hug of his own. When the hug ended, his dad asked, "So, what are your affinities?"

"I'm a Tri-Sphere with full affinity across the board," Jake replied and felt his stomach tighten at the lie. "Time, Life, and Light."

"Time? You have *full* affinity to Time?"

Jake simply nodded again. "Yeah... that's how I was able to take the shotgun out of the guy's hands and spin it around so it shot him. It was some kind of weird frozen moment."

"Damn, son... I'm proud of you. If you're as conscientious about this as you are about everything else in your life, you'll go far."

They continued to discuss the evaluation and what Jake's next steps would be now as they busied themselves with dinner. As soon as his parents gave him some space, Jake removed the harnesses and hung them on the coat and hat rack in the foyer. Returning to take his customary seat at the dining table, Jake felt buoyed in the obvious love and warmth from his parents.

CHAPTER

TEN

Mike and Jake spent the next day showing the jaguars around town. More than one child escaped his or her parents to run up to the jaguars to see the 'kitties,' much to their parents' horror. Until they processed what the harnesses meant. Then, reactions ebbed to mere anxiety. The parents fearing the jaguars made total sense; after all, an adult jaguar can do frightening things to an adult human, so what could they do to children?

But as it turned out, the jaguars *loved* children and soon sought any opportunity to interact with them. While watching them frolic among a group of kids at the park, Jake foresaw a visit to the local elementary school in their future... as soon as he acquired his own vehicle. He couldn't keep relying on Mike's generosity; his best friend wouldn't even let Jake pay him for the fuel they used going to Springfield.

And so it was that Mike delivered a very tired Jake and two exhausted jaguars to the Adams residence late Saturday evening. Jake opened the gate in the fence and watched his friends seem to drag themselves through. Both of them looked ready to drop, only moving out of sheer determination to make it to their beds in Jake's room.

Isabel arrived in Hornbeam in the late afternoon on Sunday. Most people would not have considered making the trip from the Pueblo area on a motorcycle, but—one—she loved her Indian Chief Dark Horse and—two—she was a veteran rider who knew how to make time on the highways. Most would've secured a hotel room upon arrival, or even called a friend to say they were in the area. But not Isabel. No. She went straight to the address Martha provided and arrived just in time to see a young man with an impressive build bring four large trashcans to the curb. He secured their lids before brushing off his hands and halfway turned back toward the house when he stopped and turned back. He seemed to focus on her where she sat atop her idling motorcycle for several moments before he turned and disappeared through the fence's gate.

Nothing about him screamed evil-doer, but then, it was rare that a person's evil 'shone' through to the outside. Some of the worst people she had known down through the years appeared to be people one would love to have as a neighbor. For all his brutality, Genghis Khan was a cultured and urbane individual around the supper table; just be sure not to meet him on the field of battle.

Still, though, Isabel allowed a tentative hope that this young man—this Thornton 'Jake' Adams—would be one of the good ones. Not just someone who existed, but someone who acted. The world needed more people like that, and if her people refused to step up and assume their traditional role, she would need help. Heh... not **would** need, as if it was some possibility far off in the future. She **needed** help. She was one person supposedly policing the **entire supernatural world**. Yeah... that was rough, no matter how one looked at it. If she didn't have the allies that she did or the list of favors owed to her that she did, the job would be nigh impossible.

Okay. She had laid eyes on the boy. Now, it was time to secure lodging and a training venue. If she was successful in her first choice, she'd approach the boy the next day. Decision made, she revved the engine and eased it into gear before pulling a U-turn and disappearing down the street.

~

THE WAINWRIGHT GROVE
18 May 2025, 6:35pm

BIANCA LOOKED up from the flower bed in front of her at the sound of an approaching motorcycle. Which struck her as being **very** odd. None of their friends owned a motorcycle. She sat back on her heels and waited. Beauregard was just a thought away, and she didn't mind a break from setting bulbs.

A black motorcycle with a rider decked out in a black full-face helmet and black riding leathers eased through the hedge, and Bianca marveled at the lack of reaction from the grove. At the very least, the animals of the immediate area mobbed any visitors they received, to the point that the regulars like the mail carrier and local delivery service drivers left their items just outside the hedge.

* Beauregard? * She sent her thought out, focusing on the faint link she felt with the grove's awareness.

* Yes, Mother? *

* There's something—no, someone—odd here. They just came through the hedge, and the grove didn't react. *

* Be very respectful, Mother, for you are crunchy and taste good with ketchup. *

Bianca almost snorted at Beauregard's reference to an old t-shirt from her table-top gaming youth, but where or how did he see it? The rider leaned the motorcycle on its kickstand and dismounted, first removing riding gloves before removing the helmet and revealing a classically attractive woman. Her features looked very Patrician, her hair the color of oak with a light stain. She stored her gloves in the helmet and hung that from a handlebar by its chinstrap.

By the time the visitor started walking her way, Bianca already stood and crossed the distance to meet her.

"Hello," the Druid said, "I'm Bianca Wainwright, and this is my grove. May I ask what brings you by?"

The woman extended a hand, which Bianca accepted... only to fight the urge to jerk away. She was **hot**. Her flesh felt at least a dozen degrees hotter than it should have been, so Bianca certainly didn't linger over the handshake.

"I am known in this time as Isabel Taylor," the woman said. "I am here because Martha Culpepper brought a matter to my attention. Are you aware of a mage who recently manifested in this area?"

All at once, a weight settled around Bianca's shoulders. What should she do? Say no? Say yes? Besides being literally hot, this woman exuded an aura of danger unlike anything Bianca had ever experienced. In her own grove—where her power and authority were supreme—Bianca *feared* this woman.

"Yes," Bianca answered at last. "I was there when it happened. He manifested Time, but the resonance of his manifestation was far stronger than a single-Sphere mage."

Isabel nodded. "And it should have been. He is a sorcerer, Lady Druid... what the ancient Greeks called Titans, and I am here to oversee his training. I came to you to enlist both you and your husband to teach him what each of you knows but also in the hopes of acquiring a training venue. I cannot envision anywhere else in the vicinity being as secure as your grove. If you are agreeable to the use of your grove as a training site, I am prepared to discuss compensation."

Just as quickly as the weight had settled around Bianca's shoulders, it vanished, and she erupted into a smile. "I have zero issues with sharing what I know or using our grove for his training. I had considered calling in a favor of my own with a Mind Grandmaster to remove all trace that the boy ever manifested."

"Just as well that you did not," Isabel replied. "Martha's solution is far better. She had him pick three affinities, which will be his public persona. To the world at large, he will be an exceptional Tri-Sphere with full affinities."

Bianca took a breath and huffed it back out. "Yeah, that's better than what I planned. But damn... only a Tri-Sphere? He will make every *other* Tri-Sphere look weak at best."

"We shall work on developing and practicing his restraint. He *cannot* make a mistake. Now. Let us discuss compensation."

"Well, what's your offer?" Bianca countered.

Isabel's eyes roamed over the areas of the core grove in sight. After several seconds of silence, she brought her eyes back to Bianca. "I am willing to offer a collection of now-extinct seedlings, held in magical stasis. They are sufficient in number to bring back their respective species of plants—trees, bushes, flowers, and such—that they represent."

Bianca fought to keep a straight face. She really did. But failed... utterly and completely. She *knew* she beamed like an eager child surrounded by presents, but she couldn't help it. At least she managed not to squee.

"Deal!"

A small, fractional smile brightened Isabel's features. "I suspected that might be sufficient temptation."

Sufficient temptation? Bianca almost snorted. *Any* Druid worth the title would give parts of their anatomy for the chance to bring back extinct species.

Isabel continued, pulling Bianca out of her spiraling thoughts. "I shall arrange for my associate at home to secure them for transport and delivery. Would you prefer collateral until such time as they arrive? I do not want to wait until then to approach the sorcerer."

Beauregard's warning flared bright in her mind, and Bianca quickly shook her head. "No, no. I don't believe either of us needs worry about collateral. You could've plied me with all sorts of monetary treasures or similar, but your proposal spoke directly to my heart. I would argue that you have earned some trust, which I hope will be strengthened over time."

The fractional smile expanded. "I am pleased you think so. May we negotiate for room and board?"

Bianca waved that question away. "You're covered. We have more space than we use, anyway, even with our two current guests. An old friend brought her daughter to study under us for Life and Alchemy, and she—that is, the friend—will be returning to New York within the next day or so, leaving her daughter with us. Given the nature of your visit, would you accept a polite fiction that you're a friend we met during the Restoration who's passing through?"

Isabel nodded her agreement. "Yes, that might be best, but what of the daughter? Her mother's departure will lay our falsehood bare."

"I suspect we will find a kindred spirit in the daughter, once we have the opportunity to discuss matters. Besides, we are unable to help her with her other affinities, so she might appreciate staying on and partaking of the training for those Spheres when it comes around... if you would be agreeable to such."

"Indeed. Appealing to her desire for additional training might go far in securing her as an ally. I approve of thy thoughts in this."

Isabel's slip into archaic usage did not escape Bianca's attention, but she could not discern if it was accidental or deliberate, so she kept her silence.

"When we settle into discussing the sorcerer's training, I shall inquire at that time what the daughter's other affinities are and schedule the training accordingly. Is she of an age where she won't feel slighted when he makes tasks that are beyond her seem trivial?"

Bianca's mind flitted back to Emilia's calm assertion that she would not allow failure in her life project, and she could not deny the doubt she felt in regard to Isabel's concern. "You know, I'm not certain. The best we can hope for might be his successes inspire a positive competition."

"If that is how events evolve, we shall have to ensure she does not become embittered or hostile toward the sorcerer. I have seen such happen in the past." Isabel's eyes flicked to a point over Bianca's shoulder for a moment. "But let us discuss other topics. We have ears approaching."

Bianca turned and saw Gianna heading her way with what looked to be a fruity concoction of some type. Gia arrived and said, "Gerald was kind enough to teach Emi the Wainwright Grove-approved method of making smoothies and made your favorite or so he said, tasking me to deliver it."

"Well, thank you. Gia, I'd like you to meet Isabel Taylor. We met during the Restoration after the Independence Day attacks, and she stopped by to visit since she was passing through. Isabel, this is one of my oldest friends, Gianna Harcourt."

Gia beamed. "It's so nice to meet you. I'm from New York City, so I'm rarely out here to meet many of Bianca's friends."

Isabel nodded once as if giving Gia a partial bow. "It is a pleasure to meet you as well, Gianna."

"Would you like a smoothie?" Bianca asked. "As long as Gerald's making them, he might as well make one more."

"That does sound nice," Isabel answered. "I left a motel about thirty minutes west of Topeka before sunrise this morning."

Bianca gasped, "Well, why didn't you say so? Here I was, just talking away. Let's get you a smoothie and some solid food, and then, I'll point you to a room and draw a bath. You have to be worn out from the road."

THE ADAMS RESIDENCE

19 May 2025, 7:45am

JAKE STEPPED through the gate and took a deep breath of the morning air. He always loved this time of year when the days didn't have the humidity of summer, though the temperature reached the high seventies. He looked forward to the walk to Percy's Grocery, even if he didn't look forward to the work itself.

Now that the jaguars were registered familiars, he asked if they wanted to go with him, and they promptly asked what the day would be like. Jake made it about thirty seconds into his answer before they turned without a word and went outside to lounge under one of the trees.

He set off at his normal walking pace, which should give him plenty of time to stop by the cafe he really liked for a tall cup of tea and a pastry. He easily walked a sixteen-minute mile when he put his mind to it, but after the weekend and its associated adventures, a slower pace sounded relaxing.

ABOUT TWENTY MINUTES LATER, Jake crossed the small parking lot toward his favorite cafe when a motorcycle pulled into one of the open spaces, and Jake instantly went on alert. It was the same blacked-out motorcycle and rider he'd seen when he took out the trash the night before. His certainty in that conclusion puzzled him almost as much as how his entire body tensed up, and he felt the saturation in his cells building... just like the bank Thursday morning.

The rider pulled off the gloves, then removed the helmet, and Jake hid his shock at seeing a woman's face. It wasn't that women couldn't ride motorcycles by themselves. No... it was that his subconscious had never treated a woman as a threat to him before. So, what was it about this one that made him react that way?

She hung the helmet by its chinstrap from one of the handlebars and arrived at the cafe's doors at the same time Jake did. She smiled her thanks as he graciously held the door for her, and Jake tried to be subtle in his appreciation of the view as he followed her inside.

He kept a respectful distance, not wanting to crowd her, but he couldn't believe his ears when he overheard her order. It wasn't that she rattled off a complex coffee with more flavors than he'd ever heard of... oh, no. It was her final statement that took him completely off-guard.

"And I'd like that as hot as you can make it. If it will melt the sidewalk outside, it *might* be acceptable."

The entire well-choreographed dance of everyone behind the counter came to a sudden and complete stop at those words. More than one of the cafe's *other* customers displayed their astonishment —and lack of manners—by staring at the woman. The young guy at the counter—named Marcelle and a member of Jake's high school class—stammered his reply, and the workers' dance lurched back into motion as she paid and accepted her order slip, pointing to the tip jar when Marcelle offered her the change.

Jake stepped forward to take his turn at the counter and couldn't blame Marcelle for shooting the occasional nervous look toward the woman. Without looking her way, Jake knew *exactly* where she was in the cafe, along with every other customer and worker—even the two having a quickie in the pantry—but *how* did he know all that? Was it something related to his manifestation? He couldn't remember ever having such an awareness before.

Jake stumbled through his order while his mind focused on this new awareness. As he stepped aside to allow the person behind him to order, he decided that it felt almost tangible somehow, like he should be able to grasp it with his will and manipulate it. But how? And where was it coming from?

All these changes in his life were more than a little scary.

"Jake Adams," a voice said just off his left ear. It was that perfect pitch—at least to Jake—right at the upper edge of the contralto range, and he turned to see the woman from the motorcycle standing at the edge of his personal space.

"How do you know my name?"

A slight smile—friendly and warm—curled her lips. "Martha Culpepper sends her regards."

ELEVEN

At first, Jake felt panic swelling. Martha Culpepper? Who was Martha Culpepper? Wait... the nice lady at the AEC said her name was Martha.

"Where does she work?" Jake asked.

The partial smile took over the woman's expression. "Good. Suitably wary. You met Martha at the Springfield AEC."

Relief surged. Whoever she was, this woman was *not* an immediate threat. At that conclusion and his relaxation, he felt the energy saturation draining from his being with much more rapidity than it grew.

"Okay. That was you last night outside where I live, right?"

She nodded. "I wanted to lay eyes on you as soon as I arrived in town. We need to talk."

Marcelle called, "Drinks for Isabel and Jake."

The woman turned and led Jake over to the counter. So... her name was Isabel, huh? Did anyone call her 'Izzy?' She seemed a bit intense for such familiarity, but Jake could be wrong. He collected his drink and pastry and followed her outside. She leaned against her bike and sipped at her coffee.

"They always try but never quite manage it," she remarked around a grimace.

Jake frowned his confusion.

"The temperature. I doubt it's even close to boiling. But such is the human world, one disappointment after another."

Okay. That was a little weird. Wasn't she human? She certainly looked human enough. But he wasn't going to focus on that at the moment.

"Listen, I'd love to discuss whatever Martha sent you here to discuss, but I need to get to work. We have three trucks today."

Isabel pursed her lips. "You will need to cease your human entanglements. They will only hold you back. I am here to discuss your character and your training."

Jake sighed and shook his head. "Look... it's **because** of my character that I can't talk right now. Percy Junior asked me not to quit until he could find at least two people to replace me, and I agreed. He only calls me in on truck days now, but that's precisely when he needs me."

"You do the work of two people?"

"I don't know. I know I don't get as tired as the other stockers... and I seem to bounce back from stuff like pulled muscles or sprained ankles faster, too."

Isabel nodded. "That is your Life Sphere. At your power level, your base healing is greatly increased, possibly exponentially so."

And there it was. After all these years, Jake finally understood one of the great questions of his life.

"Is that why the kids seem to have been increasing in intelligence and awareness over the years?"

"Kids?"

Jake nodded. "I rescued two jaguar cubs from a train wreck about four years ago. They started out with just raw emotional responses... hunger, fear, things like that. But now, they understand English and some really complex stuff. One of them likes to watch Daytime television with Mom."

"Ah, yes. Your Life Sphere will empower animals that associate with you for long periods of time. It just so happened to be these two jaguars, but it could easily have been a dog, a house cat, or even a gerbil."

"So, all Life mages have that?"

Isabel shook her head and took another swallow. "No. And regardless of what the Magocracy calls them, they are not your familiars. Sorcerers do not have familiars. Familiar bonds occur when a mage with full affinity to the Life Sphere and the right strength in Nature magic produces *a fraction* of what you enjoy with your jaguars. What you have with your jaguars is far closer to what Druids experience with their animal companions, except that you can have it with *any* animal. They merely need to spend an extensive amount of time in your general vicinity, although I'm sure the jaguars growing up around you certainly helped."

"Why do you keep calling me a sorcerer?"

"Because that's what you *are*. A mage with affinity to all twelve Spheres is a sorcerer."

Jake frowned. "Why wasn't that covered in the high school's introduction to magic class?"

Isabel snorted a laugh. "Probably because the last *known* sorcerer died just inside the Parthian border around 36 BC. He looked like the pincushion of an overzealous tailor by the time they finished with him."

"How do you know all this?" Jake asked. "I mean, you come across as if you were *there*."

"I wasn't there when the sorcerer died, but I did speak with people who were. And I know all this because I've been alive a *very* long time, Jake. That's something you'll have to come to terms with, too. Sorcerers don't age, at least not at a rate anyone ever measured. They can be killed, yes... but they do not age or suffer disease."

That... that was a serious pill to swallow. How could he not age? He grew up, didn't he? Wasn't that—by its very definition—aging?

Jake closed his eyes and shook his head. "That... that's a lot to take in. I'm going to need to process that. How do I get in touch with you?"

Isabel pulled a cell phone out of a pocket and tapped at the screen for a couple seconds. Moments later, Jake's phone blared the ringtone for a new text message.

"That's me," Isabel replied. "Call me when your shift is over."

"Jᴀᴋᴇ," Percy Junior's voice pulled Jake's attention from directing the forklift, and he threw a 'hold' signal. He turned to Percy Junior, who continued, "Officer Stannyk is here with a couple suits. They're looking for you. Go ahead and take a break."

Jake nodded absentmindedly as he headed toward the break room. Officer Stannyk? Oh... Mike! Mike so rarely used his last name that Jake didn't often think of it. His friend had made the joke more than once that he was going to find a nice woman with a solid American name and change **his** name when they married. Jake wasn't sure he believed his buddy, but at the same time, Mike really didn't like his family name. It wasn't as bad as that foster girl in eighth grade; she had to go through life as Mary Butt.

"Hey, Mike," Jake said as he entered the break room and went straight to his friend. They clasped forearms in the medieval tradition and patted each other's shoulders, before turning to the other occupants of the room—a man and a woman, both wearing well-tailored power suits.

"Jake, this is Howard McCabe and Fiona O'Rourke. They are attorneys representing the fund set up to disburse the rewards if the robbery gang was ever apprehended, which I think it's safe to say they were."

The two attorneys stepped forward, and when he shook hands with the lady, he felt **something** tingle between them. It was odd. Not like a static electricity spark or anything like that. No. It was almost as if his subconscious responded to her somehow.

"It's nice to meet you both," Jake said. "Apologies for meeting in a grocery store break room."

"Oh, think nothing of it," Fiona replied, and Jake almost lost his mind to the purr of her Irish brogue. "We've both practiced law in dangerous locales... haven't we, Howie?"

Well, it certainly seemed like *they* knew each other.

Howard chuckled. It sounded rueful with hints of pain. "Oh, yes... more than I care to remember." He focused on Jake. "We met while in the military. Fiona was Navy JAG, and I was Army. We kept in touch and decided to open our own practice together once we reached our respective limits. Like the man said, one can dance on the edge of a knife only so many times and still walk away. We were lucky so, *so* many times. A lot of people we knew weren't."

"But, let's move on to better news, shall we?" Fiona indicated her briefcase.

Jake gestured to the closest table, and he diverted to clock out while the attorneys and Mike sat. When Jake assumed his seat, the lawyers opened their cases and withdrew a staggering amount of paper. They laid their respective stacks in front of them, then set aside their briefcases.

"Yes, this is a rather impressive stack of dead trees," Fiona said, her lips curling enchantingly in a slight smile, "but there is a silver lining to the dark cloud. The regional representative of the Magocracy looked into the case when word broke that the mage foiled the gang as part of his manifestation, and apparently, the Magocracy believes it is in need of some good press. Just this morning, it notified the Secretary of Magic that the **Magocracy** will cover all taxes related to the reward, so for all intents and purposes, this will not qualify as income for you. You will keep the full sum in its entirety. As part of our fiduciary responsibility for the funds, we shall engage an accountant to calculate the taxes for this amount and provide that finding to the Magocracy. Any questions so far?"

Jake could only shake his head.

"I believe the regional Magocracy rep said something about

desiring a meeting and possibly a photo op as well," Howard remarked.

Panic threatened to spear his heart with its icy claws. "I... I'm not sure I'm ready for that. I mean, I just found out Thursday that I'm a mage. And apparently an exceptional Tri-Sphere at that. It kinda feels like the world's still spinning a bit."

"We totally understand," Fiona remarked, jumping back into the conversation and lulling Jake back to heaven with her voice. "If you would like, I am happy to intercede on your behalf with the Magocracy and anyone else who desires contact once the dispensation of the rewards are announced. I fear you'll find yourself a minor celebrity for a day or so, and what with the desert of quality entertainment coming out of Hollywood these days, you might even find yourself offered deals for your story."

Not even Fiona's angelic voice could stave off the panic then.

"Nope. Nope! I don't want any of that. Damn... I'll have to hide until it blows over."

"I recommend against that," Fiona countered. "Hiding and trying to avoid the media is the equivalent to them of blood in the water for sharks. They will convince themselves you have something reprehensible to find, and they will hound you, your family, your friends, and even your general acquaintances to find it. And if they can't find anything, they'll collect enough ambiguous quotes from neighbors, former teachers, former girlfriends, former boyfriends, classmates, or whoever will talk to them to paint a picture of what you *might* be hiding. If I may be so bold, I suggest you be... boring. The records of your evaluation are private, and the media can't even get access to the camera footage from the federal building in Springfield to make B-roll out of your arrival or departure. If you had waited to get evaluated, it might have led to an altogether different outcome, especially if there had been time to get set up in the parking lot and along the streets with their camera crews, so points to you for how you handled that."

"It was Mike's idea," Jake replied, nodding his head toward his friend. "Friday was his day off, and he convinced me that we might as well get it out of the way since I had to do it regardless."

"Then, you have a very good friend," Fiona replied. "Now, unless you have further questions, we should proceed to the paperwork. I'm afraid there's a bit of signing involved."

A SHORT TIME LATER, Jake was very thankful for his full affinity to Life with its accelerated healing. He signed his name or wrote his initials in so many places across so many copies that he should've gone through at least four pens and developed acute carpal tunnel or something.

"There now... that wasn't so bad, was it?" Fiona asked, her voice almost a purr, and Jake wondered if he could encourage debate, just to have more time to listen to her voice. "But without further ado, we present to you—Thornton Adams—one cashier check for the combined sum of six-hundred-fifty thousand dollars. Three of the four criminals have already had their arraignment where they pleaded guilty, which met the criteria for conviction. Your friend—beyond helping us find you—is here to escort you to the bank."

Looking at the check, it hit Jake again just how much money that little slip of paper represented. It was frightening in a way. Maybe even life-changing...

"And if you should ever find yourself in need of legal representa-tion," Fiona continued, sliding a business card across the table, "I do hope you will consider the firm of McCabe, O'Rourke, and Associates. We are licensed to practice in many of the Midwest states and are expanding our portfolio, both in licensure *and* specific subsets of law."

Jake accepted the card—though frankly felt at a loss as to why he would ever need legal representation—and thanked them for their time. They stood, and Mike and Jake walked them out of the store. Once in the parking lot, they bade each other farewell, and Mike led

Jake over to his patrol car, where he broke several state and local regulations by having Jake sit in the passenger seat.

As soon as the doors latched and Mike tapped the push-button start, he turned to Jake. "Dude, if you haven't already, you should totally look at the back of that card she gave you."

Jake frowned. "What? Why?"

Mike rolled his eyes as he shifted the car out of Park. "Humor me."

Jake fished the card out of his pocket and looked at it. The front side contained the address, office phone number, office fax number, and work email for Fiona O'Rourke. He turned the card over and slumped back against the seat, feeling more than a little dumbfounded. There, in flowing script that approached calligraphy in its artistic quality, was a phone number that did *not* match any of the numbers on the front of the card plus the words, 'Call me.'

"Uhh... what?"

Mike grinned. "It's her number, right? They insisted on seeing the security footage, and during the second run-through, they asked about your evaluation. I'm sorry, Jake; I told them about you being an exceptional Tri-Sphere without thinking. Anyway, a couple minutes later, I noticed her writing something on the back of a card."

"But... but she's what... mid- to late-thirties at least? Isn't she too old for me?"

Mike pulled out of the parking lot and onto the street, turning in the direction of one of the two banks in town... coincidentally, the same where Jake earned his reward money. Once the police cruiser was safely in the traffic flow—such as it was—Mike answered, "First off, Jakey... let me clue you into something you apparently have not learned yet. You're a *guy*; a woman in her nineties *might* be too old for you, depending on your age at the time and your goals for the relationship. Now, that is totally offset by your full affinity to Life; you're looking at a three-hundred to four-hundred-year lifespan, easy. And *that* is if you don't take care of yourself, eat shitty fast food, and do everything that would normally kill a human in forty years or so. Compared to that, what's ten years, plus or minus? Especially when there's a **very** excellent chance you'll outlive her and any **grandchildren** you have with her... unless they end up with full affinities to Life as well?"

Whoa. That kinda drove the matter home. He wouldn't just outlive his parents. He'd outlive the great-grandchildren of everyone he grew up with... like Mike. That was going to take some adjustment.

"I've never been one for wildly sowing oats, Mike; you know that."

"Oh, yeah... trust me, I know. And I'm not saying go crazy... unless that's what you want. It's not like you can catch anything, either... lucky bastard. So, you could one-hundred-percent go as crazy as you want to go, with leaving children behind the only real risk. But we're wandering away from my point. Who cares that you're ten, fifteen, or maybe even twenty years younger than she is? She's interested in you at some level, and she's been around the block enough that I doubt she's one for the types of games Jolene plays. After a certain point, those tend to fall by the wayside."

Jake frowned as Mike turned into the bank's parking lot. "Just how did you get to be so wise, Mike? We're the **same** age."

Mike chuckled and replied with his trademark cocksure smile. "Just because we're the same age does **not** mean we're at the same level of experience. Ladies love a man in uniform, and it's my experience they're not too picky about what **type** of uniform it is."

Jake just shook his head and opened the passenger door. By the time he walked around the car, Mike stood at his elbow and walked almost in step with him.

"So, are you going to call her?"

"I dunno," Jake replied as they entered the bank. "I'll think about it. I mean, she's not even from around here, right? I'm still having trouble seeing what's in it for her."

Mike snorted. "I can tell you **exactly** what's in it for her, except we're in public, and most people frown on that kind of language in mixed company."

Jake just shook his head again as he felt his cheeks heat. When Mike got going, he almost *always* embarrassed Jake past the point of recovery. And that was when Jake noticed every teller smiled and waved to them as they entered. Every. Single. One. And their eyes lingered, just not on Mike.

Mike led him toward the new accounts desk as if he hadn't noticed Jake's predicament. He stopped at the balustrade separating the administration area from the teller lobby and said, "Hi, Sally... Jake needs some help with his checking account. Do you have a minute?"

Sally looked up and smiled at seeing Mike and then held her smile when she turned to Jake. "Sure thing. Come on over and have a seat."

NOT TOO MUCH LATER, Mike and Jake walked out of the bank, and Jake had converted his entry-level checking account to the highest-interest-bearing checking account they had *and* opened a high-interest savings account for half the reward funds.

"So, when is your shift over today?" Jake asked as Mike eased the cruiser out of the bank's parking lot and back into traffic.

"Four-thirty... why?"

"Feel like helping me pick something big enough to take the jaguars with me if we need to go anywhere beyond walking distance?"

Mike grinned. "I don't mind at all. I'll drop you back off at the grocery store, and you be thinking of what you'd like to try. You might want to have the jaguars with you for anything you test drive, just to be sure they fit and are comfortable in it."

Jake nodded. "That is an excellent idea. Thank you."

"You're welcome. Oh... and call Fiona. Granted, Fiona's no Maureen O'Hara, but she'll do until that fine lady strolls along."

Mike stopped for a red light, and Jake turned to regard his friend. "You do know Maureen O'Hara is dead, right? I'm pretty sure she died while we were in high school."

Mike dismissed that with an indifferent wave as he drove under the green light. "Details, my man. Mere details."

CHAPTER

TWELVE

Parking Lot of Percy's Grocery
Hornbeam, Illinois
19 May 2025, 3:35pm

JAKE WALKED out of the grocery store and withdrew his phone from his pocket. He considered the card Fiona gave him and almost called her, but he remembered Isabel's calm insistence that he call her as soon as his shift was over.

His shift was now officially over... until the next truck or trucks came in. So, a week or so.

He tapped the control to call the number from the text message —which he would totally save to his contacts, just hadn't done so yet—and listened to the call ring. On the second ring, Jake heard the click of an accepted call, followed by, "Draco Investigations."

"Oh, uhm, I maybe called a wrong number. This is Jake Adams."

"This is Isabel. You didn't call a wrong number. Your shift over?"

Jake nodded, even though she couldn't see it. "I'm walking through the parking lot now."

"Okay. Good. Are you hungry? I'm hungry enough to eat a buffalo, and no, I don't much care whether it's an American buffalo or a Cape buffalo. Want to talk over food?"

"Sure. That works," Jake answered. "I'm supposed to meet my friend, Mike, when he ends his shift to look into getting a car."

"You'll want to make sure it's large enough for your jaguars to be comfortable. Are you planning to take them along?"

Jake smiled. "Mike already raised that point, yes."

A slight pause, then she said, "You know, I think I'd pay money to see a car salesman react to a couple jaguars trotting onto the lot. Mind if I tag along?"

Jake turned it around in his head a couple times, but he couldn't see how that could have a down-side. "Nope. Don't mind a bit."

JAKE ARRIVED at Marci's diner just as an Indian Chief Dark Horse coasted to a stop in the open parking spot beside him. Isabel removed her gloves and helmet and gestured for Jake to lead the way. Jake smiled at seeing his favorite booth available and led Isabel to it. Before sitting, Isabel unzipped her riding jacket and draped it across the helmet that she rested against the wall in the corner of her bench seat.

They didn't even have time to get settled before Marci arrived, order pad in hand.

"Hiya, Jake. Who's your friend?"

Jake flushed with embarrassment. "Oh... uhm... she's a trainer the lady at the AEC put me in touch with."

Marci's eyes went as round and large as teacup saucers. "You're a *mage*? When did this happen? Why haven't I heard of it?"

"Uhm, you kinda have. I manifested during the attempted robbery Thursday."

Marci's mouth rounded into the 'O' of surprise. "*That* was you? I've heard that something pretty freaky went down. What happened?"

Jake glanced to Isabel and mouthed 'Sorry' before turning back to Marci. "Well, apparently, I'm a Time mage, plus Life and Light. When I manifested, I was able to reverse the shotgun in the guy's hands right after he pulled the trigger but before the firing pin struck the shell's primer. He basically shot himself with his own firearm."

"That's kind of major, Jake. Are you okay?"

"Yeah, I think so. I don't like that I felt forced into the situation. I suppose I could've taken the shotgun and pointed it at the ceiling, but I'm not sure that would have de-escalated the situation as quickly as the other robbers seeing their buddy blast himself into oblivion. Some of the buckshot even clipped a couple of them. I could've used the manifestation to leave the bank, but what would that have meant for everyone else stuck in there? I would've preferred that the situation ended with no one dead, but there were many worse outcomes than how it played out. Could I get an iced tea, and what would you like, Isabel?"

Mentioning a drink order knocked Marci out of her gossip mode, and she laid down a couple menus and sets of utensils before leaving to get their drinks.

"Sorry about that," Jake said once they were alone.

Isabel waved away his concern. "Think nothing of it. That will be your life for a while, and I recommend you maintain all of your former commitments until the media decides you're too boring for ratings. From what I've seen of the town, that shouldn't take more than a week... two at the outside. But... let us discuss the world you have now joined."

She waited until Marci returned with their drinks and took their food orders. Isabel surprised Jake and Marci both by ordering six steaks from grass-fed beef—rare—and four thawed but uncooked chickens. Jake felt like a poser when he ordered his usual burger and fries.

Isabel watched Marci leave, her expression a frown that betrayed contemplation. "Hmm... I hope that's enough. I haven't eaten more than snacks since Friday."

After few more seconds' thought, Isabel turned to Jake, once more the eminent authority in full control and ready to share her knowledge and understanding. "Crafters are—for the most part—as much a part of our societies as any other profession, with the exception that what crafters do is part of them... unlike pretty much any trade, skill, or profession among 'regular' humans. Anyone can learn to be a blacksmith, but only a *mage* can then imbue power into something created through blacksmithing. Which is why the premiere blacksmiths have full affinity to the Earth Sphere. The truly top tier blacksmiths have affinities to Earth, Fire, and Life. They're rare for whatever reason. But I digress...

"Take every fairy tale or legend or myth, and if you could trace it back far enough in its evolution, you'll find a measure of truth. You might not recognize the truth for what it is, such as your case where the reality is at such odds with the picture Greek mythology paints of the Titans and Olympians, but you would still find truth. Which means that Fae, Shifters, Dwarves, Elves, Vampires, and more are all real, and they exist even now to varying degree.

"Out of all of the supernatural races and/or creatures, the Elves have it worst; they are almost exclusively a race of Druids, and the natural unmarred world has been shrinking for ages. Many Elven enclaves would make Third and Fourth World countries look damn appealing at times, and unless something is done within the next millennium, they will probably die off completely.

"Another aspect to being a sorcerer you need to understand is that, if knowledge of your existence gets out to the wider world, there are groups that will *hunt* you until multiple sources with multiple layers of evidence prove your death. And you might be surprised by who they are. Griffons. Chimeras. Centaurs. Pegasi, Unicorns, Alicorns. And several more. All of the mythological or fairy tale creatures that were hybrids? All created by sorcerers... who treated them as glorified science projects—without much science, really—and then cast them aside for the next interesting project. To this day, they all have a rage-fueled hate for sorcerers. If they learn a sorcerer exists once more? They will erupt out of their seclusion and do whatever it takes—regardless of the consequences or collateral damage—to eradicate you from the world, and they will embark upon that crusade without a second thought."

Isabel stopped speaking as Marci and two of her servers arrived to deliver their food. Isabel accepted her six rare steaks and four uncooked chickens with a smile and, once she and Jake were alone, dug in with a will. Jake took her focus on the food as a pause in the discussion and proceeded to enjoy his own.

Jake leaned back from his empty plate and saw that Isabel was— at most—halfway through hers. He took the time to retrieve his phone and send Mike a text to meet him at Marci's before leaning back against his seat to savor the pleasant lack of hunger.

It wasn't long until Isabel placed her final empty plate on top of the stack and sat back with her own sated expression. After a couple seconds, though, she leaned forward once again, her former—and Jake suspected *usual*—intensity returning to her entire demeanor. She gestured at her stack of plates as two of Marci's servers came by and bussed the table.

"That's something else you need to understand. One of the first things we discuss will be your eating and exercise habits. You need to eat... *a lot*. Possibly as much as most shifters do. It never comes into play for most mages, but the single most determining trait that will control what you can do is your body's constitution. Most people would say it's education and intellect for mages, and for anyone else, that's true. Even a quad-Sphere cannot channel sufficient power to overcome their normal dietary habits, and as they advance in mastery, they become increasingly more efficient, accomplishing more with less raw power. So the limiting factors for **every other** mage on the planet are what they know and what they can visualize. With me so far?"

Jake nodded. "I think so."

"Good. Unlike your lesser cousins, you can channel phenomenal power; you would probably shatter one of those comical power meters the Magocracy uses without much effort if you ever tried it. But if your body isn't well fed and well cared for, you will tear yourself apart trying to fill a thimble with water.

"Now, if you remember, I also mentioned exercise, which goes hand-in-hand with your diet. Let's say you have the most horrid eating habits possible for a human, but somehow, you manage to take exceptional care of yourself in terms of exercise. That's almost a paradox, really, but I suppose it could happen. Hang on... let's flip that. It will illustrate my point better. If you have or devise the absolute perfect diet for the human body and you both love it and follow it religiously... *but...* do nothing to maintain your body exercise-wise, you will still burn yourself out. And you will do so somewhere on the spectrum between a candle flaring up and the atomic bomb the United States used on Nagasaki. Mount Vesuvius? The eruption that buried Pompeii? It wasn't a natural eruption. The eruption that destroyed Pompeii was the direct result of a sorcerer's child—what the ancient Greeks would've classed as an Olympian within their mythology—who had taken such poor care of himself that he basically came apart at the seams. I was very young at the time, and I remember my parents discussing it."

Jake sat back and let that knowledge wash over him. Who was she that she knew all this? Or maybe the question should be **what** was she?

"So, forgive me for asking, but how can you live over two thousand years? If I hadn't **stopped time** last Thursday, I'd be a lot more skeptical... but we're still coming close to hitting my wall of belief."

Isabel gave him a tolerant smile. "That's totally understandable, and you should feel comfortable with me before we get to the discussion of a formal mentor-apprentice agreement. I'm a dragon, Jake. One of the last generation that hatched."

Jake's jaw dropped, and he simply stared at Isabel in silence for... well... he wasn't really sure how long he sat there staring at her.

"I obviously can't show you here, but I have arranged access to the Wainwright Grove as our training venue and my residence during your apprenticeship. Once we're there and away from prying eyes, I will prove to you that I am what I say. Is that fair?"

Jake nodded, still a little overwhelmed by the thought that he might be sharing a table with a ***dragon*** of all things. "Yeah... totally fair."

"What's totally fair?" Mike asked as he arrived at the booth.

"Oh... uhm..." Jake tried to figure out something that would have the ring of truth while not revealing his dining associate was the apex predator of the ***world***. "Isabel and I were just discussing how she wants to tag along and watch the salesman's face when we take the kids car shopping."

Mike erupted into a huge grin as he snagged a chair from a nearby table and placed it with its back against the booth's table before he sat. "Yeah, that's going to be epic. If I could arrange to film it in secret with my bodycam, I would ***totally*** do that. Anyway, sorry I'm so late. We had a domestic that turned into a major shit-show; for a while, I was afraid I'd never get out of there. So... Isabel, is it? Nice to meet you. I'm Mike Stannyk, Jake's best friend."

Isabel nodded in greeting. "Well met, Mike. I am a friend of a friend of Jake who offered to help him navigate his new status as a Tri-Sphere. While my affinities do not ***precisely*** line up with his, what I do have is a rather extensive network of contacts and associates on whom to call."

"Friend of a friend, huh? Anyone I know?"

Jake chuckled and shook his head at Mike's protectiveness. "Kind of. Martha at the AEC introduced us."

All traces of suspicion vanished from Mike's demeanor. "Oh... she ***introduced*** you?"

Jake fought the urge to glare at his best friend. "Not that kind of introduction, Mike."

"Well, damn... and here I thought you might hook a brother up and pass me Fiona's deets."

Isabel's eyes narrowed. "Fiona? Is that Fiona O'Rourke by chance?"

"Yeah," Mike replied before Jake could stop him. "I've been telling my boy here he needed to use the number she gave him."

"I see." Isabel turned her head just enough to focus on Jake. "I would be... wary... of her were I in your position."

She flicked her eyes toward Mike so quickly Jake almost missed it as Marci came up behind Mike and slapped his shoulder.

"Mike Stannyk, how many times have I told you that you're violating the state's fire code by blocking the aisle like you are?"

Mike looked over his shoulder, and Jake watched him give Marci his patented 'sad puppy' face. "But Marci, what's a poor guy supposed to do when even his best bud in the whole world won't scoot over for him?"

Marci rested her hands on her hips and just shook her head. "Nice try, Mike, but I'm not buying it. I saw you go straight for the chair."

Jake grinned and slid over until he was against the wall, leaving more than enough space for Mike to move.

Mike looked at the newly vacated space for a second or two before he gave a much-put-upon sigh and returned the chair to its place before sliding into the booth with Jake.

Marci nodded her approval and retrieved her order pad. "Good job, Mike; thank you. I wouldn't care, but I've heard the fire marshal is in town today. Neither one of us need a write up, especially since you're an officer. Now, what'll you have?"

CHAPTER
THIRTEEN

The trip to the dealership was not as enjoyable as Jake and Isabel hoped. The saleslady didn't bat an eye at the jaguars, but Jake suspected it was the 'Registered Familiar' harnesses. They did a couple test drives, and Jake ultimately settled on the current model of the Explorer. He gave the finance officer the letter of credit from the bank in town, and after saying goodbye to Mike, Jake drove off with the back two rows of seats folded flat to make ample room for the jaguars.

FOLLOWING Isabel to the Wainwright Grove, Jake realized he would need to practice his driving a bit, especially with a vehicle the size of an Explorer SUV. He felt like he was hugging the yellow line all the way out of town, and as soon as there was an actual berm, he began easing the vehicle's right wheels off the pavement to get a feel of where they were in relation to what he could see through the windshield.

It wasn't long until Isabel led him out of town and down a road that quickly turned to gravel after leaving the town's incorporation limit. After no more than ten minutes traveling down the gravel road, a massive hedge became the horizon and grew steadily closer. Within a hundred feet or so, the hedge looked at least ten feet tall, with an archway sized for delivery trucks sculpted to match the road.

As he passed through the hedge, Jake felt *something* brush his mind, his soul, or maybe both. Not even a moment later, he received a greeting.

* Welcome home, Titan. I am Beauregard, the sapient spirit that serves as the core of this grove. We shall speak anon. *

Jake felt considerable gratitude toward the jaguars. If they hadn't conditioned him to hearing random voices in his head that weren't his own, he might have driven his new SUV through the hedge, instead of the archway. He eased the SUV to a stop beside Isabel's motorcycle and took a couple deep breaths after shifting into Park. Just from that limited communication, Jake somehow sensed that whoever or whatever Beauregard was contained a staggering amount of power.

He exited the SUV to find Isabel directing a curious expression his way.

"Something that called itself Beauregard welcomed me home, which was a little weird since I don't live here."

Jake popped the rear lift gate so the jaguars could hop out and then closed it as Isabel replied, "Be very careful around entities such as Beauregard. They often operate according to their own agenda, and they cannot always be trusted."

* I dispute thy characterization that I cannot be trusted, Lady Dragon. The Titan's safety and well-being is my purpose. Soon will I set matters in motion to ensure the grove passes to him when the time for that comes. I regret that it will be sooner than I would like. *

"Why?" Jake asked without thinking.

* Because, Titan, for stewardship of the grove to pass to you... those I term my 'parents' must be dead. *

"Now, wait a minute. I don't want you killing anyone," Jake hissed, trying to keep his voice from carrying.

Nay, Titan. They are not destined to die by my agency. And nay... you cannot change their fate. We already travel that chain of decisions and reactions, and when the moment comes, they shall be beyond my help.

Isabel adopted a thoughtful expression. "Just who set you to this purpose? And how do you know these outcomes are fixed?"

Lady Dragon, Gaia Herself warned me of what shall come to pass when She offered me my task.

The nugget of an idea formed in the back of Jake's mind, and he immediately envisioned walling it off from all access but his. He had no idea if the idea was viable, and to make matters worse, he didn't know how long he had to train up enough that the idea **might** be viable. All of which meant that he wanted to keep the idea and anything even remotely related to it away from 'public' access.

Motion off to his right caught his eye, and he saw some people heading toward the parking lot. Isabel headed toward them, and Jake fell in behind her with the jaguars on either side of him. He realized in short order that he recognized two of the people... after a fashion. One of the women was from the bank last Thursday, and the hot... er, **very attractive**... young lady was at the bank, too.

When everyone converged, Isabel said, "Gerald and Bianca Wainwright, I would like to introduce Jake Adams. Martha Culpepper recommended the both of you as potential trainers. I encountered him on the edge of town, looking a bit lost, and offered to escort him back here. The jaguars are his familiars, Smokey and Bandit. Jake, these are Gerald and Bianca Wainwright, Gianna Harcourt, and her daughter, Emilia Harcourt."

They exchanged handshakes all around.

"I don't think I've ever encountered anyone with **two** registered familiars before," Gianna remarked. "That's rather impressive."

"Martha at the AEC said I'm an exceptional Tri-Sphere with full affinities across the board," Jake explained.

Gianna nodded her understanding. "Ah, yes... that would prob- ably do it."

Bianca smiled as she said, "Gerald and I also agreed to teach Emilia, whose training will be starting as soon as Gia gets tired of us. We have no issue adding another, as long as you're okay with it."

"I don't mind at all," Jake replied. "I mainly hoped to introduce myself this evening and learn if you were agreeable to training me. Oh... uhm... I should probably ask your fee."

"Are you local?" Gerald asked.

Jake nodded. "Yes. My parents and I live on Whittaker Street."

Bianca made a dismissive wave. "Well, then... since you won't need room and board, I see no reason we can't put off discussion of our fee until we're ready to start. Do you mind leaving us your contact information?"

"Not at all," Jake answered. He gave them his cell number and email address before bidding them good evening.

EMILIA WATCHED JAKE LEAVE. She hoped she wasn't being too obvious about it... but... she probably was. There was **something** about him that made her feel all warm and fuzzy, and she found herself wondering what it would feel like to be snuggled up in his arms in front of a lazy fire.

It was obvious to anyone with mage senses that he was powerful —even for an exceptional Tri-Sphere. She knew—**knew**—that she wasn't supposed to care about that. But she couldn't help the little thrill that ran through her as she considered the chances of landing him.

The more she thought about it, she hated that thrill. It was the same kind of buzz she was sure the gold-diggers of the world felt when they found a wealthy scion who wasn't all that world-wise. She wasn't **that** kind of person... or at least, she had never thought she was.

Maybe it was that Jake wasn't full of himself? Could that be it? She was only twenty-three, but it seemed like she'd seen every permutation of the male ego possible during her high-school and college years. It was something she and her friends had bemoaned many times; why were so many guys such complete jerks? Assholes, even?

But Jake didn't give her that vibe. If anything, his dating life was probably a little stunted. Hornbeam didn't seem to have much of a mage population, and his Tri-Sphere strength gave him an aura that would make the average person more than a bit uneasy.

With a heavy sigh, her heart went out to him. That had to have been rough, growing up around here. She'd need to be careful. He might not even realize there were signals girls sent guys to show their interest.

WHEN JAKE ARRIVED BACK HOME, he took the time to show his parents the SUV and insisted they drive it if they wanted. His dad wasn't much of a car person, but his mom put it through its paces. Once they had their fill of the 'new car smell,' they went inside for dinner, and after sharing an enjoyable meal with his parents, Jake went to the backyard. He didn't know when Gianna was leaving, and he itched to experiment.

The backyard had a tile patio, complete with a (mostly) round brick grill that came up to waist height and was roughly three to four feet across. Pipes allowed air to circulate through the grill's base, below the mesh-covered platform where the fuel rested. The metal grate of the grill came off for cleaning and fuel stacking, and Jake leaned it against the bricks. He grabbed three loose bricks that his father had in case of repairs and arranged them like a 'Y' on the fuel platform, then broke off a small branch that hadn't come back from the winter from one of the trees in the backyard. He stood the branch upright against the fuel platform of the grill and arranged the bricks to hold it in place. Then, he added a couple squirts of lighter fluid, and he was ready to go.

A match lit the fluid-soaked branch tip aflame, and Jake sat in the lawn chair he brought a little closer to the grill, concentrating on the tiny fire. After a few moments, he thought he felt *something*, and he closed his eyes to concentrate on the new sensation that hadn't been there until lighting the branch aflame.

Over the next few seconds, Jake's connection to the flickering fire grew, and when he felt that saturation effect happening in his cells again, he tried willing some of the energy in his cells into the thumbnail-sized flame that slowly ate the branch.

He was not prepared at all when the tiny pinprick of flame flared up to the size of a three-foot bonfire. The sight captured Jake's attention because it was so comical. The huge bonfire perched atop a branch about half the thickness of his wrist. In the span of three seconds or so—but no more than five—the now-larger flame consumed the branch and warmed the bricks. A few seconds after that, the bricks glowed a dull red. When the edges of the bricks began looking a little spongy, Jake realized he still felt a tiny thread of energy passing from him to the fire. With a startled gasp, he cut the thread, and the bonfire-sized flame vanished.

He leaned back in the lawn chair and considered how else he might explore his new reality. An idea struck him, and a smile curled one side of his mouth. Mike was always going on about how the Fireball spell was some kind of rite of passage for a mage with the Fire affinity. Jake stood and walked around the backyard, glancing at the neighbors' houses and the back windows of his parents' house. There didn't *seem* to be anyone watching.

He retrieved his phone from its pocket and looked up Fireball on MageNet. He mainly wanted a description of what the spell *did*, not necessarily the spell's text and gestures which the spells' page also helpfully provided. Hrmmm... according to the spell's description, it created a peach-pit-sized ball of fire that flew to its target, whereupon it heated to a temperature based on the mage's strength and expanded at an exponential rate to a maximum radius that was *also* based on the mage's strength. Huh... that didn't *seem* too difficult.

Jake returned to the lawn chair and began turning the problem over in his mind of how to create the effect without being trained to cast the spell. Was that something sorcerers could do? He didn't know, but touching the burning tip of the branch with his energy seemed like it would get easier with more experience. So... did that mean that sorcerers didn't *need* spells?

He worked through trying to build a construct for the Fireball spell in his mind for several minutes until he *thought* he had it just about right. But when he stood to convert thought to action, a memory flashed to the forefront of his mind. He wasn't supposed to have Fire affinity, and if someone saw him trying this, it would mean trouble for him, for Martha, and maybe even others.

No.

He went into the house and retrieved a blank notebook that he accidentally bought when looking for a ruled one. It had been in the stack for ruled notebooks, and he hadn't paid close enough attention to the packaging. He further hadn't bothered to look when he tore open the packaging, so he was left with what was pretty much a sketchbook he didn't need.

Until now.

He rummaged through a catch-all drawer in his room until he found an old set of colored pencils and then took the sketchbook and pencils back to the lawn chair in the backyard. He withdrew the orange and black pencils and started sketching his idea for the Fire-ball construct. He used the orange for the actual Fire components and the black for annotations, making up a kind of shorthand and symbols on the fly that he defined in black on the pages' margins. It wasn't until the last remaining daylight faded around him that Jake noticed a tiny fireball hovering over the sketchbook at around the height of his forehead.

The sight startled him quite a bit, and he almost panicked... until he remembered a stray thought some time back that he wanted more light to see. Jake closed his eyes as he concentrated, and sure enough, there was a whisper-thin tendril of energy connecting him to the tiny fireball.

Shit! This 'hiding in plain sight' stuff was going to be more difficult than he first thought.

Jake quickly severed the energy tendril, and the tiny fireball vanished. He collected his pencils and sketchbook, then dashed inside the house to resume work in his bedroom where he could turn on a light without using magic.

THE NEXT MORNING, Percy Junior called to say that they had a truck coming in that was off its regular schedule, asking if Jake could come in to work the unloading and stacking. Jake looked at his sketchbook with its elastic band to keep it closed as he debated. He wanted to keep working on his notes, especially since he woke up with a few ideas he wanted to record.

But... the more he considered the matter, he didn't like compromising his word—his ethics and values and integrity—just to play with what was essentially a new toy. Okay... maybe he shouldn't think of it as a new toy, but at that specific moment, that's all it seemed to be to him. Once he learned some of the more utilitarian aspects of magic, he felt certain the 'toy' evaluation would change.

So, he told Percy Junior he was on the way and ended the call.

THE REALIZATION HIT him as he climbed into his vehicle that he was going to have to join a gym or something if he wanted to keep his body in the tip-top condition he enjoyed right now. Relying on the new vehicle would make him lazy and complacent... but it was such a time-saver that he couldn't *quite* help himself.

For some reason, that morning, the jaguars decided to accompany him. While possibly being a little weird, in terms of the change in pattern, their status as registered familiars allowed them to explore the town with relative freedom now... as long as Jake was close to defuse any misunderstandings, of course.

JAKE DECIDED to visit Marci's as he left Percy's. There hadn't been too many incidents with the jaguars following him around and watching what he did and how he did it, but those that had happened were a little on the hair-raising side. Like Bandit not paying attention and almost getting his tail run over by the forklift. After the stressful day, Jake felt he had earned a pleasant meal and the peace that Marci's inspired in him.

Marci's had a patio for outdoor dining, and rather than trying to claim his favorite booth with the kids in tow, Jake chose that instead. People occupied only a couple of the tables, but much like at the grocery store, Jake and the kids drew attention as they sauntered onto the patio and chose their table.

Sitting there, in the shade of the patio's awning, Jake realized he hadn't contacted Fiona yet. Isabel's warning about Fiona followed close behind, and once again, he felt conflicted on the matter. He'd hold off on the call and give the matter further thought, maybe ask Isabel when it was just them. He hoped she'd elaborate more if they were alone.

On the other hand, he could always call Fiona and listen to her side of whatever it was... then compare that to whatever Isabel said. He wasn't sure if that was the right path, though. The sad truth was that he knew so little of his new reality that he had no way of deter-mining the best path for him. Even if the mere *memory* of Fiona threatened to turn him to jelly right there on Marci's patio.

Hrmmm... decisions, decisions.

He lifted his phone and took the time to save Isabel's cell number as a contact, then called her. She answered on the second ring.

"Hello, Jake. I wasn't expecting to hear from you today. What's on your mind?"

Jake screwed up his courage and threw caution to the wind. "Are you in a position where you can talk? I'd like more information on why you think I should be wary of Fiona O'Rourke."

Silence ensued to the point that Jake wondered if the call dropped.

"Fiona O'Rourke is not what she seems, not that any of us are," Isabel explained. "In her case, though, it is far more complex. She is —at the very least—half Fae, and the Fae have a very rocky history with mages. I promise you that a date with her will be unlike anything you have ever dreamed of, and at the same time— depending on how much Fae is in her ancestry—you might not live long enough to pine over her. The Fae are not as closely tied to the natural world as the Elves are, but all the 'progress' humans have achieved has certainly curtailed their power. And they tend to lure humans—especially powerful humans like mages—into situations where their power can be stripped from them and transferred to the Fae realm, if they're patriotic. If they're not, the Fae doing the draining will simply keep it for themselves. The unfortunate part of all this is that there's no way to know if she has designs on your power until she has your mind so fogged you don't even realize you're dying."

Yikes. That did not sound fun at all. "So, I shouldn't pass her info to Mike, either?"

Jake heard a contemptuous snort before Isabel said, "If she gave her number to you with Mike present, giving her number to him would be an insult. Possibly dire, depending how pure of a Fae she is."

"Okay, so what do I do with her number, then? She acted like she really wanted me to call her."

More silence.

"If you feel you must contact her, pass me the details if you decide to meet. I will arrive ahead of time and make sure she does not enthrall you. With your power, she would have to work at it for a while to ensure you'd be willing to follow her to your deathbed."

Okay. That made sense. "Thank you, Isabel. I appreciate your thoughts."

"You're welcome, Jake. That's why I'm here."

Isabel ended the call before Jake could do so, and he placed his phone on the table and withdrew Fiona's card from his wallet. He still stared at the handwritten number on the plain white reverse when the server delivered his and the kids' meals.

CHAPTER

FOURTEEN

Jake leaned back against his seat on Marci's patio and half-smiled. The food here at the diner was so, so good. Yes, Jake loved his mother's cooking, but at the same time, there was just something about the food from Marci's diner. And he really appreciated how they cut the jaguars' raw steaks into small cubes to make eating in public a less traumatic affair for everyone else... including Jake.

He looked at Fiona's card again and sighed. Yeah, he really felt compelled to call her. As far as he knew, no one else had ever shown any level of interest in him at all. Might as well find out where he stood with her.

Jake saved all the contact information—including her business info—into a new contact record before tapping the entry for her mobile number. The call rang three times before he heard the voice that threatened to turn him to jelly, "Fiona O'Rourke."

"Hi, Fiona. It's Jake. You probably don't remember—"

"Oh... now, now, Jake. You shouldn't be so hard on yourself. I absolutely *do* remember you. Thank you for calling. I should probably play hard to get, but the truth of the matter is that I've been wondering if you'd call. Hoping for it, actually."

"Thank you. I'll consider you hoping I would call a compliment."

"You should, good sir," her voice dropped to throaty purr. "You really should."

Jake would never have admitted—not even to Mike—what the sound of her purring voice did to him. He was **very** glad he was sitting down and not driving.

"So, now that we're talking, what do you have in mind?" Jake asked and immediately realized his mistake.

The purr continued, "So, so many things, Mister Adams. My associate and I just returned to the office, and our case load is such that I would be a horrible partner if I just disappeared off to Hornbeam. I don't suppose I might entice you to visit me?"

"There is always that chance. When were you thinking?"

"It's a damn shame I don't have a Spatial mage handy, because I would **love** to say right now. But I probably should not allow myself to sound so eager. Proper lady and all that. May I check my calendar to see when I have the fewest work commitments and send you those dates?"

"Of course, Fiona. I'm not one to risk anyone's professional life. Would texting you my email address make it easier to send me those dates?"

Fiona's reply was immediate. "Oh, yes... much. I love all my smartphone does for me, but sadly, that love is unrequited. In the love-hate relationship we have, I love it, and it hates me."

Jake couldn't keep from chuckling. "Well, then... as soon as we end the call, I'll text you my email, and we'll go from there."

"It has been a pleasure hearing from you, good sir. Thank you again for the call."

The call ended with a click this time, and Jake quickly put action to his words by sending Fiona his email address. Mere seconds later, she confirmed the receipt and promised a swift response with possible dates.

Bandit looked up from where he lounged on the patio floor. * Are you choosing a female, Jake? Shouldn't my sister and I meet her? *

Smokey expressed her thoughts on Bandit's presumption with a no-claws slap to Bandit's shoulder. * *Shut up, fur-butt. Jake's our friend, not our cub. He doesn't answer to us.* *

A number of other diners glanced their way when Smokey slapped Bandit, but when further violence did not seem forthcoming, they returned to their plates and conversations. Jake considered the matter and decided it was—perhaps—time they left. He didn't want the kids to get rowdy and alarm people. True, odds favored them taking a nap after a meal, but Marci's patio wasn't the place for **that**, either.

"All right, you two. Can I trust you to wait for me if I go pay for the food, or should you come with me?"

* *We'll be good.* * Smokey was quick to answer. * *I'll keep an eye on fur-butt.* *

Jake managed to hold it together until he stepped into the diner before the laughter overtook him. He couldn't imagine his life now without the kids, and they certainly made it **interesting**. He managed to catch the register without a line, and paying for their food was quick. He waved goodbye to Marci as he returned to the patio and collected the jaguars before heading home.

Jake had just hit the button to raise the lift gate at the back of the SUV when his phone chimed the notification tone for a new email. He checked it as he exited the vehicle and smiled at seeing a rather impressive list of potential dates for his visit to Topeka. He would have to discuss the matter with Isabel before making any firmer plans, but so far, he felt rather good about the conversation. He really hoped she wasn't out for his power; she seemed like too nice of a person for such a thing to ruin it.

He opened the side gate that allowed the kids to go straight to the backyard and then decided to use it himself and go in the house through the back door. He told his parents hello, giving his mom a hug as he passed her, and retrieved his sketchbook and pencils from his room before returning to the backyard.

Jake moved a lawn chair to the jaguars' favorite tree, and they all lounged in its shade while Jake drew more diagrams of spell 'blueprints' in his sketchbook. He was staring off at nothing in particular as he considered his Fireball sketch when his eyes landed on the grill, on the air holes. Air—specifically oxygen—fueled a fire and made it hotter. What would adding an Air component to his fireball design do for it? It was something a regular mage couldn't do unless she or he possessed affinities for both Fire *and* Air, but it was certainly something he wanted to try. So, he flipped to a new page and promptly began sketching. It wasn't long before snoring from either side accompanied the sound of his pencils as he wrote and drew.

THE WHISPERED *whoosh* of flame above his field of view coupled with the extra light over his sketchbook told Jake it was time to go inside. At the rate he was going, he'd blow his cover in no time... unless he moved somewhere far more secure. He wasn't sure he especially *liked* the idea of taking over the Wainwright Grove, especially if it meant the Wainwrights were dead, but there was no denying how much it would protect him from peeping toms—otherwise known as busybody neighbors—and allow him to study his abilities in peace.

That train of thought led him right back to his idea. If Gerald and Bianca were 'destined' to die and if those events were indeed fixed points in time and could not be avoided or changed, was there any reason they had to *stay* dead? He started to sketch his new idea, but he stopped himself... for a couple reasons. First, there was the small matter of not knowing how to access or utilize his Life affinity in a conscious, deliberate manner; he suspected it was very similar to how he used Fire, but there was always the chance he was wrong. Second, if he wrote down his idea, anyone who gained access to the sketchbook would be able to read it, and he wasn't all that sure he wanted to risk people discovering his plans, especially in this instance. For now, his idea would have to remain stored in what he hoped was a section of his mind protected from any eavesdropping.

That was something else, too. As a Mind mage, could he now read people's thoughts? It seemed like every other show or movie nowadays included a Mind mage for interrogations, but how realistic was that? After all, there were many, many websites devoted to delineating all the ways shows or movies made mistakes, so what were the chances using Mind mages was another? The more Jake considered it, the more it seemed that using a Mind mage would fall under the purview of requiring a court order... with all kinds of supporting evidence that it was necessary. He wasn't sure he liked the idea of anything else being the case.

~

THE WAINWRIGHT GROVE
   Hornbeam, IL
   21 May 2025, 9:35am

EMILIA WATCHED with very mixed feelings as her mom enfolded Bianca into a goodbye hug. As soon as the goodbyes were said, Gerald was going to drive her mom into town to catch the train to Chicago. Her mom already had a ticket for the trip and a flight from O'Hare to LaGuardia.

On one side, the past few days had given Emilia amazing insight into the mother she *thought* she knew. Beauregard had never revisited the topic of her mother not being the simple librarian she'd always believed her to be, and Emilia hoped she could coax further details out of *someone* sooner or later.

On the other hand, though, this would be the first time she'd ever been so far from the only parent she'd ever known. From what her mother said, her father died in a hit-and-run not long after her first birthday. Emilia couldn't imagine a more unassuming name than Wilbur Harcourt, but her mother swore up, down, sideways, and backwards that she couldn't imagine having married anyone else. Even twenty-odd years later, her mother claimed she had yet to meet anyone who possessed the sheer vibrancy of Wilbur.

Emilia wished she could have known him. In true 'young' fashion, neither her father nor her mother made any recordings of them, at least none that her mother admitted to her. Photos, yes. The collection of their wedding photos alone could fill the photography section of a major metropolitan library, and Emilia's absolute favorite photo showed her father holding her not long after she was born.

Movement pulled Emilia out of her thoughts, and she saw her mother standing in front of her. Emilia put on her best 'I will be okay' smile and pulled her mom into a tight hug. Her mom returned that hug strength for strength.

When they stepped back from each other at last, Emilia saw her mother's eyes glistened with moisture. Unshed tears. She suspected hers did the same.

"I've never been this far from you," her mother said, a slight catch in her voice. "You'll call me?"

Emilia smiled and fought the urge to sniff back her tears. "Yes, I will call."

"It's not just for you, you know," her mom replied. "The first few days will be rough on me. I miss you already."

"I'll be okay, Mom. I promise."

Her mom nodded, but Emilia could see the worry that still struggled to claim her.

I give thee my word, Disciple of Harpocrates. So long as she resides here, this grove and all its creatures will be ash ere thy daughter comes to harm. This I swear before Gaia and the Known Powers.

"Thank you, Beauregard," her mom said, her voice so soft Emilia almost didn't hear it.

Gerald called from the parking lot, "Sorry, Gia, but if you want to take the train to Chicago, we'd better get going."

"Coming," her mom replied and pulled Emilia into one last, *fierce* hug before she pivoted on her heel and dashed to the car.

Emilia stood her ground and watched her mom stop at the car just long enough to look back. They exchanged waves, and seconds later, they were gone, rolling down the gravel road toward the Amtrak depot in town. She stood her ground, watching the car grow increasingly smaller to her eyes until she couldn't see it anymore.

Bianca approached and stood a respectful distance away, almost seeming to stare off in the direction Gerald had driven with her mother. After several seconds, she spoke at last. "I was beginning to think she'd never go back to New York. She spent all last evening on the patio spinning out excuse after excuse why she could stay a few more days. Now, don't get me wrong; I love your mother like a sister. She will *always* be welcome here as long as I have anything to say about it, but we couldn't get down to brass tacks as long as she was here."

"Oh? What do you mean?" Emilia asked.

Bianca turned to her, a strangely sly smile curling one corner of her mouth. "I'm sure you felt at least some disappointment when you realized that Gerald and I would only be able to teach you the Life Sphere and Alchemy. No, don't bother denying it. I was young once, too, and it was a couple weeks after my evaluation before I truly came to terms with the fact that I would forever be limited in my magic. That just didn't jive with the power I felt saturating my body. But it's your lucky day, week, or month. Take your pick. Isabel and I have an offer for you on the condition that you will never speak of it to anyone under any circumstances and that you will further secure the knowledge in your mind once you gain sufficient mastery of your Mind affinity to do so. What say you?"

"Uhm... shouldn't I at least know what I'm agreeing to before I agree to it?"

"Absolutely," Bianca replied. "You should never agree to something blindly. But... I'm afraid we don't have that luxury this time. What we offer to share with you is worth *at least* one person's life if it ever became common knowledge, possibly dozens more lives on top of that. I can tell you this much; you stand at the edge of a once-in-a-lifetime opportunity. Besides, I think you already know about the situation... at least to a certain degree. I think I was the only one who noticed your window was open that evening your mother, Gerald, and I sat on the back patio discussing matters."

Emilia fought to keep her expression controlled. She was talking about bringing her in on training the Titan! Did that mean the Titan was who she thought it was?

"I accept," Emilia said, figuratively stepping into the conversation before Bianca's final syllable faded from the air.

"That was a little hasty," Bianca remarked. "Are you *sure* that's your answer? Like the woman said, you can't unring this bell."

Emilia nodded, eagerly nodded. "Oh, yes. I'm very certain. It's about the Titan, isn't it? Who is it? Is it Jake from the bank? He stopped by the other evening with the two jaguars, right?"

Bianca chuckled at Emilia's enthusiasm. "Yes. He is the Titan, and Isabel isn't an old friend who's passing through. Neither Gerald nor I knew her prior to her arrival Saturday evening."

"Then, who...?"

"The Wainwrights and I have a mutual acquaintance in Martha Culpepper of the Springfield AEC," Isabel answered as she arrived. "Martha contacted me regarding a mage who possessed all twelve affinities, as attested by every evaluation crystal in their facility. Now that we can begin discussing training, I will offer Jake Adams a Mentor-Apprentice contract, and as you have already agreed, you shall assist us in training him while being a fellow student. I will arrange and structure his training so that the immediate lessons benefit you both, which will allow you to master all of your affinities before you leave us. I will wager that neither Johns Hopkins nor Harvard's medical school will want to pass up a Tri-Sphere who is certified as Grandmaster even in her strong affinities."

Emilia could not keep the surprise from her expression. "I didn't think it was possible for a mage to certify as Grandmaster if she or he did not possess full affinity with a given Sphere."

"For anyone else? Probably not. But you will be training and learning alongside the first sorcerer in over two-thousand years, and not even I possess all the requisite knowledge to train him. Once we move past the basics, I will have to venture home to claim certain volumes from my parents that they bequeathed to me. It is fortuitous that I asked for them all those ages ago, as those tomes are now of supreme value."

"May I ask what they are?" Emilia fought to keep the hopeful curiosity from her voice.

Isabel smiled. "They are the collected works of several sorcerers who were known to be either singular teachers or visionaries pushing the boundaries of what the sorcerers understood about their powers. Once I return with them, I shall pass them on to Jake, as the start of his library."

Emilia nodded, and a thought occurred to her. "I'm not sure I want the fame or notoriety of certifying as Grandmaster in affinities that are merely strong. Could you teach me how to throw the exams to certify as Master in Mind and Spirit?"

"Of course."

At that, Emilia clapped her hands together and rubbed them vigorously as she asked, "So... when do we start?"

CHAPTER
FIFTEEN

The Adams Residence
 21 May 2025, 9:50am

JAKE LOOKED over his sketchbook and smiled at the several pages he'd filled in the short time since he first started. He couldn't wait to show Isabel what he thought of as progress and ask for her opinion on all of it. He gathered the necessities for a shower and was halfway to his bedroom door when his phone rang. He tossed everything on the bed and retrieved the phone. It was Isabel.

"Hello?"

"Hello, Jake. Are you ready to get started?"

Jake blinked. "So soon?"

"Gerald took Gianna to the train depot this morning. In fact, you might meet them somewhere along the way, unless you take your time."

"Wow," Jake remarked, his thoughts swirling. "I was just about to hop in the shower. I could head that way right afterward, though."

Isabel replied, "That will be fine. We have much to discuss."

· · ·

JAKE HUSTLED through his shower and gathered the jaguars. They seemed more excited to visit the grove again than he was to start training. He grabbed a quick sandwich before everyone loaded into his SUV. It wasn't the most wholesome breakfast, but he remembered Isabel's caution about eating and exercise. Then, they were off to the grove.

It was a pleasant drive, and Jake felt he was starting to get a handle on the whole 'driving' thing as they left the town behind and trundled down the road that soon turned to gravel.

What do you think will happen today? Smokey asked, as she poked her head between the driver and passenger seats.

"I'm honestly not sure," Jake replied. "I imagine there will be a considerable amount of introductory stuff. We'll ask Bianca if it's okay for you two to explore the grove."

That would be nice. I'm not sure we're suited to magic studies. I have no doubt it would be very interesting, but we lack thumbs and the capacity for speech.

"Would you like me to ask Bianca or Isabel if there's a way you can talk to more people than just me?"

That would be lovely. We love you, Jake. I doubt we would've survived long without your intervention, but it would be nice to thank your mother for the food without bothering you with it.

Jake smiled. "We will just have to see what we can do about it, then. It may not be right away, but I'll mention it today."

Smokey rubbed her jaw against his arm and disappeared into the back of the SUV.

THEY ARRIVED at the Wainwright Grove and found Bianca, Isabel, and Emilia waiting for them. Jake parked and pressed the button to raise the lift gate. The jaguars jumped out and trotted around to join him as he grabbed his sketchbook and exited the vehicle.

135

"Hello," Jake said as he and the jaguars met the ladies.

He noticed Emilia hung back a little, but Bianca showed no such reticence.

"Welcome back," Bianca replied. "I'm glad you brought your friends. I was hoping you would."

"We have a number of matters to discuss," Isabel remarked, diving right into the business.

Jake nodded and made eye contact with Emilia, saying, "It's nice to see you again."

Emilia gave him a slight smile in return. "I'm told we'll be training together."

Now that he'd greeted everyone as his manners demanded, he turned to Isabel, asking, "So, what's first?"

Isabel held his gaze in silence for several moments before she answered, "We should discuss the Mentor-Apprentice agreement. Formalizing our arrangement will afford a certain measure of protection through obfuscation while recording the terms of our agreement."

"Okay. And what terms are those?"

"Payment for my time, instruction, and use of my contacts... for one."

Jake fought the urge to sigh. "And just what will this cost me?"

Isabel stood in silence for several moments, then said, "Five favors that I may call upon at any time until they are spent, and barring any world-threatening circumstances, I will be very flexible in the timing and manner of delivering on those favors."

Jake started to nod but stopped himself. "I see. And Bianca, what's your price for using the grove?"

"That price has already been paid," she replied.

He turned the matter over in his mind for several moments, but the fact of the matter was that he needed this training. He needed Isabel's expertise.

"Very well," Jake said after a few moments' thought. "I agree."

Isabel smiled. "Excellent. May I ask what you carry?"

Jake lifted his sketchbook with a smile. "I wanted your opinion on this. An idea came to me the other night, and I happened to have this sketchbook handy."

He handed it to Isabel and watched as she freed the front cover from its elastic band. When she saw the first diagram, a hiss escaped her lips. She flipped to the next page, very careful of the paper as if it would crumble at her touch. Her eyes narrowed as she flipped deeper and deeper into the sketchbook. When she reached his final sketch, she went back to the first page and looked through it all again.

Jake started to feel a little uncomfortable with her long silence.

After the second look-through, she brought her eyes up to meet his, saying, "You did this?"

"Yes," Jake answered, adding a nod.

"Without any reference?"

"No. No references," Jake replied. "Well, no references beyond checking MageNet for what the Fireball spell did."

"I do not know whether to be elated or terrified that you have started your first grimoire with no more knowledge of your talents than you have. What experimenting have you done?"

Now, embarrassment surged through Jake. "Uhm... well... I lit a dead tree branch on fire with lighter fluid and then fed the fire some of my energy once I felt a resonance with the flame. It was about the size of a candle flame when I started and flared into a bonfire when I fed it my energy or power or whatever the proper term is."

Isabel immediately pivoted to Bianca. "Is that area with a rock cliff the closest fire-safe area you have?"

Bianca shook her head and pointed to a tree not far away. "That tree is an invasive species and is not compatible with the surrounding ecosystem. I've been meaning to remove it for some time, but simply haven't taken the time to do so."

Isabel turned back to Jake. "Your sketch of a Fireball. Alter your vision for the effect until it's a bullet, arrow, or bolt. Then, throw your energy at the tree and will it into the Flame Projectile construct."

"No special words or gestures or anything like that?"

Isabel's dismissive wave came complete with a contemptuous shake of her head. "No. Those crutches are for your lessers."

"Hey, now," Jake countered. "None of that. Just because I need your instruction and expertise does not give you license to denigrate other mages."

Isabel's contemptuous demeanor vanished in an instant, replaced by a minuscule smile and an exaggerated nod that seemed closer to a slight bow. "You have passed your first test, sorcerer. Now... Flame Projectile to the tree. We're waiting."

Jake turned to face the tree, examining it and the surrounding plant-life. It didn't take him long to see what Bianca meant. The tree jutted upward toward the heavens out of an almost perfect circle of death. He skimmed over his first Fireball diagram and worked through altering the design to a bullet. He felt his body saturating with energy the deeper he went into the preparation, and at the last second, he tried a further alteration. Looking over the design in his mind, he didn't see any obvious problems, so he lifted his right hand and pointed that palm toward the tree.

The energy saturation flowed out of his legs and core, down his arm, and into his hand. In the span of an eye-blink, the energy concentration reached a kind of critical mass. A pointed cylinder of pure flame about the size of a fifty-caliber bullet formed in the air, hovering in front of Jake's palm. Over the next heartbeat or so, the construct finished forming and launched toward the tree almost faster than one could follow with the naked eye.

Halfway to the tree, Jake's last-second alteration activated, and the core of air inside the flame bullet lost its shield and fueled the flame. Over the second half of the distance, the bullet that had been the regular color of a campfire flame—orangish red—blossomed into blue-white. Bianca and Emilia both gasped at the sight.

The moment the flame bullet struck the death tree, Jake pushed what felt like a fist-sized amount of his energy into the flame bullet, and a cylinder with a half-inch diameter and a depth of over six inches instantly became ash. The blue-white flame then exploded to engulf the tree, and over the course of perhaps five minutes, all that remained was a pile of ash in a modest crater at the center of the death circle.

All at once, a crushing wave of vertigo and weakness—with shaking hands thrown in—dropped Jake to his knees. His vision tunneled down to an area no larger than a dime seen from a distance of six feet. The jaguars were at his side instantly, pressing to either side, as Emilia screamed and Bianca rushed to her house.

Isabel withdrew a cylinder of glucose tablets from a pocket, popped off the cap, and shook four into her palm... which she held out to him.

"Eat these. Now."

Jake scooped the tablets into his mouth with a violently trembling hand and used what felt like his last scrap of energy to chew them and swallow. By the time Bianca returned with orange juice and dark chocolate, he started to feel vaguely human once more.

"Here," Bianca said, holding out the juice and chocolate. "The tastes are horrible for each other, but that doesn't matter at the moment."

Jake devoured the chocolate in no more than three bites and washed down whatever remained with the orange juice. After a few more minutes passed, he felt recovered enough to stand. He wobbled a bit as he did so, but he managed the feat.

"And now, you understand the cost of experimentation before you're ready," Isabel remarked. "Yes, what you did was **very** impressive. I doubt anyone short of a dual-Sphere with full affinity to both Fire and Air could duplicate it. But until you've trained your body to channel that power, it will knock you on your ass faster than a pro boxer. Remember this, the next time you feel like experimenting."

Emilia looked from Bianca to Isabel to Jake and made the circuit several times until she asked in a hesitant voice, "Will I be in danger of that?"

Bianca and Isabel both gave her a reassuring smile. Isabel answered, "No, child. Of those present, only Jake is in danger of channeling more energy than his body can sustain. It is one of the risks of being what he is."

"A sorcerer," Emilia remarked.

"Yes," Isabel replied. "This is an important topic to discuss right now. I have yet to gauge your level of competitiveness, but you run the risk of killing yourself if you attempt to compete with Jake, especially as he grows into his power. The more affinities a mage has, the more powerful the mage is... yes?"

Emilia nodded. "Some scholars have hypothesized that each affinity after the second leads to an exponential increase in baseline power."

"I fear your people's attempts to quantify mages' relative strength is doomed to failure," Isabel countered. "It is a complex balance between raw power, knowledge and understanding, and imagination. I am uncertain that even 'exponential' in your mathematics is accurate."

"How do you feel?" Bianca asked Jake.

Jake nodded. "Better. Either a little tired or a little hungry... can't really tell which."

Isabel turned to regard Jake for a moment before giving a decisive nod. "We should eat, then allow you to nap. You were on the cusp of what I believe modern medicine terms a diabetic coma. From this point forward, you should increase your daily caloric intake to a baseline of roughly four thousand calories and increase that still further during those times you practice learning your power."

Jake froze and gaped at Isabel. "*Four thousand*? Seriously? That's twice the average recommendation."

"Yes, but the average person is not bending reality to her will... now is she? Unless you desire your metabolism to start breaking down your muscles for protein, you would be wise to heed my words. During days of heavy practice, your minimum should be six thousand calories or more, preferably eight thousand if you can manage it."

Jake shook his head, disbelief dominating his expression. "Eight thousand? No way. I'd look like some big blob inside of a month."

Isabel turned and met Jake's eyes with her own. "With the practice regimen I have planned, I will be amazed if you gain five pounds over six months."

Without another word, Isabel turned and resumed her journey to Bianca's house. The jaguars stopped on either side of Jake and leaned into his legs, adding their silent support and regard. His collapse must have scared them, because they didn't 'say' anything... just pressed against him.

After a couple moments, Jake resumed his walk toward the house. He didn't want to give the impression he was having second thoughts. He wasn't... well... not really. He needed to learn how to be who and what he was now.

~

ROSSMART
A few miles west of Quapaw, Oklahoma
21 May 2025, 11:45am

DEPUTY US MARSHAL HANNAH GAINES surveyed the scene, then stepped back outside the convenience store. It wasn't the worst crime scene she'd seen, not by a long shot, but the thick, oppressive arcane residue only served to intensify the ghastly smell of the poor victims' corpses. She was fortunate that her affinity with the Air Sphere allowed her to filter out the worst of it. This was the tenth such incident in less than a month, and whatever—or whoever—it was headed east.

One might have thought that the FBI would have jurisdiction

over federal law regarding the supernatural within the United States, but such was not the case. The United States Marshals dated back to the very founding of the country... 24 September 1789, to be exact. And part of their earliest mandate was to enforce—and oversee the enforcement of—all federal laws governing the supernatural within the country's borders. The task force investigating the string of arcane-related murders was Hannah Gaines's first command within the US Marshals' Arcane Division.

Hannah was one of the rare exceptional Tri-Spheres, possessing full affinity to Air, Mind, and Spirit, and she approached her sixth year with the Marshals and her eleventh year in law enforcement overall. She walked over to the closest of her government-issued SUVs. Her fellow deputy marshal, Luis Alvarez, had a map of the continental US spread across the hood. As she neared, she saw he had a yard stick and his colored pencils, marking the latest attack and adding it to the jagged line he'd drawn. Sure, computer modeling could do it so much faster and more accurately, but Luis liked having case notes and maps that he could touch.

"How bad?" he asked when Hannah stopped off to his right.

"Bad," Hannah replied. "A cashier, two teenagers, and an elderly lady. All looked like they were devoured."

Luis winced. "So, whatever this is, it's moving east... and it seems to be moving east at a pretty good clip. Here, let me show you something."

He put one edge of the yardstick on the large dot that represented Los Angeles—its port being the site of the first incident—and positioned the rest of the yardstick, drawing a 'trend' line across the country.

"The monster that's doing this has yet to deviate too far from this line... no more than ten to fifteen miles in either direction. Springfield, Missouri. Hornbeam, Illinois. Cincinnati, Ohio. Lexington, Kentucky. Even Norfolk, Virginia, is within fifteen miles of this line."

"And whatever it is kills the cameras before it gets within range of any of them," Hannah growled. "I **do not** like flying blind."

Luis knew what the response would be, but he felt compelled to say it anyway. "There's always Isabel Taylor up in Pueblo. She's supposed to be our escalation call for anything supernatural."

"No. I will not roll over and bare my throat on this. Besides, what's a private investigator going to do? Take pictures of it cheating on its spouse?"

Luis shook his head. "There's a reason she's our escalation call, Hannah. Granted, I don't know what that reason is, but it's right there in our operations manual. If there is even the slightest chance we are in over our heads on something, we are to contact Isabel Taylor at Draco Investigations right away. You're lead on this, and I'm not trying to be insubordinate... but Hannah, can you even identify the arcane residue in there?"

It took all Hannah's willpower to keep from losing her cool. Yes, she was the only mage on the task force. Yes, she was only thirty-five. And **yes**, she had no idea what was doing this. A tiny voice in the back of her mind whispered that maybe Luis was right. Maybe she **should** call this Isabel Taylor, but the idea of doing so galled her in the extreme.

Then, one of the last things her father ever said to her forced its way to the forefront of her mind: sometimes, it's better to eat a little humble pie than bull your way into something and get people who depend on you killed. He'd been a soldier during the Gulf War back in the 1990s, and that conflict haunted him for some reason that he never discussed with his daughter.

"Fine," Hannah said, her voice devoid of its former ire. "I'll make the call."

CHAPTER
SIXTEEN

Wainwright Grove
Hornbeam, Illinois
21 May 2025, 12:00pm

Isabel led them into the backyard of the Wainwright residence. After a hearty lunch, Jake no longer felt like he might need a quick nap, so she decided it was time to establish her credibility.

"Emilia, you may be wondering what my credentials are that I know so much about the arcane world while not being a crafter myself."

Emilia's lips quirked in something between a smile and a grin. "You could say that. There's no 'Isabel Taylor' listed in the Magocracy database... at least none that matches your description. There was an 'Isabel Taylor' who lived in London, but that was over two hundred years ago."

Isabel stopped at the edge of the paved patio and looked over the large, open grassy area. It was about fifty yards to the tree line and maybe seventy-five yards long. It **should** be large enough. She turned to face the others.

"Yes, and she was such a dear soul, too," Isabel replied. "I took her name when I needed a new identity in the late Victorian era."

Bianca and Emilia both frowned. Emilia said, "That's not possible. You don't look that old, and only a Life mage could live so long."

Isabel smiled, chuckled even. "Oh, dear child. How little you know of the world you inhabit. Life mages are not the **only** creatures of this planet who live longer than humans. Please, step back and do not leave the paving stones until the change is complete."

"Change?" Emilia asked. "What change?"

Reaching behind her with her left hand, Isabel produced a cell phone and extended it to Jake. "Jake, please hold this for me. If it should ring, tell me who calls before you answer."

"Got it," Jake replied as he accepted the phone.

The jaguars ventured out of the house and moved to Jake's side as Isabel turned and walked away from the patio. When she was about halfway to the tree line, Isabel stopped and gauged the size of the grassy area once more. She still thought it should be sufficient, but she hadn't asked Kai to measure her lately. She knew the fifty-yard distance to the tree line was good enough, but the seventy-five-yard width was the source of her concern. She didn't **think** she was longer than that, nose to tail... at least she hadn't been prior to moving to North America... but that was over three hundred years ago.

Well, no time like the present to find out...

JAKE STOOD IN SILENCE, holding Isabel's phone, and felt the jaguars press against him. He placed the phone on the planter wall to his right and patted each of them while he waited for Isabel's big reveal. Out of the three humans present, he was pretty sure only he had the vaguest idea of what was about to happen.

After a few more moments of examining the grassy area, Isabel turned so that they were on her right and closed her eyes. He felt... well... he wasn't sure. It was almost like an explosion of tightly constrained power, and it manifested as an enormous flash of bright, white light. Bianca and Emilia reacted to the flash, but if they felt the explosion of power, they didn't show it.

When the flash of light faded, Jake couldn't help but gape at the sight. A massive dragon—straight out of Western legend—stood in the grassy area behind Bianca's home. She—assuming it was indeed a *she*—looked to be maybe eighty to a hundred feet long, and when she extended her wings, her right wing extended past the edge of the pavers and onto the patio, while the left brushed the trees at the far side of the grassy area. Her scales were the color of aged red bricks with striations of flame orange and gold running irregularly through each scale. Two massive horns extended back over her head from just above what would be the forehead on a human, and her tail tapered to a point that looked sharper than a razor.

After a few moments of stretching her wings, the dragon pulled them back to her sides and turned toward her audience. When she lifted her feet to take steps, Jake saw that each foot ended in thick toes with claws that looked capable of rending tank-grade armor.

"Is - Isabel?" Emilia asked. The sound of her voice made Jake think she was just at the cusp of terrified panic.

"Yes, child," the dragon replied in a voice that resonated against Jake's bones but sounded surprisingly similar to her voice when in human form. "You cannot speak my actual name without harming yourself, so please, continue to address me as Isabel."

Jake smiled as he examined Isabel in her true form, and he said, "You're beautiful, Isabel."

"Thank you, Jake," Isabel replied, then turned back to Bianca and Emilia. "I am about twenty-two-hundred years old. Calendars were none too accurate for my earliest years, and the conversion from the Julian to the Gregorian calendar merely complicated the matter."

Isabel's phone rung. Jake grabbed it and—upon glancing at the screen—said, "It's the US Marshals."

"Answer it, please," Isabel replied.

Jake thumbed the controls to accept the call and put the call on speaker before saying, "Draco Investigations."

The speaker broadcast a woman's voice, responding, "This is Deputy US Marshal Hannah Gaines. I'm trying to reach Isabel Taylor."

"One moment please." Jake thumbed the 'mute' control and looked to the dragon. "What should I say?"

"Hmmm... tell her I am momentarily unavailable and will return her call within ten minutes."

Jake took the call off mute and repeated Isabel's words.

"Very well," Hannah replied. "Thank you."

The call ended, and Jake returned the phone to the planter wall.

"I would have preferred to offer you each a ride, flying around the grove, but it seems the Marshals have need of me," Isabel remarked. She stepped back from the patio and recited a series of words in a language unlike anything Jake had ever heard. Moments later, the Isabel Taylor he met in the diner parking lot stood at the edge of the pavers. She crossed to the planter and retrieved her phone, then turned to face them. "My people are the ultimate enforcement of the laws that govern the supernatural world, and I do not mean human laws that touch upon the supernatural. When the vampires or the shifters or the fey or any of a dozen different species fail to police themselves, then doing so falls to the dragons... which essentially means me, since most of my people sleep the centuries away in their respective lairs. Excuse me, please; they would not have called if the circumstances were not dire."

~

AFTER TAPPING the most recent call in her phone's call list, Isabel lifted the phone to her ear while Jake and the others looked on. She heard one ring before a woman said, "Deputy Marshal Gaines."

"This is Isabel Taylor, Marshal. I apologize for missing your call. I'm afraid it was somewhat unavoidable."

"I don't know what a private investigator from Colorado is supposed to do, but our operations manual lists you as our escalation call. And... well... I have a case that I can't help but feel should be escalated."

Isabel turned the matter over in her mind for a heartbeat. The Marshals **never** called her. Well... that wasn't quite true. They called her about the rogue vampire preying on the railroad camps back in the late 1800s and three times since then, and every time they called, it had always been something preying on humans.

"How many bodies, Marshal?" Isabel asked.

Silence extended for a few seconds before Hannah replied, "How... how did you know?"

"I have yet to be called in on one of your agency's cases that did not involve something preying on humans. I was merely playing the odds."

Hannah said, "Oh. I... see. And the answer—for the current crime scene at least—is four."

Four. Not good. "How recent?"

"No more than ninety minutes."

Isabel frowned. There **might** still be time. "Do you have a Spatial mage handy? I'm in Hornbeam, Illinois, and unless you're very close, I doubt we'll have time for more conventional transportation."

"Yes. We have a Spatial mage assigned to the office in Springfield."

This might not be too bad, then. "Very well, Deputy. Make the call. I am currently located at the Wainwright Grove, and I recommend your mage arrive **outside** the grove's hedge... just for the safety of all concerned."

"I don't understand, ma'am," Hannah remarked.

Isabel fought back a chuckle. No... of course, she didn't. "When you have a few moments of downtime, do a federal records search on 'Beauregard' in relation to the Wainwright Grove."

"I will, ma'am. If you'll excuse me, I need to make that call."

"Goodbye, Deputy Marshal. We shall speak anon."

Isabel ended the call and returned the phone to her hip pocket. "Well, it seems I must leave you for a time. The Marshals have a case with at least four bodies, and they are escalating the situation to me. A Spatial mage will arrive shortly to conduct me to the current crime scene." She paused and directed an appraising expression toward Jake. "Jake, as a sorcerer, there are few—if any—supernaturals that will be able to stand against you once you fully grow into your power... especially in a one-on-one confrontation. Have you given any consideration to what you will do with your gifts?"

Jake chuckled. "I'm still coming to grips with the idea that I *have* power. Why?"

"You have it within you to be an incredible force for good or evil in the world. A symbol of hope or a symbol of terror. I know that I—along with a number of other people who are aware of the Titan's existence—hope and pray that you will be a force for good. I would like for you to accompany me and participate in this case as part of your training so that you have an idea of what you may face one day."

"My only question is whether I should take the kids," Jake replied, gesturing toward the jaguars.

Isabel considered them and ultimately shook her head. "No. They are on record as being the familiars of Thornton 'Jake' Adams. To operate in the world as a sorcerer, I recommend you cultivate a separate identity, because as we discussed, there will be many who hunt you... for myriad reasons."

Jake turned to Bianca and Emilia. "Bianca, do you mind watching a pair of rambunctious jaguars for a while?"

The jaguars seemed to perk up at the idea of spending some time at the grove.

"Of course not, Jake," Bianca replied. "The grove and I will take excellent care of them."

Emilia took a half step forward as she asked, "May I accompany you?"

"What are your affinities?" Isabel asked.

"Full affinity to Life, Strong in Mind and Spirit as well," Emilia answered.

Isabel turned and looked toward the archway in the hedge that allowed access to the grove. She neither saw nor sensed the Spatial mage yet, but it wouldn't be much longer. At least, she hoped it wouldn't be much longer. After a moment of consideration, she turned back to Emilia, saying, "It will not be pretty... whatever it is."

"Pre-med," Emilia replied. "Might as well get used to it."

"So be it. You may accompany us. Now, we should go to the hedge. The Marshals' Spatial mage should arrive soon, and I would prefer the mage not risk Beauregard's wrath."

JAKE KNELT in front of the jaguars and pulled each of them into a one-armed hug, which he held for a couple heartbeats. When he broke the hug and leaned back, he said, "I don't know how long I'll be gone, so I want you to be good for Bianca. Okay?"

We'll be good, Jake. Smokey replied. *I'll keep an eye on fur-butt.*
*

You'll keep an eye on me, huh? I'll be good, too! Bandit replied.

"Would you rather wait for me at home with Mom and Dad?"

Bandit looked over his shoulder at the grove for a moment before turning back. *I suppose we could if you wanted us to wait there.*

"Okay. I'll call them and let them know we'll be a little while on a training trip. Be good for Bianca."

Both jaguars bobbed a nod, and Jake rubbed their ears before he stood. He looked to Bianca, saying, "Thank you for watching them."

"Think nothing of it, and you should probably hurry."

Jake nodded and turned, then jogged to catch up to Isabel and Emilia. He arrived at their sides just as an oval-shaped section of reality began swirling like a two-dimensional whirlpool. After a couple seconds, the center of the effect seemed to draw away from them, and when it started to snap back, it disappeared in a flash of light that left a young woman in business-casual attire. She stood about five-and-a-half feet tall with wavy, sandy blond hair.

She took two steps toward the trio and revealed a holstered sidearm as she withdrew a wallet-style identification folio. She opened it and held it up for everyone to see, revealing a Deputy US Marshal badge and a photo identification card as she said, "Hello. I'm Deputy US Marshal Carol Bergman. I'm looking for Isabel Taylor."

"I am Isabel Taylor, and these are students who will accompany us."

Carol frowned. "I wasn't informed of any students. This is a classified—"

Jake felt **something** fade into existence, and it seemed to be centered on Isabel. When she spoke, her voice carried the tiniest hint of the power and resonance it had in her dragon form.

"Child, your agency no longer has authority over the case. Per your own regulations, the moment I accept the call, the case is **mine**. As such, I will decide who has access to it. Do you understand?"

By the time Isabel finished speaking, the color had long since fled from Carol's complexion, and her eyes were wide. "I... uhm... I will have to confirm this with my chain of command."

"Then, do so with celerity," Isabel replied, her voice back to 'normal.' "Every moment you waste makes my task all the more difficult."

Carol withdrew a cell phone from a belt holster under her left arm, and she looked at it, her expression becoming a grimace. "No bars? Really?"

"I shall take full responsibility," Isabel said. "Conduct us to the crime scene; then, report it to your chain of command."

Carol returned the phone to its holster with a huff. "Fine. I probably wasn't going to last long with the Marshals anyway. Okay... so, we'll be going to a road-side convenience store a few miles west of a small town in Oklahoma. Gather around, everyone."

Jake and Emilia moved to stand closer to Carol as the deputy marshal withdrew a small notebook from yet another belt holster. When she opened it, Jake saw that each page had a name written at the top with a little plastic baggie stapled to it. Carol flipped through the notebook until she arrived at a page with 'Hannah Gaines' at the top. She opened the baggie and retrieved a tuft of hair.

"Wait..." Emilia said. "If she needs a link to her destination, how did she teleport here?"

Carol's head shot up, and her expression drifted toward a glare.

Before the deputy marshal could say anything, though, Isabel explained, "Spatial mages with at least Strong affinity do not require a link to their destination within a certain distance, and that distance is greater if the mage has Full affinity. I suspect that our destination is close enough to her unassisted limit that Deputy Marshal Bergman is wisely choosing to guarantee a successful portal, instead of attempting to force the issue on bravado and hope. She demonstrates excellent professionalism in this regard."

Carol's expression shifted from a burgeoning glare to almost surprise. "I always like to use a connection when there's more than just me going... unless the hop is absurdly short. No one has ever called it professionalism before."

Isabel turned to the deputy marshal. "Then, those who do not are fools. Please, proceed."

Carol placed the tuft of hair in the palm of her hand and closed her eyes. Jake felt **something**, but he wasn't sure what. He closed his eyes and focused on the feeling. The more he concentrated on it, the more it felt like Carol reached toward their destination somehow. All at once, he felt the link between the two places form, almost like someone had carved a path through space-time between the two points. Then, a sense of raw power exploded, and the link between them and their destination snapped like a rubber band against one's wrist. Jake felt a sudden lurch that sent his inner ears into almost open rebellion, and he weaved on his feet.

A hand clutched his shoulder in an iron grip right before Isabel said, "Open your eyes, Jake. It will help with the disorientation."

Jake opened his eyes and saw they stood on the outskirts of a road-side convenience store with both charging stations and old-style fuel pumps. He saw a couple sheriff cars, a couple Oklahoma Highway Patrol cars, several blacked-out SUVs, and a square-box ambulance chassis with 'Medical Examiner' stenciled on the side. Emilia stood close, but Carol was already thirty feet away as she walked to a cluster of people in similar business-casual attire standing with a cluster of uniformed officers.

"I think I sensed what she did," Jake whispered as he brought his left hand up to cover his lips.

Isabel smiled. "Good. That's good. Maintain awareness of your senses. Now... let's go see why they felt it necessary to call me."

CHAPTER
SEVENTEEN

RossMart
A few miles west of Quapaw, Oklahoma
21 May 2025, 12:45pm

THIS WAS NOT the first grisly scene Isabel had faced. She was over two thousand years old, after all, and humans had made a thorough study of war across many of those years. But so far, such scenes always impacted her. Sorrow that more lives had ended before their time. Compassion—tinged with regret—for the next of kin who would have to face this. Of all the things she had done in her long life, notifying loved ones of an unexpected death was not one of them. She hoped it never was, despite the twinge of guilt such a hope incited.

Her eyes sought out the wounds on the victims' bodies next. She noticed two types right away. Claw marks and... rents in the flesh. Something strong tore away sections of the corpses' tissue.

There was little more her eyes could tell her, so she closed them and released her grip on the magic that held her in human form. Not too much. Just enough that her draconic senses came to the fore, specifically her sense of smell. A deep breath drew a cornucopia of scents through her nostrils, and she discarded all those she expected to find. One scent remained, and she recognized it in an instant.

Her eyes shot open, and she pivoted on her heel, searching the assembled officers for the one she wanted. There!

Isabel crossed the convenience store's parking lot to approach the trio of deputy marshals. "Deputy Marshal Bergman!"

The three deputy marshals flinched as if their boss caught them goofing off during work hours, and all three turned to face her.

"Yes, Ms. Taylor?" Carol asked.

"I need you to return my apprentices to the Wainwright Grove at once," Isabel said.

Carol blinked, then frowned. "Excuse me? What am I... your personal taxi?"

Isabel glared at the woman. "You are a Spatial mage assigned to me for the duration of this case, are you not?"

Carol swallowed a scowl. "Yes."

"Then, if I tell you to teleport to Manhattan for a dozen New York City bagels, you will damn well do it, and if you have a problem with that, I am happy to address the issue with the director of the Marshals Service."

Carol sneered. "You don't have—"

Deputy Marshal Gaines stopped her with a hand on her shoulder. "Carol, if you're about to say she doesn't have the authority, you should read the operations manual. She is *our* escalation call. Our director is *hers*."

Carol turned to her associate, and her shoulders slumped in resignation when she saw the expression on Hannah's face. "Fine. Which one?"

"Both. Wait here, and I will collect them."

Without waiting for Carol to respond, Isabel pivoted and crossed the distance to Jake and Emilia in short order.

"What is it, Isabel?" Emilia asked.

"You both need to return to Wainwright Grove at once," Isabel answered. "I recognize the scent of the creature that did this, and Jake will be in grave danger if he stays."

"Why?" Emilia asked. "What did this?"

"A griffon, and if it becomes aware of Jake's presence, it will slaughter everyone here to kill him. I hope it is just the one; I only detected one unique scent."

"So, more than one would be a danger to you?" Jake asked.

Isabel frowned. "In this form, possibly, but in my true form, no. There is very little in this world that can harm me when I don't hide behind one of the shorter-lived forms. You should call your parents when you return to the grove. It is not safe for you to stay with them until I resolve the matter of this griffon."

"And you're saying I'll be safe at the grove?" Jake asked, his voice hinting at disbelief.

Isabel nodded. "Oh, yes. Not even an entire clutch of griffons would choose to fight Beauregard for you, but I will do what I can to end the threat before it is even aware of you."

"Why is Jake in danger?" Emilia asked.

"He can tell you once you're safe behind the grove's hedge. Now, we have tarried long enough. You need to go."

Isabel turned and led them back to the trio of deputy marshals. By the time they arrived, Carol had a portal waiting for them. Isabel waited for Jake and Emilia to step through and the portal to close before she turned to the marshals.

"Were all the previous scenes like this one?" Isabel asked.

Hannah nodded. "Yes. All of them."

"A creature did this, not a human. To be exact, a griffon. I would examine the other scenes, but it's possible sufficient time has passed for the scent to have dissipated... which means I cannot confirm that the *same* griffon is responsible for all the sites."

"A griffon?" Carol asked. "You expect us to believe a mythical creature did this? What's next? Dragons exist, too?"

Isabel considered her options. She never minded honest, healthy debate among her team, but she did not like Carol's attitude. Fine. Perhaps a lesson was in order. She relaxed the magic holding her in human form, focusing the weakening to happen around her eyes. She knew her eyes would very soon become fiery orange orbs with black, vertical slits for pupils, and she looked to each deputy marshal in turn as she said, "We existed *before* griffons."

Carol's complexion went white as a piece of copier paper, and her eyes rolled back in her head as she collapsed to the ground. Her associates stood frozen in place, too stunned by Isabel's revelation to catch her before she hit the ground.

Once she felt she'd made her point, Isabel weaved magic back over her eyes and regarded the two deputies who were still conscious. "I can count on one hand the number of humans in the western hemisphere who know that dragons are real. If you divulge that information to anyone—even your president—I will eat you, whoever you tell... and possibly your immediate families also, depending on when I had my last meal. Do you understand?"

Both deputies nodded.

"I shall take those nods as your agreement," she said. Pointing at the unconscious Spatial mage, she added, "and I suggest you be sure *she* understands as well."

Isabel turned and returned to the convenience store. She had a griffon to hunt.

Wainwright Grove
  Hornbeam, Illinois
  21 May 2025, 12:58pm

As Jake stepped through the portal and stood once more just outside the hedge of Bianca's grove, he stopped and closed his eyes, focusing on the portal behind him and his sense of it... both its formation as well as how Marshal Bergman held and maintained it. He needed to sit down with his notebook and work out some thoughts, but he felt even more sure than before that he had an excellent start on understanding how to use his Spatial Sphere to create portals. Which set him off thinking about how else he might use it.

He must've stood motionless with his eyes closed too long, because he heard Emilia say, "Jake? Is everything okay?"

He opened his eyes and smiled. "Yes, thank you. I just got a little lost in my thoughts. I know Isabel said I need to stay here at the grove because of the griffon, but if I'm going to do that, I need a few things from my house. Let's go check in with Gerald and Bianca, and I'll see if the kids want to go back to the house with me."

Uncertainty dominated Emilia's expression, but she didn't voice whatever thoughts she had on the matter. Instead, she turned and led the way through the hedge.

The moment Jake passed through the hedge, he felt a presence touch his mind. * Welcome home, Young Master. Where is the lady dragon? *

* The marshals contacted her about a multiple murder scene in Oklahoma, one of a series that started in Los Angeles. Isabel determined a griffon is behind the killings and sent me back here, saying I wasn't ready to face even one griffon yet. *

* The lady dragon was wise to do so. Griffons can be vicious predators. While you have vast untapped potential, I agree that you are not yet prepared to face that particular fight. Rest assured, Young Master, that you shall not come to harm within my domain. *

* Thank you, Beauregard. I appreciate that. *

The conversation with Beauregard carried Jake past the parking spaces and halfway to Bianca and Gerald's house. He was still some thirty feet from it when his jaguars came bounding around the house and ran up to him.

* You weren't gone long. * Bandit said, then turned to Smokey. * He wasn't gone long, right? You're better with clocks than I am. *

Smokey chuffed, expressing exasperation, resignation, and possibly relief all at the same time. * *No, fur-butt. He wasn't gone long, and I know you could do better with the clocks and so many other things if you just tried.* *

* *Why? I have you and Jake. It leaves more time for fun.* *

Smokey shot back a soft growl and gave her brother another slap. Then, she turned to Jake. * *Is everything okay? When you left, you seemed to think you might be gone a while.* *

Jake went down to one knee and pulled them each into a one-armed hug for a few moments before letting them go. "I was going to explain everything to Bianca and Gerald, so let's wait. That way, I won't have to explain twice."

The jaguars both bobbed a nod and moved to his side when Jake stood. When he lifted his head, he saw Emilia standing with Bianca and Gerald on the porch, looking his way.

He led the jaguars across the remaining distance, greeting them by saying, "So, did they give you any problems while I was gone?"

"You weren't gone that long, Jake," Bianca countered.

Jake leaned over and gave Bandit a friendly pat on his shoulder and rubbed along his side while replying, "Oh, yes, I was. Bandit is an engine of chaos and mischief the likes of which you've never seen."

"Well... be that as it may," Bianca said, "I'm pretty sure they spent the time you were gone exploring the grove. So, what brought you back so soon?"

Jake took a deep breath and puffed out his cheeks for a moment as he blew it out. "The marshals contacted Isabel about a quadruple homicide at a convenience store in Oklahoma. When she examined the scene, she determined right away that a griffon was responsible for the killings and told me in no uncertain terms that I was to return here, where I'd be safe until I learn more about what I am and what I can do."

Gerald and Bianca looked to one another, both of their expressions unsettled. After a moment, they turned back to Jake, and

Gerald said, "A griffon, huh? I wonder what set it off. It's been something like two hundred or three hundred years since the last time a griffon came out of hiding."

All Jake could do was answer with a shrug. Prior to Isabel seeking him out, he never realized griffons existed outside of the storybooks. "Isabel told me that I should stay here until she deals with it, but I don't want to put you out or impose."

Bianca shook her head, shutting down that idea almost with prejudice. "No. Not at all. If Isabel says you're not safe outside the grove with this thing prowling around, you won't be outside the grove. We have all kinds of space in the house that we don't use more than once or twice a year, so it's no imposition at all to set you up a room."

"It's probably not a bad idea just to give him the room for the duration of his studies," Gerald remarked. "Never know when it might be needed."

"Yes. I like that idea," Bianca agreed, nodding.

Jake sighed. "Well, if you're certain I won't be an imposition... okay. I do need to run home for a little bit, though. I need to pack some things and talk with my parents. It won't take too long, and I was going to ask the jaguars if they wanted to ride along with me."

Bianca and Gerald shared another look; then, Bianca spoke. "I do not doubt the jaguars' commitment to you or that they would defend you at a moment's notice, but I'm not certain it's wise for you to be by yourself. Take Gerald with you. Emilia and I will work on prepping your room while you're gone."

His expression must have revealed his reticence, because Gerald spoke up, "Look, Jake, I know people see only the Life Grandmaster and healer when they look at me, but I also have a strong affinity to Shadow. I'm not worthless in a fight, and unlike you, I have over twenty years' experience mastering my magic. I am honestly very doubtful that the griffon can reach Hornbeam from even the Oklahoma border in the short amount of time it has had, but if it helps

Bianca relax a little bit for me to go with you, is that really such a bad thing?"

"No, I guess not," Jake replied. "Are you okay to go now?"

Gerald smiled. "Sure. Just let me get my wallet. I never feel right if I leave the grove without it."

It took no time at all to get loaded into Jake's Explorer and depart. The first couple minutes passed in silence, before Gerald ended it.

"So, Bianca and I discussed a few things while you and Emilia were gone. I would normally just wait to discuss this with both of you at the same time, but I'm confident Bianca has already broached the topic, especially given the situation with the griffon. We think it's time to begin your training in the Life Sphere for both of you, especially since we have no way of knowing how long Isabel will be busy. We think the most important thing you can do right now—aside from beginning your study of the Life Sphere—is to start training your body to channel and maintain the enormous power you're capable of drawing."

Jake nodded his understanding. "I guess I'm still coming to terms with my new situation. It doesn't seem all that real yet."

"Trust me, lad; it's *very* real. Bianca and I know several mages with at least a strong affinity to both Fire and Air, and we're of the mind that it would have taken two mages—maybe three—working in concert to do what you did with that tree. Yes, you paid a price for it, but you still did it."

There was no doubt in Jake's mind that he had destroyed the death tree. On the one side, he felt a certain amount of pride that his idea for an air-fueled firebolt worked as well as it did. But at the same time, he did not enjoy driving himself so far into hypoglycemic shock to do it. Yeah... he had a lot of practice in his future.

GERALD ENJOYED the stories Jake shared about raising the jaguars during the drive to the Adams residence. He and Bianca first met Frank and Sarah Adams when they moved to Hornbeam as part of the resettlement efforts.

After pulling into his parents' driveway, Jake shifted the vehicle into Park and set the emergency brake as Gerald exited the vehicle. Gerald heard the back hatch rise, and the jaguars were out of the back and waiting for Jake before the young man completed his exit from the vehicle.

A silence descended as Jake led them through a gate in the privacy fence and into the backyard. The jaguars immediately broke off to lounge in the shade under the sole tree in the yard as Jake went to the back door of the house, calling out to his parents as he stepped through the doorway.

Sarah Adams peeked around the corner and smiled. "Gerald Wainwright, it has been too long. How are you and Bianca?"

"We're just fine, Sarah," Gerald replied. "How are you and Frank?"

"Oh... getting along, getting along. What brings you so far from the grove?"

"Well, I will be training Jake in the Life Sphere, along with the daughter of a close friend from back east, and Bianca and I would like Jake to stay with us for a little bit while we work through all the basics of being a mage."

By this time, Jake's father had stepped into the kitchen and offered his hand to Gerald. They shook hands while exchanging a warm greeting.

Frank—Jake's father—nodded his agreement. "If you and Bianca think staying at the grove is best for Jake until he gets a better handle on his power, I'm all for it. Sarah and I both love him being home every night, but he's twenty-five. He has to spread his wings sometime."

"I'll go pack a few things while you three talk," Jake said and disappeared deeper into the house. The sound of his heavy footfalls going upstairs carried through the house.

Once Jake was out of earshot, Sarah directed a concerned expression to Gerald, "So is Jake really okay? We've been a little worried about him ever since the situation at the bank."

"Bianca and I haven't seen any reason to be worried, Sarah. Jake expressed some concern about practicing what we teach him here, because he didn't want to risk hurting anyone. All the houses around here are so close together that it really isn't the best place for a new mage to study and practice his powers."

"Oh. I... well, we didn't realize any of his powers were that dangerous," Sarah replied.

Gerald shook his head. "Oh, they're not... not really. But by staying out at the grove for a while, Jake won't have to worry about collateral damage if he loses control of something. Neither Bianca nor I worry about that happening, mind you, but Jake does. This will help him have enough peace of mind to build a good foundation of confidence and control."

A slight frown furrowed Sarah's brow. "I never thought of it that way."

"But it makes perfect sense," Frank interjected. "He has to be somewhere he feels safe enough to learn all the ins and outs of what he can do now. Thank you for helping, Gerald. What do we owe you?"

Gerald shook his head. "You don't owe us anything. This has all been handled through the Magocracy; given how Jake made headlines with his manifestation, they wanted to ensure he had the best instruction possible. They don't want any mage to fail, but certainly not Jake... not that he would, anyway. The boy has a good head on his shoulders."

The sounds of Jake heading back downstairs reached the kitchen, and it wasn't long before he came into view with a suitcase and a duffle bag. "Okay. I think I have everything I'll need."

Gerald stepped back and enjoyed how Jake hugged both of his parents before collecting his luggage once again. He shook hands with both Sarah and Frank while Jake watched and then backed out of the house as he said his goodbyes. Jake whistled for the jaguars as he led the way back to the Explorer.

CHAPTER

EIGHTEEN

Bianca and Emilia both looked up from their seats as Gerald led Jake and the kids into the house. Bianca smiled when Gerald crossed the distance between them and delivered a quick—yet heartfelt—kiss.

"I was thinking we'd do a sandwich buffet as a late lunch, and we still have two steaks in the fridge that we can cut up for Bandit and Smokey," Bianca said when Gerald broke the kiss. "What do you think, Ger?"

He nodded. "That sounds fine."

Bianca unfolded her legs and stood as she asked, "Do you mind getting started on that while I show Jake to his room?"

"Not at all. I may draft Emilia to help."

Bianca walked to the stairs that led to the upper floor of the residence and waved for Jake to follow her. They climbed the stairs, and as he turned at the first landing, Jake noticed the jaguars padding softly toward the kitchen behind Gerald and Emilia and wondered how well Emilia was prepared to resist Bandit's sad kitty eyes when he didn't want to wait for food.

"You have a beautiful home," Jake remarked, following Bianca onto a balcony that overlooked the great room below and taking in how the soft wood that made up the walls seemed to reflect the light more than absorb it. He had seen wood-paneled rooms in the past that always felt dark, regardless of how much light the space had.

Bianca stopped at a door on her right and worked the latch, swinging the door wide on silent hinges. "Thank you. It's very special to us, especially since we spent so long growing it."

Jake froze mid-step as he blinked at that revelation. "You... **grew**... your house? How does that work?"

"I am a Druid, you know. It doesn't take any more effort to encourage plants to grow in a specific way than it would have to build it by hand."

Jake scanned the walls that he could see, his eyes focusing here and there on natural curves and strong lines that he doubted even a master woodworker could have produced, and all at once, he saw the truth of her words.

"I... I'm not sure I have the words for how amazing this is."

Bianca shrugged. "Well, you're seeing it now... after it's settled and finalized. I was still learning how to be a Druid when we started the house and made more than a few mistakes that taught me as much as a handful of successes. This will be your room. We have scads more guest rooms, so we want you to think of this as your space. It will be waiting for you anytime you care to use it."

"Wow... thank you, Bianca. That's... you're too kind."

Bianca made a dismissive wave as she entered the bedroom. "Think nothing of it. We want you to consider the Grove to be as much of a home and refuge for you as it is for us. Not just for the immediate circumstances, but as long as you want it. So, you have the bed, there, and a writing desk in that corner. The little sitting area has windows that overlook the back patio. To your right, here, is the ensuite. Full bath and shower with a door leading to your closet, which can also be accessed through the door on the far wall. The carpet should be plush enough that the jaguars won't need pet beds, but we can run back to your house if they do."

"I appreciate that, but I packed a couple blankets they like to use for bedding. I'll set them out and let the kids arrange them however they want." Jake carried the suitcase and the duffle bag to the foot of the bed and set them on the floor, then crouched and withdrew his sketchbook and pencils before turning back to Bianca. "If you and Gerald don't mind, I have a few ideas I'd like to record before we get too deep into the initial training."

"We don't mind at all, Jake."

"Thanks! I'll work on that after we eat, then. I've suddenly realized I'm more than a little hungry."

Bianca started to leave but stopped and turned back to Jake. "I know this is a bit awkward, but given what Beauregard said about the eventual fate of the grove, I thought you should know that Gerald and I have instructed our attorney to prepare a Transfer on Death deed. It will ensure the grove passes straight to you on our deaths, bypassing probate."

Jake nodded... then shrugged with one shoulder. "Yeah... I'm not really sure how to process that. You and Gerald seem like awesome people, and I'd just as soon the fate of the grove not be an issue for quite some time to come."

THE MEAL WAS PLEASANT, even with Bianca encouraging Jake to make three sandwiches before she let him eat in peace. Afterward, Jake helped clear the table and wash the dishes, despite Bianca's insistence that she had it. Jake's opinion was that he could help clean up the mess that he helped create.

As soon as the necessary post-lunch chores were complete, Jake returned to the table and laid out his sketchbook and colored pencils. Looking over the available colors, he wanted to use gray for notes on the Spatial and Time spheres, but he saw that wouldn't work as soon as he tested it on a corner of the page. There wasn't enough contrast between the paper and the mark. So... without any other serious option, he settled on black for both his diagrams and his annotations. He didn't like that, but he didn't see how he had much of a choice.

Jake delved into his thoughts, drawing out the best diagrams he could to represent what he had felt as Marshal Bergman created and maintained the portals. As with his previous work, he put the diagrams on the left page with unique marks that corresponded to annotations on the right page. The world around Jake ceased to exist while he worked through his thoughts and memories, and when he leaned back against his seat at last, the day had progressed toward early evening.

He blinked and looked all around, drawing the attention of Bianca, Gerald, and Emilia.

"Finally come up for air, did you?" Gerald asked.

Jake felt his cheeks heat with just a touch of embarrassment. "Yeah... I guess so. I'm sorry I held up your teaching."

"Think nothing of it," Gerald replied, adding a dismissive wave. "It's important to get that kind of thing off your mind as quickly as you can. Besides, we still have some time before dinner, so we can start on the basics."

Jake nodded his agreement and closed the sketchbook, securing the front cover with the built-in elastic strap. Then, he returned the pencils and the sketchbook to his room before coming back to sit in a plush armchair across from Gerald.

Gerald looked from Jake to Emilia and back again before he said, "Very well. Emilia, I apologize if what we're about to discuss is old news to you. The very first topic we need to cover is how to exercise your bodies to enhance and maintain your ability to draw on your power. This is one of the cornerstone techniques that will improve your overall efficiency and allow you to access and use more power for less effort. Are both of you with me so far?"

Jake and Emilia answered, "Yes," almost in unison.

"By the time a mage reaches Master-level certification in a Sphere, he or she has often developed their own, personal method for doing this. What I am about to help you learn and practice is the method my mentor taught me... more years ago now than I care to consider." Gerald paused, closing his eyes and taking slow deep breaths while resting his head against the chair's back. "Close your eyes and push all senses to the back of your mind except for my voice and your awareness of your body. Focus on that awareness and allow my voice to become a part of the surface background.

"Before we can begin, we must first learn to sense the power within us. Oftentimes, mages have said it feels like a pit of energy resting within their cores. Only you can determine how your power feels to you, and sometimes, mages must attempt drawing on their power in a kind of 'slow motion' to single it out from the noise that is the overall sense and awareness of our bodies. Try to locate your power now, and tell me if or when you succeed."

Jake was not one for meditation, so the idea of tuning out his surroundings except for the sense of his body was a foreign concept. Emilia's happy exclamation that she found hers mere moments after Gerald stopped speaking did not help matters. The problem was that it seemed like he felt his power *everywhere*. All throughout his body, and not localized in one specific place. He shook his head as he concluded that he must be doing something wrong, because nothing Gerald said suggested that he would feel his power saturating his entire body.

So, faced with initial failure, he decided to attempt the 'slow motion' draw. He didn't know how to draw his power into a greater saturation, so he fell back on *doing* something with it. But whatever he did had to be safe for everyone and everything around him, so rather than call on his Fire affinity, he re-worked the mental diagram for his Fire-based reading light into one that drew on the Light sphere. Once he felt confident in the framework's design, he pushed a trickle of power into the construct and focused on identifying the power's source.

"That... that can't be right," he muttered.

"What can't be right, Jake?" Gerald asked.

His eyes still closed, Jake did not see the pinprick of pure white light above his head that grew in both size and intensity at a gradual rate as he fed a trickle of power into the construct.

"I'm trying to feed a trickle of power into a light construct to locate my core, but it's like the draw is some kind of mesh or web across my entire body."

Silence extended for long enough that Jake decided to increase the power he sent to the construct. When he did so, the strands of the energy mesh he felt thickened as the trickle increased to a flow comparable to that of a kitchen faucet.

"Uhm, Jake?" Gerald said, his voice tentative.

"Yeah, Gerald?"

"Do you mind terminating your light construct?" His voice still carried hints of wariness and caution.

"Don't mind a bit. Why?"

When Gerald didn't answer right away, Jake opened his eyes and flinched. A sphere of bright, pure white light hovered about six inches above his head. It looked to be about the size of a basketball and left a large off-colored spot in his vision after glancing at it.

Closing his eyes once more and concentrating on the energy tether connecting him to the light sphere, a thought occurred, *Huh... I wonder if I can drain the power out of a construct.*

With that thought in mind, Jake reversed the flow in the tether and immediately felt the power he'd fed to make the sphere flow back into his mesh. Soon enough, there was no power left to drain, and the tether fizzled into nothingness... but... as long as Jake held his focus on the energy mesh within him, he found he could sense it without effort.

A smile curled his lips as Jake opened his eyes. The moment he processed the others' expressions, though, the smile faded. Wariness. Something akin to disbelief. Awe.

"What?" he asked, breaking the silence.

Gerald and Bianca shared an unreadable look, before Gerald said, "Jake... walk us through what you just did, step by step if you please."

"From the beginning?"

Gerald answered with a nod.

"Okay." Jake closed his eyes and took a deep breath. "So, I tried separating awareness of my power from the general awareness of my body, but that wasn't working. It seemed intertwined or woven through me to the point that it was indistinguishable from the rest of me. The way you describe it, I thought I should feel my power separate from me somehow, and that just wasn't the case. So, I decided to try the 'slow motion' thing you mentioned and modified my fireball diagram to draw on Light, since I didn't want to risk harming anyone or anything.

"When I tried feeding a trickle of power into the light construct, I found... well... I guess the best word for it is 'mesh' or 'web.' The web itself isn't my power, though; it was more like the plumbing through which my power flowed to feed the trickle. It started off thin and faint, like cobwebs you see, but when I increased the trickle to something close to the full flow from a kitchen faucet, the web intensified and gained definition."

He heard Gerald ask, "Have you ever heard of anything like that before?"

Jake opened his eyes and found Gerald looking to Bianca.

Bianca shook her head 'no' as she answered, "Every mage I've ever spoken with and every account I've ever read always refers to one's power manifesting as a pit in the mage's core that varies in size, according to the mage's strength. No one has ever said *anything* about some kind of web or mesh."

"Do you know why the light construct faded instead of just vanishing?" Gerald asked.

Jake nodded. "Yeah... I drained the power I'd fed into it back out of it when you asked me to terminate it. I didn't know if that was possible and decided to try it."

As silence took over the room, Bianca and Gerald shared another uncertain look. Gerald must've communicated a silent question, because Bianca simply shook her head slowly.

Gerald turned back to regard Jake and Emilia for a moment

before focusing on Jake. "I don't really know what to do with that. As far as I know, mages can't drain power out of an established construct. At least... I've never heard of one doing that. Uhm... okay, then. I'm not sure how the next step will work for you, Jake. It may be fine, or you may have to develop a work-around for your unique situation. Now that you've identified and localized your power, I want you to draw it into yourself and push it around your body as if you're directing a bead of mercury in a bowl. This will—for lack of a better term—burn pathways that are less resistant to the flow of power, and the more time you practice this across years, the lower the resistance will be. Try it now."

Jake closed his eyes and took a deep breath as he laid his head back against the chair. He released the breath as a slow sigh and tried to collect a squeeze-ball-sized node of power to push around his body. Except nothing happened. No matter what he tried, it was like he tried to catch fog in his hand.

As he continued to try to do as Gerald asked, his focus slipped, and instead of a 'handful' of power, he latched onto the center of the web. Before he thought anything of it, Jake tried to push the center of the web from what felt like the core of his torso to his shoulder. He felt resistance.

Ah, ha! Progress at last!

He 'tightened his grip' on the web's center and put all his willpower behind his intent to push it into his shoulder. All at once, the web's center came free with what felt like a *pop*, and all resistance vanished as the sensation of a red-hot iron poker traced along his skin and followed the path of the web's center.

He gasped at the pain and felt sweat erupt across his torso and forehead.

"What is it, Jake?" Gerald asked.

Jake released the center of the web, and it snapped back to its original location with a sensation not unlike a rubber band snapping against his skin. The searing heat vanished.

"Oh... wow. So, I figured out how to push my power throughout my body, and you don't know how right you were when you called it 'burning.' It felt like someone was tracing the path of my power with a red-hot poker pressed against my skin. I even started sweating. In fact, my skin is still tingling like the burn hasn't faded yet."

Once again, Gerald and Bianca shared a look laden with uncertainty and wariness.

"Do you mind removing your shirt, Jake?" Gerald asked at last.

Jake answered with a shrug and doffed his t-shirt. Gerald, Bianca, and Emilia all gasped.

"What?" Jake asked as he looked down... and did a double take at the sight of his chest. Faint lines formed a spider web across most of his torso, almost like a fractional tattoo. The center of the web blazed an angry red like a second-degree burn and capped a line of burned flesh that curved up between his pecs to his right shoulder. As he watched, the red faded from his shoulder down as his body healed. Jake watched, unable to look away, as the red faded to pink and then to his normal skin tone. By the time he finished healing, the gray lines of the spider web had faded from his torso as well.

"Uhm... yeah..." Gerald vocalized as he stared at Jake's now-healed chest. "Until we have a chance to consult with Isabel, Jake, I think you should avoid that particular exercise and practice creating spheres of light instead."

"Okay. I can do that," Jake replied as he pulled his shirt over his head.

Gerald turned to his other student. "How about you, Emilia?"

"I managed to push my power around my body, and it did feel warm as I did it. But I don't think it was anything close to what Jake experienced."

"Very good," Gerald remarked. "Practice that several times throughout each day until you can shift your power without feeling any effects. For now, get a good night's sleep, and we'll start on an overview of the Life sphere tomorrow morning."

CHAPTER
NINETEEN

The Wainwright Grove
Hornbeam, Illinois
22 May 2025, 8:15am

JAKE SAT on the edge of his bed, staring at the contact he had open on his phone. Fiona O'Rourke. They hadn't settled on a day for him to visit her in Topeka, and given the griffon threat, that possibility seemed unlikely for the near future.

He sighed.

He didn't want to do this, but he felt like there was no other choice.

He tapped the number he'd marked 'Personal' and lifted his phone to his ear.

Fiona answered almost immediately. "Hi, Jake. How are you?"

"I'm doing well enough, Fiona. I was calling about—"

"Jake, please forgive me. I know I sent you that huge list of possible dates we could meet up, but it's been nine kinds of crazy here. I'd love to have lunch with you or something, but it's going to be a bit difficult to make that work right now."

Holy cow. Jake wasn't prepared for the flood of relief that cascaded through him. "It's totally okay, Fiona. That's why I was calling. My mentor got called away to consult on a case that turned out to be a series of griffon attacks, and she doesn't want me leaving the Wainwright Grove until she can get the griffon sorted."

There was a pause just long enough to process as a pause. "There's a griffon on the loose? Shit... that explains so much. Hang on. How did you know it was okay to discuss the supernatural with me? It's kind of a no-no to expose the poor, wittle humans to it."

He chuckled... couldn't help it, really. "My mentor told me you have at least some Fae ancestry, so I figured it was okay."

Fiona sighed. "Yeah... okay. Fair enough. Do me a favor, though, please? Don't bandy that about too much. The government already knows because of my military service, but I try not to advertise it."

"Deal. I won't mention it again."

"And your mentor is right. I sensed the Wainwright Grove from the grocery store parking lot that day we met. I doubt even a full clutch of griffons would attack the grove to get a mage, even if he is an exceptional Tri-Sphere. Hrmmm... tell you what. One of my clients in this case from hell is a Spatial mage, and I have a rare opening this Saturday evening. Since you're not supposed to leave the grove and since I could feel it all the way in Hornbeam, how about I portal over to you for dinner? That diner not too far from the grocery store was rather divine."

Jake turned the idea over in his mind. He couldn't deny the appeal of having dinner with her, and if she was right about how large of a presence Beauregard cast (not that he was going to tell her about Beauregard), the town would probably be safe enough.

"All right. You talked me into it. The diner is Marci's Diner, and what time would you like to meet?"

"Let me text my client and see if she's available for hire to portal me there and back, and I'll let you know. Okay?"

"Sure thing. I hope the case gets better."

He heard Fiona's fervent agreement in her tone. "You and me both, Jake. Bye for now."

The call ended before Jake could respond with his own 'Bye,' and he stood and stretched. It was time to face the day.

The pleasant smells wafting out of the kitchen encouraged his spirits to brighten as he entered the dining area and chose a seat. Emilia sat a couple chairs away, engrossed in her tablet. Soon enough, Gerald and Bianca laid out a fine spread for the day's first meal, and the four of them sat to partake of it.

"So, Jake... tell us a little about you," Bianca encouraged as they all pursued a morning meal.

Jake shrugged as he slathered a bagel with cream cheese. "You seem to know quite a bit about me already if you're laying out bagels with chive-and-onion cream cheese." He took a bite to allow him time to order his thoughts, then continued. "I suppose the most important piece of information is that I'm adopted. I never delved too deeply into it, since Mom and Dad are all the parents I need, but I have no idea who is responsible for me existing. By the time I was old enough to understand that I'm not theirs in a biological sense, it didn't really matter how they came to have me. I'm not even sure if anyone knows *where* I was born."

He watched Gerald and Bianca share another look. Part of him thought to ask them what it was about, but the majority vote indicated another bagel was in order. The breakfast conversation turned to other topics, and soon enough, Gerald gathered them once more in the great room.

"Today, we begin our exploration of the Life Sphere," he began once everyone was seated and comfortable. "The simplest explanation is that it allows you to sense and manipulate living matter. Here's an excellent example. The Life Sphere—specifically the Nature subdomain—will allow a mage to stimulate growth in a seedling to the point that you have a tree that looks hundreds of years old in less than a week. However, once loggers cut that tree and run it through a sawmill, the Life Sphere can no longer touch it. The lumber then falls under the sway of the Earth Sphere, as it is natural non-living matter. Please, don't ask me **why**. As far as I know, no mage as far back as our records go has ever explained it. Just like why Light Sphere mages can't control fire created by focusing intense light through a magnifying glass. The obvious answer is that one is fire and one is light, but that does nothing to touch on the **why** of it. We good so far?"

Everything seemed straightforward to Jake, and he nodded his assent.

Emilia said, "The only applications of the Life Sphere that come to mind are healing- or growth-related. Does it have any offensive capability?"

"Not as such," Gerald replied, shaking his head. "I suppose one could use it to create a tumor or something, but that would not save you in a situation like the bank where Jake manifested. You can't even use it to stop a heart; doing that requires the Death Sphere. Your question is yet another instance where the Magocracy does not possess an explanation or understanding of why."

All at once, a thought burned its way across Jake's mind, and in that instant, he **knew**. He knew beyond any doubt why the Spheres came with irrational limitations or abilities.

"It's because they're pieces of the whole," he said, barely more than a mumble as his mind raced through the implications of the thought.

Everyone in the room focused on him. Gerald said, "Explain, please."

"The 'Spheres' as you call them were never supposed to exist on their own," Jake answered. He scanned the room and, finding the jaguars lounging in a corner, pointed to them. "Modern mages are like **them**. Mutants. The result of hundreds—if not thousands—of years of sorcerer blood getting diluted through reproduction with plain humans or other mages. That's why the Spheres don't make sense. They're pieces that were never supposed to exist on their own.

Would an elephant's trunk make sense if you'd never seen an elephant—had no idea what the overall animal was—and had only the trunk to examine?"

"Well, damn," Gerald remarked, astonishment saturating his voice. "How has no one ever realized that?"

Bianca laughed. "Because we haven't had a sorcerer in recent memory. I wish Isabel were here to discuss this, too. She has actually seen them." She moved her focus to Jake. "You will set the arcane world on its ear if you ever come out to the general populace. The current Merlin—which is the title used for the elected leader of the Magocracy—is only a Tri-Sphere; imagine what would happen if Jake demonstrated mastery over all twelve Spheres before the Convocation."

Jake frowned. "The Convocation? What's that?"

"The ruling body of the Magocracy, with one Grandmaster for each affinity," Gerald replied. "As it stands now, the Magocracy divides the mages of the world based on their strongest affinity. If a mage has only one full affinity, they are grouped in that Sphere; if a mage has two, he or she makes a choice which of them they join. And so on for strong and weak affinities. Because I only have full affinity to the Life Sphere, the Magocracy classes me as a Life mage, and as I have earned Grandmaster certification, I am now qualified to run for election to the Life seat in the Convocation."

"I guess I should've paid more attention to the structure and function of the Magocracy in school," Jake muttered. "I just never thought I'd **need** that knowledge."

"I'm a bit surprised Martha at the Springfield AEC didn't have you choose your so-called 'primary' Sphere during your evaluation, since she recorded you as an exceptional Tri-Sphere. Once the records of your registration worm their way through the Magocracy, the Time Grandmaster will be beside himself to have you choose that as your primary. Time is the rarest affinity by a significant margin, so they're always excited about potentially adding to their roster."

Jake turned that thought over in his mind for a few moments, then asking, "Does it matter how many mages a given Sphere has?"

"No, not at all," Gerald answered. "Well... it's not **supposed** to. Each grandmaster only gets one vote, but mages are just as human as non-mages. There have been jealousies and attempts to restructure the Convocation to grant more votes to those Spheres with more members at various times in the past, but so far, nothing has ever come of it."

Jake nodded his understanding. He knew—beyond any doubt—that he wanted nothing to do with the Magocracy. He was grateful that they had chosen to pay the taxes on the reward monies, but that was just a publicity stunt.

"The Magocracy paid the taxes on the rewards from the bank crew," Jake said. "Do I need to worry about them coming to me somewhere down the line and trying to say I owe them something for having done that?"

Gerald pursed his lips and directed a look to Bianca.

Bianca lifted her eyebrows and angled her head to the side for a moment as if she shrugged without moving her shoulders and answered, "It is not outside the realm of possibility. Like Ger said, we're all human. I've not heard of anything like that happening, which probably just means that news of it hasn't reached me, but the Magocracy has traditionally been very good about keeping out the kind of scum who would do that. They are very careful in policing their own, especially given what we can do. The Mind mages have it the worst; you would not believe the strictures and regulations they live under."

"I would love to take you to my clinic or the hospital in Hornbeam," Gerald remarked.

"Oh?" Jake asked, frowning. "Why is that?"

"It's the most common way of teaching Life mages how to access and use the Sphere. Even where the both of you are right now, you should be capable of healing cuts that would require minor stitching," Gerald answered. "Like most Life mages, I am also licensed to practice medicine, except that the Magocracy accredits my license which makes it valid anywhere in the world."

Emilia gaped. "Are you serious?"

Gerald simply nodded. "No Life mage who pursues a career in medicine is ever certified and/or licensed through local authorities. There is a department within the Life Sphere administration that acts as a medical board for all medical disciplines and fields. They cover it all... everything from EMTs all the way up to neurosurgery."

"What if a Life mage doesn't pursue a medical career?" Jake asked. "Do they get in trouble if they use their Sphere to help people if they witness something like a car crash or... if someone falls?"

Both Gerald and Emilia shook their heads. When Gerald saw her respond, he gestured for her to answer.

"They covered just such an occurrence in one of my Pre-Med classes at NYU," Emilia explained. "Anyone with a documented affinity to the Life Sphere who does not possess formal medical training comes under the jurisdiction of the Good Samaritan laws. So, if you witness a wreck or someone falling or whatever, you are free to render aid without being held liable for any unintended harm. Honestly, in your case, I don't see how there could be any harm, though. All the documented cases they covered in class had to do with Good Samaritans not having the power to heal some of the more grievous injuries or wounds, resulting in partial heals that had to be corrected later."

Jake frowned. "Partial heals? How could a mage partially heal someone?"

"The most memorable example they gave in class came from a massive car wreck out in Oregon, something like fifteen years ago now. There was a Life mage in the traffic that was stopped because of the wreck but not involved in the wreck itself, and she rushed in to start helping people. The first five or six, she handled just fine, but she pushed herself so much that she ran her mana well dry and passed out before the healing could draw on her life energy to finish the job. The person she was healing ended up having a shin with a slight curve to it because the healing stopped abruptly and prematurely. The first responders found an unconscious mage and a crash survivor in the midst of a panic attack because the bottom half of his leg looked like a parenthesis."

The mental image of that alone was enough to encourage Jake to swear off responding to emergencies, and before he thought, he said, "Well, I suppose that beats a bracket... or curly brace."

Emilia blinked, and both Gerald and Bianca erupted in laughter.

Once everyone regained their composure, Jake asked, "So, why can't you take me to your clinic or the hospital?"

"Because of the griffon threat," Gerald answered without hesitation. "I can't help but feel it's more than my life is worth to take you outside the Grove until Isabel deals with the griffon."

The strange presence—almost a weight—settled on the area, announcing Beauregard's arrival or attention.

* Father, the visit is necessary to the Titan's development. Take him... and Young Mistress. I shall send protection with you and intercede on your behalf with the dragon. *

Gerald and Bianca shared an uncertain look.

Bianca asked, "What do you mean by protection?"

* A raven from the grove shall act as my proxy. In the event that Father, the Titan, or Young Mistress come under threat, I shall respond with all necessary force. *

Bianca and Gerald both paled just enough to notice.

"We didn't realize you could reach that far beyond the grove," Gerald remarked.

* The Mississippi and the Ohio rivers are the limit of my reach east, west, or south, Father. To the north, my reach extends twenty-five miles. *

Bianca sagged in her chair, everything about her betraying the depths to which Beauregard's revelation overwhelmed her. "How... how long have you been so powerful?"

* Years, Mother. It is necessary if I am to fulfill my role. *

"And what role is that?" Gerald asked.

* Ensure the safety and existence of the Titan's sanctuary, Father. As

long as I exist, none shall harm him while he stands upon my land. Go. Educate him in the ways of the Life Sphere. All of you shall be safe. *

Gerald and Bianca still looked a little stunned. After a handful of moments, Gerald shook his head as if to clear it.

"So be it, then. Both of you should make preparations to head into town; we'll leave as soon as you're ready," he said.

Emilia surged to her feet and dashed upstairs. Everyone still in the great room heard her door close, as it faced the balcony that overlooked them.

Jake looked over his clothes and shrugged. "I'm ready to go right now. Should we take the jaguars?"

Gerald turned his gaze toward the lounging felines. "Not just yet, no. A hospital isn't the place to create the kind of stir they will."

A SHORT TIME LATER, Gerald led Emilia and Jake through the main entrance of the hospital in Hornbeam. Like every other building in the main parts of Hornbeam, it was part of the construction to rebuild in the wake of the Independence Day attacks of 2001. The hospital itself served as a satellite facility for a regional medical center farther north, focusing on emergency medicine, diagnostics and imaging, outpatient procedures, and limited in-patient care.

An older lady and gentleman staffed the reception desk, and they both smiled their greetings as Gerald approached.

"I didn't realize you were on the schedule today, Dr. Wainwright," the lady said.

Gerald smiled. "I'm not, at least not really. I'm training these two mages in the Life Sphere, and I thought I'd bring them to the emergency room to get them started."

Over the next few minutes, Jake and Emilia both filled out several forms that Gerald countersigned before the lady at the desk handed them each a clip-on badge that labelled them as trainee mages in the Life Sphere. Then, Gerald showed them how to sign in and set off down the hall, following the signs for emergency.

As soon as they crossed into the emergency section, Gerald went straight to the nurses' station. A young woman looked up from her workstation and smiled.

"Hi, Dr. Wainwright. What brings you to this neighborhood?"

Gerald smiled. "Hello, Sally. I have a couple Life mages I'm training. We just started today, and I thought I'd show them how it works in the real world. Who's working, and do we have anything low-stress I can use for a demonstration?"

"Doctors King and Parker are working the unit today, and we have a broken arm in One, difficulty breathing in Three, and a hemophiliac with a nasty laceration in Five. Both doctors are in Five, and they've already called for blood from the bank twice." Sally glanced around before she rose from her chair just enough to lean closer to Gerald, then whispered, "You might want to stick your head into Five first and offer. We don't have a Life mage in-house today, and you should've seen the trail when the paramedics brought in the bleeder. I'm amazed the patient's still alive."

Gerald nodded once and winked, then turned toward Exam Room Five and waved for Jake and Emilia to follow him. He knocked twice on the closed door with a plate above the doorframe labeled '5' in large type before opening the door.

The scene in the exam room looked rather grim to Jake's eyes. A young woman he had seen around town lay on the hospital bed, and blood flowed from her right shin, soaking the sheets, bed, and anyone getting too close. An older woman Jake presumed to be the patient's mother sat in a chair by the wall.

A man and woman in scrubs on either side of the hospital bed looked up as the door opened, and Jake watched both of them relax as soon as they recognized Gerald.

"Dr. Wainwright... are we glad to see you," the female doctor said. "We have a hemophiliac, age nineteen, with a deep laceration on her shin. The blood is washing out the clotting factors before they have a chance to stop the bleeding."

"This is Emilia Harcourt and Jake Adams," Gerald replied. "They are both Life mages with full affinity who I am training. Emilia is Pre-Med."

Both doctors stepped back as the man said, "Please, take over, and we'll call down to the bank for more units once you've stopped the bleed."

Gerald motioned for Emilia and Jake to both step closer to the patient as he addressed the patient and her presumed mother, "Is it okay if my students observe the healing process?"

The patient was well on her way to unconsciousness, and her head lolled to one side. Her mother, on the other hand, jerked several quick nods. "Yes, please!"

"Okay. As you both have an affinity to the Life Sphere, it is important to note that you are immune to all known pathogens. That is fortunate, because we are unable to heal through latex or nitrile gloves. In order to work, we must have skin-to-skin contact. So, step over here and touch the patient's ankle or shin, please."

Jake couldn't shake his nervous unease at the thought of touching the patient. Sure... the person may have only been a patient to Gerald and Emilia, but Jake saw a pretty, young woman. Memories of every girl or young woman who shied away from him flashed through his mind, and it took all his willpower to step forward and lay his hand across the arch of her foot.

"Now," Gerald continued, "close your eyes and focus on the patient. Draw upon your affinity to the Life Sphere, and you should be able to feel her injuries. I would go into greater discussion, but this is a bit of an exigent situation. Pay careful attention while I repair the laceration."

Jake felt Gerald exercise power, and through his power, he 'saw' the injury repair itself. He also couldn't help but notice the subtle wrong-ness he felt in the patient's blood and bone marrow; he could tell it was **wrong**, but he didn't know enough to understand the nature of it. He needed an example of someone who wasn't a hemophiliac... so he placed his other hand on Gerald's wrist and reached out with his senses to compare the patient to him.

The exact difference became apparent at once. One of the young woman's genes did not match the same gene in Gerald. Jake stopped focusing on Gerald's repair of the laceration as he delved into the imperfect gene. He reached the limit of his understanding in rather short order, but he felt like it might be possible to correct the gene, thereby curing the young woman of hemophilia. He didn't want to forget his sense of the imperfect gene, so he quickly excused himself, moving to the room's sink to wash his hands thoroughly before stepping outside the exam room.

Jake returned to the nurses' station, and Sally grinned when she glanced up and saw Jake standing in front of her.

"Well, you're not green or tossing your cookies, so that's pretty good for a first time," she said. "What brings you back to my domain?"

"May I please have a piece of printer paper and borrow a pen or pencil?" Jake asked.

Sally looked a little askance at his request but handed him pen and paper. Jake turned the paper to landscape orientation and set to sketching the damaged gene without delay in the first fourth. Then, he sketched the same gene he observed in Gerald on the second fourth. As soon as he finished with that, he closed his eyes and delved into his own body, seeking that specific gene; it didn't take him long to find it, and after a few moments of careful study, he opened his eyes and sketched his gene next.

He lifted his eyes to Sally and found her giving him the hairy eyeball, then said, "This will probably sound a little odd, but do you mind taking my hand? I'd like to get a sense of your genes that control the body's clotting factors."

Sally pursed her lips for a moment, then sighed and nodded. She extended her hand as if to shake, and Jake took it in his, closing his eyes once more. It took him no time at all to locate the gene sequence he wanted, and he spent sufficient effort and focus to commit it to memory. Then, he released Sally's hand and drew it in the final fourth of the paper beside the sketch of his.

"Look," Sally said, "you should know you're not the first to follow this line of thought in regard to hemophilia. A number of Life mages have even tried curing it, but none of them have ever succeeded. It's usually the case that they either make it worse or have no effect on it at all. I don't want to burst your bubble, but at the same time, I didn't want you giving anyone false hope."

Jake nodded absently as he looked over his sketches, saying, "I understand. Thank you."

Then, he pivoted on his heel and strode toward Room Five, arriving just as Gerald and Emilia stepped outside.

"What happened to you?" Gerald asked. "I wanted you to experience how Life mages repair an injury like that."

Jake held up the paper where Gerald could see the sketches. "I think I can cure her hemophilia."

Gerald did not look optimistic. "Many have tried without success... but... none of them had your power, either. Let's say you're right, though, and you succeed where everyone else has failed. Can you afford the notoriety that would bring?"

Jake stopped and turned the new consideration over in his mind several times. As certain as he was that he could cure the young woman's hemophilia, he wasn't sure he understood his power enough to be confident in his certainty. The idea that he might be wrong and make her condition worse—or possibly kill her—horrified him. And the idea of even a whisper of notoriety outright terrified him.

"You're right," Jake said at last, "but I'm keeping these notes for future reference."

Gerald smiled. "I wouldn't have it any other way. Now... let's go see someone about a broken arm."

CHAPTER

TWENTY

Wainwright Grove
   Hornbeam, IL
   22 May 2025, 6:47pm

A LIGHT BREEZE ruffled Jake's hair as he sat in one of the patio chairs behind Gerald and Bianca's house. His legs stretched out in front of him, and a lap desk rested across his thighs. Bandit laid on the patio to his left, and Smokey laid to his right. The diagrams, notes, and thoughts on the pages of the notebook held his focus.

The sound of footfalls drew his attention, and he saw Emilia pull a chair around so she could face him... and rub her feet in Smokey's fur. As Emilia settled in the chair, Smokey shifted her position to present her flank, and Emilia smiled as she rubbed her feet along the jaguar's ribs.

"Their fur is so soft and warm," Emilia said.

Jake nodded. "It is that. When they were cubs, I made the... well... it wasn't a mistake, per se. I made the decision to let them sleep in my bed with me. They started out as little bundles of fur who were afraid and not understanding why their mom wasn't around anymore, and it seemed to help calm them if they could snuggle with me."

"Aww, that's so sweet."

"Yeah... you'd think so, right up until you have two adult jaguars trying to climb in bed with you every night. It took me a little bit to explain to them why they didn't exactly fit anymore. But when we have really nasty thunderstorms, I still get a bed full of jaguar. So, what's on your mind?"

Emilia shrugged. "You just seemed distracted ever since the hospital, and I thought I'd ask if you wanted to talk about it. Not everyone is cut out for medical stuff. We had a class where we had to sign up as pre-med volunteers, and I think the class roster shrunk by half, the first time we walked into a hospital and saw open wounds."

"I can see that, but the blood didn't get to me. I don't think it ever has. No... what got to me was understanding **why** the girl had hemophilia. I could literally **see** the difference in her genetic structure, especially when I compared it to Gerald or Sally at the ER desk. I can't shake the feeling that I could cure her hemophilia."

"Then, why didn't you?"

Jake pursed his lips for a moment and sighed. "A couple things, really. Number one, what if I couldn't? What if I tried and made the situation worse somehow? Nobody wants that. And number two, if I actually did cure her hemophilia, what would we do or say? From what Gerald says, not even a handful of Life Grandmasters working together can cure genetic diseases. Oftentimes, they just create worse problems."

"But you're not other Life Grandmasters, are you?" Emilia asked, her eyes focused on Jake. "Sure, you still need to be careful until you develop your endurance for magic, but Jake, there's no telling **what** you'll be able to do. I've seen how Gerald and Bianca share looks when you ask questions or talk about what you feel or experience."

"Do you think I should've tried to heal her hemophilia?"

Emilia grimaced and shrugged. "That's not an easy question.

Before you try tackling anything like a genetic condition, I'd like to see you much further along in your development. Specifically, I'd like you to be able to channel your power without going into hypoglycemic shock. Until you're at that point, I don't think it's wise to do anything beyond practice making light spheres."

"Say... would you mind taking my hand?" Jake asked. "I'd like to compare your genetics to Gerald's."

"Sure, why not?"

Emilia leaned forward and extended her hand toward Jake. He leaned forward and took her hand in his, closing his eyes so he could concentrate on her DNA. It took a second or two, but he soon 'saw' her body's genetic blueprint. He almost gasped at the sight. Emilia had certain sequences on certain strands that Gerald didn't, and when he focused on his own DNA, he found still yet more sequences neither Gerald nor Emilia had.

After a few more moments, he released Emilia's hand and leaned back against his seat, saying, "Huh."

"Huh, what?" Emilia asked.

"You have a couple sequences in your DNA that Gerald doesn't have and vice versa. I have sequences in my DNA that neither you nor Gerald possess. I wonder if those sequences have any connection to mage abilities."

Emilia's expression seemed torn between shock and awe. "You... you think you might understand what gives us our abilities?"

Jake fervently shook his head. "No, I didn't say that at all. I said you have pieces of genetic code that Gerald doesn't, just like he has pieces you don't, and I have pieces neither of you do. I'm nowhere *near* saying I understand why we're mages. Right now, I'm a caveman looking at a burning tree that was struck by lightning. Don't ask me how to make fire on command."

Emilia giggled. "You are many things, Jake Adams, but a caveman isn't one of them."

Jake didn't know a whole lot about girls... that is... women, but he suspected that getting them to laugh was a good first step. It struck

Jake that he had never cared about doing well with any other woman or girl; until Emilia, they had always shied away from him.

"Say," Jake said, his tone hesitant, "do you mind if I ask you a question that might seem a little weird?"

She scrunched her eyebrows as she regarded him but ultimately shrugged. "You can ask me anything you like, but I always reserve the right not to answer."

"I'm not really sure how say this, so I'm just going to spit it out. You're the first woman that isn't my mom who doesn't shy away from me, and I was wondering why."

Emilia beamed. "Oh, that's easy. You're such a powerful mage that your aura is very off-putting—eerie almost—like an old, haunted house. It doesn't surprise me at all that the average person would keep you at a distance, and I doubt they even understand why. Only another mage can sense your aura."

"So, that's why all the girls around town always looked at me weird?"

Emilia shrugged. "Probably, but you are a bit of a hunk. That may have played a part, too."

Jake blinked. Did... did she just say what he thought she said? She thought he was a hunk? That was good, right? "Uhm... the whole 'hunk' thing is good, right?"

A faint flush colored Emilia's cheeks as she looked down and to the side. She worked her lower lip between her teeth, but she nodded. After a few moments, she said, "Yeah. That's a good thing."

Jake nodded his understanding. He redirected his attention to the notes in his lap and found he couldn't muster the motivation to keep working on them. He decided instead to focus on chatting with Emilia.

~

WAINWRIGHT GROVE
Hornbeam, IL

23 May 2025, 8:22am

THE FOLLOWING MORNING, Jake came downstairs after showering at the end of a run with the jaguars and found Gerald and Bianca chatting with a woman in business-casual attire who looked to be about the same age as Fiona. As far as he knew, he'd never seen her before, but he had the impression or sense that she was a mage.

"Ah, here he is now," Gerald said. "Jake, this is Callista McMahon. She is the Magocracy rep for the state of Illinois, and she drove down from Springfield last night to speak with you this morning."

When Callista stood to greet Jake, Gerald and Bianca joined her. Jake did his best to keep from betraying the sudden nervousness he felt, but that was something he'd need to get past. Especially as he developed his power. So, he put on his best smile and approached her, extending his right hand.

"It's nice to meet you," he said. "You didn't have to drive all the way down here, just to meet me."

Callista's eyes seemed to sparkle as a smile tugged at the corners of her mouth. "It's nice to meet you, too, and I disagree, Mr. Adams. But even if I didn't, the Magocracy certainly does. Besides, I don't get enough excuses to get out of the office."

Gerald gestured for everyone to resume their seats as Jake struggled to figure out what came next. One thing was certain, though; he wasn't about to be 'Mr. Adams.'

"Please, call me Jake." In the end, he decided to foist off his dilemma onto her, especially since he was hungry enough that the armchair in which he sat was starting to look tasty. "So, what comes next? I grew up thinking that I'd never be a mage, and I'll be honest that all this has hit me kind of cold."

Callista nodded. "That is perfectly understandable, and we at the Magocracy sympathize. It's simply rare that a mage's manifestation makes headlines, so when one does, the Magocracy prefers to take

191

more of a direct role in ensuring the new mage gets set up for success."

It seemed like there was a lot of politician-speak in there to Jake. Lots of words. Very little substance. It didn't give him much to work with.

"Well, I certainly appreciate the Magocracy paying the income taxes on the reward money," Jake said. "That was both nice and very beneficial."

"You had every opportunity to walk out of that bank and leave everyone else to their respective fates, and yet... you didn't. Yes, the pacifist elements of society would probably prefer that you had found a non-violent resolution to the situation, but the simple fact is that you used your manifestation to help others... if not save their lives outright. The Magocracy believes that all mages should be productive contributors to society, and you provided an excellent example of that. Now... have you given any thoughts as to your long-term goals?"

All kinds of thoughts, but he wasn't sure he should mention them. "Not really. I'm still coming to grips with my change in status, and Gerald just started training me and Emilia in the Life Sphere yesterday."

"Exceptional Tri-Sphere, yes? Full affinities to Time, Life, and Light?" Callista almost purred as she spoke. "I must say that is a... unique... combination. I can't say I've ever heard of it before."

Well, crap. Now, Jake wondered if he should've chosen something else for his affinities. Or at least asked Martha if there were any patterns to the manifestations before he chose. Not knowing how else to respond, he threw a one-shoulder shrug. "Well, at least I'll never have to worry about needing a flashlight."

Callista laughed, and Jake saw the skin at the corners of her eyes wrinkle as she smiled in its wake. "No, you certainly won't. Tell me about your first day of training. Anything stand out?"

"Gerald healed a deep laceration while we watched. That was

interesting. I'm not sure if I want to pursue a career in medicine, but I won't deny the appeal of never needing a first aid kit, either."

"A few Life mages have found it... tricky... to heal themselves," Callista remarked. "At least until they achieve Master certification with the Sphere. There are a lot of moving parts to healing, if you will, and pushing through your own pain response only complicates that."

Jake nodded. That made perfect sense. "Are you a Life mage, too?"

"No, I'm afraid not. I'm a dual-Sphere, strong affinities to both Earth and Shadow."

Jake leaned back in his seat and interlaced his fingers in his lap. On the one side, he felt like meeting the state's Magocracy rep was kind of neat and interesting, but he still didn't see the advantage for her in driving to Hornbeam from Springfield. For that matter, how did she even know he was at the Wainwright Grove? Did she stop by his parents' place first?

"So... please forgive me if I'm being a little obtuse, but I'm still trying to wrap my head around why you drove all the way down here to meet me. I heard what you said, and I even understand the words. But it didn't seem to have very much substance. Can you help me understand?"

Callista held Jake's gaze with her own for several moments. Then, glanced to Gerald and Bianca and then to the jaguars before resuming eye contact with Jake. After a few more moments of silence, she said, "Abigail filed a report about your irregular evaluation, Jake."

Jake felt his blood run cold, and he fought to prevent any reaction from appearing in his expression or mannerisms. He felt the jaguars start to react, but he begged them to keep lounging as if they didn't care or understand what was happening around them.

"Really? What's so irregular about being an exceptional Tri-Sphere?"

Callista smiled. It was slight but wholly genuine. "You are cool... very cool. I'll give you that. If Abigail hadn't demanded to have her veracity assessed by a Mind master, it would be incredibly easy to believe you and Martha over her. It would not be the first time her excitable nature has gotten the better of her. But she's right, isn't she, Jake? Every crystal in the AEC turned white when you touched it. That's unheard of."

Gerald and Bianca looked like they wanted to slink away and leave Callista and Jake to confront each other. There was no doubt at all in Jake's mind that he could overwhelm her if she proved hostile, totally leaving aside how *Beauregard* would react. Overwhelming her would put him deep into hypoglycemic shock, but there was no question he could do it.

Jake sat motionless, not seeming to react as he tried to piece together just how he should react. More than a small part of him wished Isabel was there. He had no doubt that she would know how to handle the situation... but she wasn't there. And she wouldn't be in time.

"So, if a Mind master verified Abigail's honesty, what happens to Martha?" he asked after a few silent moments.

Callista's eyes betrayed her surprise for a lightning-fast finger-snap. "That's your response? I tell you that I have verified proof you falsified your evaluation, and your response is to ask about Martha Culpepper?"

Jake broke eye contact with her and looked around the great room of the Wainwrights' house. Once again, it struck him just how beautiful a home Gerald and Bianca had. He knew Callista would need convincing. After all, she seemed to think he faked his evaluation, regardless of how impossible that was supposed to be.

Fine. So be it. He would convince her, but not inside.

He turned to Bianca and focused on her, tapping into that part of him he used to 'talk' with the jaguars.

*When you follow us, bring several of those emergency glucose tablets, please. *

Bianca's eyes shot wide, and the color drained from her face. It seemed she received his message.

"Callista, let's step outside. There's something I think you want —or maybe just need—to see, but you can't see it in here."

The Magocracy rep frowned as Jake stood, making no movement to follow. "Oh, really? And just why can't I see it here?"

Something about Jake's expression as he looked down at her from where he stood shook Callista to the very core of her soul. Then, he answered and piqued her fear toward terror. "Because I don't want to harm the house if I lose control. I'm still very new to all this."

Callista shot a quick look toward the Wainwrights, but they sat easy and relaxed. As if whatever was about to happen was a normal, everyday occurrence. Faced with no other apparent option, she stood as well, saying, "Fine. Let's go."

JAKE LED Callista and the jaguars outside. He felt Gerald and Bianca trailing them, but they were far enough behind that he suspected they'd grabbed first aid supplies, complete with those emergency sugar tablets. He wasn't looking forward to what came next, but he didn't see any other way around it.

As he stepped around the house, on his way to the burnt circle where the death tree had stood, he ran into Emilia. She took in his expression and demeanor in an instant, then noticed the woman behind him she didn't know.

"Is everything okay, Jake?"

Jake nodded. "Yeah. Just need to show Miss Magocracy Rep something. You might want to stand back with Gerald and Bianca. Could be risky."

"Jake..." her tone laced with caution and stern reproof as she hurried to keep pace with him as he walked "...what are you doing?"

He chuckled, but it was a resigned chuckle. No mirth. No happiness. "You'll see. Stay with Gerald and Bianca, please."

Jake led the small procession to the circle and stood in the very center, where the death tree had loomed over that corner of the yard when he first visited the grove. He turned to face everyone, making and holding eye contact with Callista.

"You say I falsified my evaluation."

Callista nodded. "I do."

"You're wrong. Martha falsified my record."

Callista crossed her arms across her chest. "I don't believe you."

"You will."

At that, Jake closed his eyes and focused on that web of power that flowed throughout every cell and fragment of his body. He decided to start with Fire, since he was more familiar with that than any of his 'official' Spheres. He reconfigured his fireball framework to create only a peach-pit of pure flame and sent a trickle of power into it... just enough to achieve his intent. The surprised gasp he heard told him he succeeded.

Then, he moved to Water. Reconfigured his fireball framework and fed a trickle of power to the new design. Another gasp as a peach-pit-sized sphere of water condensed out of the air's moisture and started following the tiny fireball on its circular path.

When he reached for Earth, he felt a resonance with the woman standing no more than fifteen feet away, and he heard a soft muttering, "Oh my..."

He held three, tiny spheres aloft now—Fire, Water, and Earth— all progressing in a Ferris wheel path in front of him. He didn't put more than the tiniest trickle of power into them, but regardless, he was starting to feel the strain.

His manifestation of Air was nothing more than a small, swirling cyclone. It wasn't too visible on its own, but when it passed in front of something—like Jake—it stood out due to contrast.

Jake's next addition was an orb of pure Light, then an orb of Shadow. And he really felt the strain, then... even though none of the tiny spheres drew more than a trickle of his power. He couldn't think of a way to add Life, Death, Space, or Time... but that was maybe just

196

because it was becoming a tad difficult to think and maintain the Ferris wheel of Spheres.

He opened his eyes and found Callista staring at the tiny spheres slowly circling a point of Jake's choosing. Her arms hung at her sides, and her expression made him think of a terrified animal faced with an apex predator. He decided to prove one last Sphere and touched that part of his mind he used to talk with the jaguars.

So, Callista, did I really falsify my evaluation?

The color drained from her face, and her eyes rolled back in her head as she collapsed to the ground. Jake severed all the tendrils of power, and his Ferris wheel of Spheres vanished as if they never were. He sagged but didn't collapse. He certainly **wanted** to collapse, though. Oh... how he wanted to.

The jaguars were at his sides in a heartbeat, and Gerald, Bianca, and Emilia joined them not even a second later. Bianca handed Jake four glucose tablets, and he tossed him in his mouth. He crunched and swallowed two, letting the other two dissolve.

"Are you okay?" Emilia asked.

Jake nodded. "Yeah. I'd love a nap, but I don't feel too drained."

Gerald looked at him with a speculative expression. "If that's the case, I think we just found how you can practice drawing your power. When you can hold that..."

"Ferris wheel of Spheres?" Jake asked.

"Sure. I guess. When you can hold that for fifteen minutes, increase the size of the individual spheres."

"All right," Jake replied, his voice betraying his exhaustion, "but what do we do with her?"

CHAPTER
TWENTY-ONE

Her first sensation was something warm and wet and rough rubbing the side of her face over and over and over again. Then, she realized she lay on something just soft enough to be very comfortable, and a slight breeze wafted across her face. It was so faint that she wasn't sure she would've noticed without the assistance of the moisture on her cheek.

Whatever rubbed her cheek moved her whole head every time it went from jaw to hairline. It didn't feel like any cloth or compress she'd ever experienced, and for the life of her, she could not think what it could possibly be.

"Bandit!" She recognized Jake's voice, except it carried exasperation. "Stop licking the Magocracy rep."

She forced her eyes open, and it took all her willpower to keep from screaming at the sight of a melanistic jaguar dominating her field of view. He did not look ashamed or chastised at all as he turned away and sauntered over to lie down beside his sister.

Jake came into her field of view, then, walking around the foot of the couch on which she laid. He carried a damp cloth and held it out to her.

"It's a washcloth damp with cool tap water. I was going to lay it across your forehead, but you probably have a better use for it now."

She accepted the cloth and scrubbed from the side of her neck all the way to her hairline. As she did so, Jake sat in the armchair across the coffee table from her.

"Sorry about that," he said. "Bandit apparently felt it necessary to find out if you tasted as good as you smell." He lifted his hands in the universal gesture of surrender. "His words, not mine... I promise."

She shot the big cat in question an appraising look. "Is that so?"

Bandit lifted his head from where it rested on his forepaws and did a very good job of moving his head up and down in an exaggerated human nod.

"And did I?"

Another exaggerated nod... just in time for his sister swat him with her paw and give him a look that reminded Callista very much of the exasperated looks she'd given her brothers down through the years.

"Am I seeing things? Did the white one just swat the black one and give him an exasperated look?"

Jake smiled. "No, you are not seeing things, and yes, Smokey just swatted Bandit. She does that from time to time. Neither one of us are all that certain he'll ever learn. At this point, it's probably more choice on his part than ignorance. How are you feeling?"

"I feel... okay... I guess. A little bewildered. I don't remember laying down on the couch."

"What's the last thing that you do remember?"

Callista closed her eyes to concentrate on her memories. She drove down to Hornbeam to assess the apparent perpetrator of the first falsified evaluation in the entire history of the Magocracy. She had a lovely time verbally sparring with him until she felt he was far enough on the hook, and she told him why she was...

Faster than someone snapping their fingers, it all came back in a rush, and she suddenly felt far too close to this... this... whatever he was. She knew she looked like a cornered prey animal as she frantically searched her surroundings for the doctor or the druid or anyone who could save her, but she didn't see anyone. She was all alone with... him... and his two jaguars.

"Okay, so you do remember." Resignation dominated Jake's voice, but there were hints of other emotions, too. Regret, maybe?

"Of course, I remember." Her voice was almost a snarl, and she instantly regretted that. When one finds oneself facing an apex predator, it was probably a tiny bit unwise to antagonize said predator. "So... what happens now?"

"I'm not sure."

Not sure? How could he be not sure of what happened next? Didn't he hold her life in his hands? What... was he waiting for justification to kill her? To let her live?

"How the—" She stopped mid-thought and closed her eyes, then forced at least a veneer of calm, reasoned discourse into her demeanor. "What makes you say that?"

Jake sighed. "Well, the only reason we're in this mess is because your system wouldn't let Martha record twelve affinities. She didn't think it would go well for me if she could, anyway, and I have to admit—based on your reaction alone—she was probably right. I don't know what comes next; I really don't. Do I pick two more Spheres and you update my record? Do you send Abigail's report along with one of your own up the chain in the Magocracy? You tell me. What's the best way forward here?"

Callista almost hated herself for what she was about to do, but she had to know. Know without any doubts.

"There's another option. You could... kill me."

Jake's expression went from confusion highlighted by hints of being overwhelmed to disgust and revulsion faster than she'd could remember ever seeing someone's expression change. He fiercely shook his head, saying, "No. That will never be an option. I didn't want to kill the robber in the bank. Yes, that was the choice I made, but all of my other options were equally bad or worse. Horribly bad in a couple cases. You're welcome to be terrified of me all you want, but do not think for even an instant that I will ever consider harming or killing you to be viable options."

All at once, the tension and fear faded from her. Whatever else he was, Jake Adams was no threat... not to her, anyway. But that still left them with the question of what to do next. On one side, the choice was obvious: run the report up the chain. It might mean trouble for Martha Culpepper, but then again, it might not. After all, she was correct that the Magocracy's registration system didn't allow for twelve affinities. It didn't allow for even half that.

But what would pushing the report through the Magocracy mean for Jake? That was the question she wasn't sure she wanted to answer. Because she felt almost certain that Martha's conclusion there was right on the money, too. The Magocracy would never give him any peace if they knew. They'd want to analyze him. Blood samples. Tissue samples. Maybe even sperm samples.

She wanted to say the Magocracy's leadership was good and altruistic and sought only the safety and betterment of mages every-where. But a small voice in the back of her mind whispered such dreams were fallacy. The Magocracy did an excellent job of keeping their in-fighting out of the public view, even in this modern informa-tion age where **everything** ended up on the internet. But past a certain level of the bureaucracy, everyone knew the truth. The only desire the grandmasters of the Conclave possessed was more power. And more than one of them wouldn't bat an eye at sacrificing others to get it.

Callista pulled her focus back to Jake. "I'll quietly bury Abigail's report. She gave me a hand-written note of all things, so that part will be easy. I don't think she'd do an end run, because she's had issues before and she's making a name for herself as something of a problem child, but if I feel she will try to push this, I'll reach out to a contact and have it dealt with."

Jake's eyebrows shot up. "Dealt with? Just how will you deal with it? Not kill her, I hope."

"Oh, goodness, no," Callista replied, shaking her head. "A

number of Mind mages owe me favors, so it won't be too difficult to find one who will pull this from her mind and leave her thinking she went on a two-day bender after a hard week at work."

"Why are you doing this? I mean, why not push the report up through the Magocracy? If you did it right, I can't help but think it would almost be a golden ticket for you."

Callista shrugged. "It might, and then again, it might not. The Magocracy is largely stable. Yes, there's political in-fighting and everything you'd expect of an organization as large as it is. But on the whole, it's a stable, known quantity. I don't mind rocking the boat, but a mage with all twelve affinities? That's not rocking the boat; it's capsizing it. There's no telling where the revelation of your existence would end."

Jake sighed and nodded. "That makes a lot of sense. And I suppose you'll want a favor of me at some point in the future?"

"Oh, hell no. I'm going back to my office in Springfield, destroying that note, and doing my damnedest to forget I ever heard your name. I can tell you're a nice guy and all, but you terrify me down to my bones. I know how much more capable a Tri-Sphere is over a dual-Sphere, so I can't even imagine what you'll be able to do once you've mastered your power. I only hope you stay one of the good guys, because it'll be my head—my literal head on the block—if you ever go bad. Maybe even Martha's, too."

Before Jake could say anything else, she pushed herself to stand and made a hasty departure. She knew she was being rude, but she wanted to get as far away from this guy as she could. Just being in the same room with him edged her toward a panic attack.

Jake watched Callista stride down the walk to the parking area. She didn't say goodbye. She didn't look back. As soon as she was in her car, she left, and once she passed beyond the hedge, Jake heard the whine of an electric motor under load.

He heard the door open behind him, and Emilia soon stood at his side. "So, how'd it go?"

"I'm... I'm not sure. She said I terrified her down to her bones." Jake heaved a sigh. "I don't want to terrify anyone."

Emilia laid a hand on his shoulder. "I'm not sure you'll be able to avoid that, Jake. Especially once the world becomes aware of you."

"I thought the plan was to lay low and act like I only had three affinities."

"You stepped up and saved everyone at the bank from being hostages. I'm pretty sure laying low isn't part of who you are. Besides, could you really stand by and watch some mage terrorist harm people if you could stop it?"

No... he couldn't. Jake knew himself well enough to understand that, at least. There was no way he'd just step back and watch something like the bank robbery. Especially if the bad guy had the locals outmatched. That didn't happen often, but when it did, it was usually a huge kerfuffle for all involved. What would it be like to be an agency's escalation call, like Isabel was for the Marshals?

"So, what was that wheel thing you did for the Magocracy rep?" Emilia asked after several moments of silence. "It looked really cool."

Jake felt his cheeks and ears heat with embarrassment. "Oh... uhm... she said I falsified my mage evaluation, so I wanted to prove to her that I hadn't. If I could've figured out how to do something like that with the Life, Death, and Spatial Spheres I would have. She already had proof of my Time affinity."

Emilia frowned. "How'd you prove an affinity to Mind?"

Jake touched the same part of his mind he used to communicate privately with the jaguars and sent her a thought.

Like this.

Emilia jumped back, her eyes wide. "What? What was that?"

"It's how the jaguars communicate with me, and I can communicate the same way when I want a private conversation. One of us— meaning me, Bandit, or Smokey—can also loop both of the others in for a 'group call,' for lack of a better term."

"Holy shit... can anyone with an affinity to Mind do it?"

Jake shrugged. "How am I supposed to know? I don't know anything about what is or is not possible for mages... remember? I'm kinda making this up as I go along."

"Well, you're doing an impressive job of it."

Jake fought the urge to scoff. "Thanks, I guess. Has Gerald said anything about what's next for our training?"

"Nope. I think he was waiting for the situation with the Magocracy rep to play out."

A phone rang deeper in the house, and a few moments later, Gerald and Bianca came outside.

"There's been a massive pile-up on I-57," Gerald said. "The hospital wants everyone with even a weak affinity to Life on-hand to help with the wounded, so let's go."

"Are we going to join the first responders on-site?" Emilia asked.

Gerald's eyes flicked to Jake for a second, and he shook his head. "What do you think, Jake? I can get us into the first-responder teams, if you think you're up for it."

"I want several tubes of glucose tablets on-hand, just in case, but sure. Let's go."

Not more than fifteen minutes later, Jake, Gerald, Bianca, and Emilia exited Jake's SUV at the command area for the emergency response. A couple people set up folding tables and a pavilion while others laid out stacks of triage tags and boxes of nitrile gloves and face masks. As soon as the two folding tables were set, a person laid down a printed overhead image of the pile-up.

"Okay, people," the woman working with the overhead image said. "What's the ETA for Fire & Rescue, and when are the state police going to shut down the northbound lanes?"

"Hey, Kim," Gerald said as he and his people approached the pavilion.

The woman leaning over the printed image looked toward Gerald and immediately broke into a smile. "Oh, thank goodness you're here, Gerald. Bianca, good to see you. Who are the new faces?"

"This is Jake Adams and Emilia Harcourt," Bianca replied. "Gerald is training them in the Life Sphere. Jake and Emilia, this is Kim Thomas; she's with the local Office of Emergency Management."

Kim nodded a greeting to Jake and Emilia as her eyes locked on the two cases of glucose tablets Jake carried. "I appreciate your willingness to help, Jake, but if your blood sugar is that bad, I'm not sure we want you here."

"Oh, you want him here, Kim," Gerald countered. "Trust me on that."

"We have enough problems…" Kim's voice trailed off as she made eye contact with Gerald. She remained silent for a heartbeat or two before speaking again. "You sure, Gerald? And I mean really sure?"

Gerald simply nodded. "I wouldn't have brought him if I wasn't completely certain he'd be an asset. He will pair up with Bianca and Emilia will pair up with me."

"All right. You haven't let me down yet. Grab some triage tags. Then, get out there and work your magic."

Gerald and Bianca led Jake and Emilia over to the supplies and helped them with sticky labels on the backs of their shirts that labeled them 'Life Mage Emergency Response' before doing the same with each other. A corresponding name tag went on the front of their shirts once they'd filled in their first names with a permanent marker. As soon as everyone was ready, Gerald collected a radio for each pair, and they headed into the fray.

CHAPTER
TWENTY-TWO

The air was thick with smoke, screams, blaring vehicle horns, and the occasional shriek of tortured metal as it carried the sounds of the injured or dying. There were no scorch marks or sounds of gunfire, but the first thought in Jake's mind as he surveyed the edge of the pile-up was that he now stood on the fringe of a warzone.

Part of him recoiled from it. Wanted to flee. Run away and only face those aspects of his power that made him smile or that he thought were cool.

And yet...

He couldn't help but think that situations like this were the price... no. Not the price. The counterpoint to exploring his power in fun or cool ways.

He took a deep breath and steeled himself for all that he was about to see and experience. Then turned to Bianca. "You might want to switch with Gerald. You and Emilia can work with the people who are less injured while Gerald and I handle the serious trauma."

Bianca stopped and turned to face him, looking deep into his eyes as if she gauged his soul. "Are you sure about that, Jake? The farther into the pile-up you go, the worse you'll find."

"I can give a chance to those who might not otherwise survive. Isn't that what all this power I have is for? And besides, Gerald's medical degree will let him quickly point out the worst cases to me."

"If that's what you want it to be for, sure... but there are many Life mages who aren't cut out for emergency response. They can't handle the violence or the stress or the knowledge that their choices might mean life or death for others."

Jake nodded. "I understand, but I feel like it's the right thing to do. I'll be up ahead. Please, send Gerald to catch up with me."

Without waiting for Bianca's response, Jake jogged ahead. He didn't care about the cars with people who were only woozy or with minor injuries. The paramedics and other first responders could handle them just fine.

He found his first major case not even fifteen yards ahead. A minivan with a soccer mom rear-ended a construction company truck. Somehow, the soccer mom ended up with a piece of rebar speared through her left shoulder and the seat behind her. She was the sole occupant of the minivan, and her expression betrayed her agony.

Gerald arrived at his side just as he withdrew one of the tubes of glucose tablets and popped four into his mouth. He chewed two right away and allowed the others to dissolve.

Gerald laid a hand on his shoulder. "This is a red tag if not a black, Jake. Are you sure?"

Jake merely nodded as he lifted his hand to the driver's window that somehow had not shattered from the impact and called on the Earth Sphere. He didn't consciously direct the power as he pulled his fingertips diagonally across the glass from the top-right to the lower-left, instead focusing on his desired result; the glass flowed with his fingers, almost like he unzipped the window.

As soon as the glass laid over the side of the car door like a quilt or blanket, Jake reached into the car. The woman must have sensed him somehow, because her eyes fluttered. "Please... tell... tell my children... I love... them."

Jake smiled and winked. "Tell them yourself."

He then wrapped his left hand around the rebar as he placed his right hand against the woman's neck. He rolled his shoulders and closed his eyes, focusing on how he wanted to evolve the base framework he used for magic. Focusing the Earth Sphere on his left hand and the Life Sphere on his right hand seemed so far beyond him, but he refused to fail.

He felt the rebar's structure or matrix start to shift almost at the molecular level or deeper as he pushed pure Life into the woman. His strength waned faster than water passing through a sieve, and he gasped, "Glucose. Whole tube, please."

Gerald's hand cupped around several tablets appeared in front of him, and Jake opened his mouth and tilted his head back. He chewed them all and accepted a second batch, allowing those to dissolve.

Energy surged through him, and he knew he'd pay the price later. But that didn't stop him now.

The rebar protruding from the back of the driver's seat severed itself and thunked to the floorboards as the rest withdrew from the woman, peeling back in individual strands of iron like an unraveled licorice stick. As soon as the iron was free of the woman's shoulder, the Life energy flooded the wound and catalyzed sufficient healing that she was no longer in immediate danger.

Jake pulled back and sagged against the minivan. He glanced at Gerald, seeing his mentor's eyes wide. "How long?"

Gerald shrugged. "Not long. Ninety seconds maybe? Two minutes at the outside."

"Damn. It felt longer."

Gerald chuckled and secured a triage tag to the side mirror of the car where it would flap in the wind and draw attention. He touched the woman's neck for a moment, then nodded and made some notes on a second tag that he tied to her necklace. He turned back to Jake, giving him an appraising look. "Ready for more?"

Jake pushed away from leaning against the minivan and popped another glucose tablet. "Nope, but let's do it anyway."

Gerald smiled and fell into step beside Jake as they resumed searching through the pile-up for people in need of medical attention.

~

Hours later, it was all over but the clean-up. Jake, Emilia, and the Wainwrights sat around a table with Kim Thomas, drinking water while Jake popped the occasional glucose tablet. Up on the highway, wrecking crews worked to remove the cars and clear the road, but the first responders had already removed the people—both survivors and not—from the scene.

Kim sat in a camp chair, periodically sipping from her water bottle like it contained hard liquor. She stared at the ground as she slowly shook her head. "Five. Out of all of that, only five people died, and Fire & Rescue didn't have to use the Jaws once. Not once. Damnedest thing I've ever seen."

She pulled her gaze away from the ground and eyed Jake as he popped another glucose tablet like it was candy, then turned to Gerald. "There was one car with its whole side opened like a banana peel, Gerald. No stress fractures in the metal. No nothing. What the hell went on out there?"

Gerald shrugged, his mind going back to watching the car peel open shortly after Jake laid his hand on it. The boy nearly collapsed after that one, but how was he supposed to tell Kim? "Does it really matter?"

"Yes. No. Hell... I don't know. I'm glad we're walking away from this with only five fatalities, but what am I supposed to say if the Magocracy shows up asking questions? One of the paramedics who responded was a Light mage, and she told me there was some serious power getting thrown around out there. It unsettled her, Gerald... a lot... and she's an army vet. She's seen some wild stuff."

Jake watched Gerald fumble for an answer or explanation, and he contemplated a very unwise idea. On the one hand, it seemed sheer folly to include anyone else in his secret, and yet... and yet... a part of him wanted certain key people to know he was available for situations like this pile-up.

He made eye contact with both Gerald and Bianca and asked, "Do you trust her?"

Gerald and Bianca both frowned for just a moment, then their eyes shot wide. Gerald found his voice first. "Jake, are you sure about that?"

"If I'm going to be one of the local first responders, people like Kim need to know what they're getting when I arrive at a scene."

Now, Bianca joined the discussion. "Jake, that's very admirable, but aren't you worried about your secret getting out?

Through all this, Kim's attention ping-ponged back and forth between Jake and the Wainwrights, and at the mention of a secret, she frowned. "Wait... what secret?"

Gerald sighed. "Kim's good people. Most OEM directors are, but Jake, some of them are just in it for the power of the office. They like that they're 'in the know' about what's happening around the town or county or what have you."

"I understand, Gerald, and I'm not saying I want to announce myself to the world. I'm nowhere close to that. Heck... I burned through two whole cases of glucose tablets in what... one hour? Two? Granted, several people went to the hospital who would've gone to the morgue, but if Beauregard and Isabel are right, I'm not even up to entry-level power for what I am. As I learn more and practice, I'll become both more efficient and more capable with my power. Why shouldn't people like Kim know about me?"

Kim stood up and lifted her hands, gesturing like she wanted to take control of the discussion. "Okay, people... someone needs to tell me just what the hell y'all are talking about."

Jake pulled his focus away from the Wainwrights and made eye contact with Kim. "That 'serious power thrown about' that the Light mage sensed?" He lifted his hand and waved it. "That was me. I brought glucose tablets because I haven't trained my body to draw and/or generate too much power yet, and any time I do something big or complex or both, my blood sugar doesn't just bottom out. It vanishes. That piece of rebar peeled like a banana? It impaled a woman through her left shoulder, and I went through a whole tube of glucose tablets removing the rebar and healing her enough that she could reach a hospital. Well... okay... I think I healed her a tad more than that, but still."

Gerald snorted. "Jake, you pushed so much power into her I'd be amazed if she even needed a transfusion when she arrived at the hospital. She definitely won't have any scarring or even need stitches."

Kim stared at Jake, her jaw moving as though she wanted to speak but said nothing. After a handful of seconds, she found her words. "Gerald, how much did you heal?"

He shook his head and pointed at Jake with his thumb. "I don't know about Bianca and Emilia, but I kept an eye on Jake and told him who would survive to reach a hospital and who wouldn't. I wanted him to be a little more measured in his healing, but he pushed at least a little power into everyone we found and made sure they all could get out of their vehicles."

Kim turned to Jake. "What the hell are you?"

"My mentor says that I'm a sorcerer. Beauregard out at the Wainwright Grove calls me a Titan, the same word the ancient Greeks used for sorcerers. But labels are largely meaningless. What I am is a mage with full affinity to all twelve Spheres."

"Bullshit. I may be a mundane, but even I know that there hasn't been a mage with more than five affinities as far back as the Magocracy records go."

Jake looked to Gerald and Bianca. "Ferris wheel?"

They both nodded.

Emilia stood from her chair and walked to the edge of the pavilion. "I'll be lookout."

Jake stood also and held his hand out to Gerald. "Four tablets, please."

Gerald withdrew the tube from his shirt pocket and popped the cap off, shaking out its last four tablets. He passed them to Jake before he reseated the cap and tossed the now-empty tube into a nearby trashcan.

Jake rolled his shoulders to stretch them as he popped all four glucose tablets into his mouth, crunching two and allowing the other two to dissolve. He felt a rush of energy fill him and pushed power into the Ferris wheel framework he built while sitting in the pavilion of the mobile command center. Unlike his demonstration to Callista—where he added each Sphere individually—a circle of six tiny orbs blinked into existence and began to slowly rotate.

Kim stared at the Ferris wheel as the color drained from her complexion.

Jake produced a slight smile and touched the part of his mind he used to communicate with the jaguars. * I hope you'll forgive me for only demonstrating seven Spheres. I haven't designed a proper show for Life, Death, Spirit, Spatial, and Time yet. *

The pupils of Kim's eyes dilated to the point that the irises were just a thin band of color, less than a heartbeat before she weaved on her feet. Jake feared she about to pass out, but she rallied, her eyes locked on the Ferris wheel of Spheres like she didn't know what to make of it.

Kim still looked a little wild around her eyes as she turned to focus on Jake, and there was a slight tremor in her voice. "Y - you're still developing your power?"

Jake replied with a nod. "I didn't even know I was a mage until the attempted bank robbery in town the other day. I manifested my Time Sphere when the lead robber tried to shoot me with his shotgun."

Kim just shook her head, her entire expression a mask of stunned disbelief. "If you can do all this **now**, you'll be... I can't even imagine it."

"So... would you like my contact information?" Jake offered a weak smile.

Kim snorted a laugh. "Now, what kind of question is that? Of course I want your contact info."

"Okay, but here's the deal. Don't publish my number or what I can do in any county records. I've always heard that there's a tradition where the outgoing president leaves the incoming president a letter. I don't know if that's true, but that's how I want you to handle my info. Share it with whoever takes over for you when you leave the OEM... as long as that letter doesn't go into the county archives or anything. Can we agree to that?"

Silence reigned under the pavilion for a handful of seconds before Kim nodded. "We have a deal."

CHAPTER
TWENTY-THREE

Hornbeam, Illinois
24 May 2025, 8:15am

IT WAS A BRIGHT MORNING. The sky dawned clear and cloudless, and the sun highlighted the horizon. Jake sat behind the wheel of his SUV, his destination less than one hundred feet away. His stomach roiled at the thought of his intent, but he knew he couldn't go another day without having this conversation.

He exited his vehicle and trudged up the walk to the house. The morning paper laid on the stoop, and he collected it as he approached the door. Just as he lifted his hand to knock, the interior door opened, revealing Mike Stannyk in a robe over pajamas, a steaming coffee cup in his hand.

Mike blinked, frowning at the unexpected sight of Jake on his stoop. He looked at the watch on his wrist—thankfully the opposite wrist from the cup—and returned his attention to his guest.

"Sorry for stopping by unannounced, Mike. Was I right that today's your day off?"

"Yeah, Jake. What's going on?"

Jake fought his nerves, taking a deep breath and slowly exhaling. "Do you mind if we talk? There's something I need to tell you."

Mike retreated into his house, waving for Jake to follow. Mike led him to the dinette on one side of the kitchen, gesturing to one of the four chairs. Jake sat and rested his arms on the table.

Silence dominated the room for several moments until Mike broke it. "So, what's the deal? I can tell whatever it is has you all torn up."

"Mike... I... well, I wasn't fully honest with you at the AEC the other day. I'm not a Tri-Sphere."

Mike frowned again. "Okay. Maybe I'm not awake enough yet, but that kinda implies you have more than three affinities. And why would you go around saying you're only a Tri-Sphere if you're not?"

"My evaluator at the AEC... do you remember her? Martha?"

"Yeah. A little older, but she seemed like a nice lady."

"She suggested I pick three Spheres, and she would register me as an exceptional Tri-Sphere." Jake sighed and shook his head. "I'm not doing this right. Mike, I have all twelve Spheres."

Mike's eyes narrowed. "Bullshit. Is this some kind of prank? Did someone put you up to this?"

Jake didn't reply as he pushed back from the table and stepped about three feet away. Mike's house had high ceilings, so he didn't feel like he needed to worry on that front as he recreated the Ferris wheel Sphere by Sphere, like he had for the Magocracy rep. It wasn't long until six small orbs spun in a lazy circle in front of him.

"I only see six, Jake."

* *I don't know how to demonstrate Life, Death, Spirit, Spatial, or Time, Mike.* *

Jake quickly reached his limit for holding his Ferris wheel, and he released it before his blood sugar started collapsing. Still, though, it tired him as if he had just run the 100-meter sprint, and he returned to the table, sagging into his seat.

"I should have told you sooner, Mike. I'm sorry. Time got away from me, and I realized I had screwed up when I told Kim Thomas after the pile-up yesterday."

Mike sat in silence for several more minutes, just staring at the top of the table. Eventually, he brought his attention back to Jake. "You know... it honestly makes perfect sense that you'd keep this fairly close. I have no idea how the world would react to a twelve-Sphere mage. As far as I know, there has never been one."

"From what Isabel told me, the Parthians killed the last one... or at least the last *known* one."

"The Parthians? Seriously? That's..." Mike frowned, his expression almost shouting that he worked on the mental math.

"Around twenty-one hundred years ago."

Mike shook his head. "Damn. Why now?"

Jake blinked. "Huh? What do you mean?"

"I mean... why after all these centuries is there another twelve-Sphere mage? What happened?"

"You expect me to know?"

Mike sighed and shook his head. "Nah... not really. It just boggles the mind, you know? I wish you could've known your parents; I mean your biological parents. I bet they were twelve-Sphere mages, too."

"Isabel said people called them sorcerers."

"Okay. Sorcerers. But think about it. When a mage has a child with a regular human, it's rare for the child to be as strong of a mage as the crafter parent. The only way you could be a sorcerer is if *both* of your parents were sorcerers, too."

That made sense. But if it was true, how many sorcerers were in hiding around the world? Or was it possible that his biological parents were not in fact sorcerers but possessed the proper genes so that Jake 'won' the genetic lottery? And that was assuming the odd gene sequences in his DNA were why he was a sorcerer.

"I'm wondering if maybe my parents *weren't* mages at all."

Mike blinked. "What makes you say that? I thought we established that your parents pretty much *have to be* sorcerers."

Jake shook his head. "The more I think about that, it just doesn't track. If they really were sorcerers, why did they put me up for adoption? I would've thought they would want to guide me through all this, help to keep me from bumbling around like I've been."

"Bumbling around? Seriously?" It looked as though Mike exerted effort to pull his eyebrows down from his hairline. "Jakey, you already have a reputation among the county EMS, even though none of them know who you are. The Light mage paramedic who responded to the pile-up has been talking non-stop about someone capable of peeling open a car like a sardine can. The nearest Earth mage who might—*might*—duplicate what you did is a sixty-something Grandmaster, and she works for a construction company just outside of Chicago."

"Really? That's the closest Earth mage?"

Mike heaved a sigh and rolled his eyes. "Is that the only thing you took away from what I just said? She's not the closest Earth mage, just the closest who might have a chance at duplicating what you did... and even then, it's iffy. The paramedic has seen that Earth Grandmaster at work, and while she might be able to do what you did for two or three cars, you manipulated almost twenty in some small way... all while healing people of injuries ranging from the equivalent of paper cuts all the way up to cases where anyone else would've left a black card and moved on."

Jake nodded. He didn't need Mike to tell him what he'd done. He'd been there doing it, after all. Still, though, it all felt a little unreal to him still. Like he was in a lucid dream where he could control and modify the landscape at will.

He remained silent for long enough that Mike reached across the table and nudged him. "Come on, buddy. Use your words. What's going on in that head of yours?"

Jake replied with a partial grimace and heavy sigh. "I... I don't know, Mike. Having to get used to something like this... well... I'm not sure I'd wish it on anyone, you know? People like me created whole species. How do I process that? Especially when most of them would happily kill me just because I'm like whoever created them?"

"Whoa, whoa, whoa... hold on there. Who said anything about creating whole species?"

"Isabel. She said sorcerers created centaurs, griffons, chimeras... pretty much all the so-called 'mythical' creatures that look like a mishmash of other things. She also said they all would embark on a crusade to see me dead if they knew I was a sorcerer, especially given how new I am. They'd probably still embark on the crusade if I had full mastery of my power, but it would be more like a suicide mission, then. At least, that's what Isabel led me to believe. She said she witnessed a full-fledged sorcerer handle several mages—one of them a Quad-Sphere—without exerting himself; for some reason, Caesar had one traveling with him during the invasion of Gaul."

Mike blinked, then frowned. "Just who is Isabel that she knows all this stuff? And she witnessed Caesar's invasion of Gaul? Jakey, that's farther back there than the Parthians... or at least a contemporary of them."

Well, shit. He was so caught up in his head that he hadn't watched his words. That wasn't good. What would Isabel say when she found out? But there was no turning back now. If he tried messing with Mike's memory, he'd probably just cause him to stroke out or something.

"Isabel isn't everything she seems, Mike. First off, she's my mentor in all of this, but secondly and probably more importantly, she's also a dragon."

"A dragon." Mike's voice was flat. No inflection. No emotion. Might as well have screamed that he didn't believe Jake. "I know you've said some pretty wild stuff, Jakey, but a dragon? Really?"

"She showed me. When she broke the spell that bound her to human form, she almost filled the Wainwright's back yard. Her wingspan is over seventy-five feet when she has them fully extended. Honestly, she's kind of beautiful."

Mike closed his eyes and pinched the bridge of his nose as he shook his head. "I don't know what to make of all this. I really don't. I mean, it's one thing to find out my best friend is some kind of super-mage, but dragons and griffons and centaurs and shit? I dunno, man."

"May I try something?"

Mike jerked his focus back to Jake, a little wild around the eyes. "You're not going to mess with my mind, are you? Try to take the memories away?"

Jake just shook his head. "Nah... I haven't had any formal training with the Mind Sphere yet, just what I've learned on my own. I don't want to hurt you. What I'd like to try is give you my memories of Isabel in her true form."

Mike sat there for several moments, simply staring at him in silence. It was just starting to become awkward when he shrugged. "Sure... why not? What's the worst that could happen?"

Jake felt Mike was entirely too trusting, but he wanted to try this before his friend changed his mind. He called forth the memories he wanted and accessed the part of his mind he used to communicate with the jaguars, pushing those memories to Mike over the same 'channel' he had used during his demonstration earlier.

He wasn't sure he was having much success until Mike's eyes shot wide and his jaw dropped.

"Holy shit, Jake! She's a damn dragon! You stood less than an arm's length away from a freaking dragon!"

The fact that Jake had just passed him a memory with full sensory details seemed lost on Mike for the moment as he erupted out his seat and started stomping around his house, waving his arms and otherwise freaking out that dragons truly did exist.

He'd never seen this behavior from his friend, so Jake just leaned back against his chair and watched. Part of him wondered if he should try to intervene and calm Mike down, while another part of him felt Mike was fully justified in freaking out. Truth be told, he wouldn't have minded freaking out right along with Mike... except that he'd been thrown into the deep end of pool and was past the shock of it all. By now, he was mostly numb.

It didn't take Mike long to realize he was the only one freaking out between the two of them, and he stopped mid-rant, his arms still half-raised where he'd been gesticulating wildly.

"Uhm... I'm being a bit silly, aren't I?"

Jake shrugged. "Dunno. There have been so many shocks to my system over such a short amount of time that I'm admittedly numb to it all... or... well... at least most of it. I'm sure there's something still out there waiting to ambush me that will send me right over the edge into a screaming fit."

Mike took a deep breath and lowered his arms. He released that deep breath as a shuddering sigh. Then, when no better alternatives presented themselves, he trudged back to the table and resumed his seat there.

"So, what do you need from me?"

"I'm not really sure, Mike. My biggest concern was that a relative stranger knew my secret before you did, and I wanted to fix that. Now that you know, I expect you to contact me if I can help you, just like I told Kim Thomas."

Mike grinned. "Yeah... I can see how it would be handy having access to a sorcerer."

"A half-trained... no. Not even that. An eighth-trained sorcerer."

"Awww... come on, Jakey. Don't be that way. Always remember to be patient. Don't try to do in a week what it would take anyone else a month to do. Just keep practicing and pushing yourself. You'll be better before you know it."

Jake nodded as he dropped his eyes from meeting his friend's gaze. "I know, but sometimes, it seems like I'm not making much progress."

Now, Mike cut loose a full-on frown. "How can you say that, man? You've been a sorcerer for... what... nine days? Seriously, bud...

it's only been nine days since you manifested, and you're already peeling rebar like a banana. You need to work on your perspective if you think you're not making progress."

Nine days? Really? That didn't seem right. Wasn't it... Jake's thoughts trailed off as he tallied how many times he'd slept. He didn't take naps, and those times he had passed out didn't count. So, yeah. It seriously was only nine days since he started all this. Maybe Mike was right about his perspective.

Still, though... that didn't change the fact that he needed to keep getting better, needed to keep working on mastering his power. It seemed like everywhere he looked, the world was going downhill faster than people could save it. It wasn't up to him alone to save the world, but maybe, he could take something off Isabel's plate and help her hold back the downward spiral a bit.

The problem was that he didn't know where to go next. He understood the Life Sphere well enough. Oh, sure... he doubted he would qualify as Grandmaster—or even Master—anytime soon, but he knew how to heal people. Wasn't that all there was to the Life Sphere? His thoughts drifted to Bianca, and he realized that, no, healing people probably wasn't all there was to the Life Sphere. But what other subsets of the Life Sphere were there besides nature magic?

Damn... it would be really awesome if this stuff was written down somewhere.

Jake pulled out of his thoughts and found Mike watching him while he ate a bowl of cereal and milk. Jake blinked. He hadn't even processed that Mike left the table.

"Ah, ha... there you are. Did you reach any world-altering conclusions?"

Jake snorted. "Sorry about that. Do you know if there are any books on the different Spheres and their subsets?"

"Oh, I'm sure there are." Mike shrugged. "But good luck getting the Magocracy to grant you access to them, especially if you want to read up on Spheres you have no recorded affinity with. Have they started pestering you to choose your 'primary Sphere' yet?"

Jake winced. "I'm honestly not sure they will. I... uhm... kinda terrified the state's Magocracy rep almost to the point of a nervous breakdown. She did pass out for something like an hour or so when I showed her the Ferris wheel of Spheres."

Mike froze with a spoonful of cereal half-way to his mouth. "You did what? When did that happen? Why didn't you tell me?"

"Uhm... I just did. I'm pretty sure it happened the same day as the pile-up. She drove down from Springfield because she believed she had evidence of someone filing a falsified evaluation report. The way she talked, I guess she thought I coerced Martha to record that I was a Tri-Sphere when I wasn't. And while that is what happened, it's also not what happened. Or at least, it didn't happen the way she thought it did. She didn't believe me when I told her I had all twelve Spheres, and I stumbled into creating the demonstration I gave you to prove it to her. I really need to figure out how to demonstrate the other Spheres, just to be sure people believe me if I ever have to do that again."

"Jake... buddy... trust me on this. If you ever have to prove you're a sorcerer again, the Ferris wheel of Spheres is just fine. The four elements, Light, Shadow, and Mind. That's seven Spheres right there, and that's sufficiently unprecedented that it's not such a big leap to believe you have the other five."

Jake frowned. "You sure?"

"Oh, yeah... I'm sure. Trust me. What you have right now is enough for ninety-nine percent of the people you'll need to convince. The only hardliners you might encounter will be from the Magocracy, and I honestly agree with the idea that you don't want to attract their attention anyway."

"Okay. Thanks, Mike. I probably ought to head out and let you get on with your day."

Mike stood with him and walked him to the door. "Don't worry about it, buddy. Stop by any time."

One heartfelt man-hug later, Jake left Mike to salvage what was left of his morning, while his thoughts focused on returning to the Wainwright Grove. He needed to learn what else there was to the Life Sphere.

CHAPTER
TWENTY-FOUR

His conversation with Mike swirled through Jake's mind as he drove back to the Wainwright Grove. He'd always known he was adopted, but by the time he was old enough to understand that, he no longer cared who his birth parents were. The parents he'd grown up with were the only parents he'd ever needed.

But the thought that his birth parents might be out there somewhere...

If that was true and if they were sorcerers like him, why did they give him away? Why did they leave him to figure all this out on his own?

The more he thought about it, he admitted to himself that his parents—if they were sorcerers—might not have known that he would grow up to be one, too. But then... if that was true... did they give him up because they didn't want a 'normal' child, or did they give him up because a 'normal' child wouldn't have survived with them?

Too many questions and not enough answers.

Jake was within sight of the roundabout that served as the end of the paved road going out toward the Wainwright Grove when he realized that he wouldn't be able to concentrate on his studies as long as this hung over his head. He needed answers... at least some kind of answers... before he could put all this behind him.

He pulled his SUV off the road and grabbed his mobile. His parents' home phone was the top of the list in his favorite contacts, and he tapped it before returning the phone to its cradle. The SUV's hands-free system took over the call, and he soon heard ringing over the speakers.

There was a small click, followed by his mother saying, "Hello?"

"Hi, Mom. How are you and Dad?"

"Oh, we're fine, Jake. How are you?"

His gut twisted at the thought he might hurt his parents with his questions in some way, but he couldn't shake the feeling that he needed to know. "I'm okay, Mom. I was calling to ask if you and Dad had any plans this afternoon."

"No, dear. We're just puttering around the house today. Why?"

"I thought I'd bring the jaguars by and say hello."

There was a slight pause. "Jake... is everything okay?"

"Everything's okay, Mom. I'd like to talk to you and Dad about a couple things, and it's been a few days since Smokey and Bandit have visited."

"You're always welcome here, Jake. You know that."

"Thanks, Mom. I know. I'll load the jaguars into the SUV and head over. Okay?"

"Sure, Jake. See you soon."

Jake ended the call and pulled back onto the road. In no time at all, he passed through the hedge and stopped in the Wainwrights' parking area. He pressed the button to raise the powered lift gate and exited to locate his furry friends.

IT DIDN'T TAKE him long to find them lounging in the shade of an oak tree. They were stretched out on a quilt with Emilia between them, lazily swirling her fingers through their fur. He couldn't help but notice she wore a string bikini top and short denim shorts, so short and tight, in fact, they almost looked painted on. He made it all the way to the edge of the blanket before Emilia looked up.

"Hi, Jake. We wondered what happened to you this morning."

"I went to talk to my friend Mike. It bothered me that I told Kim Thomas about what I really am but hadn't told him."

Emilia frowned and sat up. "Are you sure you can trust him?"

"I'd trust him with my life. We've been friends for years. I was going to go over to my parents' for a little bit and wanted to ask the jaguars if they wanted to go as well."

Bandit gave a lazy flip of his tail, but Smokey pushed to her feet and padded over to stand by Jake. After a couple moments, Bandit gave a slight chuff and pushed himself to stand as well. He mirrored Smokey's position on the other side of Jake.

Emilia leaned back with her hands and forearms flat on the quilt-covered ground as far back as her elbows. She looked up at Jake showing hints of a playful expression. "Do you think you'll ever want me to meet your parents?"

Jake's mind locked. "Uhm... isn't that part of dating? I've always heard that's one of the things that happens when dating starts getting serious."

Emilia didn't change her posture at all, but a soft, pleasant smile curled her lips. "I've heard that, too."

Jake didn't know what to do or say. Was she really flirting with him? If she was, was she serious? Or just playing around?

"Uhm... so... I'm not sure what to say right now."

Emilia kept her smile as she shrugged, which made it a challenge for Jake to maintain eye contact with her. "Just be honest, Jake. There's a reason people say it's the best policy."

"I... well... I like the idea of you meeting Mom and Dad. But... well... I've never dated, really, and I'm concerned I'd hurt your feelings through ignorance."

Emilia beamed up at him. She stood and moved to about half her arms' length from him. "I have news for you, Jake. Each person in a relationship will accidentally hurt the other at times. There's no way to avoid it. The important part is to be sure it's never intentional or malicious." She paused for a moment, her eyes locked on his. "We can work through anything else."

It wasn't lost on Jake that she'd just said 'we.' He held his eye contact with her in silence for a few more moments, then spoke. "I'm going to ask Mom and Dad about how they came to adopt me. My mind is locked on whether my biological parents were sorcerers, and I feel like I won't be able to concentrate on learning the Spheres until I see what I can learn about them. Would you like to come with me?"

Another smile brightened her entire demeanor. "I'd love to, Jake. Let me pull on a t-shirt and more appropriate shorts. See you at the parking lot?"

"Sounds good. That'll give me time to get the kids settled."

Emilia stepped off the quilt, then turned around and bent over to take hold of it. Jake couldn't keep from looking, and he certainly enjoyed the view. Emilia made no mention or reaction as she straightened and began folding the quilt as she headed toward the house. Jake and the jaguars followed a short distance behind her, and something Mike had said a few times came to the forefront of his mind: I hate to see her go, but I love to watch her leave.

They parted ways at the patio, Emilia going inside and Jake leading the jaguars around the side of the house. Jake thought about the sudden change in his relationship with Emilia, but Smokey interrupted.

* I like her, Jake. I think she would be good for you. *

* Do you have any idea what brought about the sudden interest? *

Smokey chuffed, and the mental accent suggested it was her version of snorting a laugh this time. * Oh, Jake... her interest is anything but sudden. We spent most of the morning discussing her interest in you. *

Jake stopped cold and stared at Smokey. It was a heartbeat or two before the jaguars realized he stopped, then looked back to him. * Really? She chats with you? How? *

The same way we communicate. Once she learned you use your Mind Sphere to speak with us, she tried it.

I agree with my littermate, Jake. She would be very good for you. There was no trace of the customary juvenile playfulness that normally accented Bandit's thoughts, which only strengthened Jake's suspicion that the playfulness was just an act.

What about the fact that I'm a sorcerer? Won't that complicate things?

Smokey shook her head as she chuffed again, and this time, Jake felt it was more out of exasperation. *Humans overcomplicate matters far too much. What you are will only be an issue if you make it so.*

Jake nodded as he resumed walking to the SUV. Was Smokey right? Was he overcomplicating things? Probably. Maybe he should talk it over with Emilia.

It wasn't long at all until Emilia joined Jake and the jaguars in the SUV, and Jake backed out of his parking spot and left the Grove. They rode in silence for a handful of minutes until Jake spoke.

"So... may I ask you a question?"

Emilia glanced his way and smiled. "Sure."

"Why the sudden change? I mean... it has seemed like we were just fellow students since we met, but now..."

Emilia's smile intensified. "Jake, I promise you it wasn't sudden for me. I've been dropping hints like a klutz drops everything trying to get your attention. I finally discussed the situation with Smokey and Bandit, and Smokey suggested I take the first step myself. She's of the opinion that there haven't been too many women in your life."

Jake shook his head. "I'm pretty sure I'm the only mage in town, and I always got the vibe from girls in school and later women that they didn't like me or were uncomfortable around me. I think we talked about that... hrmmm... I think it was the evening before the Magocracy rep arrived."

"Yeah. I remember it now." She snickered, then blushed. "Honestly, a part of why I like you is that overwhelming feeling of power you radiate. Yeah... a normal girl would be totally weirded out by it, but for a mage who knows what it is... well... for me at least, it's comforting. I know it's the twenty-first century and that women can be independent and don't need a man to be complete and all that stuff. But at the same time, I've always been attracted to guys I thought could step in and protect me if I was out of my depth, and you, Jake Adams, could walk all over damn near anything on the planet... especially once your master your power. That's very comforting to someone like me."

"Someone like you?"

Emilia nodded. "Dad died while I was still a baby. I have a couple pictures of him holding me, but that's it. I never had the same experience growing up that my friends did. Dad was never there to take care of me. Mom did a great job; I'm not saying she didn't. It's just I've always felt I had this space in my life that Dad should've filled, and I've kinda been looking for the right guy who could partially fill that while still being my partner... you know?"

"I understand... or... at least, I think I understand. I doubt I could ever truly understand without living with it. I never gave my birth parents a second thought until the conversation today with Mike, about how they must be sorcerers too. If they are, I'd like to find them and ask why they didn't keep me and raise me and help me through all this."

Emilia gave a heavy exhale and shook her head. "I can't even imagine what it must be like getting thrown into the supernatural world like you have been without anyone to guide you. Mom was always talking with me and trying to help me get ready for when I manifested, since she was certain for some reason that I would... even though Dad wasn't a mage. I don't know if it's been mentioned yet, but when only one parent is a mage, it's rare for any of the children to be even a single Sphere. And here I am a Tri-Sphere. Are either of your adoptive parents mages?"

Jake shook his head as he hit the turn signal to turn onto the street that would take him to his parents' home. "Not that I know of. They never said anything about it or did anything about it while I was growing up. I... I don't know how they'll take that I lied to them about my affinities. I don't think I've ever lied to them before."

Emilia reached over and touched his arm. Jake thought it was supposed to be a comforting gesture, but it set off a fire in his nerves unlike anything he'd ever experienced. And it wasn't necessarily a **bad** fire, either.

"Jake, I'm sure they will understand once you explain what you are. They're your parents. They love you. They want you to be safe more than anything."

"I guess so. I didn't like doing that, and I think I'll feel better after coming clean about it." He fell into silence for a few moments. "So... you decided to make the first move. I feel like I should tell you that I have a dinner appointment this evening with Fiona at Marci's. I'm not trying to play you both against each other, but it's just that I've had it scheduled for a couple days."

"I appreciate that, Jake. Not many guys would've been upfront about something like that."

"So... what do you want out of this? Or maybe the better question is what are your expectations?"

Emilia smiled. "What I want is to go on a date or dates with you. See where it goes. What I expect is that you'll have a bit of a learning curve, since I'll be your first multiple-dates woman, but I like dating men, and I want to experience dating you."

"Hey... what makes you think you'll be the first woman I go on multiple dates with? After all, Fiona has a head start on you, given tonight."

Emilia began her reply with a confident, suggestive smirk. "Oh, I'm certain I have what it takes to hold your attention, Jake Adams."

Jake grinned. "Okay. I can work with that. Will you help me learn what dates are? I want you to have fun and enjoy the time."

"Sure." Emilia's smile broke into a grin. "We can talk about it. If we were back home in New York, we'd start by hanging out at an eatery or something. Maybe a coffee shop. Or we'd go see a show or a concert. There's always events and things going on in the city somewhere. Here... we'll have to figure it out."

Jake grinned. "I wish I was further along with Spatial. I could take you back home to New York for a visit."

"Oh, that would be so nice, Jake. So, so nice. It's great here, and Bianca and Gerald have been so welcoming... but at the same time, it's not home, you know?"

"Well, no... not really. This town *is* my home. It's the only place I've ever known. Mom and Dad moved here right after they adopted me and never took any trips while I was growing up. I don't know why. No summer camp or anything like that, either. I never thought we were hard-up for money, but maybe we were. A kid isn't always aware of that, I guess."

Emilia reached over and patted his arm again. "It'll be okay, Jake. You have all the time in the world, from what Isabel was saying. You can see whatever you want to see."

A SHORT TIME LATER, Jake turned into the driveway at his parents' house. Even though it hadn't been very long, he still smiled at seeing nothing had changed. He shifted into Park and set the e-brake to keep the weight of the SUV off the transmission, then pushed the button that activated the powered lift gate. The jaguars were outside and waiting for him beside the driver's door by the time he was unbuckled.

Jake led them to the fence's gate and chuckled as he unlatched it. "Mom and Dad can take the fence down for the front yard now. If Bandit and Smokey will be at the Grove with me, they won't be here to terrorize the mail carrier or random passers-by."

"Maybe they like it, too."

"Maybe. I just remember how I worked all summer one year to pay for this when the kids were close to their full size. Even as cubs, their claws and teeth were plenty sharp, and they were insatiably curious. Still are, but at least they've learned enough to have an appreciation for things they shouldn't put their noses or paws to. It took me a little bit to teach them the poison symbol. But I'm pretty sure they can read English now and possibly even understand why they should not drink drain cleaner."

The front door of the house opened before they were halfway across the yard, and Jake's parents came out to meet them. Jake beamed a smile, this being the first time he'd seen them in a few days... the longest he'd ever been away from them. As soon as the tight, heartfelt hugs were finished, they turned to Emilia, and Jake's mom led the charge.

"And just who is the pretty young lady, Jake? You've never brought anyone home before."

"Mom, Dad, this is Emilia Harcourt. She's also studying with Gerald and Bianca. Emilia, these are my parents, Frank and Sarah Adams."

Emilia smiled, it showing in her eyes, as she stepped forward and shook hands with Jake's parents. "It's so nice to meet you both. Please forgive Jake for springing me on you. I sort of invited myself along."

Jake's mom gave her a curious expression—one eyebrow quirked upward—with a pinch of playfulness in her voice. "Oh, you did? You simply must tell me all about that."

"Oh, I'm not sure there's much to tell, really." A blush colored Emilia's cheeks. "I'd been trying to get Jake's attention for a while, and Smokey suggested that I should probably make the first move. She told me she'd never known Jake to show any interest in relationships."

Jake's parents both chuckled as his mom replied, "Well, thank goodness for Smokey. I've always liked her."

Bandit leaned into their circle and nudged her hand with his nose.

"Oh, I like you, too, Bandit... but you're far more of a force of nature than your sister."

Bandit replied with an eager nod before backing away and darting off toward the backyard.

"Well, come on inside, both of you." Jake's dad gestured toward the door as he spoke, partially turning that way himself. "Jake said something was on his mind, and whatever it is, I'm sure it's best not to discuss it on the porch."

Jake approached the front door of his childhood home and held it open for Emilia and his mom. His dad clapped him on the shoulder and nodded toward the open doorway, and Jake took the hint. Soon enough, they sat in the living room of the house, his parents in their respective recliners and Emilia with him on the sofa. She didn't lean against him by any means, but she certainly was closer to him than an uninterested person would've been.

Silence reigned for several moments after everyone found their seats, and Jake's dad ended it. "So, son... your mother said there was something you wanted to discuss. Might as well get it out there, and we'll help you however we can."

Jake took a deep breath as he nodded, releasing it as a heavy exhale that wasn't quite a sigh. "Mom, Dad... well... I'm sorry about this. I came to admit that I lied to you about my evaluation. I'm not an exceptional Tri-Sphere."

A silence seemed to settle on the room as both of Jake's parents regarded him with no expressions whatsoever. Then, just as the silence was starting to become oppressive, they both erupted in smiles, as Jake's mom spoke.

"Of course you did, honey. You can't just go around telling everyone that you're a sorcerer."

CHAPTER
TWENTY-FIVE

Claws of ice speared Jake's heart. It felt like half of it wanted to beat a thousand times a second, while the other half couldn't manage more than a beat a minute. His lungs froze. His breath died somewhere in his chest. His brain locked up like an ancient computer with bad code.

"How... what..."

He shot a glance at Emilia, and she appeared just as gobsmacked as he felt.

His dad patted the air in front of him in what many would've called a calming gesture. But Jake didn't feel especially calm afterwards. "Yes, son, we know. When you came home and told us you went to the AEC, it was too much of a shock, or we would probably have told you then. We weren't sure whether you'd manifest or not, and we hoped you would tell us first. We... that is, your mother and I... discussed how we wanted to handle your manifestation many times."

Jake still couldn't find his voice. His mind was such a seething swirl of thoughts that it was difficult to focus.

Emilia found her voice just fine. "Wait... what do you mean that you didn't know whether he'd manifest or not?"

Jake's parents looked to him, as if asking the silent question of how much he wanted her to know.

He just gestured at Emilia and nodded.

Jake's mother took over. "We always wondered what we would say if you ever asked us how you came to be with us. We had the adoption talk early on and thought that would force the issue, so to speak, except you never brought it up. You seemed to accept that we adopted you without ever digging into who your 'real' parents were."

That jerked Jake out of his swirling thoughts in the span of a finger-snap. "I know who my real parents are. They raised me."

Both of his parents looked a bit misty-eyed at that, and his mother continued. "Yes... well... the truth is that you came to us under very odd circumstances. We wanted children from the time we married, but we could never have our own. We tried all the medical options, but they only led to miscarriages and heartache. Pastor Ralph—back in Dallas—knew of our desire and situation, and one night, he called us. He told us to come over to the church and hurry. We went over there, of course, and found him in the sanctuary with a couple police officers and Francine from Social Services. They stood around a woven basket that... that held you. You were a newborn... or close enough. You certainly weren't a month old yet. Pastor Ralph explained that he came to the church that night to prepare for a service the next day, as he usually did, and found you at the base of the altar. He convinced Francine to send you home with us as foster parents, while the authorities looked for your birth parents. And when no trace of your birth parents was ever found, we adopted you."

Jake frowned. "I don't understand. How was that odd circumstances? All kinds of stories exist of babies being left at churches."

"Son, Pastor Ralph found you inside a locked church. There were no signs of tampering or forced entry, and the security cameras—sad that a church needs them—didn't show anyone entering the building all day before Pastor Ralph entered that night."

Okay... yeah... that was more than a little odd.

"So... where did I come from?"

"We don't know," his mother replied, "but you were not alone in the basket. Oh, sure... as long as the police and Social Services were there, it was just you wrapped in a blanket—your favorite blanket in fact, the one you keep on the nightstand by your bed—but as soon as we started the process to adopt you, Pastor Ralph brought us some items. He said they had been in the basket with you, and he didn't want the police or Social Services taking them and losing them."

Jake blinked, then gaped at his parents. "Seriously? You're telling me a pastor of all people tampered with evidence?"

His dad chuckled. "Oh, yes. Here... give me a minute, and I think you'll see why."

Jake watched his dad stand and cross the room to a large landscape painting that covered a section of wall almost in its entirety. They'd always told him it was a work by a distant ancestor. Jake didn't know whether it was or it wasn't, and being adopted, the ancestor would have borne no connection to him. All this and more went through his mind as he watched his dad slide his hand along the left side of the frame until he reached a point somewhere between a third and halfway from the top to the bottom. He flexed a finger, and a very audible click echoed through the room.

Jake gaped once more as the painting swung out on silent hinges, revealing a safe whose door looked three feet square. It had both a keypad and a fingerprint reader. His dad pressed a thumb to the reader as he keyed in an impressive series of numbers—at least sixteen—before unlocking the safe and swinging the door wide. From the safe, he withdrew four items: a leather pouch about the size of Jake's fist, a folded piece of paper, a thick sheaf of papers that looked different from the first, and a stone about the size of Jake's fists clasped together. Someone had etched or engraved all manner of runes and glyphs and symbols into the stone.

The items in hand, his dad turned and laid them out on the shin-high coffee table in the center of the room before returning to his seat. Jake started to lean toward the items, but his dad stopped him with a gesture.

"Son, you need to be careful with that sheaf of papers. It's not paper. It's papyrus. Before you really learned to walk, we asked a professor from the University of Chicago to visit us, and she was astounded that the papyrus was so well preserved... and... not degrading like she thought it should. Of course, we never told her that it was only so many months old from our perspective. The last time we had it out of the safe, it still felt sturdy and strong. Just please be careful when you handle it. Okay?"

Jake nodded and leaned forward, lifting the top sheet to examine it. The writing seemed to be in Latin! He jerked his head up to look at his parents. "Are these why you had me take Latin in school?"

His mother simply nodded. "The folded piece is Pastor Ralph's translation of the top page. You'll probably want to translate all of it yourself, but in the interests of speed, you might want to start with his piece."

Jake returned the sheet of papyrus to the stack with care before he lifted the folded paper from the coffee table. He unfolded the paper and began to skim it. He wasn't through more than a handful of words, though, when it felt like the world dropped out from under him.

"This... this... it can't be right. This just can't be right."

Emilia leaned forward and touched his arm. "What is it, Jake?"

Jake cleared his throat and lifted the translation. "'My son, I do not have the words for how it tears at my heart that you will never know your mother and me. If we are successful, you will be safe, happy, and well cared for. That is all any parent could want for their child. Please forgive us for sending you away, especially so very far, but the world has turned against us at last. We would rather risk the very fabric of reality than leave you to be slaughtered by some ravening horde of filth-covered farmers or worse. Before we discuss matters almost as grave, know that we love you with all that we are, your mother and I, and were it possible, we would have kept you or traveled with you.'"

"'Traveled with you?' What does that mean?" Urgency saturated Emilia's tone.

Jake leaned forward, returning the translation to the tabletop, and grabbed the leather pouch. As he moved it, something inside clinked. Jake carefully untied the strings and reached inside. He felt coins. He pulled one into the light. Emilia gasped when he held up a golden disc to glint in the light.

"Unless I'm very, very wrong... this is a Roman *aureus*."

His dad shook his head. "You're not wrong, son. We had one authenticated. The pouch holds fifty Roman *aurei* in near-mint condition. Well... forty-nine plus the one in your hand. They are almost pure gold and worth many, many times over the value of the gold for their historical significance alone."

The color drained from Emilia's face as she glanced back and forth from Jake to his parents, her head and eyes jerking faster than hummingbirds flit from point to point. "I'm feeling a little over-whelmed here, people. Can someone tell me what all this means? Please?"

"I'll need to drag out my Latin textbooks and dictionary to work through the rest of what I'm sure is a letter from my birth parents, but all this points pretty solidly to one conclusion... at least to me."

Emilia turned to Jake, looking rather wild around the eyes. "And that is?"

"*Civis Romanus*. I am a Roman citizen... or at least a contempo-rary." Jake frowned and turned his focus back to his parents. "But you still haven't explained why you thought I might not manifest. There's nothing in that translation that says anything about a sorcerer."

Now, his parents looked a little embarrassed. His mother was the one to speak. "You weren't the only one learning Latin, Jake.

Remember how we had you teach us the lessons as we helped you with your homework?"

And just like that, understanding clicked, hitting him like a two-hoof kick from an enraged donkey. "You translated the rest of the letter, didn't you? Where is it?"

Now, his parents looked really embarrassed.

"Son, we... well... I tossed it in the fireplace in a fit of rage. Your mother saved the papyrus from me, but by the time I calmed down, our translation was nothing but ashes." Jake watched his dad clench a fist and his jaw. "Those selfish fools risked **everything** to send you forward through time. The way they described it, it could have ended with total success—being you arrived healthy and hale and with your power intact—to utter failure—being they ripped the very fabric of reality apart and caused the end of everything... not just Earth, son, **everything**—or anything in between. You could've arrived healthy and hale but a normal human baby, or you could've been physically deformed or mentally damaged. After understanding just a fraction of the risk they took... well... many times, I have knelt by your bed as you slept and thanked God you arrived safe and whole. And then... you manifested."

Jake sat back, teetering between aghast and disbelieving. The idea that his biological parents would risk all of creation to send him forward through time seemed not only incredibly reckless but also selfish and inconsiderate. His next thought stamped down the swirling emotions; did they truly understand enough about sorcery and the nature of reality to accurately predict the risks? He didn't know enough yet to gauge the truth of the statement or lack thereof.

But he couldn't deny that—someday—knowing enough about it to decide for himself would be cool and awesome and incredible.

And in that moment, Jake's perspective and awareness of what he was finally clicked into place. He would have to tiptoe through the world, because what would be a hammer from any other mage—even a true exceptional Tri-Sphere—could easily be a nuclear blast from him.

People like him created **species**. And from what Isabel said, they did it as little more than curiosity experiments and then left them on their own to fend for themselves. Regardless of the morality or compassion displayed in that, the fact remained that—again, someday—Jake could easily have the knowledge and power necessary to create species of his own.

That scared him. More than a little bit, if he was being honest with himself. Just what would his limits be once he fully mastered his power?

"Oh." His dad's monosyllabic vocalization drew Jake out of his spiraling thoughts. "That stone. If your mother and I translated the letter correctly, it is everything from a tutor to a grimoire... whatever a grimoire is. They described it as their best attempt to give you all the knowledge and reference you'll ever need, on the off chance you actually manifested as a sorcerer. They said your blood would both unlock it and activate it."

Oh... oh, my. If all that was true, did Jake even need Isabel or the Wainwrights anymore? The more he thought about it, Jake felt that —yes—he did need Isabel. If for no other reason than to have someone to talk to, someone who could understand being the only one of his kind. Okay... so, yes, Isabel wasn't truly the only one of her kind, but she was the only one still active from what she said or implied. It kind of gave them something in common.

And there again, he still needed the Wainwrights, too. They could serve as a sounding board for whatever knowledge of the Life Sphere or nature magic the stone imparted. A kind of 'is this true' or 'does this make sense' check to keep him from going off and doing something exceptionally stupid.

Jake didn't feel like he was the type to do that, but at the same time, Life happened.

His mind finally started to settle, and he made eye contact with his parents in turn. "Thank you both for this. I can't deny that I'm so excited to see what the stone holds and to translate the letter myself, but I also want to be very clear that—regardless of what I find or learn—you are my parents. You are who I think of when I think of home. Nothing will ever change that."

His mother clasped her hands together over her heart as she rapidly blinked her eyes. "Oh, Jake, honey. We know. We never thought for a moment that these people would supplant us."

"I'm glad." Jake smiled softly. "Well... I feel bad about this, but I'd like to take the stone and see what it tells me."

His dad grinned. "Of course, son. You wouldn't be you if you didn't. Just don't forget to stop by and visit from time to time... okay?"

"There's no danger of that at all."

He saw his mom's eyes flit to his right for a moment before she smiled, too. "And we wouldn't mind seeing Emilia more, either."

Emilia laughed right along with Jake as he nodded and said, "I think... maybe... we might be able to arrange that."

They stood, and Jake gathered up the items that were his inheritance, letting Emilia carry the coin purse and Pastor Ralph's translation of the first papyrus sheet. His parents saw them to the door, and he whistled for Bandit as they left the house. Smokey stayed right at his side as they walked to the SUV, and by the time the lift gate at the back was up, Bandit was there to hop in beside his sister.

Jake claimed the coin purse from Emilia, handing her the papyrus, and placed it and the stone in one of the second-row captain's chairs. Emilia placed the folded paper on top of the papyrus in the passenger-side captain's chair before she climbed into the front passenger seat.

It was a good five minutes of riding in silence before Jake turned to her as they sat at a traffic light. "So, what do you think?"

Emilia sighed. "Honestly, Jake... I'm not sure what to think. It's almost too fantastical to believe. I've never heard of **anyone** able to send items—let alone people—forward or backward through time. It's just insane... and yet... you have a leather coin pouch with fifty Roman *aurei* in it. I'm no coin expert, but they look real. And that

papyrus... I almost wish we could let my mom look at it. She'd probably know whether it was real or not."

There was something in her voice though that made Jake think
she questioned the wisdom of actually doing that. "So, why don't
you think it would be a good idea to show it to your mom?"

"What?"

"I'm not sure, but I think I sensed a hint of hesitation. That
makes me curious."

Emilia took a breath and sighed. "Yeah... well... Beauregard has
led me to believe I don't know my mom as well as I thought."

"How so?"

"Well, he twice called her 'Disciple of Harpocrates,' whatever
that is. I don't know Beauregard that well, but I can't help but feel
there was truth and meaning there. He knows something about
Mom that I don't, and I think Gerald and Bianca know it, too."

That settled kind of heavy around Jake's shoulders. He had never
expected Gerald and Bianca to reveal all their secrets, but at the same
time, it would've been nice if they had opened up about anything in
their lives or experience that affected—or might affect—him.

But the more he thought about it, he knew has wasn't being fair.
There was no conceivable way to predict what might or might not
affect him, so were they just supposed to sit him down and tell him
their life stories? No... the proper way to handle this was to sit down
with them and lay everything out, then see what they did or said.

Yeah, that sounded—and felt—like the best plan.

But first... he had a date with Fiona.

CHAPTER
TWENTY-SIX

Wainwright Grove
Hornbeam, Illinois
24 May 2025, 4:17pm

THE PEACE and serenity of Bianca's grove washed over him again as he shifted the SUV into Park and pressed the button to turn it off. As much as he loved his parents and where he'd grown up, there was something about the Grove that felt inherently *right*. He couldn't explain it... and wasn't even sure he wanted to. The air was fresh with floral scents and pine and mint, and everywhere he looked, Nature spread out before him in all its beauty.

He wouldn't mind living in a place like this, but he would prefer that he could have a similar place and not take over the Grove after the Wainwrights' deaths... as Beauregard had intimated was his fate.

"You okay?" Emilia asked as she laid a hand on his arm. "You don't have to do this right now, you know."

Jake shook his head. "No. I despise waiting. I'd rather talk all this over with them right now and get past it than have it sitting on my shoulders for who knows how long. Besides, there's always the chance Gerald or Bianca will have some excellent insights."

"Can I be there with you when you awaken the stone?"

What? Didn't she realize that it could be dangerous?

"Are you sure that's what you want? I mean... we don't know what the stone will do when I drip my blood on it... if anything. It could be dangerous, or it could be literally nothing."

Emilia moved her hand from his forearm to take his hand. "Yes, but I'd like to be there for you if you'd let me. You shouldn't have to face this alone. But all that aside, no one else in the world has ever seen anything like this... at least not they've openly admitted. If you don't mind me being here, I'd love to see it, too."

He wasn't all that sure he should face it in any other way but alone. Like he told her, they had no idea what the stone would do. It could be incredibly dangerous, totally inert, or anything in between. He wasn't sure that getting Emilia hurt would be a great first impression with her mother, either.

"Let's talk all this over with Bianca and Gerald and see what they think before we make any concrete plans."

"That's probably the best path. I wish we could discuss it with Isabel, too."

Jake snorted a breath. "You and me both, but there's no telling how long she'll be hunting that rogue griffon. Come on; let's go see if Gerald and Bianca have some time."

THEY FOUND the Wainwrights on the patio, lounging in Adirondack chairs with comfy cushions. They each held a glass of iced tea as they chatted amiably with their guest... who just so happened to be Isabel herself. They turned as Jake and Emilia stepped outside the house. Gerald and Bianca both smiled their welcome. Isabel regarded Jake in silence with a non-expression.

Just as the silence edged toward awkward, Isabel broke it. "I thought I was clear that you needed to stay here at the Grove for your safety."

"You were very clear, but..."

Isabel interrupted him with a mild glare. "If I am to be your mentor, you should respect my opinions more."

Before Jake or anyone else could respond, the presence Jake had come to recognize as Beauregard settled over the patio.

* Lady Dragon, the Titan was not careless on a whim, and he did not disregard your directive lightly. In fact, it was only when I assured both him and Father that I could protect him anywhere in Hornbeam that he chose to visit the hospital for his first lesson in the Life Sphere. Since then, he has made a handful of trips outside the Grove... all under my protection. *

Silence reigned for several moments.

"It was not your place..."

Before Isabel could finish her statement, grassy earth rose up into a vague humanoid shape in the back lawn and trudged forward to stand between Jake and Isabel.

* You are wrong, Lady Dragon. It has been, is, and always shall be my place to safeguard the Titan. That is the charge I accepted from Gaia, and if I must, I will protect him from you as well. *

Jake fought to keep his expression as close to neutral as he could manage. He didn't see how anyone could miss the ginormous gauntlet Beauregard just tossed at Isabel's feet, and he didn't want to do anything that might influence the outcome of the confrontation. An attempt to de-escalate could just as easily incite as succeed.

Tension blanketed the patio like a thick fog. To Jake, it seemed like everyone waited to see how Isabel would react. He was sure the Wainwrights didn't like the idea of the dragon fighting Beauregard for many reasons, not the least of which being property damage.

In the end, worries proved unfounded.

Isabel sighed. "Yes. You are correct, Beauregard. My apologies. It would be rude of me in the extreme to attempt placing myself between you and a task given by Gaia Herself. And... it would be very poor repayment of Gerald and Bianca's excellent hospitality. I ask both your and Jake's forgiveness."

* In mine eyes, you ask needlessly. It is not something rising to the severity of needing to seek forgiveness, for I grant it out of hand. *

Jake nodded and pointed at the Earth construct with his thumb. "Yeah... I'm with Beauregard on that. Don't worry about it, but if you do, I forgive you. I'm very glad you're here, too. Did you get the griffon?"

The Earth construct Beauregard animated trudged back to the grassy yard where the ground re-absorbed it.

Isabel growled. "No. I was able to track its scent a goodly distance, but I never saw it. It's still heading roughly east but was angling more southeast the last scent I had of it. It may bypass Hornbeam completely, but it still needs to be stopped. I will keep hunting it, but I thought to take a day at least to relax and rest while checking in with you on your studies."

Jake grinned. "That's why I'm glad you're here. I was going to discuss all this with Gerald and Bianca, but I really wanted to include you, too."

"Very well. What did you wish to discuss?"

Jake pulled one of the small tables over to stand between the Wainwrights and Isabel. It was about knee-height, just perfect for reaching when lounging on the patio. It had an octagonal top made of frosted glass inside a metal frame with curved metal legs welded to the base of that frame. Jake opened the small bag his parents had given him and laid out the items that were his only physical inheritance from his birth parents. At the sight of the papyrus and engraved stone, Isabel gasped.

"Tell me what is in the leather pouch, please."

"Here. I'll show you." Jake grabbed the pouch and untied the strings before reaching inside and withdrawing a single coin, which he handed to her.

An expression of desire flitted across Isabel's expression at the mere sight of the *aureus*, and the longer she held it, the more she looked like she wanted to kiss it or make love to it somehow. Soon, though, she closed her eyes and shook herself, reaching the coin back to Jake.

"Take it, please. I... it has been so long since I've seen such a coin that wasn't in my hoard that I find myself desiring to add it."

Both Gerald's and Bianca's expressions betrayed their curiosity, but Gerald spoke. "May I ask what it is?"

Before Jake could turn and hand them the coin, Isabel answered. "It is a Roman *aureus* in near-mint condition."

Bianca gasped as Jake laid it in her hands. "It's authentic? You're sure?"

Isabel chuckled. "If there is one topic you can trust a dragon to know well beyond any human authority, it is precious items, like rare metals or even rarer coins. I have more *aurei* than I can count in five years, but I still hunger for that one. Such is the curse of my people."

"How did you come by it, Jake?"

"Well, therein lies a tale..."

Jake settled in a regular patio chair that he moved close to the table and told them the entire story. Everything from the fact that he was adopted by Frank and Sarah Adams to the exact circumstances his parents had told him of just that day, plus the items his birth parents sent with him. By the end of it, Gerald and Bianca simply sat in their chairs, hovering between astounded and almost disbelieving.

Gerald turned to Isabel when Jake finished. "Is... is what he said possible? Could the sorcerers of old have sent him forward through time to escape the people and creatures hunting them?"

"It... it would not surprise me. I do not know that anyone ever charted the full extent of their powers... even the sorcerers themselves. Beyond that, these papyrus sheets are certainly authentic... as is the Latin. The handwriting, the spelling, the phrasing... all of it supports the conclusion that this letter was written by a native Roman of the middle to late Republic."

Bianca sighed. "I wonder who they were. I almost wish you could have known them, Jake."

Jake shuddered. "I appreciate that, but if even half of what Isabel has told us is true about sorcerers, part of me is glad they didn't come through with me. I mean... can you imagine what it would've been like for someone with their powers to be loose on the world right before the Independence Day attacks? Isabel, were there any *good* sorcerers?"

"I'm sure there were. The law of averages almost insists that it must have been so. But no one ever heard about them. It was always the... bad actors, as you say... that drew attention."

Gerald turned to Jake. "Have you activated the stone yet?"

"No. I wanted to see what everyone thought about it, and Emilia asked to be with me when I did. I wanted to ask all of you whether you thought that was wise."

"It is not." Isabel's voice was as implacable as a granite cliff. "First, there is no guarantee that anything will happen. But if something indeed does, we cannot know whether they built in protections to ensure only sorcerers could access the knowledge they bequeathed you. And there is even the chance that whatever is built into the stone won't even detect or be aware of her presence. There's no way to know, which means there is inherent and incalculable risk... perhaps to the both of you. And that is not even broaching the topic of whether she'd have a frame of reference for whatever it disclosed to you."

Emilia frowned. "What do you mean?"

"I am not saying or implying that you are in any way deficient, child. But it is a simple fact that modern mages are not even a shadow of the sorcerers. The Spheres as you know them were never meant to be separate, and they interact with each other and interweave to such a degree that even one of your Grandmasters of Life would look a mere aspirant beside a sorcerer in full command of his or her power. The sorcerers created entire species, child; what modern mage can even come close to claiming that?"

Jake scratched at his chin as he thought about it. "So... what you're saying is that whatever the stone tells me might not even be appropriate at all for Emilia because she doesn't have access to all the Spheres like I do."

Isabel replied with a firm nod, "Yes. Exactly."

Emilia turned to Jake. "Well... if you'll have me, I'd still like to be there with you. I understand and accept that there may be some risk involved, but I still say you shouldn't have to face it alone."

Jake fought to keep his expression neutral. *He* wasn't nearly so blasé about the risk to her, especially if something within the stone harmed her because she wasn't a sorcerer or blood relation. But how to go about convincing her of that?

"Let me think about it, okay? I'm still not comfortable with placing you at risk."

Emilia merely nodded.

"How many of those coins do you have?" Gerald gestured at the small leather pouch.

"Fifty in total, but I'm not sure what they're worth."

Isabel stared at the leather pouch almost hungrily. "Those are from the Republic era and, as such, have around eight grams of gold in them... assuming they are from the time of Julius Caesar. They are in excess of ninety-nine percent purity, which means—at today's market prices—they're worth around $439 in US currency. However, their historical value—especially to a collector—is much, much higher."

She pulled her eyes away from the pouch with obvious effort. Everyone watched her battle with her desire for the coins, and Jake turned over the idea of giving them to her. On the one hand, they were part of his 'inheritance' from his parents, and he would never get them back. Beyond that, it wasn't like they were making any more. But on the other hand, Isabel's desire for them was an almost palpable presence.

Jake reached over and claimed the coin purse from the table. He shifted the purse in his hand until it rested on his palm, and he extended his hand toward Isabel.

"Here, take them."

Isabel wasn't the only person who betrayed shock. She stared at him wide-eyed, then her eyes flicked to the coin purse and back to him several times. "Do not toy with me, baby sorcerer. You would not enjoy the outcome."

"I'm not toying with you, Isabel. I have no idea what do with them, besides put them in a safe. Would you appreciate having them? Would you value them?"

"Oh, yes. I love each and every item in my hoard as if it were the only item I owned. Are you certain this is what you want? Dragons *never* part with gold once they have it."

Jake nodded. "I understand. I don't sense anything from them. I mean... I don't think my parents embedded any magic in them or anything like that. So, you can have them if you want."

Isabel's hand shot toward the coin purse and froze mere millimeters from it. "No. It is the custom of my people that matters such as this must be an equal exchange. Value for value. I have not claimed these coins through right of battle. What do you want for them?"

Uh... what? How was he supposed to answer that? He hadn't even known they existed before yesterday, and in a sense, they weren't even real to him yet. Maybe that was why it was so easy for him to part with them. But he respected Isabel's ethics and beliefs, so... what did he want for them? What could she give him that would be even close to equal value to him as the coins obviously were to her?

"I... I don't know. I'm not sure."

Isabel pulled her hand back—again, with apparent effort—and settled back in her seat. "When you agreed to my mentorship, you promised me five favors as payment. I am willing to reduce those to four."

Yes... that was an excellent offer. But at the same time, those favors could easily be learning experiences for Jake, too. They could be valuable to him ways that lay outside paying Isabel back for her mentorship. On the other hand, though, one of them might get him killed. There was just no way to know. Still...

"With respect, Isabel, I don't think that's a good deal for me. Many would say it was, I'm sure, but I can't shake the feeling that those favors will prove just as valuable learning experiences for me as your mentorship."

Now, Isabel pulled her eyes away from the coin purse without effort at all. She regarded him with an appraising expression in silence for several moments, before hints of pride peeked through. "Very few would see those favors as such, Jake. You are perhaps an even more singular human than I first thought. So be it. As neither of us have the necessary knowledge to devise an appropriate payment to you for these coins in this moment, I shall instead offer you one favor for every ten coins, redeemable under the same terms as mine are from you."

Gerald and Bianca both tried to hide their gasps.

Jake turned the matter over in his mind a few moments before nodding and offering a handshake. "Yes. I think that's fair. I agree. Fifty *aurei* for five favors."

Isabel accepted Jake's hand and gave him a respectable hand-shake, after which Jake placed the coin purse in her hand. She quickly untied the cord and emptied the coins into her other hand. Given Isabel's expression as she stared at the coins, Jake was a little surprised she didn't break into a riff on 'my precious.'

After several moments of gazing lovingly at the coins in her hand, Isabel returned them to the pouch and tied it shut with the drawstring. She quickly stood, picking up her phone from the side-table. She walked toward the corner of the house as she tapped on the phone, before lifting it to her ear.

As she turned the corner, Jake heard her say, "Kai... it's Isabel. I need one of the couriers we trust to meet me in Hornbeam. I have exceptionally precious cargo that must be secured in the hoard as soon as possible."

CHAPTER
TWENTY-SEVEN

Jake looked at the stone he held in his hand. He marveled at how... *normal*... it felt. The textured, unpolished surface of a hunk of rock that came out of a hillside somewhere. Probably Italian. He ran his thumb over a section of engravings. Odd runes or glyphs that held no meaning for him.

What did they mean? What would happen when he activated the stone?

According to his parents, the message was that his blood would activate it. Since it didn't light up at his mere touch, it must mean that he had to prick him thumb or something. He certainly wasn't going to be all melodramatic and slice a gash across his palm.

He wasn't stupid.

With a slight sigh, he pulled his focus away from the stone and its oddly comfortable weight. Gerald, Bianca, and Emilia watched him from their seats around the patio. Gerald and Bianca conveyed no emotion; they just regarded him in silence. Emilia watched him with open eagerness and expectation.

Those feelings made sense. He'd be lying if he said he didn't feel the same. But that wasn't all he felt. Not by a long shot. No... there was a thread of worry and concern interwoven with the rest. He feared what he'd learn of his parents. The created races and species —the griffons, the chimeras, the centaurs, and all the rest—supposedly hated his kind for how sorcerers treated them. Across two thousand years, they still held onto their hatred.

In some ways, it seemed almost unbelievable to him.

"Well? What are you waiting for?"

Jake brought his attention back to Emilia who sat on the edge of her seat, looking for all the world like she was about to start hopping up and down like an eager puppy. He smiled. "Impatient, are we? Why do you care so much?"

That dampened her enthusiasm a bit, and she settled down. "Honestly? I'm hoping there will be something in there that will help the blood disorder that killed my friend. But... I'm also eager for you to learn more about who and what you are."

"Yeah... that would be kinda cool."

Gerald stood, prompting Bianca to follow suit. They shared a look and turned smiles toward Jake and Emilia.

"You kids be careful. Sure... it feels inert right now, but there's no telling what that stone is capable of. What its creators weaved into those markings."

Jake nodded. "We'll be careful. I won't let anything harm her."

Bianca gave him a fond smile as Gerald nodded. Then, they entered the house, leaving Jake and Emilia alone on the patio.

"Come on, Jake. There's no point in stalling now."

Jake almost felt like Emilia would prick his finger for him if he waited much longer. He set the stone back on the patio table and retrieved his pocketknife. It wasn't much, just a little folding-blade pen knife that he used to open boxes or the mail. Still, though, it was sharp enough to do the job. He soon had a bead of blood welling up on his thumb.

He set the knife aside and retrieved the stone. Then paused.

This was it. The moment of truth. The point of no return.

The blood on his thumb started to run, but before it could drip to the patio tiles, he brought his thumb and the stone together, swabbing as much of it as he could with the blood he had. He and Emilia both froze, waiting for something to happen.

For what seemed like ages, there was only the chirping of crickets in the distance. Nothing else.

Then...

In a flare of power that set Jake's body afire, the runes and markings on the stone exploded in kaleidoscopic radiance. Every color in existence and then some lit up the evening. There was no sound. No taste. Nothing but the colors.

After a few moments, the luminal fury faded until the stone merely glowed, the markings pulsing a slow rhythm. But that wasn't all. Oh, no...

Jake and Emilia now sat on benches in an open-air space. A small pool occupied the center. The space held two doors that led out of it, a door over Jake's left shoulder and another on the opposite side of the pool. Instead of late afternoon, the ambient light and temperature suggested early morning, and the air felt different. A touch more humidity, perhaps, with a light breeze.

The door beyond the pool opened to reveal a man and a woman. Both bore the olive complexion of Mediterranean descent. She wore a dress with sandals. He wore a toga, and that toga bore a thick, purple stripe that ran diagonally from his left shoulder to his right hip.

Their expressions betrayed surprise at seeing Emilia, but they refocused on Jake quickly enough. The woman smiled. It was warm, welcoming, and full of what Jake could only think of as a mother's love. The man looked on him with an expression that carried both respect and pride... not pride in himself as such but more like pride in the young man before him.

He lifted his hand in greeting. "*Salve, Fili.*"

Jake blinked.

Emilia looked back and forth from Jake to the two people. "Uhm... what did he say?"

The words sounded familiar. **Very** familiar. Where had he... oh!

Jake smiled and lifted his hand. "*Salve, Pater. Salve, Mater.*"

He turned to Emilia. "They're speaking Latin. He said, 'Hello, Son.'"

He felt a faint flare of power from the man and turned back to them. The woman took a cautious step forward, her eyes wet with unshed tears. "Oh, Gaius... we feared we would never see you again."

Jake's expression betrayed his surprise. "You speak English now?"

"No, Son." His father's expression suggested restrained amusement. "But you now hear us speak it. A simple effect so that we may converse. If you will permit us—once we have established a modicum of trust—your mother and I can share in your knowledge of the world. Your life. Experiences. Languages. But that can wait. We understand that we are strangers to you."

His mother focused on Emilia, a slight smile trying to peek out. "And who is your friend, Gaius?"

"Oh... uhm... this is Emilia Harcourt. She's a fellow student where I am, and... well... we're talking about maybe dating."

His mother's expression lit up. "That's good. How old are you? You look a man."

"I'm twenty-five. I only just learned of the stone and everything you sent with me today. I... I manifested about nine days ago, and I am a full sorcerer. Your letter suggested several things were in doubt."

His mother shot his father an exasperated look that reminded Jake so much of his adoptive parents. Then, she faced him once more. "Give your father half an hour, and he'll fill the day. Most of the dire outcomes he predicted had no chance of coming to pass... and yet... he insisted on pontificating about them past the point of reason."

It took all Jake's willpower to keep from laughing. Oh, goodness... his father was a **pedant**. Out of all the things he expected... that wasn't anywhere on the list.

"Now, Claudia... that isn't exactly accurate. In the proper circumstances, all of the possible outcomes were equally valid. You know that, just as well as I."

His mother—Claudia, apparently—pivoted on her heel. She almost glared at him. "Yes, Flavius, I do... and I also know that those 'proper circumstances' of which you speak are about as common as multiple suns exploding... at the same time. Yes... it happens, but not very often. Besides... is this really what you want to discuss when we have our adult son standing right there?"

His father looked properly abashed as he cleared his throat. "No... uhm... perhaps not. We can revisit it later... at another time."

"I should think so." Claudia turned back to face Jake and Emilia, rolling her eyes as soon as Flavius couldn't see. "Please, come inside and be welcome, both of you. We have much to discuss."

Jake and Emilia hastened to follow his parents into what he was slowly deciding was a Roman villa... or at least a re-creation of one. The clay roofing tiles, the atrium... all manner of little details suggested that was what this structure was. The room inside the atrium was furnished as a sitting room or parlor with cushioned chairs and lounges. His parents gestured for them to be seated.

Emilia glanced from Jake to his parents and back again. "May I ask some questions?"

Claudia nodded, her expression and demeanor suggesting warm regard. "Of course, child."

"You're his parents?"

Another nod. "Yes. The people of the time were hunting us, spending horrid amounts of lives for every sorcerer they killed. It seemed far too great of a risk to try hiding in the outlands, so we developed an alternative."

"You keep calling him Gaius. What is that?"

Now, she blinked her confusion. "Why... it is his name. Gaius Aternius Magius. What did you think it was?" Seeing the surprise betrayed by both Jake and Emilia, she turned to her husband. "Flavius... did you or did you not include our son's **name** in the letter like we discussed?"

Uh oh...

Flavius looked down and away. "Uhm... well... that is... I... honestly, I don't remember Claudia. There was simply so much to cover, you see. After all—"

Claudia rested her elbow on her knee and placed her forehead in her hand. "You mean to tell me that you spent whole *pages* prattling on about horseshit like how we risked the end of all creation by sending him through time, but you failed to mention our son's *name*?"

If they weren't sorcerers in full command of their power, it would've almost been funny.

"Claudia... my love... there were important matters..."

Jake could clearly see the tension in his mother's jaw as she rubbed her forehead, her other hand a tight fist.

"Save it." Claudia spat the words as if they were the vilest epithets. "We shall discuss this... later."

She took a deep breath and obviously put effort into pushing aside her heightened emotions, looking to Jake once more with a (mostly) pleasant smile. "I trust you have not spent the past twenty-five years nameless. Please tell me that is not so."

Jake noticed Emilia pressing her hand to her mouth and looking away, and he too had to admit to a certain amount of effort required for a straight face. "The people who took me in and adopted me named me Thornton Adams, but I mostly go by Jake."

"Thornton Adams Jake." Her tone implied she turned the name around in her head. Considering. Evaluating. "It is not the worst name I have encountered, not by a long chalk. I will endeavor to address you thus, but please forgive my occasional lapse. Time does not exist here, you see. So to us, it seems as if we just sent you on your way mere moments ago."

"Where is 'here' if you don't mind? It looks like what I know of Roman villas, but..."

Claudia nodded, her slight smile tinged with sadness. "It is a replica of our home on the outskirts of Herculaneum. We could bring nothing with us. Everything you see is something we created here."

"Okay. And where or what is here?"

Now, Flavius grinned. "It is... well... a soul space inside the stone for lack of better terms. You are not physically here, neither of you. And you are interacting with our souls... our spirits."

"So... you can't leave this space?" Emilia asked.

Both of his parents shook their heads, almost in unison. Claudia spoke. "Sadly, no, child. Would that we could."

Flavius lifted a hand, his index finger extended. "That... may not be entirely true. I have postulated that we could indeed leave this space and the protection of the stone glyphs, but we would need bodies and a sorcerer capable of tying our spirits to those bodies. Otherwise, we would be pulled to the afterlife or perhaps afterlives, same as any other recently deceased."

Jake's fingers itched for his notebook. The blank one where he sketched all his ideas, and the one place he never **ever** thought about recording his idea for how to save Gerald and Bianca from the supposedly set fate Beauregard had hinted. He still wanted to chat with the awareness about that, but... like everything else... there hadn't been time.

Something in his expression or demeanor must have betrayed him, for his mother zeroed in on him like a hawk. "What is it, my son? What is thy need?"

"You just said we weren't here physically, so it's foolish anyway." Jake shook his head, as if to dismiss the thought.

His mother offered the kind of soft, loving smile he'd seen on his adoptive mother so, so many times. "Speak thy need, Son."

"I have a notebook that I use to sketch ideas. It's where I designed my fireball framework and a handful of other things. I had an idea about getting you both out of here, and I want to be sure that I don't lose it."

His parents shared a look, then turned to him. Their demeanors radiated a heady mixture of awe, paternal pride, and disbelief. His father spoke. "You are but nine days into your heritage, and yet, you have already started a grimoire? That... that... it's unheard of."

"'Unheard of.'" His mother scoffed. "That's like saying it's unheard of for water to flow uphill. Son, focus on your... notebook, as you call it. Remember its every line and contour. Inhale its very scent... both natural and mystical."

Jake closed his eyes and tried to do as his birth mother bade him. It was a challenge. So many things he realized he took for granted. But after a few moments, he felt like he held the sense of it in his mind.

He heard that parental pride in her voice. "Yes... yes, that's it. You have it. I can see it, myself. Now... will it to be here, with whatever writing implements you use with it."

A familiar texture and weight filled his hands, and Jake opened his eyes, grinning at the plain notebook and box of colored pencils he held.

"How? I thought this a spirit realm?"

"Just as with both of you, those are not physically here. They are a thread, connecting your awareness and power to the physical objects wherever they await you." His father lifted a hand with the index finger outstretched. "But... do not assume them worthless. Open the cover, and you will see all your notes and writings. Make a mark, and you will find it in the book when you leave here."

Emilia simply grinned. "That is unreal. How did you do that?"

"Through the confluence of what you call the Spirit, Mind, and Earth Spheres, child." Claudia's tone was patient and kind.

Jake sighed, pulling his focus away from the notebook and pencils. He made eye contact first with his mother and then his father. Something in his thoughts must have leaked through, for his mother turned to him, her expression and demeanor dominated by concern. Before she could say anything, he spoke. "I owe you both an apology. The woman who offered to be my mentor out in the world told me things about sorcerers that painted all sorcerers in a... well... an unkind light. When I activated the stone, I did so expecting the worst, and it wasn't fair to either of you. I'm sorry."

His mother was out of her seat and across the room almost faster than the blink of an eye. She knelt in front him and pulled him into a tight embrace, and he couldn't believe how *right* it felt. "You owe us nothing, my son... ***nothing***. Your mortal mentor did not lie. There were sorcerers—many, if I'm being honest—who were cruel and uncaring, not giving a moment's thought to the consequences or ramifications of their actions. But just as the most brutal of humanity is not wholly representative of them, so were they not wholly representative of us. Each of us—sorcerer, human, and all the rest—are what we make of ourselves. They *chose* that path... and damned us all because of it."

She held Jake until he released those feelings and nodded. The way she kissed his forehead before returning to her seat stirred *something* deep inside him. Something that was both a memory... and not... all at the same time. She squared her shoulders as she sat and looked on him with the loving warmth and regard only a mother has. "Now... tell us of the thought you desired to record in your grimoire."

"You said you couldn't leave here without bodies, so it seems the most obvious answer is to create them for you. Once they're ready, we take you out and tether your spirits to them. I don't know how to do that... yet... but I will one day. Isabel—my mentor out there—told me sorcerers are functionally immortal, so it's not like I don't have time."

His parents shared another look before turning back to him. His father spoke. "You would do that for us?"

"Of course. You're my parents, right? You're good people? You wouldn't become a plague on the world? Why wouldn't I do that for you? I'd like for you to meet the two who took me in and raised me as their own. I'd like you to see what the world has become. I'd like you to be part of my life, and I'd like to be a part of yours. And... well...

frankly, it feels weird leaving you in here to be my own private resource when you could have your lives back."

His parents shared another look, and when they turned back to him, he saw tears in his mother's eyes. "You are a better person than we could've ever hoped for, Son. Thank you. Success or fail, know that your desire means so much to us."

"As long as you're here, we might as well have our first lesson." His father's voice was also a bit thick with controlled emotion. "Speak the question that is your greatest need."

For a moment no longer than a finger-snap, Jake felt his mind spiraling out into analysis paralysis. He recognized it, though, and the sheer idiocy it represented. The answer was so obvious that it would hide a sore thumb.

"How do I practice training my power? There was... well... an emergency situation the other day, and I helped. But to do that, I carried around sugar tablets that I used as batteries, for lack of a better term, to keep my power from bottoming out my blood sugar."

His parents shared another look, and his mother voiced their confusion. "It... we understand your words but perhaps not their meaning to you. Will you show us what you experienced?"

Jake shrugged. "How?"

"Put yourself back in that moment and push the memories to us." She must've noticed his stray thought of the jaguars, and she beamed. "Yes! Exactly like how you converse with your companions, except send the whole experience and not just the thoughts."

Jake nodded and closed his eyes, calling forth his memories of the highway pile-up. His experiences. His thoughts. His feelings. And especially how the merest effort with his power drained him to the point of exhaustion without the glucose tablets. Then, he gathered it all up and touched that part of his mind he used to speak with the jaguars and sent the thought packet to his parents.

They both beamed, their expressions leaking parental pride. His mother said, "That you succeed so well in no longer than you've had your power is uncanny, almost unbelievable."

They fell silent, and Jake assumed they examined the packet he sent them. After a few moments, their expressions revealed shock.

His father simply stared at him in bewilderment while his mother addressed the issue. "Gaius... apologies... Jake. Why are you using your life energy to power your desires... your frameworks, as you call them?"

Jake blinked. "What? I don't understand. How else would I power them?"

"All reality is but energy given form, Son." His father's voice still carried hints of disbelief, but he wasn't condescending or arrogant about it. "When you leave here, open yourself to it. Don't try to make it fit into these arbitrary labels the lesser—forgive me... the mages—have given them. Their reality is not yours, and you are limiting yourself by relying on it. Yes... it is necessary to expend *some* of your energy to catalyze the change you wish to make, but use the energy inherent in the world around you for the vast majority of the change. If the energy for a desired effect could be described as one hundred parts, the energy that comes from you should be no more than ten."

Jake blinked. It was both overwhelming and stupidly simple. Holy shit... no wonder mages—even Quad-Spheres—couldn't compete with true sorcerers. He turned to Emilia who looked just as gobsmacked as he felt. "Have you ever heard of anything like this? Not the matter and energy stuff... I mean using energy external to us."

She simply shook her head.

Claudia lifted a hand to draw their attention. "And with good reason. The mages cannot sense the energy around them, let alone use it. The few who have tried that we know of... well... it did not go well for them."

Huh... interesting. Now, he wanted to ask his parents if a sorcerer could modify a mage to give them whatever he or she lacked and make them a sorcerer. But he wasn't about to voice that as long as Emilia was with him. That was another project he kept secret from the world.

Something in his mother's expression—around her eyes mostly —suggested she'd picked up hints of it. But if she had, she made no other mention of it.

Then, another thought struck him. "Say... since Emilia came with me, can I bring others? Like... say... non-magical people? Regular humans?"

His parents shared another look, and his father gave a 'why not?' shrug. "It should be possible. There's nothing inherently dangerous in activating the stone. It might not be as easy for them as it is for you or a mage, but there shouldn't be any lasting effects... harmful or beneficial."

His mother frowned, and he felt her curiosity. "Why, Son?"

"Because I don't want to wait until I can take you to the world for you to meet the people who raised me."

His mother swallowed hard, her eyes glistening again. "We would like that and welcome them with open arms. But we have kept you long enough for now. Please, visit as you can."

Jake grinned. "Oh, I will. So... uhm... how do we leave?"

"How else do you leave someone's home?" His father gave him a 'duh' look that Jake felt was teasing. "Through the front door."

CHAPTER
TWENTY-EIGHT

Jake once again felt like he sat in a chair on Gerald's and Bianca's back patio. He felt his weight pressing against the chair. He felt the slight dampness of the evening air on his skin and breathed in the floral scents from the flowerpots that decorated the area and were lovingly cared for by Bianca.

He looked all around, and he settled on Emilia. She gazed at him with an expression of joy and wonder. Then, he realized that he held something. He looked down and grinned at the sight of his notebook and pencils in his hands.

"Did that really just happen?" She almost bounced in her seat. "Did we really visit your birth parents in their spirit realm?"

He smiled, then laughed and lifted the notebook and pencils. "You tell me. I remember it, too... so either we both did or we both shared the same hallucination." A thought struck him, and his smile turned into a grin. He opened the notebook and flipped to the last occupied page. There, he saw the quickly jotted notes about trying to create bodies for the spirits of his birth parents to inhabit. He couldn't keep from grinning, and then, another thought occurred to him. "Come on. I want to test something."

He was out of the patio chair like a shot and halfway across the patio before he realized everything he left on the table. He turned and took a half step back toward the items but stopped. Emilia's confused frown was the last thing he saw as he closed his eyes and tried opening himself up to the energy all around him. It felt like he brushed it—or it brushed him—several times... but it seemed almost elusive. Like it was playing with him somehow.

He held out his hand, palm up, and pushed a smidge of his energy out through his palm. An offering to the world at large. Bait, if you will. Then, he felt it. The faintest resonance. He opened himself to *that* and felt the very fabric of reality unfold before him.

It was overwhelming. Awe-inspiring. Terrifying.

He rotated his hand and cupped it as if to catch a ball and nudged the energy, passing it just a smidge more. He heard Emilia's gasp a mere heartbeat before he felt the mass of the stone smack his palm. It didn't hurt, and he quickly gripped it to keep it from falling. He opened his eyes once more and grinned at Emilia's expression.

"I think I might be on the right track."

She stood and retrieved the papyrus and folded note, shaking her head as she approached him. "I'll say you are. I can't believe how much power I felt from you right then. I didn't feel you *use* it; it was more like I stood beside a full-pressure firehose trickling like a kitchen faucet."

"Wow... really?"

"Yeah... most mages can sense each other to a certain degree. That was just freaky. It was like the stone just leaped to your hand of its own accord."

Jake turned and nodded for her to follow. "Come on. I'm going to ask Gerald if he'll take me back to the emergency room... or maybe the cancer ward. I want to test something."

Emilia's expression hovered somewhere between a smirk and a grin. "Don't you have a dinner date?"

He stopped mid-stride. "Damn. Yes, I do. Thank you for reminding me. But I really, really want to test this."

"You can always test it tomorrow, Jake. The hospital will still be there."

CHAPTER
TWENTY-NINE

Marci's Diner
    Hornbeam, Illinois
    24 May 2025, 5:55pm

JAKE LOOKED up at the sound of the bell over the door ringing and smiled when he saw Fiona enter. He waved to her and, as she approached the booth, stood out of respect. A smile dominated her expression as she stepped close and gave him a hug. He felt that strange tingle that he had when she touched him before, and when she gave him a quick kiss on his cheek, it was almost like there were literal electrical sparks.

After the kiss, Fiona stepped back and slid into the booth, then leaned forward. "Hey, you, it's good to see you. How has everything been going?"

Jake shrugged. "I'd be lying if I tried to tell you there's not a learning curve, but I suppose that's to be expected."

"Oh, yes. I could tell you stories, but..." She waved her hand to indicate the moderately busy diner.

Jake nodded his understanding. While crafters were an accepted part of society, not all the supernatural races were. Matter of fact, he wasn't sure that the general class on magic in high school had touched on **any** supernatural races. And yet... he had proof of two (dragons and griffons) and indirect proof of several more (Fae and all the other hybrid races Isabel had mentioned).

Marci came and took their drink orders, giving Jake a wink after side-eyeing Fiona, and disappeared back into the production areas of the diner. A few moments later, one of Marci's servers arrived with their drinks and took their food order.

"So, you said you have a rough caseload right now?"

Fiona nodded around the straw of her drink, mid-swallow. "Yes. It's rough more because of the nature of the cases than because the cases themselves are actually difficult. Just because someone feels they've been wronged and should sue doesn't automatically guarantee that they have an actionable case, regardless of their thoughts in the matter. Howie and I have tried to explain that the case has no legs, but they won't listen. We're pretty much at the point of just telling them we can't help them. Lawyers have a bad enough rep in our society without actually playing to the ambulance-chasing stereotype."

"I can see that. On top of the clients' chances, you also have your professional reputations to consider."

"See? What's so difficult to understand there? But that's enough shop talk. Tell me about your mage affinity studies. I've always been fascinated with mages. Not to the degree your friend Officer Stannyk seems to be, but still..."

Jake grinned. "Yeah. Mike's a major fanboy where mages are concerned. Gerald Wainwright has been teaching me the Life Sphere, and I can also make a light orb."

"Have you had any formal training with the Light Sphere, yet?"

He wasn't sure how much he should tell Fiona about what he could do. Isabel seemed to have concerns about her. His memory of the phone call where she said that Fae like to drain mages to steal their power replayed in his mind... almost crystal clear. Still, though... he didn't like lying.

"No. Not yet. My training so far has centered around the Life Sphere, since Gerald Wainwright is so available."

Fiona beamed. "Incredible. Most mages, in my experience, need training in each individual affinity. That you can take what Gerald teaches you and extrapolate that into accessing and utilizing your Light Sphere, too... well... I have very high hopes for you. I must admit that your affinity combination is *very* odd. Time, Life, and Light. I don't think I've ever encountered another mage with those affinities."

Jake hoped his rising anxiety didn't show in his expression... and... that she had no way of hearing or sensing his heartbeat. "It's just the law of averages, right? Given that there are only twelve Arcane Spheres... we must have worked through all the combinations by now."

Fiona chuckled. "Sure. It's easy to think that, but if you spend any time perusing the Magocracy records, you'll see that affinities tend to group together. The elemental affinities are the most common, followed by Life, Death, Light, and Shadow. Spirit and Mind are next in rarity. Spatial and Time are the second rarest and rarest, respectively. And overall, affinities tend to group along those lines. Tri-Spheres—especially exceptional Tri-Spheres with full affinities across the board—tend to have a common, an uncommon, and a rare affinity. You have two uncommon and the rarest. That's unheard of."

Jake had no idea what to say to de-escalate the situation. Fiona's gaze focused on him unblinking, as if she could divine the answer to the puzzle that was Jake Adams from across the diner's table. There was too much he didn't know about her intentions and about her in general to trust her with his secret... and there was no way to get that information right then, not sitting in a diner with several occupied booths within earshot.

"Well... I... I don't know what to say. Like the cartoon sailor said, 'I am what I am.'"

She threw back her head and laughed, drawing a few looks from around the diner. When she settled down, she beamed a huge smile. "Oh, you are certainly something, Jake Adams." Then, her expression shifted to one of consideration and question. "But what is that?"

Before Jake could put together an answer—any answer—her beaming smile was back, and she shot him a wink.

Jake gave her his best non-committal smile in reply.

They continued to chat, mixing in veiled (or not-so-veiled) flirting, until their food arrived. At several points during the conversation, an odd expression flitted across Fiona's face, but it vanished almost as quickly as it appeared, which didn't leave Jake much time for a good look to try to interpret it.

By the time they finished eating, the diner was filling up, and Fiona looked at Jake with an expression he could only describe as equal parts demure and sly. "It's getting a little crowded in here. Want to go for a walk?"

Jake smiled and shrugged. "Sure. I'm good with that."

Marci met him at the register, where he paid for himself and Fiona, and they left the diner in a companionable silence. Once they were easily out of earshot of anyone without a parabolic mic, Fiona turned to him as they walked.

"There's something about you, Jake. I've honestly never felt anything like it. You are *not* an exceptional Tri-Sphere... I don't care what the Magocracy says."

Jake shrugged and gave her his best 'I know nothing' smile. "I don't know what to say, Fiona."

They now stood on the sidewalk, a good twenty-five yards from the diner, and Fiona stopped and looked him square in the eye. "Jake, you might not understand what this means, but I'm partial Fae. My great-grandmother was the youngest daughter of a noble family. I can sense mages. I sense the difference between single-Spheres, dual-Spheres, and Tri-Spheres. I don't know what the hell you are, but you're no Tri-Sphere. The power I sense from you is nothing like any mage I've ever encountered. I thought it was just because you

270

were so new, that day we met, but no. If anything, it's almost like the power I sense from you has settled in... or perhaps matured in some way."

Before Jake had time to process her words fully, she stepped close and pulled him to her for a deep, full kiss. Almost instantly, he sensed some kind of strange draw that felt like it pulled at his power, much like how it feels to block an operating vacuum cleaner's hose with your hand. His vision started to tunnel, and he did the only thing he could think of. He treated the draw like one of his frameworks and connected it to the ambient power that he now felt all around him.

He knew the instant he was successful.

The draw stopped, and Fiona's eyes shot wide with sheer, unmitigated terror... less than a heartbeat before a concussion like a thunderclap erupted between them. It ruffled Jake's clothes, but it sent Fiona skidding backward with only the back edges of her heels touching the pavement. She didn't stop until her feet caught on the far sidewalk, where she toppled over like a felled tree. Before Jake put one foot off the sidewalk where he stood, she sat upright, though she weaved unsteadily as she did so. The weaving slowed, then vanished altogether.

She was back on her feet by the time Jake stood at her side, and she took one look at Jake and turned, hurriedly walking away... coming as close to running as she could without actually doing so. She fished her phone out of her purse, made one call, and stepped through a portal that opened almost immediately.

Even after the portal closed, Jake stayed rooted to the sidewalk, staring at the space Fiona had occupied mere moments before. He wasn't sure what had just happened, but he suspected Fiona wouldn't be calling him for a second date anytime soon.

Jake crossed the street and returned to the diner's parking lot to retrieve his SUV before he headed back to the Grove. He made a side bet with himself on just how far from the SUV he'd get before either Emilia or Isabel corralled him to ask about the date.

. . .

AS IT HAPPENED, he made it all the way to the porch of the Wainwrights' house. Emilia sat in one of the Adirondack chairs Gerald and Bianca kept there, and when he climbed the steps and entered the porch, she looked to him wearing an expression that was equal parts curiosity and anxiety.

"So... how'd it go?"

Jake chuckled as he waved his hand for her to follow him. "Not so well that I want to repeat myself telling the story. Come on. Is Isabel still here?"

The anxiety vanished from Emilia's expression as she jumped to her feet and moved to his side, taking his arm in hers. "Yeah. She's inside talking with Gerald and Bianca. It really went that badly?"

"Just wait for the story. Then, you can tell me."

THE WAINWRIGHTS and Isabel turned to them as they entered the great room and found seats. Their expressions all suggested appraising curiosity.

"I asked Emilia to wait for me to come inside, so I could tell everyone how it went in one go." Jake sat on the sofa and sagged back against it, prompting Emilia to do the same. She even went so far as to snuggle into his side. He took a deep breath and released it as a heavy sigh before he continued. "So, the dinner conversation went well enough. We had some banter, and it was fun. But when the diner started filling up, Fiona suggested we go for a walk. She stopped us twenty-odd feet from the diner's parking lot and told me in no uncertain terms that I am most assuredly not an exceptional Tri-Sphere, because her Fae heritage allows her to sense mages and she had never sensed another mage like me. When I didn't rise to the bait, she moved in for a kiss. It was a far more serious kiss than she'd given me thus far, and I actually felt my power start draining. But... it felt like the draw when I power one of my frameworks, so instead of letting her continue drawing on me, I bypassed my life force and connected her straight to the ambient power. I essentially became nothing more than a piece of pipe in a waterline."

He sighed again, shaking his head. "The next thing I know, the draw just stopped. No tapering, no nothing. It just stopped cold, like someone flipped a light switch. Then, there was a concussion, like a really big thunderclap without sound that threw Fiona away from me. She skidded all the way across the street before her feet caught the far sidewalk. She took just long enough to get her bearings before she jumped up and fled back through a portal."

Isabel leaned forward in her seat, her expression intense. "Did she create the portal herself?"

"No. She made a call from her cell, and then, the portal appeared."

Isabel leaned back, nodding as she relaxed. "Good. That's very good."

Jake glanced between Isabel and the Wainwrights, his lack of understanding dominating his expression. "Mind telling me why?"

"Only full-blooded Fae or their immediate offspring have sufficient power to create portals on their own. If she made a call to get a portal, she's at least another generation removed."

Jake frowned as he went back over their dinner conversation. "Yeah... she said she's the granddaughter of a noble or something."

Before Isabel or the Wainwrights could speak, Emilia tightened her arms around his as she smiled at him. "So, I have you all to myself now?"

Jake shrugged the shoulder of the arm that didn't have Emilia holding onto it. "Sure... why not?"

"Goodie." Emilia surged up and gave him a quick peck on the cheek before settling back.

CHAPTER

THIRTY

Hornbeam General Hospital
Hornbeam, Illinois
25 May 2025, 1:35pm

JAKE BRAKED the SUV to a stop in a parking space reserved for doctors. Gerald placed his placard on the dash where it could be seen through the windshield, while Jake and Emilia exited the vehicle. They gathered at the sidewalk that separated the parking lot from the roundabout ambulances used to deliver patients to the emergency room.

"Are you sure about this, Jake?" Gerald regarded him with a neutral expression.

Jake nodded. "My parents—that is, my birth parents—told me what I've been doing wrong. That's no fault to any of you, because the knowledge and experience you've shared is all you know. It just also happens to be wrong for me. I *think* I know what I need to better practice using my power, but without testing that, I won't know for certain. So, I might as well help some people in the process."

"That's very admirable, but what if you're wrong? What if you try to help someone but make it worse... and make it worse in a way Life mages can't fix?"

Jake sighed. "Yes, I suppose it's possible, but Gerald, I feel like I have to try. It's almost a compulsion."

Emilia chimed in, defending Jake. "You should have seen the telekinesis. He was halfway to the patio doors, and he called the stone to him. It suddenly just leaped across something like fifteen feet to his waiting hand."

Gerald looked back and forth between them for several moments, then nodded. "Okay. We'll see how it goes. Let me speak to the patient first and be sure we have their consent. I may even swing by my office and get an experimental procedure consent form, just to be safe."

"Whatever works for you." Jake just shrugged. He didn't care so much about that part of it. He had this odd feeling of certainty, like when he thought about trying to cure that girl's hemophilia. Somehow, he simply *knew* he could do this.

THE EMERGENCY ROOM looked even busier than the first time Jake had seen it. Almost every seat was full, and nurses and doctors rushed to and fro in a frenetic dance that only made sense if one knew the steps. When Gerald approached the desk, the nurse looked up, and her distress vanished as she betrayed an intense relief.

"Oh, thank goodness, Doctor Wainwright. I don't know why you're here, but we need you. There was a scheduling foul-up, and we've been without a Life mage for the past four hours. We're doing what we can, but we've come close to losing a few that would've been easy otherwise."

Gerald didn't waste any time. "Where do you need us?"

"There's a stabbing victim in Three. It's... well... it's not good."

Jake was already on the move before he remembered his promise to let Gerald speak with them first. He stopped and waited, following

Gerald into the room with Emilia. And the moment he surveyed the scene inside the exam room, his immediate reaction was to swallow the fury that threatened his calm.

Three people occupied Room Three who were not medical personnel. A young woman not much older than Jake lay on the exam table. Another woman a little older and a woman about middle age each held one of the woman's hands; the family resemblance between the three was almost painfully obvious.

At their entrance, the medical team looked up, and relief washed through every single one of them like a palpable wave. Two doctors stood over the woman's wound, and the woman spoke. "Oh, thank heavens. Ma'am, that's Doctor Wainwright; he's a Grandmaster of the Life Sphere."

Now, the two women holding the unconscious woman's hands showed relief as well.

Gerald went to scrub up and spoke over his shoulder. "What do we have?"

"A twenty-seven-year-old female who is nine weeks pregnant. Her supposed boyfriend stabbed her when she told him the news."

Jake **almost** asked for a name. Instead, he focused on the unconscious woman, trying to reach out with his new awareness without closing his eyes.

Gerald returned to the center of the room and faced the two women. "As Doctor Halliwell stated, I am a Life mage, certified Grandmaster. These are my students, and I would like your consent for them to assist me."

The middle-aged woman bobbed a quick nod. "Yes, please. We fully expect she'll lose the pregnancy, but if you can save her..."

There... he had it. Jake 'saw' the wounds, saw the damage all the way through the woman's body... both as individual tissue layers but also as a whole. Her body fought to heal itself, fought to save the life it harbored. He almost spoke, almost made a pithy comment about doing more than just saving the would-be mother, but he remembered something his adoptive mother had said once: Always under-promise and overdeliver.

While Gerald called Emilia over to experience once again how he used the Life Sphere to heal, Jake hastily threw together a framework of what he wanted to achieve in his mind. He was no medical professional, but he could feel the damage done to the woman and her child. With his new understanding of how his power worked, it seemed like it would be so easy to heal them... both her and her child.

He closed his eyes as he focused on the energy around him. He fed a tiny trickle of his power into the world, creating a connection between himself and that energy, then reversed the flow. Drawing it inside and feeding it to his framework.

It didn't take long—no more than a few seconds at most—for the framework to feel like it overflowed with power, and Jake released it, pushing it out of him back along the pathways of the energy he felt flowing into him.

The non-mage doctors jumped back, each making a startled exclamation as they jerked implements away from a wound that closed itself before their very eyes. They both turned to Gerald, seeing that he had yet to touch the woman as all Life mages had to do to heal anyone.

Just as the doctors drew breath to speak, Jake gasped and staggered backward until he collided with the wall. Sweat erupted from his forehead and flowed down his face like a massive waterfall. Every inch of his being felt like it was literally on fire. Like he was a tiny extension cord trying to pull three-phase power. He didn't understand why he wasn't melting... or self-immolating.

Emilia was by his side in an instant, laying the back of her hand on his forehead. "Ger... I mean, Doctor Wainwright... he's burning up! I've never felt someone this hot."

One of the nurses grabbed a laser thermometer and stepped close enough to get an accurate reading. She frowned. "That... that can't be right. He'd be dead."

"What does it say?" Gerald asked.

"One seventy-three."

While everyone else jabbered, Jake slowly felt the heat fading. After a few more moments, it was enough for him to stand upright under his own power. "Check it again, please."

"One fifteen. How are you conscious? A fever like that should have you out of your mind."

Jake didn't answer. He just gave her a soft half-smile. "Check it again, please."

"Ninety-nine. This is insane."

Not caring at that point, Jake looked to Gerald and gave the man a wry, almost self-deprecating smile. "Well... guess we know what I need to practice now."

The two non-mage doctors shared a look between themselves before the woman spoke. "Doctor Wainwright, what is he talking about?"

Gerald shook his head. "Later. Let's get an ultrasound in here. We do have a patient, after all."

When they turned back to the reason they were all in the room, it was apparent that she was waking up. The non-mage doctors shared another look before the man said, "How is that possible? She was under full anesthetic. She shouldn't be waking up yet."

Jake didn't realize how loopy he felt until he spoke again. "I guess it purged the anesthetic when I healed her, since it was foreign to her system."

Everyone in the room turned to stare at him in varying stages of disbelief.

"Hello," a soft voice interjected. "What's going on? I lost the baby, didn't I?"

The focus snapped back to the woman on the exam table, and Gerald quickly stepped to her side. "We just sent for an ultrasound. We'll soon know for sure... okay?"

She nodded, looking a little loopy herself. "It doesn't feel like I lost the baby, but I guess I wouldn't know. Or maybe it's like that phantom limb syndrome I've read about. Does that happen when a woman loses a pregnancy, too?"

There was a quick double-knock on the door, followed by its opening to admit a pair of people with a mobile ultrasound machine. One of them pulled Gerald off to the side while the other worked to set up the machine and prep the young woman.

Jake was just able to hear her almost frantic whisper. "You need to get out there, Doctor Wainwright. It's crazy."

Gerald frowned and leaned close to her ear, but Jake still heard his whispered question. "What is it? What happened?"

"Not sure, but it sounded like everyone in the ER suddenly healed."

Gerald turned back to the patient and who Jake assumed to be sister and mother. "If you will excuse me for a moment, I need to check something while the techs handle the ultrasound."

He then pivoted on his heel and grabbed Jake by the arm, almost dragging him out of the exam room...

...and into pandemonium.

Everywhere they looked, people were talking or cheering or shouting. Some hugged doctors or nurses. A few kissed them. It didn't seem to matter that the medical personnel were just as bewildered as the would-be patients.

Gerald pulled Jake over to the nurses' station, with Emilia close behind them, and confronted the charge nurse. "What's going on out here?"

She looked up and just shook her head. "Damned if I know, Doc. Everyone just suddenly healed. It didn't seem to matter if it was a cold, a broken bone, or what. I've never seen anything like it."

Gerald turned to Jake. His expression cycled through exasperation, accusation, and disbelief almost faster than the eye could follow.

Jake didn't know any better than Gerald and simply offered a half-hearted shrug. "Oops?"

Shaking his head, Gerald stepped far enough away from the

nurses' station so she couldn't overhear and turned to Emilia. "Get him out of here... before people start asking questions. I'll get a cab or rideshare once I've sorted out this mess."

IT WAS ALMOST midnight before Gerald returned to the Grove. He looked half-dead as he entered the house and found Bianca, Isabel, Jake, and Emilia all waiting for him. He didn't say a word as he went straight to the wet bar, poured three fingers of single-malt Scotch, and tossed it back like he was doing shots at a college frat house. He looked across the room at Jake, staring at him in silence for several moments, then poured another three fingers and tossed that back too.

He placed the glass on the counter near the sink and went to sit in his favorite chair. He still hadn't said a word.

The silence extended past the point of becoming awkward until it became apparent Bianca had had enough. She almost glared at him. "Well? What happened?"

"He healed the first three floors of the hospital... at least the sections of the floors centered on the ER. It seemed contained to a sphere with a radius of about a hundred and fifty yards. There was guy up on Two who went into cardiac arrest at almost the same time as whatever Jake did. The code cart had just come through the door when the patient jerked back to life as if nothing had happened. People are going to be talking about this for *years*, Jake. They won't talk about anything **but this** at the hospital for the next few months."

"So we must teach him focus and control," Isabel interjected. "Understandable... and a process I remember very well from my own youth."

No one seemed to know what to say to that.

Emilia looked hesitant as she lifted her head. "How was the stabbing victim?"

Gerald snorted a laugh. "What stabbing victim? If they hadn't taken pictures when she first came in, there'd be no proof it ever happened. She's fine. The baby appears to be fine. No scarring. No signs that give any indication she won't be able to have another child if she wants. It's like it never happened."

Emilia's expression betrayed her joy. "I'm so glad she didn't lose the baby."

"By all rights, she should have. Not even all the Life Grandmasters working together could've saved that baby. I probably could have saved her uterus and reproductive ability... probably..." Gerald's voice trailed off as he stared at Jake. "And I thought your Ferris wheel of Spheres was the most amazing thing I'd ever seen. Do you know what happened?"

Jake shrugged. "The closest I can come to figuring it out is that I didn't exclude everyone else from my focus. That's the only thing I can think of. So, instead of just healing that woman and her baby, I must have flared the healing out in a sphere like you said. That's probably why the fever hit me. I'm not used to channeling that much power."

"Why didn't your blood glucose drop, though? It always has before."

"I didn't use *my* energy this time. I just acted as a conduit."

Gerald and Bianca both blinked their lack of understanding.

Jake sighed. "That's what my birth parents said I was doing wrong. Sorcerers don't power their... designs... or maybe effects? Anyway, they don't power what they do with their own energy, like mages. They draw in energy from all around them and use that to do whatever it is."

"Your birth parents?" Bianca's question was almost a gasp. "When did you meet them?"

"While Emilia and I were inside the stone." Jake grimaced. "Well... when our awareness or consciousness or something was inside the stone. I don't really understand it, honestly, but the stone is a kind of spirit vault. Their spirits are in there, but there's no passage of time. To them, it's like they just sent me away. They... well, my birth mother was a little shocked to see me grown."

Bianca just shook her head. "Unbelievable. I've never heard of such a thing. How did you even have time to talk with them? We weren't inside the house for more than a minute before you came in all fired up for Gerald to take you to the hospital in spite of your pending date with Fiona."

"I don't know anything about that. If I had to guess, it was like we talked with them for a half-hour or so."

Gerald turned to Isabel. "Have you ever heard of anything like this?"

Isabel was very slow to respond. "Not that I am aware, no."

"So... what do we do now?" Emilia asked.

Gerald snorted. "I don't know about the rest of you, but I'm going to bed. I am beyond exhausted."

Bianca stood as he did and left with him, and it wasn't long before those who remained went in search of their rest as well.

THIRTY-ONE

Wainwright Grove
Hornbeam, Illinois
26 May 2025, 8:35am

JAKE SAT at the kitchen table after breakfast. His mind swirled around and over everything that had changed for him in the past... well... eighteen hours, really. He now understood why accessing the Spheres had always been so draining for him. A part of him wanted to rush out and try all kinds of things... see what all he could do with his new understanding. But that was a very small part. It was the eager, happy child who gave not a thought toward consequences.

He didn't feel that he was in any special danger, nothing new anyway. He still wanted to stay under the Magocracy's radar, keep them from being aware of him for as long as possible. It was probably too much to hope that he would 'hide' from them forever, but the better he was at being a sorcerer when they finally learned of him, the better his overall situation would be.

A part of him even wished he could somehow go back to being

just Jake, but he knew that was impossible. Besides, as registered familiars, the jaguars were safe. He could keep them with him. That might not be the case if he could go back to being just a twenty-something stocker at the town's grocery store. The government seemed to frown on random people keeping large predators as pets... even though they weren't technically pets.

It didn't take long for his mind to settle on the core thought that seemed to color everything he did lately. What was he supposed to do with his life? Knitting and bridge didn't really seem all that satisfying to him. It never had, really, but it definitely didn't now.

But he felt sure he wasn't the only person struggling with the question of what to do with his or her life. He simply had exponentially more options than most, and that didn't even take into account his supposed lifespan. That was something else to ask his parents about... well... his birth parents. Was it true that he was functionally immortal?

Isabel entered from the back patio and crossed the room to sit at the table across from him. She watched him eat in silence for several moments. "While we wait for the griffon to reveal itself again, I see no reason not to continue your training."

"What about the marshals? Don't they expect you to be out there hunting it?"

Isabel shrugged. "Griffons are among the oldest of the hybrid races. While this specific griffon may be young, the race as a whole are master hunters. Unless we are fortunate enough to obtain a feather or blood or something that will allow us to track it magically, it is very unlikely we'll find it before it's ready to be found. If they want to waste time and money scouring the countryside and be horribly out of position when it strikes again, let them. The griffon will reveal itself when it wants to reveal itself, and very little will make it change its mind."

That was a... well... unfortunate situation. Jake had hoped Isabel had a way to settle the matter in short order, but his mind went back to another topic. "You said last night that you remembered learning focus and control. May I ask about that?"

"You think breathing fire or appearing human is a natural reflex for us?" Isabel gave him a half-smile. "Controlling one's flame is all about focus and control, and I practiced until I was one of the best. My flame can be anything from the full cone of fiery death down to a superheated line of flame whiter than anything you've ever seen."

"So, when you control your flame like that, it takes all the heat of the full cone and packs it into that line? Is that why it's so much hotter than the cone?"

Isabel smiled. "Very good. Yes, that's exactly why. Don't expect to apply a lot of science to it, though. Dragons are as much magical as natural creatures, and magic tends to defy all of the humans' scientific laws. But... come with me to the backyard. It is time to begin your training anew."

Jake pushed himself to his feet and followed Isabel. He almost couldn't believe his eyes when he stepped through the patio doors. In the grass beyond the patio, a field of candles sat atop small pedestals. There had to be fifty of them, at least.

"What is all this?"

Isabel stopped at the edge of the patio and turned to face him. A mischievous smile curled her lips. "I want you to light a candle. It cannot be one along the edge closest to us. Choose which candle you will light and light it... without melting the candle or any around it."

At first, Jake didn't see the challenge. Anyone could light a candle, right? His attention settled on a candle near the center of the mass that had a blue dot on it. He didn't know why that candle out of all the rest had a blue dot on it, but it made for a handy point to focus.

He rolled his shoulders and stretched his back and arms in an effort to clear his mind. Then, he brought his fireball framework to the forefront of his mind and modified it to deliver just a trickle of heat. He wasn't sure how much heat it would take to light the candle, but he figured it was better to undershoot the mark than overshoot it... at least in this case.

As he had at the hospital, Jake pushed a tiny trickle of his energy into the world around him and then pulled that trickle back and a hair more that he fed into the framework. Then, it was just the small matter of applying the framework to his chosen candle.

Nothing happened. At least... nothing *seemed* to happen.

Jake thought he saw a tendril of smoke rise up from the candle's wick, but he was far enough away and the maybe-tendril of smoke was so small that he couldn't be sure. He still had the framework applied to the candle wick, so he sent more power from the world around him into it.

A *poof* of fire flared up like a charcoal briquette slathered in lighter fluid. The heat was so intense that his target candle and every other one around it for two rows out became puddles of wax.

Isabel regarded him in silence for a moment. "Well, it seems you have the focus half down. We just need to work on your control."

"I don't understand. I would've sworn I only pushed a trickle of power into my framework after the first attempt."

"And that is why we practice with wax candles. When you can light one—and only one—candle, we will move on to the next exercise."

Jake sighed. "I'm going to hate candles by the end of this, aren't I?"

Isabel offered a slight smile. "There's no way to know, but I've had a very personal dislike of hay bales since the time I was a hatchling for much the same reason. But fear not. I purchased several cases of candles. I need only a few moments to prepare for your next attempt."

~

WAINWRIGHT GROVE
Hornbeam, Illinois

26 May 2025, 5:35pm

JAKE LOUNGED in a pool a short distance from Gerald and Bianca's house. As with the house, Bianca had grown the pool, and whether it was the sun or some other mechanism he hadn't bothered to identify, the water was at the perfect temperature... warm enough to enjoy and cool enough to soothe after a hot day.

A tall tree shaded the portion of the pool Jake chose, and he rested his head on the shore, submerged up to the base of his neck in the water. Crickets and other insects buzzed or chirped nearby, accompanied by the occasional birdsong.

Footfalls and slight waves pulled him out of his mindless relaxation, and Jake lifted his head as he opened his eyes. Emilia stood with one leg in the pool up to her knee. She wore a green, string bikini and a playful smile when he finally focused on her face.

The water in the pool was almost as clear as crystal, so Jake knew his swim trunks were visible even if the water slightly distorted the image.

"Hi. Did you decide to come soak?"

Emilia's expression flitted between a confident smirk and a playful grin. "And what if I did?"

Jake simply shrugged. "No man in his right mind would complain about such an attractive woman sharing a pool with him."

Now fully in the pool, she lifted her feet off the bottom and swam the short distance to reach Jake. Before he had time to process what was happening, Emilia pressed herself against him and gave him a quick peck on his cheek, then regarded him with a raised eyebrow and a serious, stone-like expression. "I should hope not, Mister Adams."

For the span of a finger-snap, Jake feared he'd said or done something to make her mad or hurt her, but before he could even think about asking, she broke the moment with a happy, mischievous laugh and snuggled into his side. The water lapped closer to her chin, but she didn't seem to mind.

Considering how she pressed against him, Jake didn't mind, either.

OVER THE NEXT FEW DAYS, Isabel created a course somewhere in the Grove that Jake would have to navigate through, using focus and control. It was slow going and frustrating at times. More than once, Jake wanted just to pull the power for his framework from within himself, since he **knew** he had ultimate focus and control with that. He'd already demonstrated it, but it always came back to needing glucose tablets to offset the energy usage.

Plus, if he was honest with himself, he wanted to impress his birth parents. He had visited them several times since learning how to access their spirit vault and shared his progress with them. Oftentimes, they asked how his practice was going before he had the chance to mention it.

He hadn't asked his adoptive parents to go with him into the spirit vault yet. He was a tad worried that something might go wrong, since they were plain humans without any trace of arcane affinities. It was something he'd have to test. Maybe Mike would enjoy meeting his birth parents. It probably wasn't fair to his best friend to use him as a guinea pig, but if he explained the full situation to Mike and did his best to help his friend make an informed decision, it might work.

In between her studies and his, Jake enjoyed a handful of dates with Emilia. He'd never enjoyed spending time with a girl... no, woman... even close to his age before, and the experience was a very pleasant surprise. They were both in their mid-twenties, but it took effort sometimes to remember that Emilia might prefer 'woman' or 'young woman' to 'girl.'

Either way, her company was a definite improvement to his life.

The griffon had either gone to ground or gone back to wherever it called home. There had been no more attacks since the incident in Oklahoma, and sometimes, Jake couldn't help but wonder what the deal was with that. The griffon had made an almost straight line from Los Angeles to Oklahoma but then... just... stopped.

If these creatures were as intelligent as Isabel claimed they were, there was a reason it stopped. But whether Jake or anyone else would ever **know** that reason was anyone's guess. He didn't like the mystery. Then again, he didn't imagine the Marshals liked it any more than he did. Upwards of twenty people had died because of the griffon—assuming it was the same griffon and also assuming that all the incidents were indeed griffon attacks—and something like that going unsolved never sat well with anyone.

But Isabel was adamant that there was no way to track the griffon unless it chose to be tracked, so the whole situation was in a kind of limbo.

~

CITY PARK
Hornbeam, Illinois
16 June 2025, 8:53pm

JOLENE LOVED TO RUN. She had been a track star in high school, and she kept up her regimen even after graduation... unlike so many of her former teammates. She enjoyed running at any time of the day, but especially preferred the twilight. Something about the slow transition from day to night appealed to her. Energized her.

Her feet struck a steady cadence as she ran the jogging path that weaved through the town's park. It was a familiar trail, but that was fine with her. It freed her mind to concentrate on—or consider—other matters.

Like Jake Adams.

She hadn't seen much of Jake lately. Mister Hendricks at the town's grocery store said Jake had quit when he told the young man that he'd finally hired three stockers to replace him. It was a bit of a bummer, since the store's parking lot was the one place she'd been able to see him... if only from a distance... but she supposed she should be happy for him if he moved on to bigger and better things.

He'd always been the odd kid in school. Always quiet, maybe shy. He helped anyone who needed it, but there was always something different about him. A strange, unsettling feeling whenever she was too close to him. It was... well... she'd never felt anything like it with anyone else. Not even those classmates who had manifested as mages. Cori Andrews manifested as a Tri-Sphere, and Jolene had never felt anything from her like what she felt from Jake.

That might have been one of the reasons she was so interested in Jake.

But maybe the implicit challenge, too.

Every guy in town within five years of her age—up or down—chased her skirt. Every single one... except Jake. He wasn't gay; she knew that much. But he had never displayed even the slightest interest in her or even any of the 'friends' that always seemed to glom onto her.

She knew they only hung around her because they hoped to snag one of her 'cast-offs.' Probably not the best strategy for long-term romance, but who was she to judge?

None of it helped, though. She wanted Jake. At least... she **thought** she wanted Jake. But she didn't see any way to get him. Especially since he'd effectively disappeared from town. No one knew—or would tell her—what had happened to him, not even his best friend Mike.

Just as she made the turn at the top of the small hill that made up the center of the park, a *whoosh* of air rushed over her just before she heard something heavy hit the ground behind her. She slowed and turned.

Then froze.

A massive creature stood on the jogging path behind her. The head and wings and front legs of an eagle with the body and hind legs and tail of a lion. Her head came up to the base of its neck... if she was lucky. And she couldn't tell if it looked at her like food or a toy.

It lunged, rearing up on its hind legs, and she screamed as its bony talons wrapped around her arms at the shoulders. Its *scree* drowned out her scream as it leaped and flapped its wings, lifting both of them into the air. The last thing she saw as darkness took her was a piece of paper falling to the jogging path.

CHAPTER
THIRTY-TWO

Wainwright Grove
Hornbeam, Illinois
17 June 2025, 8:30am

IT WAS another day of practice with Isabel, and he wanted to look forward to it. He always had thus far. But something unsettled him just enough that whatever it was felt like a thorn in his foot or a sore tooth. It gave him no peace at all and made simply enjoying the morning a challenge.

The knock at the door barely registered. He didn't even give it any thought as he wracked his mind for the source of his disquiet, but Bianca's voice pulled him from his thoughts.

"Jake, Mike Stannyk is here to see you."

He frowned, blinking his confusion. "Mike? But he works today."

Mike stepped into his field of view, dressed in his police uniform. He held his hat in both hands. There was something in his expression that... he looked sad. Worried.

"What's going on, Mike?"

Mike pursed his lips and looked at the floor for a moment before he met Jake's eyes again. "We have reason to believe Jolene Chesterfield was taken last night during her evening run in the park."

Jake blinked again at the non-sequitur. "Yeah... that's unfortunate, but why come to me?"

"A morning jogger found a crumpled note laying along the side of the trail near Mercy's Hill. I was first on the scene and snapped a picture. The crime scene tech said it was written in blood, and they've taken a sample to see if it's Jolene's blood." Mike fell silent and looked at the floor again for a few moments. "Jakey, whoever— or whatever—took her claims he will feast on her if the sorcerer does not meet him in two days at the trailhead a few miles northeast of town. I... I'm sorry, buddy. I can't... I just *can't* hide the note. It's already logged into evidence, and a handful of people have seen it."

Jake waved that away. "I'm not worried about that. If we're careful, I can handle it without revealing that I'm the sorcerer. Maybe. I hope."

Isabel entered through the patio doors and read the room in a glance. "What is wrong?"

"Someone took a young woman who graduated high school with us. They left a note demanding that the sorcerer meet them at a trailhead near town or they'll feast on her."

Isabel's eyes narrowed. "Do you have the note?"

Mike withdrew his phone from its pouch on his duty belt. "I have a picture. The note's already with the crime scene people."

Isabel accepted the phone. Jake could see her eyes scan from the top of the phone to the bottom, and her expression slowly shifted into an angry scowl. "This is the griffon. It has to be. But how did it learn of you?"

Jake shrugged. "How am I supposed to know? I've been laying low, here at the grove, just like you wanted."

Isabel started pacing, tapping the tip of her nose with a fingertip. "I could make myself look like you, but if the griffon has scented you, it would know immediately that I am not you."

Jake shrugged. "I think the only thing we can do is for me to meet the griffon... or whomever, if it isn't actually the griffon."

Isabel stopped and turned to face him. "No, it's the griffon. I've seen their style of writing before. If you had seen the note, it wouldn't be difficult for you to realize that the author of it took great care not to puncture or rip the page but was unsuccessful at times. That is because the author wrote by dipping the tip of a claw in blood and dragging it across the paper."

"Huh... okay. I guess that would be the only way they could write." Jake shrugged. "But that still doesn't change the fact that I need to be the one who goes to the meet."

The jaguars padded into the room through the open patio doors. They crossed the room to stand in front of Jake and looked up at him.

*Maybe so, but that doesn't mean you have to go alone. *

Bandit's mental voice was the most mature and serious Jake had ever heard.

*Bandit's right, Jake. We're going with you. We'll locate the young woman, and one of us can lead her away while the other helps you ambush the griffon. *

Jake wasn't sure he liked that idea. He was used to operating from the mindset that he needed to watch over and take care of the jaguars. As he considered it, there in the moment, he realized he still thought of them as the cubs he'd rescued. On the one side, that wasn't fair to them; he certainly knew he didn't enjoy the rare occasions when his parents still treated him like someone who was their responsibility. But on the other side, they were his closest friends, aside from Mike. He wasn't too sure he liked the idea of them risking themselves. Even for such a good cause.

Still...

Everyone had to grow up sometime... and... he needed to start treating the jaguars like the adults they were.

In the end, Jake smiled and nodded, dropping to one knee and pulling first Bandit and then Smokey into a big hug. They endured his affection in silence, which reminded him of something.

When he stood, he turned to Bianca. "Is there any way to give them the ability to communicate with others beside me? As it stands right now, I 'hear' them using what I guess is the Mind Sphere, but no one else can 'hear' them. I can also use the Mind Sphere to communicate with them silently."

Bianca blew out a breath as she leaned her head back. It was apparent to Jake she went into deep thought. Everyone waited until she brought her attention back to Jake and shrugged. "I... I just don't know, Jake. It's not something that nature magic is normally used for... at least as far as I know. This might be something where you'd want to ask your birth parents, especially since we have so much time."

"Okay, then. I know what I'm doing next."

Mike raised a hand like they were still in school. "Hang on... mind passing back over that one for the slow kids? How is Jake supposed to ask his birth parents anything?"

Jake grinned. "Mom and Dad were holding a few things for me from when they adopted me. I can explain everything later, but basically, my birth parents sent me forward through time to save me from everyone hunting sorcerers. And then... they stored their spirits in a specially prepared spirit vault. I've visited them several times over the last couple weeks."

By the time Jake finished speaking, Mike simply stared at him, his expression flickering between disbelief, astonishment, and excitement. "Can you take other people with you?"

Jake just grinned. "Sure. Wanna go?"

"Now, what kind of question is that? Of course I want to go."

Jake stood and motioned for Mike to follow him. "I have the spirit vault up in my bedroom. There are enough chairs up there, or we can use the patio or some other place."

Mike waggled his eyebrows at Jake, then broke into a grin. "We're going to play in your room, just like when we were kids, huh?"

"Has anyone ever told you that you're a rascal?"

"Many times... and usually worse names."

They situated themselves with the stone on a small end table in front of them. Jake used a lancet—like those used by diabetics to test their blood glucose—to prick his finger and swabbed his blood on the stone as he took Mike's hand in his. The engravings flared bright, and when the light faded, Jake and Mike did not seem to be in his bedroom at the Grove anymore.

Mike shot to his feet and slowly turned, taking in the atrium around them. His expression reminded Jake of a giddy child. "Oh, wow, Jakey... this is... this is incredible."

"I'm glad you like it." Claudia said from the doorway to their 'home.'

Mike spun on his heel, his eyes wide, as Jake stood and moved to his side.

Jake clapped his hand on Mike's shoulder. "Mother, allow me to introduce Mike Stannyk. He's my oldest friend, and he's extremely interested in all things crafter-related, specifically everything about mages. Mike, this is my birth mother, Claudia Aternius."

Mike shot Jake a surprised expression before turning back to Claudia. "Aternius, ma'am? You're from one of Rome's patrician families?"

Claudia smiled and nodded once. "Why, yes... we are. I am both pleased and impressed that you recognized the name, given the amount of time that has passed. It unsettled us a little once we truly understood what year it is for you now. We were not prepared for *that* much time to have passed outside the spirit vault."

"So... if you're of the Aternius family, what's Jake's proper name?"

Claudia frowned for just a moment. "I would argue that his proper name is the one he has always known, but his birth name is Gaius Aternius Magius."

Mike grinned. "That's so awesome. I love it."

Jake thought Claudia's expression was far more of a polite smile than one of true agreement or commiseration, but he wasn't sure it mattered much in the long run. She turned to him while Mike reveled in the birth name. "And what brings you to us today, my son?"

"A griffon has abducted someone Mike and I went to high school with. The jaguars I've told you about want to come with me and help, but I'm the only one who can 'hear' them. Is there anything we can do about that?"

Claudia's expression turned thoughtful for a moment. "Do you want them to be able to speak or simply communicate with anyone?"

Jake shrugged. "Why not both? I mean, if it's possible. I can think of situations where having the option of speaking verbally or mentally or both would be very useful."

"Yes... good point. Come. Let's discuss it with your father. I can think of a couple options, but he would both enjoy consulting on the question and be able to provide the best answer."

THE WORLD RETURNED in a rush of light, and Jake leaned back against his seat as Mike leaped to his feet and cheered.

"Oh, man, Jakey... that was... it... that was incredible. Your birth parents are so awesome. I loved meeting them. Thank you for that."

Jake just grinned. "You're welcome, Mike. Wanna go see if I can do this?"

"You seriously have to ask?"

Jake grabbed his colored pencils and notebook where he kept his notes and thoughts on his frameworks and then led his friend downstairs, where it seemed like no one had moved from when they left. The Wainwrights, Emilia, and Isabel were all used to the fast turn-around by that point, and Jake went straight to the jaguars.

"Would you like to be able to speak to more people than just me?"

They both nodded to answer 'yes.'

"Then, come with me outside. I have the framework in mind for what we need to do, but I can't promise it won't be pain-free. We're basically modifying your larynxes and brains. But my birth parents showed me how to include a failsafe so that you won't be harmed, and nothing will happen if it's not going to work."

The jaguars stood and padded over to the patio doors and turned back to look at him as if asking why he hadn't opened the doors yet. Jake just smiled and crossed the room. He opened the doors for them, and they led a procession out to the patio.

Gerald caught up with Jake. "Do you mind if we tag along?"

"Of course not, but I can't promise there will be much of a show."

"Oh, that's fine," Bianca interjected. "We just want to watch you make history again."

Jake snorted. "Gee, thanks. No pressure, then."

He sat in one of the patio chairs and flipped to the first unoccupied page in the notebook his birth parents and Isabel called his grimoire, then double-checked that it was indeed the first unused page. He hated skipping a page when they tried to stick together.

Then, he sketched out the framework his parents drew for him on piece of slate with chalk. His already-impressive memory had only improved since he began working with his power, and it wasn't long before he recorded the framework in its entirety. He looked it over a couple moments longer to be sure he had indeed recreated it accurately before turning to the blank page on the right side to jot down his notes, thoughts, and insights about the framework. It surprised him a bit that new thoughts had popped into his mind while he worked on the framework.

As soon as he finished his notes, he closed the notebook and leaned back against his chair, closing his eyes and concentrating on the framework in his mind. Turning it around and over, looking at it from every angle to make sure he wasn't missing anything. It didn't feel like he was.

He nodded once and opened his eyes, focusing on his jaguars. "Well, kids, are you ready to finally be heard?"

Both bobbed their heads in silent nods.

DAWN OF THE SORCERER

Jake focused on the framework in his mind and pushed a tiny thread of power into the world just to establish a more concrete connection. He then reversed the push to a pull and sent the incoming power into the framework. He had absolutely learned his lesson with healing at the hospital and made a deliberate, conscious choice to exclude everyone from the framework *except* the jaguars. It took a few moments for the framework to feel saturated with power and ready, but once it did, Jake gave it another quick once-over and released it to mold reality to his will.

The jaguars collapsed to the patio pavers.

In that first second, terror tore through Jake's emotions that he'd killed two of his closest friends. He closed his eyes and reached out to them with what he still thought of as his Life Sphere, assessing them like he would a patient in the ER.

Then...

Relief.

They were still alive. Their heartbeats felt strong. Everything about them felt one-hundred-percent healthy. In fact, the feeling Jake had from what he sensed made him think of having to reboot a computer to install new hardware.

Another minute or so passed, before there was any movement or reaction.

Smokey opened her eyes first, and she looked up at Jake, her expression full of feline adoration. "Th... thank y... you, Jake."

Everyone—from Gerald to Mike—gasped at Smokey's first spoken words.

Jake just beamed. "The way my birth parents explained it, I merely gave you the ability to speak. You'll need to practice, but before long, it should be second nature to you."

By then, Bandit was awake once more, and both jaguars stood and took the few steps necessary to reach Jake. They rubbed against him, their traditional method for expressing gratitude, and Jake slipped off the chair and pulled them both into a hug.

After a few moments, he broke the hug and returned to his seat. Bandit looked up at him. "Y... yes. Thank you, Jake."

Jake looked forward to surprising his parents the next time he took the jaguars to visit. He couldn't wait to see their expressions when one or both of them said hello the first time.

Mike stared at the jaguars, slowly shaking his head as his expression flitting between amazement and wonder.

Smokey padded up to him and rubbed against his leg before backing up enough to look up at him. "Thank you for being Jake's friend."

"You're welcome, Smokey. He's a good friend to me, too." Then, Mike's expression blanked as he pivoted to face me. "Jake... we might have a problem. The abduction is on record as an active case. How are we going to handle that? I mean... none of you are active law enforcement."

Isabel stepped forward. "It won't be an issue at all. I am already working the case at the behest of the United States Marshals, and between the deputy marshals assigned to the case and myself, I'm sure we can explain things to the chief of police."

CITY Hall
Hornbeam, Illinois
17 June 2025, 10:50am

JAKE FOLLOWED Isabel and Deputy Marshals Gaines and Alvarez up the steps of Hornbeam's city hall. They had an eleven o'clock appointment with both the mayor and the chief of police to discuss Jolene's abduction. Like most of the buildings in and around Hornbeam, City Hall was less than thirty years old. It was built shortly after the town incorporated, following the restoration and resettlement efforts in the wake of the Independence Day attacks.

It was a modest building for the role it served, brick with marble columns supporting a portico. The city's police department stood right next door, and the two buildings shared a parking lot.

Jake wasn't sure he should be attending this meeting. After all, he had no official standing in the investigation at all. Isabel insisted. The marshals looked somewhat askance as well, but neither of them seemed willing say anything.

Mike met them right inside the door and introduced his captain, and together, they led the group to the conference room where the mayor and police chief waited.

Kit Donaldson was one of the first children born in Hornbeam, and he was less than a year into his first term as mayor. He and Jake had come up through the grades together and graduated in the same class. Tall and with a lithe runner's build, he seemed possessed by boundless energy. He never walked when he could fast walk, and he jogged to work every day.

Marissa Sykes—the chief of police—was almost his exact opposite. Barely taller than five-nothing, she had the average build of a middle-aged woman who spent just enough time in a gym to maintain her health and physical capability. Her bright blue eyes, natural red hair, and heart-shaped face belied the stern demeanor she had cultivated across her twenty-plus years in law enforcement.

They both looked up when Mike and his captain opened the door, and Kit grinned at seeing Jake trailing at the end of the procession. Being the consummate politician, he greeted each person in turn until he shared a medieval-style forearm clasp with Jake and Mike, a happy smile brightening his features.

Once everyone sat around the conference table, Marissa fired the first shot. "Would someone care to explain to me why we have someone who is not law enforcement or civil government in this meeting?"

Outside of the office, Jake had an excellent relationship with Marissa Sykes and her family, and he didn't take any offense to her apparent attitude and demeanor. He knew she drew a very hard line on duties and responsibilities versus private life.

"Jake Adams is my apprentice," Isabel replied without hesitation. "As I am the marshals' escalation call for these types of cases, so is he until such time as he completes his apprenticeship."

Marissa turned to me, raising an eyebrow in silent question. Then, her expression shifted into the 'O' of realized understanding. "You stopped the bank robbery as part of your mage manifestation."

"Yes, ma'am."

She nodded once. "Very well. Let us proceed."

Isabel and the marshals shared a look, Deputy Marshal Gaines nodding to her. Isabel turned to the mayor and chief. "The abduction of Jolene Chesterfield is the latest incident in a case stretching back to Los Angeles. There have been a string of murders, with the most recent attack leaving four victims in a convenience store in Oklahoma. The responsible party is a griffon."

Both Kit and Marissa blinked. It wasn't *quite* synchronized, but it was close. Kit spoke. "Griffon? You mean…"

"Yes, the mythical race that is a hybrid between an eagle and lion."

Marissa frowned. "Why haven't we heard of them before?"

"There have never been very many of them. If the world at large knew of them—or the other hybrid races—they would be on the endangered species list, based on their numbers alone. As to why you haven't heard of them, the hybrid races prefer to avoid interactions with the other inhabitants of this world. They have never been received well, and that experience has taught them to distrust people."

Kit leaned back against his seat. "Why is it active now? Are griffon attacks common?"

"They are not common. Very rare in fact. The last active griffon attacks I can remember occurred in the early 1700's in Europe."

"1700's?" Marissa repeated. "And you remember them? That makes me think you're not human… or at least, not entirely human."

Isabel gave the woman a noncommittal smile. "Chief Sykes, the world is a far more complex and wondrous place than even the mages know, but in short, no. I am not human, and no, you have no need to know what I am. It is not germane to the matter at hand."

Kit glanced at Jake and looked like he was about to speak but settled down.

Marissa drew a deep breath before slowly exhaling and squaring her shoulders. "So, what do you need from my department?"

"Nothing. Your officers are not equipped to face a griffon, and the note it left was not for you. Mark the case as turned over to the Arcane Division of the United States Marshals and give it no further thought, please."

Marissa scanned those at the table with her eyes in silence before turning to the mayor. "As much as I want to say that Jolene's case is our responsibility, Mr. Mayor, I see the wisdom in stepping back and letting those with proper experience handle this."

Kit nodded once. "Then, that's what we'll do. You'll take care of handing the case off to the marshals?"

"Yes, of course."

Kit turned his focus back to the rest of us. "Can we be of any further assistance?"

Isabel shook her head. "No, I don't believe so. Thank you for your time."

Everyone stood, and Mike and his captain led them back out of the building.

THIRTY-THREE

Jolene wasn't sure how long it had been dark, but she was *mostly* certain it was the second day after that... that... thing had taken her. She felt oddly conflicted about her captors... and yes... she was also certain there was more than one of the creatures. She would have no problem killing the one that took her nor would she miss it if she did. It was always cold and aloof—borderline hostile—every time it came around her. The one that made sure she ate, though, seemed younger and... well... nicer. There was a faint color pattern in its feathers and fur that marked it as a different creature from the one that took her from the park, and it seemed slightly smaller, too. She knew without knowing *how* she knew that the one who made sure she had food wasn't strong enough—or maybe just not old enough —to carry her like she had been carried to this abandoned shack in the remains of the national forest north of Hornbeam.

She fought her instincts to smile with all her willpower when the smaller one stayed and cooed while she ran her hand along its head and neck. The creature became absolutely kittenish when she stroked her hand along its spine.

She'd not seen much of the shack, even though she knew her

room had an exterior wall with a window looking out to the forest. She'd seen more than one of these fearsome creatures pass the window and pause long enough to regard her with a look in its eyes that communicated only too well that they'd just as soon eat her as keep her alive.

Any time she moved or one of the creatures entered the room, the floor creaked and cracked alarmingly. Dust sometimes cascaded down from the clapboards that made up the ceiling overhead, and the cot that passed for a bed barely held its own weight, let alone hers.

If she had her choice, it wasn't the type of room she wanted to die in.

Heh... she didn't **want** to die at all.

But the longer she sat in the room with no hint of a rescue, the more she accepted that her death was far, far closer than she had ever considered.

Those thoughts led to other, similar thoughts... and the inevitable navel-gazing as she considered her short life. In school, she'd toyed with the boys who pursued her, and later, she continued it with the men, playing them against each other. At the time, she'd enjoyed the power it gave her. In a world that accepted crafters as fellow citizens, little Jolene had no power to speak of... except the ages-old power of an attractive woman.

Sitting there in the dust-filled darkness, she realized all too late just how poorly she'd wielded that power.

So many men sought her attention, but precious few of them liked her... let alone loved her. With a sigh, she regarded how the faint moonlight illuminated the window and cracks in the clapboard walls, highlighting motes of dust drifting slowly toward the floor. And... she confronted the fact that hardly anyone would miss her.

A single tear escaped her iron will. This was not how she'd pictured her life ending. Not at all.

Just as she was about to give in and let herself start an extended cry, she heard something heavy hit the ground outside her room.

Mere heartbeats later, something heavy hit the wall, and for the briefest moment, she thought she saw the wall bow inward with the hit.

She shot a fearful glance to the door.

Nothing.

With the greatest caution, with all her senses focused on the door, she crept toward the window as silently as she could. Right before she approached arms' reach, she crouched down and slowed her pace even more.

It seemed like forever before she arrived at the wall, and she was sure everything around her easily heard her runaway heart. She hooked her fingers on the edge of the windowsill for balance as she slowly straightened her leg. Just as she rose to peer tentatively out the window, another head rose into view on the outside peering in.

It was a huge cat. All black with yellow eyes.

She fought with all her might to stifle the scream that threatened to erupt from her lips, but terror became disbelief when the cat smiled—actually **smiled**—at her.

* Hi! You must be Jolene. I'm Bandit. *

Jolene slapped her hand to her mouth to cover the scream she almost didn't catch as she scrabbled backward away from the window. Those words... she heard those words in her mind, as if the speaker stood at her shoulder. But... how?

The big cat angled its head to one side, as if confused by her, but otherwise waited.

Jolene returned to the window and stared at the big cat.

* Come on. We have to hurry. Jake is meeting the griffon that took you at the trailhead not far from here. Smokey is leading the other griffons away from the cabin. Can you open the window? I don't have thumbs. *

Jake... did the cat mean Jake Adams?

* Yes. I mean Jake Adams. And yes. I can hear your thoughts when I choose. Jake raised me and Smokey from cubs. He saved us from something he calls a train wreck north of town. Can we go please? I'm afraid I only incapacitated this griffon because it didn't see me coming. I need to

get you to safety before catching up with Smokey. I'm worried about her.
*

Jolene remembered the train wreck. It happened a couple years after they graduated high school, and she remembered that Jake had become even more distant than he had previously been right around that same time.

Yeah. He was caring for a couple cubs. You coming or not? *

Jolene shifted so that she half-crouched and half-stood at the window, hunched over like she was about tie her shoe. She ran her fingers along the top of the interior window, searching for a latch or clasp that kept it shut.

She found nothing.

She pressed her hands against the window right below the wooden frame at the top and pushed. The window rose enough for her to slip her fingers under it and push it all the way up.

It was a struggle. The wood was old and felt like either the window or the window frame had warped over the years. But she made enough space for her to climb through... and stand on the corpse of one of her guards.

A spike of fear pierced her heart, and she crouched low, examining the corpse. She couldn't really tell in the moonlight, but she didn't **think** it was the griffon that was nice to her.

There's a young one on the porch, acting like it's guarding the front door. *

Did it suspect her escape attempt and aid her without seeming to?

How should I know? I'm not about to go ask. Come on already. *

The black cat that was larger than any jaguar Jolene had ever seen turned and softly padded away from the cabin and into the forest that surrounded it. Jolene followed as quietly as she could.

THE DEEPER THEY went into the trees, the darker it became. All too soon, moonlight was in short supply on the forest floor. Her rescuer and guide all but disappeared, and she resorted to grabbing the cat's tail and holding it, just so she knew where it was.

Without any warning, her foot caught on something. She tripped, lurching forward as her grip tightened on the cat's tail.

Hey! Buy a jaguar dinner first!

The near-impenetrable darkness all around her was frightening, but the cat's sudden thought forced her fear to retreat. She fought the urge to laugh.

She grinned and whispered, "Don't worry. You're not my type."

A soft chuff reached her ears as she sensed amusement radiating from the cat.

What seemed like a short time later, they broke through some underbrush, and she found herself on the edge of large meadow. And all at once, she knew where she was. This was the clearing medical helicopters used to evacuate injured hikers or campers. Her relief soared when she saw a woman about her age step out of the underbrush on the far side.

Go. Her name is Emilia. She'll see you safely back to town.

Without another thought, the big black cat vanished back into the darkness of the forest.

All her fear and worries gone, Jolene jogged across the clearing at a steady pace. About halfway across the clearing, a large shadow engulfed Jolene just as Emilia looked up toward the sky, terror overtaking her expression. Jolene knew the woman's terror could only mean one thing, and she dropped into a forward shoulder roll.

Air whooshed over her once again as a large griffon hit the ground a few feet in front of her. It jumped and spun around as it *screed* its frustration at being denied. Its feet touched the ground facing her just as Jolene came up from her shoulder roll.

The beast was too close. There was nothing she could do.

The griffon opened its beak as it drew its head back, and Jolene closed her eyes, resigning herself to her fate.

But death didn't claim her.

Another *scree* pierced her ears from above and behind her, and she opened her eyes just in time to see a smaller griffon strike her would-be killer with talons, beak, and claws.

Jolene stood transfixed, unable to look away, as the griffons fought over her. One seeking to kill her, the other save her.

A harsh whisper—more like a hiss—reached Jolene's ears. "Come on!"

She looked away from the fight and saw the woman—Emilia—waving her arms in a 'come on already' gesture. Given her frantic movements, it might have been better named as a 'hurry the hell up' gesture.

But Jolene didn't want to leave her friend. Already, in the short time they'd been fighting, she saw several wounds on the smaller griffon. There was no doubt how the fight would end. She hated the thought of leaving the smaller griffon to its fate.

A hand closed around her wrist, and she looked up to see Emilia at her side. She said not a word as she pulled Jolene into motion, almost dragging her across the remaining distance of the field to the tree line.

"Wait!"

Emilia only stopped once they were in the trees. "What? You want to get carved up just like the cub?"

"It's my friend. It was nice to me. I don't want it to die."

Emilia shot a glance over her shoulder and sighed. "I'm not sure anyone but Jake could prevent that now."

Jolene frowned. How could Jake prevent someone from dying? And why would he face a creature like this for her? But then, it settled in what Emilia said, and she turned back to the clearing.

The smaller griffon lay on its side, swatting feebly at the larger one. Even Jolene could see it didn't have much strength left.

She turned to Emilia. "Please... can't you do something?"

Emilia shot her a glance that spoke volumes and precious few of them kind. She hissed a whisper, "Just what am I supposed to? I have affinities to Life, Mind, and Spirit. Not exactly the most combat-focused affinities out there..."

EVER SINCE SHE FIRST MANIFESTED, Emilia felt content in her evaluation. She wanted to pursue a career in medicine, which made affinities to Life, Mind, and Spirit the perfect combination for her.

But like she'd just hissed at Jolene, those weren't exactly the most combat-oriented Spheres.

And she needed combat right now.

She wished Jake was with them. *He* wouldn't have... her eyes shot wide as she realized her answer. It wasn't perfect, but few things were. She took a deep breath, closed her eyes, and touched that portion of her mind that she used to chat with Smokey. Right as she did, she pushed as much power as she dared into what would've been a full-throated shout.

* Jake, help! *

CHAPTER

THIRTY-FOUR

Jake exited the SUV and scanned the trailhead around him. It was the first time he'd ever been there. He knew of it, of course, but this wasn't one of the trails he preferred. It was a cloudless night with a full moon that looked like it hovered just a few hundred yards above the countryside. It made for a very well-lit, very bright night.

It was strangely peaceful. Three vehicles occupied spaces around the otherwise-vacant lot. Crickets chirped all around him, and just as a personal test, he closed his eyes and concentrated on his senses. The world opened up around him, and he became aware of every firefly, every cricket, every bat in the sky.

It felt so odd to him... and at the same time... very cool. He felt connected to the world around him in a way he never had before... well... at least not before he learned he could do this. He simply stood in place, eyes closed, and focused on his awareness of the world around him.

He smiled. But then, something entered his awareness that pulled the smile from his expression. It was large and flew toward him, just skimming the treetops.

At almost the exact stroke of midnight, the griffon touched down in the center of the trailhead's parking lot. It was a large, fearsome predator, and it was beautiful. From what Jake could see, its feathers possessed a faint, mottled pattern. It regarded him with undisguised hostility.

A housecat moseyed into the parking lot, walking under the guard rail that formed the lot's boundary. It sauntered along the side of a vehicle, and the griffon looked at it for a moment, then returned its focus to Jake.

*So... you are the sorcerer I have been sent to kill, not that it is any great imposition. *

Wait... what? Someone **sent** it?

"Who sent you?"

*Why should I tell you? You will die here tonight, sorcerer, and the world will be a better place without you in it. *

"You killed those people at the gas station in Oklahoma?"

*I do not know what this 'gas station' is, but if you mean the building in the great plains, yes. I killed them and many before them. You were stupid to come alone. Surrender, and I will make it quick. *

"Where's Jolene? I want to see her, make sure she's safe. When you let her go, we can get on with this."

*You are such a fool. This is not one of your tales. You do not get to make demands. Now that the bait has served its purpose, it will be a feast for me and mine. I only needed to draw you out. *

The griffon pawed the ground, revealing its impatience. But why? Was it simply that eager to kill him and feast on him... as creepy as that sounded? Or was there something else?

But it seemed the griffon wasn't inclined to monologue and gloat. Which was unfortunate. Jake feared it had said all it was going to say and diverted some of his attention to preparing a new framework he had practiced with Isabel all day.

Just as Jake was about to try another attempt to get information, a new voice touched his mind.

*I got her to Emilia, Jake. I'm going to help Smokey. There were a lot more griffons than we thought. *

Jake couldn't help it. He grinned.

The griffon's eyes narrowed as it took in the change in Jake's demeanor. * *Are you so eager for death?* *

"Oh, I'm not the one who's going to die tonight."

* *Ah, the fallacy of youth. I am older than you can imagine, sorcerer, and you do not even have a proper teacher. What threat do you pose to me?* *

Jake chuckled. "Oh, more than you think, actually... but I'm not the one you need to worry about. You were wrong, you know; I didn't come alone."

The griffon's eyes narrowed once more, and Jake sensed confusion coloring their communication. In the corner of his eye, the housecat started to grow, and he grinned again as he pointed at it. When the griffon finally turned to look, the cat no longer had fur and seemed to have scales.

"Funny thing... you think Jolene is the bait for me, and in a way, I suppose she is. But what you failed to understand is that I am also the bait for **you**. My associate here would like a word."

By now, Isabel was her full size and looked down on the griffon as she towered over it. The griffon shot Jake a look that carried more than hints of fear and made to lunge at him. Just for pure theatrics, Jake lifted his hand and snapped his fingers as he fed power into the framework. The griffon locked on Jake's fingers and didn't seem to notice the ground beneath it surging upward to enclose its feet.

It didn't take long to realize its mistake, though.

The griffon looked down and flapped its wings as it *screed* its frustration. The ground did not yield. It was no longer loose dirt. It felt like solid stone.

"Who sent you to kill the sorcerer?" Isabel's voice was a both the voice Jake knew and not. "If you tell me true, I will grant you mercy."

The griffon *screed* again as it fought the stone that held it. It seemed wholly focused on its bonds, paying no mind to Isabel's offer.

* *No! Not again! We will never be the playthings of sorcerers again!*

*We have fought too hard... lost too many! We will die before he claims us again! ***

Isabel moved in for the kill, but Jake lifted his hand. The immense dragon saw his movement and stopped.

Jake crossed the distance between them and stopped to stand in front of the griffon but out of its reach.

"I don't want to claim you or your people. You are right that I am young and very new to my power, but I carry no animosity toward you or yours. I would help your people if I could."

The griffon stopped its struggles, focusing on Jake once more. Glaring at him. * *Lies! I* know *what you want. He told me!* *

Jake sighed and shook his head. "I'm sorry. You've been manipulated. I didn't even know griffons existed until I went to the... the building in the great plains, as you put it. I do not want to be your enemy."

* *But... but... you are a sorcerer. Your kind made us for nothing more than amusement and cast us aside when you tired of us.* *

"Were you there? Did you witness it with your own eyes and senses?"

* *No, but every griffon knows— ** *

"Every griffon knows what they've been **told**. Are there any griffons still alive that witnessed their creation and treatment at the hands of the sorcerers of old?"

The griffon held its silence.

Jake waited several moments. "Well? It's a simple question. Do any griffons still live who witnessed your creation and how the sorcerers of the time treated you?"

* *No. Not for many generations.* *

"Okay. Let me ask you something else. Suppose that... oh... let's say your parent. Suppose that one of your parents wronged another griffon in some way. Before you were even conceived. Is it fair or just or right for the griffon who was wronged to hold you accountable for your parent's actions? Especially when you didn't even exist yet?"

The griffon lowered its head, refusing to make eye contact with

Jake. * *No. That is not our way. You... I... you truly have no wish to claim us? No desire to toy with us? Force us to submit against our will?* *

Jake fought the urge to laugh. He knew the griffon would misinterpret it. "I'm twenty-five years old. I just found out—at most six weeks ago—that I am not just a mage but a sorcerer. Then, I find out griffons exist. Doesn't it make more sense that I'm tiptoeing around the edge of being overwhelmed? I just want to live my life and learn about who and what I am. I bear you and your people no malice. Curiosity, yes. I'd love to know more about you, but no malice, no ill will."

* *If all is as you say, how were you able to bind me so easily?* *

Now, Jake did grin and gestured at Isabel. "The dragon is my mentor. We practiced this all day, just so I could hold you and not hurt you."

The griffon turned to Isabel. * *The sorcerer speaks true?* *

Isabel nodded once. For her, it was a regal, majestic action. "He does."

* *I... I wish I had time to consider your words. The hatred of sorcerers... it is almost bred into us from the egg. I do not think we have ever considered that we might be wrong.* *

"Oh, I'm not saying you're wrong; for all I know, the sorcerers who created the griffons were utter bastards. But I do know you're wrong about **me**."

* *The human is in an abandoned structure just over the hill. I flew straight here from it. She is unharmed. I... I think a young one who insisted on coming has taken a liking to her. Others came with me. I ask that you let them return home.* *

Jake pulled his power from the framework. It was structured in such a way that the 'stone' dissolved back to dirt and gravel as soon as the framework held no power.

The griffon... well... it squawked when it felt the stone leave its feet. It was clearly surprised, and once again, Jake fought an urge to grin.

"Get the others. Go home. Don't harm any more humans."

The griffon jerked its head up to look first at Jake then at Isabel then back to Jake. * *I... I do not understand. Is this some kind of trick?* *

"No. It's no trick. Just as I am not what you thought, you are not what we thought. You're not the true criminal in this. Yes... we would like for you to tell us what you know about whoever set you to this task, but it's not required for your freedom. Your fear for your people carried across your words when you spoke of what you expected me to do. You made some terrible mistakes, but I truly believe you made them for the right reasons. You'll have to live with the fact that you killed people who bore you no malice and were no threat to you for the rest of your life. Their families don't even know you or your people exist. How would killing you help them?"

The griffon regarded him in silence for several heartbeats. * *You are truly not what we have come to believe the sorcerers were. I... my shame is complete. I will take my people and go... return to Aerie... and never bother the humans again.* *

"That's all I ask. They have no part in any of this."

* *What if the young one desires to stay? He has become entirely too fond of the human.* *

Jake grinned. "Oh... I'm sure we can work something out."

The griffon bobbed its head in a nod and turned, leaping into the air and taking flight.

Jake and Isabel watched it go in silence for several moments until Isabel spoke.

"This is not how I expected the night to end."

"Me, neither, but I think it could've ended a lot worse."

Jake felt a surge of power, and Isabel the woman stood beside him once more. She regarded him with an appraising expression for several minutes.

"Yes, it could have. Shall we return to the Grove?"

"That sounds amazing. I'm up past my bedtime."

They crossed the parking lot to Jake's SUV in silence. Just as they reached the vehicle, the jaguars slinked out of the night. Jake stopped to give each of them pets and rubs, then opened the back hatch for them. He wasn't sure what fallout there would be from the jaguars rescuing Jolene, but that was a matter for another day. Besides, he suspected the Grove was about to adopt a young griffon. It would be interesting to see where that led.

Just as Jake was about to close the hatch with the jaguars inside, a pulse of power touched his new sense. It was faint, but he heard Emilia's voice in his mind.

Jake, help!

CHAPTER
THIRTY-FIVE

Jake ran through the possibilities that Emilia was bait for a trap... but arrived at the conclusion that it largely didn't matter. Leaving aside his desire to date her, he wouldn't leave anyone in need of help if he had any say in the matter.

But how much time did Emilia have? The clearing where she was supposed to meet Jolene was not easily accessible from the trailhead... by car or foot or paw. An idea came to the forefront of his mind. It was risky. Possibly *very* risky. But it was also the fastest way to reach her.

After all... the shortest distance between two points is a straight line.

Jake closed his eyes and focused on two thoughts. His sense of self and his sense of Emilia. He built a framework around those two thoughts that would open a portal between them. He touched the ambient power and saturated his new framework with it.

Then, he released the framework.

A hole in reality appeared, beginning at a point slightly above Jake's head and moving in a straight line to the ground. Almost as if space-time was unzipping itself. When the 'zipper' reached the ground, the opening widened and took on the shape of an arched doorway that looked out on Jolene standing beside Emilia. They looked off to the right, beyond what the portal could show him.

Jake stepped through the portal, Isabel and the jaguars following. When everyone was through, Jake severed the power to the portal, and it winked out of existence as if it had never been.

Jolene gaped at their arrival. Her jaw worked as if to speak, but no words emerged.

"What's happening?" Jake asked.

"Jolene didn't want to leave without helping her new friend... who is the young griffon currently having his ass handed to him nine ways from Sunday," Emilia answered, jerking her chin toward the meadow they faced.

Jake turned and saw what she meant. Two griffons fought, one large and fully adult while the other was little more than a plucky early adolescent. The adolescent fought with fierce conviction, but that never stood up to experience, knowledge, and skill... which the adult griffon apparently had in spades. Left to their own devices, it wouldn't be long before the older griffon killed the younger.

Right, then.

As much as he felt it wasn't his place to intervene, Jake was not about to allow someone to die for doing the right thing, not if he could prevent it at all.

And prevent it, he could. Easily so.

He took a few steps forward as he focused on quickly assembling the framework in his mind for the effect he wanted to achieve. He'd have to time it just right, but his intuition told him he'd have his moment soon enough. It was a simple matter to saturate his framework with power once he had it formed to his liking, and it all came down to waiting for the right moment.

Soon enough, the adult griffon sent the adolescent rolling through the meadow. The plucky youngster made a valiant effort to stand and continue the fight, but while his spirit was willing, his body had taken too much punishment. It was obvious that he couldn't get back to his feet in the time he had... or at least, **thought** he had.

The moment there was enough distance between the griffons, Jake released his framework. A power-rich aura of Life energy settled on the young griffon, healing in mere heartbeats what would've taken months even with the best care. At the same time, the grassy meadow swarmed up to enshroud the adult griffon's feet in boots of solid earth just as the air around its body solidified to complete the prison.

The youngster pushed himself to stand and gave himself a look-over. If Jake wasn't projecting, he thought the young griffon's manner suggested surprise and perhaps bewilderment. The adult betrayed surprise, too, along with a healthy dollop of rage; his full-throated *scree* seemed fit to wake the dead five counties over.

Before anyone else could do anything, a collection of dark shapes swooped out of the night sky and landed in the meadow. Griffons. Easily a dozen, maybe more. The apparent leader approached the group of onlookers, making a point of walking between the two combatants, and stopped a respectful distance away from Jake.

* I thought we had an accord. I thought you swore you had no plans to entrap us. *

He heard a gasp over his left shoulder, suggesting that the griffon broadcasted his mind-speech to everyone.

"We do, and I did," Jake replied. "When I arrived, the two griffons were fighting, and the adult had damn-near killed the youngster. I stopped the fight to give us time to figure out the situation."

The young one moved to the apparent leader's side and looked up at him unafraid. ** The sorcerer speaks the truth, Father. **

Father? Well, damn... that meant the situation would go either really, really well or really, really badly... and probably in **very** short order.

The griffon who had met Jake and seemed to be the leader regarded the youngster for a moment before turning back to the onlookers. * *If this is true, who killed one of us back at the abandoned structure?* *

Bandit padded forward and faced the griffon full-on. * *That was me. He was pacing right outside the window where you kept Jolene. I didn't realize I'd killed him, though. I regret that. I just wanted him incapacitated long enough to get Jolene out of there.* *

The griffon regarded Bandit for a moment in silence, then deeply bowed. * *Then, rest well knowing it was as you desired. She woke up not long ago, none the worse for wear. Her pride was a bit wounded, but that is healthy for all of us from time to time.* *

Bandit's apparent tension vanished, and he gave his version of a smile. * *I'm glad she was just unconscious. I didn't want to harm her, just make sure she couldn't stop me from getting Jolene.* *

The griffon leader turned to the ensnared adult. * *Come. It is time to return to Aerie. The sorcerer is not what we thought, and we have much to discuss.* *

For a moment, Jake feared the adult griffon wouldn't listen to reason. After a tense handful of seconds, though, he bobbed his head once in a nod, and Jake severed the power to the framework that ensnared him.

The young griffon padded up to the leader and nuzzled at his side. * *Please, Father... may I stay with the nice person? She's my friend.* *

The leader looked down at his offspring in silence for the longest time, then looked to Jake. * *I understand that the humans of this world like to exchange hostages to help ensure the good behavior of their allies. I think they call them emissaries. Would you accept my young one as an emissary?* *

Jake managed not to sigh. "Emissaries aren't hostages. They are people who choose to serve as representatives to help facilitate communication between allies. I'm sure your young one would be welcome at the grove, where Jolene could easily visit without the world at large getting involved. But I want everyone to understand that he is free to come and go between your lands and the grove as he desires... as long as he can do so without alerting the world to your existence."

The young griffon gave a happy chirp and trotted over to Jolene. For the moment, their eyes were level with each other, but the griffon wasn't fully grown yet.

The griffon leader seemed to sigh and gave a small, almost invisible headshake. Jake recognized it as the ages-old wordless lament of all parents whose children chose a questionable friend. He walked forward and brushed his cheek along the crown or crest of his child's head, prompting an almost-feline purr before he turned and returned to the other griffons.

The adult Jake had ensnared in chains of earth and air darted looks from the leader to Jake and back, like he expected a sneak attack at any moment. But when his leader kept walking and Jake gave him a nod, the adult joined the griffons.

Almost as one, they flapped their wings and leapt into the air, and soon, they were merely small dark spots, barely visible against the night sky.

Jake turned to survey his group and found them looking to him now. He wasn't sure he was ready for that, but maybe it was just an 'in the moment' type of thing.

"Well... like they say in the movies, our work here is done."

He decided to flex his muscles and adjusted his portal framework to open three at once. One led to the trailhead where his SUV waited in the parking lot. Another led to the Wainwright Grove. The third opened to the second trailhead that wasn't too far away and revealed Mike Stannyk leaning against the fender of his police cruiser.

"Jolene, Mike will see you home. He'll probably insist on a quick checkup at the emergency room for the police report, but that's nothing major." Jake turned to the griffon. "You and Emilia and anyone else who wants to can take the center portal straight to the Wainwright Grove. We'll deal with proper introductions later, because I'm all kinds of tired. Anyone who wants to ride back to the Grove with me can join me at the SUV."

No one made to move until Isabel walked through the center portal. Then, the jaguars went to the SUV as Jolene went to Mike. Emilia surprised him by waiting for him and walking at his side through the portal to the SUV.

The portals closed the moment Jake passed through his, and as soon as he pulled the key fob out of his pocket, Emilia claimed it.

"You've been throwing around a lot of power tonight. I haven't. I'll drive us back to the Grove."

Jake wanted to argue with her. He really did. None of his favorite stories ended with the hot young woman driving off into the sunset while the hero dozed in the passenger seat... but he didn't have the energy to argue with her. He was rather beat.

With a graceful silence, he nodded and trudged over to the passenger door.

THIRTY-SIX

Wainwright Grove
Hornbeam, Illinois
19 June 2025, 8:35am

THE MORNING after meeting his first griffon, Jake sat in one of the chairs on the back patio. The remains of his breakfast sat on the patio table in front of him. Morning birdsong filled the area, and a slight breeze tugged at his hair and shirt sleeves. But he didn't notice either the birds chirping or the breeze. Not really.

His mind swirled around and over and through the events of the night before. Part of him felt like... well... maybe, it was a little too soon for the 'building a bridge' metaphor. But he certainly felt like they'd at least selected the location for the bridge's abutments. He hoped they had, anyway.

A part of him wished all the hybrid races could come out into the open. Reveal themselves to the world. But he had a suspicion he knew where that would end.

Big game hunting was alive and well in American culture (at the very least). Conservatism was just another stupid idea from some stupid liberal nutbar with no idea how the world **really** worked.

Jake snorted a chuckle. Yeah... he could just hear someone saying that on one of the hunting shows that seemed to play non-stop in a few of the public establishments around Hornbeam. He didn't agree with that sentiment... not at all... but he felt fairly safe in thinking he was in the minority when it came to American opinions regarding the value of conservatism. Maybe not, but he wasn't about to hold his breath, either way.

No... despite how much he would like for hybrid races to have a place in the public awareness, he understood that it was probably best that they remained hidden like they did. If they hadn't hidden themselves away back in Antiquity, it would be different. But now? After all the centuries that had passed? He didn't see how revealing themselves to the world would go well for them at all, especially since the humans who thought they were the sole sapient life on the planet would wonder where these hybrid races came from, and Jake suspected the hybrid races would be only too eager to throw his subset of the crafters—the sorcerers—under that particular bus.

But were they right to let the griffon responsible for all those deaths just leave? Was that right course?

Jake was so deep into his thoughts that he wasn't even aware when Isabel approached and sat in the patio chair ninety degrees to his left around the patio table. Her voice did pull him out of his thoughts, though.

"So, you seem a bit pensive this morning. What's on your mind?"

Jake did his best not to grimace. "I'm wondering if we did the right thing in letting that griffon who'd killed all those people just fly off into the night with the others. I'm honestly very conflicted about it."

Isabel leaned forward and rested her elbows on her knees. She took a deep breath and slowly released most of it as a sigh. "Jake, one of the most difficult things for me to grasp early on in my life was that the scope of my people's lifespan is fundamentally different from every other creature on this planet... including humans. When I was a young hatchling, I remember hearing others discuss a Great Dragon Graveyard, but I've never seen it with my own eyes... because a dragon hasn't died in my lifetime that I know of. Now, it's easily within the realm of possibility that—far off in some forgotten and deeply buried lair—there is an ancient corpse of a dragon that is slowly decaying because he or she died while they slept the centuries away, and we're such solitary creatures that... well... **no one knows**.

"It took me a little while to come to terms with the idea that I have outlived entire civilizations and probably will continue do so. The dragon that helped me learn to control my fire breath was over seven thousand years old, Jake, and *that* was over two thousand years ago. The last time I visited my family, a couple centuries ago or so, that dragon was still alive and well."

The way Isabel casually brushed off whole *centuries* like humans would off-handedly mention *years* really hit Jake in that moment. Part of him wondered why it hadn't penetrated his awareness before, but that question was largely pointless overall.

"And Jake?" Isabel asked, pulling his attention back to her.

"Yeah?"

"Your lifespan has the potential to equal mine... if not exceed it. No known sorcerer ever died of old age, and there were several who were older than some dragons."

That little tidbit really set Jake back. How old were his birth parents when they chose to enter the soul vault? Were they two of the older ones? He leaned back against his seat as he tried to wrap his mind around being that old. In the end, he gave up, shaking his head as he realized he had no way to conceptualize living that long.

It was like Isabel knew what he thought. "Don't feel bad about having difficulty understanding that. I didn't have a frame of reference for it until I outlived the Roman Empire... and all the other nation-states that have arisen and fallen over the last twenty-one hundred years. And I brought this up as a lead-in to your concerns over how we handled the griffon.

"One of the other things I've had difficulty with over the years is maintaining that personal connection humans are so capable of. When you outlive whole civilizations, getting worked up over the fate of a handful or two of humans can—sometimes—be damned hard. The simple fact is that one of the things humans do really, really well is... die. Often at the hands of other humans. The griffon killed thirty-seven people from Los Angeles to that convenience store in Oklahoma. I didn't read all their information, but every single one of them would've died within the next hundred years... probably less since there were no newborns among the victims.

"Is it unfortunate that they died? Absolutely. Is it tragic that they died? Undoubtedly. But the crux of the issue is where do we draw the line? Sure... we could've killed that griffon for what he did. I've killed supernaturals for less to maintain peace and order as well as the secrecy surrounding the supernatural world's overall existence.

"But if we—or I—had killed that griffon, he would not have returned to the Aerie with the others to talk of a sorcerer that treated them with honor and dignity and compassion."

Isabel sighed and leaned back against her own seat. "Jake... even with how little I know you, it's obvious beyond mention that you will reveal your existence to the world to help people. And just because the hybrid races hide from the world at large *does not* mean they're unaware of what transpires in the world. The fewer enemies you have when you announce yourself, the less you'll have to worry about."

Jake sighed and nodded. "This is seriously messing with the cultural norms that I've absorbed since infancy. The idea that we should be tough on crime is so fundamental that I still feel all torn up."

"Despite how quickly humans die and how fragile they are otherwise, I have never understood Americans' seeming preference for throwing away their own people, simply because they find themselves in bad situations and make mistakes. *Every* sapient makes mistakes. Mistakes are impossible to avoid. Yes, it is important for a civilization to have a Code of Laws. Yes, it is important to ensure a fair and impartial implementation of those laws... even though humans rarely achieve that, especially here in America. But I also feel humans' perspective might change a little bit if their existence wasn't as fleeting as it is. Each generation is so short that it's far too easy to lose wisdom or awareness or understanding in an alarmingly small amount of time."

Jake looked off toward the wooded area of the grove as he contemplated Isabel's thoughts. Frankly, they shook him. The idea that ethics might depend upon one's societal frame of reference rattled him.

"Is that why the sorcerers made such a bad name for themselves?" he asked. "They lost touch with the people around them to such a degree they felt themselves outside the societies they lived in?"

Isabel shrugged. "I personally think so, yes. But there's not really any way to know for certain now. Why did you decide to let the griffon go?"

"It was apparent to me that he didn't choose to set off on a rampage. I don't know what leverage the one using him has or had over him, but I didn't like the idea of killing the griffon for something he didn't **want** to do. I sensed that about him somehow during our conversation. Plus... he didn't seem to be inherently violent. He chose to talk with us. He didn't try to attack us once we started the conversation. All that told me he wasn't a truly bad person."

Isabel stood. A slight smile tried to take over her expression as she regarded him. "Jake, I'm going to leave you with one final thought. Most children evaluate the values and belief systems they absorbed during their childhood to see if they still hold true for them in adulthood. You have to decide what matters to you, and that will probably change across the years. If I had felt allowing the griffon to live would have been a colossal mistake, I would've killed him and all his associates myself... without consulting you. For what it's worth, I think you did the right thing."

Isabel left Jake to his thoughts. And if he was being honest with himself, the talk with her had helped him sort out his thoughts and feelings. Part of him still insisted they should've killed the griffon, but doing that wouldn't have brought the victims back. It wouldn't have undone the tragedies the victims' families faced.

Maybe, he needed to step back and decide what mattered to him, where he wanted to draw the line. But the world had never been black and white. It was totally shades of gray. Perhaps, the best thing he could do was take each situation as it presented itself.

It was a difficult topic. He ultimately knew he wouldn't settle the matter in the here and now, but it was good to spend some time alone considering it. Evaluating his values, ethics, and morals against his newest experiences and deciding if they still worked for him.

~

WAINWRIGHT GROVE
Hornbeam, Illinois
19 June 2025, 9:23am

LATER THAT MORNING, Jake stood at the entrance to the Wainwright Grove with Isabel. It was a cool morning, still in the 60s. The air had that crisp, after-the-rain smell to it, but Jake wasn't aware of any rain in the area. He may have missed it, though. It wasn't like he had nothing on his mind.

Isabel paced like a caged animal a short distance away. A blind man would have known she was *not* happy. Jake let her have her space. Without warning, she stopped and whipped out her mobile phone like an Old West gunfighter. The dragon-in-disguise tapped the screen several times before lifting the phone to her ear. Moments later:

"Your deputy marshals are *late*, Director. You know what this means."

She fell silent for several moments.

"No. Do not play the time zone bullshit with me. The agreement was to be at the entrance to the Wainwright Grove at nine o'clock, local time. It is now nine-twenty-four. The US Government owes me an additional twenty-four bars of gold... assuming the deputy marshals arrive before... no. Make that an additional twenty-five bars of gold. Given our long-established and well-regarded working relationship, I will accept one-pound bars... *this* time."

Jake felt the power swell around him, and somehow, he knew—without conscious understanding of how he knew—that a portal was opening roughly fifteen feet in front of him and three feet or so to his right, well away from the hedge that bordered the Grove and *probably* at a sufficient distance to avoid Beauregard's wrath.

The portal formed heartbeats later, and the three deputy marshals Jake had met at the gas station in Oklahoma stepped through it.

"Ah... here they are. It is now nine-twenty-six. I shall submit the final statement of the government's forfeit as an addendum to my invoice for the griffon matter. Good day, Director."

Isabel withdrew the phone and tapped it once more, presumably ending the call.

Deputy Marshal Hannah Gaines, the lead officer on the griffon case, approached them wearing a scowl that really did not go well with her suit. "We're here. What's so important?"

"I am informing you that the griffon matter has been closed. No further attacks will occur."

"So, you killed it, then."

Isabel quirked her lips in what might have become a smile in another setting with other people as she held out a single piece of paper to Gaines. "The matter has been handled, and this is the official statement for your records. That is all you need to know."

"But what about my reports? You don't get to demand our presence and then refuse to—"

"Deputy Marshal, I suggest you take a moment and consider just who you address in such a belligerent tone. I do not work for you, your superiors, or even the people you swear to protect." Isabel's tone wouldn't have frozen nitrogen, but it came close.

Gaines held her silence for several moments while she clenched and unclenched her jaw several times. At last, she accepted the paper from Isabel. "Thank you for that information. Do you require anything else of us?"

"No, thank you, Deputy Marshal. But I'm sure your director will want a word to discuss punctuality, considering you have cost your government more than all three of your annual salaries combined with what I suspect was pointless posturing. Good day."

Gaines's associates looked less than thrilled with the prospect of that conversation as Gaines herself stalked back to them. Deputy Marshal Bergman created another portal, and the marshals returned from whence they came.

As silence and peace settled over them, Jake couldn't help but feel happy at how they'd resolved the matter with the griffon. Sure... if the griffon had been truly a monster, he would've accepted the necessity of killing it, but such was not the case. From the way it sounded, the griffon was as much a pawn as anything else.

After a few moments of silence, Jake turned to Isabel. "So, what's next?"

Isabel replied with a soft smile. "The same thing that's always 'next.' Train, study, explore, and enjoy life until we're needed again."

∽

THE ADAMS RESIDENCE
Hornbeam, Illinois
27 June 2025, 5:45pm

. . .

Jake, Emilia, and the jaguars headed straight for Jake's parents. They arrived without any fuss or fanfare, and Jake opened the fence's gate to let the jaguars inside. This time, they went straight to the house, and Bandit pawed at the front door as Jake and Emilia caught up at a walking pace.

Jake's dad opened the door just as Jake and Emilia set foot on the porch, and he smiled at seeing them. "Well, hello! It's been a few days. Please, come in."

He stepped away from the door and allowed them to enter, Bandit and Smokey trailing behind him as Jake and Emilia entered and closed the door. Jake's mom entered the living room and beamed at seeing them, making sure to give both jaguars pats and scratches.

As soon as his parents returned their attention to him and Emilia, Jake produced the spirit vault and placed it on the coffee table. Both of his parents looked from him to it and back again.

Jake smiled. He couldn't help it. "Mom... Dad... there are a couple people I'd like you to meet."

WHAT'S NEXT?

Do you want to stay up-to-date with the latest news about my stories and receive exclusive content?

Sign up for my newsletter.

~

The story continues in *Hyperion*.

ACKNOWLEDGMENTS

There's an old saying: it takes a village to raise a child. I don't know if that's true or not, but it certainly seems true where publishing a story is concerned. You would not be reading this were it not for contributions from several people.

No story should reach the public without passing through the scrutiny of a quality editor or editors, and TF Poist is one of the best.

I also want to thank Suzie O'Connell of Sunset Rose Books for the excellent cover. As I told her on a recent project, "I would be proud to blame you in public for this."

I'm sure there are many who will see this next paragraph and think, "Goodness, he's acknowledging his parents and grandparents *again*?" My greatest regret is that I cannot hand my grandfather, Bob Miller, a paperback copy of my novels. So, yes... the Acknowledgements page of *every* story I publish will have the paragraph that follows. Consider yourselves forewarned.

Without my grandparents, Bob & Janice Miller, I honestly don't know where I'd be today; my grandfather taught me to read and love reading, and my grandmother taught me to develop and exercise my imagination. This story (not to mention my life in general) certainly would not have happened without my parents, Vernon & Judy Kerns.

WORLDS OF ROBERT M. KERNS

For a complete and accurate listing of all publications, both currently available and forthcoming, please visit Knightsfall Press.

Knightsfall Press - Books

https://knightsfall.press/books

SO... WHO'S THE AUTHOR?

Robert M. Kerns (or Rob if you ever meet him in person) is a geek, and he claims that label proudly. Most of his geekiness revolves around Information Technology (IT), having over fifteen years in the industry; within IT, he especially prefers Servers and Networks, and he often makes the claim that his residence has a better data infrastructure than some businesses.

Beyond IT, Rob enjoys Science Fiction and Fantasy of (almost) all stripes. He is a voracious reader, with his favorite books too numerous to list.

Rob has been writing for over 20 years, published his first novel in 2018, and has no plans to stop any time soon.

Connect with Rob at robertmkerns.com.

- facebook.com/RobertMKerns
- amazon.com/author/robertmkerns
- bookbub.com/authors/robert-m-kerns
- patreon.com/nomadicnovelist